THE
PHILOSOPHER'S
FLIGHT

A NOVEL

TOM MILLER

SIMON & SCHUSTER

NEW YORK LONDON TORONTO SYDNEY NEW DELHI

Simon & Schuster
1230 Avenue of the Americas
New York, NY 10020

First Simon & Schuster hardcover edition February 2018

SIMON & SCHUSTER and colophon are registered trademarks of Simon & Schuster, Inc.

For information about special discounts for bulk purchases, please contact Simon & Schuster Special Sales at 1-866-506-1949 or business@simonandschuster.com.

The Simon & Schuster Speakers Bureau can bring authors to your live event. For more information or to book an event, contact the Simon & Schuster Speakers Bureau at 1-866-248-3049 or visit our website at www.simonspeakers.com.

Interior design by Ruth Lee-Mui
Illustrations created by Michael Gellatly

Manufactured in the United States of America

1 3 5 7 9 10 8 6 4 2

Library of Congress Cataloging-in-Publication Data is available.

ISBN 978-1-4767-7815-0
ISBN 978-1-4767-7817-4 (ebook)

FOR ABBY—

Who once asked why there were so few women in my stories

AND FOR MY MOM—

Who read to me every night when I was young

PROLOGUE

But you must never call philosophy "magic," for there is no such thing.

Traditional

A FEW WEEKS AGO, my daughter, who is nine years old and learning to fly, asked me the question I've been expecting for a long time: Why do so many people hate empirical philosophers?

She and I were out drawing koru sigils on the tomato plants in the garden, the sun hot on our backs, each of us with a little square of glass in our hand and a mister filled with distilled water. I'd spent so many hours drawing them as a boy that the rhythm came back to me automatically: four sprays to coat the glass, aim at a single seedling, then trace your finger through the beads of water, forming the elaborate curlicue that is a koru sigil. Draw it right and the tomatoes will grow to four pounds each and mature twice as fast as an ordinary plant.

That sort of miracle is the most common thing in the world to my daughter, who was born down here in Matamoros in 1930, two miles across the Mexican border, raised among malcontents and renegades, women (and a few men, like myself) who were made outlaws in the United States. All of us are empirical philosophers, or sigilrists if you prefer the common term. And what is empirical philosophy—what is sigilry—except a branch of science that we don't yet fully understand? There's no dark art to it; it's nothing more than the movement of energy to produce a physical effect. The human body provides the energy, while the sigil, drawn sometimes with beads of water, sometimes with cornmeal or sand, catalyzes the movement. You can do a thousand useful things with philosophy: make a plant grow larger and faster, send a message a thousand miles in an instant, fly. If you grew up with it, it's natural. It's right. Why would anyone want life to be otherwise?

But, of course, not everyone feels that way. Sigilry only came into widespread use around 1750 and right from the start women were better at it than men. That upset a lot of folks, who thought sigils must be some form of witchcraft. Most people, though, saw the usefulness in empirical philosophy and were content to allow it.

So it went until 1831, when we get to what every nine-year-old girl calls "the good part." And that's Lucretia Cadwallader, who at that same age, hidden away in a remote cabin in Wisconsin, illiterate and with no knowledge of empirical philosophy at all, devised a method for solidifying smoke and shaping it with her bare hands. When she traced the right glyph into a cloud of smoke with her finger, it became docile. She could make it stretch like taffy or fill an entire room or coil itself neatly in a jar. For years, young Cadwallader practiced her trade in secret, until the University of Detroit heard of her extraordinary abilities and invited her to study as a scholarship case.

Cadwallader spent three decades at the U of D engaged in endless study and experimentation, learning how to combine her smoke with chemical vapors to create complex structures. Her clouds could take on the properties of a spring or harden into a mass that struck like a fist. They could asphyxiate a man or burn away tuberculosis or bring the rain. Because she often used a pocketknife to shape her clouds, Cadwallader named her technique "smokecarving."

The leading philosophers of her age called Cadwallader's discoveries scientific breakthroughs of the highest order. Laypeople called them the Devil's work. That sort of superstition always infuriated Cadwallader—you could take a man with no notion of chemistry and have him hold a match to gunpowder or breathe ether and he'd call it honest knowledge. But if you accomplished the same physical effects by tracing out a glyph in hot ash or silver filings, he would declare it the lowest form of wickedness.

Cadwallader took on students, too, the most unusual of whom was a young male sigilrist named Galen Wainwright. Though Wainwright possessed only a fraction of Cadwallader's power, he was nevertheless quite talented for a man. He had a grand vision of forming the world's first military unit to fight using smokecarving. Cadwallader always dismissed the idea—smokecarving was a tool of peace and creation, not of destruction.

When the Civil War broke out in '61, Wainwright went to Washington, where he offered to raise a regiment of smokecarvers and defeat the Confederacy in a week. The Secretary of War laughed him right out of the city. Wainwright then made the same offer to the Confederates in Richmond, who didn't see any harm in the idea and made Wainwright a colonel. Then from every last corner of the South, Wainwright sought out men who could do empirical philosophy. Most of them were inept practical sigilrists, but they had high spirits and kitted themselves out in the elaborate uniforms of Zouaves. They called themselves the Legion of Confederate Smokecarvers.

The Legion's first action came at the Battle of Bull Run, where it brewed up a huge cloud of tear gas, intending to break the Union lines. However, Wainwright miscalculated the wind speed and instead hit a group of picnicking dignitaries who'd come down from Baltimore to watch the fighting. His attack didn't affect the outcome of the battle, but it did throw the entire North into an uproar over the "philosophical menace."

The Legion spent the next ten months fighting in one skirmish after another, putting on overwhelming pyrotechnic displays. They caused only a few dozen casualties while exhausting the South's supply of strategic chemicals. And yet the mere sight of Wainwright and his men in their baggy, scarlet pantaloons, blue silk jackets, and tasseled fezzes inspired panic in the Union army. Back in Virginia, the Legion was feted as the most ingenious weapon of the Confederacy.

Until, at last, Mrs. Cadwallader took the field. She led what came to be known as the United States Sigilry Corps: ten thousand women, all practical philosophers. They marched out of Detroit with a vast, silent, slate-gray cyclone that billowed a mile high. "Like the Israelites," wrote the overawed

Detroit Defender, "with a pillar of cloud to lead them by day and a pillar of fire by night." In reality, it was nothing so biblical, merely a supply of concentrated, premade smoke so they could strike more quickly.

Galen Wainwright knew a losing proposition when he saw one. He feinted and retreated across the length of Tennessee, before at last the Corps cornered the Legion on the night of Halloween 1862. Wainwright's display of flash and fire lasted all of fifty-one seconds before Cadwallader's women brought down a blanket of smoke that pulled the oxygen right out of the air, extinguishing his colorful flames. Nine-tenths of the Legion surrendered on the spot, but Wainwright and his most fervent followers escaped to a nearby gully to make their last stand.

Cadwallader wished to avoid killing fellow philosophers. Instead of smothering the Legion, the Corps put up smoke streamers impregnated with lead iodide, which seeded the clouds and produced torrential rains. Wainwright's final attack was washed away. He himself suffered a bad case of pneumonia and was carried back to Richmond, where he spent the remainder of the war writing his memoirs.

Nevertheless, the South fought on and the huge loss of life on both sides continued. Dismayed at the bloodshed, Cadwallader demanded to be allowed to attack the Confederacy directly. Escorted by William Tecumseh Sherman's army, Cadwallader and the Corps made their way to Atlanta. She sent ahead a brief note that read: *I will burn the city to the ground on Sunday at four in the morning.*

So fearsome was Mrs. Cadwallader's reputation that nearly the entire civilian population evacuated. The Corps surrounded the city on Saturday afternoon and all through the night, Cadwallader's women sent wisps of incendiary vapor creeping through the Confederate lines. Right on schedule, fire erupted, moving west to east, permitting enough time for the stragglers to flee but leveling every building in its wake, sparing not even the churches.

Cadwallader marched from Atlanta to the sea, burning everything in her path, cutting a swath ten miles wide. Her advance was unstoppable.

Finally, she arrived at Petersburg, Virginia, the last bastion of Confederate resistance. Besieging the city were Gen. Grant and his army, exhausted after a months-long campaign that had failed to pry forty thousand Confederate defenders from their impenetrable web of trenches.

On the morning of April 6, 1865, the Southern soldiers watched as tendrils of smoke probed their lines and vanished into the ground. They waited for an ultimatum. Cadwallader had never attacked without warning or killed unnecessarily. Surely they would negotiate a surrender.

Then, shortly before noon, smoke boiled up around the Confederates, as if from the very soil itself, covering dozens of square miles in an instant. It was a dense, black concoction that blinded men and burned their lungs. A handful of soldiers in the front line of trenches dragged themselves free and staggered toward the Union forces, gasping and screaming for mercy. Their Northern brethren were shocked, too. Cadwallader had not informed them that she was about to attack.

The soldiers trapped inside the cloud tried desperately to indicate their surrender, setting off flares, striking flags, firing cannons into the air. But within a minute or two, the city and trenches encircling it had gone quiet.

A horrified Gen. Grant found Mrs. Cadwallader and begged her to lift the smoke. She agreed and with one sigil made the entire cloud disintegrate.

The Union soldiers picked their way into the city. The streets were littered with bodies, red, foamy blood on their lips and the whites of their eyes turned gray. Forty thousand of them.

The entire world was aghast at the slaughter.

Cadwallader declined to explain her actions at Petersburg as long as she lived. Historians have wondered if she underestimated the power of her own weapons. Was there a miscommunication among her captains? Perhaps the warm temperatures that morning caused the chemical reactions to run at an unexpectedly rapid rate?

But ordinary sigilrists have always understood the truth: Cadwallader intended to win the war with a single blow. No more bloodless "demonstrations" that might allow the fighting to drag on with hundreds of thousands more dead on both sides. No, she would inspire such fear that further resistance was impossible.

She proved only too successful. During my youth, when unphilosophical folks thought about sigilry, they imagined the carnage at Petersburg. And they wondered what would protect them if philosophers ever turned on the common man.

All that sounded like ancient history to my daughter. But she admitted that there are plenty of people around the settlement here who, if you didn't know them, might seem frightening: old Dr. Synge, who has canisters of smoke in her clinic that can kill a man in ten seconds flat; Ms. Pitcairn, who teaches hovering at the school but did bad things during the Great War (and is rumored to be quite a good shot with a machine gun); and Grandma Weekes, any time she looks at you over her glasses.

"And you, Dad."

She's right. You can't blame everything on Cadwallader. You have to lay some of it at the feet of the modern heroes, the ones I knew and fought beside: Danielle Hardin and Janet Brock and Freddy Unger. And me. Because all of us made terrible mistakes—and that's a story I'd better learn to tell, too.

ROBERT A. CANDERELLI WEEKES
Field Commander,
Free North American Air Cavalry
Matamoros, Mexico
January 1, 1939

PART 1

EMMALINE'S SON

1

APRIL 1917

Though he was a famously incompetent sigilrist, Benjamin Franklin included five practical glyphs that he had learned from the women of Philadelphia in an early edition of *Poor Richard's Almanack*, as well as a simple design for a message board. In less than an hour, a woman could build a Franklin sand table using a silver penny, pane of window glass, hammer, and broom handle. This was to prove vital to the Continental Army during the Revolution.

Victoria Ferris-Smythe, *Empirical Philosophy:*
An American History, 1938

A LITTLE MORE THAN five decades after Mrs. Cadwallader ended the Civil War, I was eighteen years old and lived in Guille's Run, Montana, with my mother, Maj. Emmaline Weekes, who served as our county philosopher. In her official capacity, Ma responded to all manner of accidents and natural disasters. The rest of the time, she earned a decent living doing the kind of dull, ordinary sigilry that was in constant demand—short-haul passenger flights, koru glyphs for enlarging crops, simple smokecarving cures for asthma and pleurisy.

Much as I would have liked to help her in the field, Mother only rarely gave me the chance. I had the typical male lack of philosophical aptitude and so instead of going on emergency calls, I did the work of a philosopher's son: I kept the books, ordered supplies, cooked, and stood night watches.

On the night of April 6, 1917, I was engaged in the thrilling task of organizing handwritten invoices from the previous year when Mother stormed into the house at nine o'clock, dripping wet from the rain.

"What kept you?" I called.

"Don't even start, Boober!" she shouted. "Those cattle were scattered clear across Teller's Nook. I must have put in four hundred miles trying to track down the last ones. Mr. Collins is going to be mad as hell when he gets the bill."

Mother ran a towel over her face and graying hair. She'd taken ten emergency calls over the previous fourteen hours—a very busy day—in the midst of terrible weather.

"There's beef stew on the stove," I said.

Mother dished herself a bowl and collapsed in a chair. I'd eaten hours before.

"You've heard the news, I expect?" Mother said.

I had. After months of prodding, President Wilson had convinced Congress to declare war on the German Empire. So now America, too, would be part of the fighting that had racked Europe since 1914.

I'd decided I wanted to join up the second I heard. The army or the navy; one was as good as the other. A uniform, a chance to see the world while fighting next to the boys I'd grown up with, a real man's job.

But I knew Mother was going to be a problem. She'd spent three decades with the Rescue and Evacuation Department of the US Sigilry Corps, flying wounded and dying soldiers from the front lines back to the field hospitals. She'd done tours of duty in the Franco-Prussian Intervention, the war with Cuba, the Philippine Insurrection, and the Hawaiian Rebellion. As a result, she tended not to approve of America involving itself in other people's wars. She wasn't going to like the idea of me enlisting.

"Is there any chance you could be called up?" I asked, trying to position the conversation just so.

"Never," Mother said. "They'll mobilize a few of the younger reservists and move more active-duty women overseas. But they're not going to call a sixty-year-old lady, even if my name is still on the lists. It would be an embarrassment. No, what I'm worried about is when Wilson calls for a draft for the army."

And there was my chance.

I regretted it a little. If I'd had my pick of careers, I would have done as Mother had and served with Rescue and Evac—the best fliers in the world, saving lives instead of taking them. But that was impossible. R&E was the Corps' most elite unit. They'd never commissioned a man. And while I was a fine hoverer for a boy, the least R&E woman could fly circles around me. So, the army didn't seem a bad second choice.

"I spoke with the State Philosophical Office," Mother continued. "They expect to get two draft exemptions for essential support personnel. One of those is for you."

This was going wrong already. She must have spent months laying the groundwork for that.

"Well, that's good to know," I said. "But what I was thinking is that Willard Gunch dropped by this afternoon. He and Jack are talking about riding into town, maybe on Monday. To sign up."

"Absolutely not."

"Roddy Hutch is going with them," I continued. "Probably Eliot Newton, too. And—"

"No! How can you even think it?"

"Mother, listen—if you sign up, you get to choose. You don't have to go in the infantry."

"It's all of them that get blown to hell and flinders! In the cavalry and the artillery and the merchant marine. I could tell you stories about the burns on the sailors at Manila Bay that would make your teeth sweat."

"Jesus, Ma! I'm going to be the only man my age in Montana sitting at home. You joined the Corps when you were only thirteen years—"

"I don't care if you're the last man in the *world* sitting at home! You're not going, and I'm not discussing this." She swept up her bowl and spoon, went to her bedroom, and slammed the door.

Midnight came and went. Outside, the rain picked up and battered at the shutters. I fixed myself a cold ham sandwich and sat glumly back down in our little laboratory behind the kitchen.

Essential support personnel. I should have seen it coming. I should have rehearsed my speech better, with all its fine sentiments about duty and loyalty to one's friends and adventure. Maybe I would broach the idea of enlisting again tomorrow after Mother had had time to get used to it.

I tried to set my feelings aside as I settled in to mix up a batch of silver chloride, which we used for stasis sigilry. It was a godsend for flying when you had to strap a sick or nervous passenger to your back—draw a stasis sigil with powdered silver chloride on a client's chest and she went stiff as a corpse. No breathing, no bleeding, no experience of what was going on around her. Most important, she didn't try to help you hover by flapping her arms and throwing off your center of gravity. We were down to our last three tubes. I'd already put an order in with Harnemon's Philosophical Supplies, America's finest purveyor of philosophical powders, but they needed a couple weeks to arrange a shipment to a place as remote as Guille's Run. I would have to mix up a batch of homemade stuff to last until their delivery arrived.

I weighed out a measure of thin, feathery crystals of silver nitrate and dissolved it in a beaker of hot water. I stirred for several minutes until I had a colorless solution, then did a few calculations and poured in the appropriate amount of common table salt. A whitish precipitate formed, swirling like snow toward the bottom of the beaker. Over the next hour, I laboriously filtered out the solids, washed them, dried them over a flame, and measured the powder into tiny smoked-glass tubes, which I put safely away in their padded box.

Then I kicked the powder cabinet shut.

How did Ma think she was going to stop me if I decided to sign up? I was an adult; it wasn't as if I needed her permission. I could simply go. Tonight even. She could find any old philosopher to replace me.

I needed advice. I needed my half sister Angela.

I went back to the kitchen and pulled out my message board. It was quite a large model for the time, an eighteen-inch square of glass with a wooden frame, the underside of which was coated with silver leaf. I took a scoop of milled quartz—highly refined sand—and poured it onto the glass, then smoothed it with my board scraper. Using the four-beat rhythm that the sigil required, I traced Angela's personal glyph into the sand in the upper right-hand corner with my finger.

Ma said no, I wrote in the sand. *What nxt?*

I countersigned my own glyph in the opposite corner, drew the sigil to send, and wiped the sand level with the scraper. The same message would appear immediately on Angela's board the next time she set it to receive.

(A perfectly reasonable person might ask why it should work at all—why should the sand on a slab of glass two thousand miles away shift to form the same words I'd just written? Well, philosophy warps the laws of probability. If you watched a million plates of sand for a million years, eventually the powder on one of them would slip a little and end up resembling the letter *A*. Philosophical energy just gives it a nudge in the right direction.)

I drew sigils to bring up the conversation Angela and I had had during the afternoon.

Hows she tking it? Angela had written.

Dunno, I'd replied. *I havnt askd yet. She's prbly mad not to be joinng th fun.*

Don't joke abt tht! 4 wars was plenty. Talk lik that & she might voluntr.

Wht abt y? I'd asked. *Cld be philsphr draft.*

Nevr, Angela had said. *If they do, I'll mov to Mexco.*

Snds warm. I'll vist.

Sure, bt when are y vistng me here?

I wished I could. Six months before, Angela had run off to New York City, where a friend had found her a job as an amanuensis handling the message boards at a bank. It shouldn't have been a surprise; Angela had entertained fantasies like that for years, one exotic locale after the next. But when she'd actually left in the middle of the night with one of Mother's old duffels full of clothes and equipment, Ma and I had been stunned.

Angela's departure had left Mother in a difficult spot. Angela had been Ma's field assistant, backing her up on difficult calls and taking care of the simpler ones herself, so that Mother wasn't exhausted by the end of the day. I was a poor substitute at best, a fact the State Philosophical Board had driven home a few weeks earlier by denying me credentials as an apprentice. They didn't mind if I tagged along from time to time, but, as they put it, *We cannot find any precedent for permitting a man to serve as a state philosophical officer, even in a trainee capacity. Indeed, it seems unwise and inhumane, both for you and potential clients, to allow such a circumstance.*

Which meant Ma now did all the practical philosophy and I was nothing better than her housekeeper.

"It's not the women's work you'd hoped to be doing, is it?" my best friend, Willard, had said on my last visit to Billings, twelve miles up the road. That conversation had turned into our first fistfight in years. (I'd knocked out two of his teeth.) Willard was right, though. Something was going to have to change at home before I got in real trouble or Mother dropped dead from exhaustion.

I tried to console myself by reading a few pages from my favorite book, *Life and Death on San Juan Hill,* the memoir of Lt. Col. Yvette Rodgers, who'd commanded the first modern R&E wing during the war in Cuba. Chapter eleven—Lt. Col. Rodgers trying desperately to guide a wounded flier back to the landing field by message after sunset, the woman lost and running low on powder, when the Corps encampment comes under Spanish cannon fire. Rodgers has the clever idea to—

Out of the corner of my eye, I saw the sand shift on the message board, which I'd left set to receive under Mother's glyph. It now read:

TO: E Weekes

FR: Montana Philosophical Office, Night Desk

PRIORITY CALL. Respond immediately.

"Oh, come on!" I muttered. I didn't want to haul Ma out of bed.

Robert Weekes for E Weekes, I replied. *Details, pls?*

Original request reads: 'RA, RA, RA fam,' the State night desk answered. *Unable to reach originator by board. Glyph matches for Klein, Evelyn. Address on record is rural home approx 1.8 miles north of Three Forks.*

That was a mess. So, someone had messaged an RA—a request for assistance—for an entire family and then had failed to reply to any follow-up messages. A sigilrist might do that right before she ran out to fetch the doctor. Or for a fire. Or as a prank. The State Office seemed confident of the location, but I'd never heard of anything called Three Forks.

Wht county is 3 Forks? I asked.

Gallatin County. Best estimate of location: latitude N45° 53' 33", longitude W111° 33' 8".

I pulled out a sheaf of topographical maps and found the spot—175 miles away, well outside Mother's usual area of responsibility.

I wrote: *Confrm: to Emmaline Weekes?*

Y. No closer CP avail. Tell E sorry from us, Robert.

"Son of a bitch!" I said. Mother was going to have to cover it and it was going to take the rest of the night. On top of that, she'd be flying in the middle of a rainstorm with only the sketchiest information.

Acknowledged and accepted for E Weekes at 2:48, I wrote.

I rapped on her bedroom door. "Mother!" I called. Nothing. I opened the door and shouted her name. She continued snoring. "Flight for you, Major!"

Without entirely waking, Mother lurched out of bed, wrapped her bathrobe around herself, and shuffled into the kitchen.

"Did you say something?" she asked.

I ran back through the messages for her. Ma shook her head in disgust. "I'm supposed to be at the construction site for the hotel in Billings at six! If I'm lucky, I'll clear this in time to be a couple hours late."

Mother was fully awake now and copying the coordinates down. She spread out the large-format Montana topo map on the desk and began lining up a course. "Squeeze through the pass and sight from the church steeple in Bozeman. Roughly west-northwest." She had a straightedge and compass out and was using a cardboard slide rule to determine flight times and powder expenditure. She stopped and gave me an irritated look.

"Well, go get dressed!" she said.

"I *am* dressed," I said.

"Put on your skysuit."

"You want me to fly it?" I asked, my voice rising an octave and a half.

Mother didn't even look up from her charts. "I need a navigator and a second pair of eyes. This is already a goat rodeo and it's going to get worse."

2

Spanish conquistadors as early as 1540 mention witnessing a Cherokee fertility ritual in which medicine women drew symbols with corn pollen and were hurled into the air "as if by the hand of God." However, the hover sigil did not see widespread use until 1870, when Mary Grinning Fox substituted finely milled cornmeal for pollen and mixed in sand as a stabilizer. By redrawing the glyph while in midair, Fox learned to produce continuous thrust; by warping it, she could change speed and position, allowing for aerial maneuvers. After numerous crashes into Lake Ontario, Fox also designed the mechanical regulator to ensure uniform powder flow and rigging to secure her equipment tightly to the body.

Victoria Ferris-Smythe, Empirical Philosophy:
An American History, 1938

I SPRINTED UPSTAIRS TO my room. I'd flown high school classmates hundreds of times, but Ma had never taken me along on an emergency case like this.

I put on long johns and a heavy, winter-weight skysuit—a high-necked set of wool coveralls with padding over the ribs and shoulders to protect against harness burn—two pairs of wool socks, boots, a knit cap, gloves, and my oilskin slicker. I stuck my leather helmet and goggles under my arm.

Mother was already kitted out when I returned to the office. She was sending and receiving messages at a terrific rate.

"I don't like the smell of this," Mother said. "I knew Evelyn Klein during the Disturbances. She's a smokecarver—deadly serious woman. She has a couple of children, but I can't see this as a prank."

"Whole family got sick, maybe?" I suggested.

"Too sick to answer a follow-up message?" Mother answered. She shook her head.

"It shouldn't even be your call in the first place," I said.

"Well, we're it for all of Montana right now. A tornado hit the mining camp outside Eureka, with at least forty injured. The State Office pulled the CPs from Helena, Missoula, Bozeman, and Butte to evacuate casualties and left us to cover everywhere else."

"Jesus," I said. "They could have warned me."

"They're still trying to scramble everyone. The problem for *us* is that we don't know how many of the Kleins we'll be flying. If it's more than two, I'll need you to carry the lighter ones."

"Okay," I said, but my voice wavered again.

"You'll do fine," Mother said. "I'll take you as a passenger on the way there so that you're fresh for the second leg. If you have to carry someone, we'll put her in stasis. You'll barely even notice her."

I wished I felt as confident as she sounded.

We gathered equipment. I rolled up a Montana map and put it in a carry tube, adding a slide rule, trigonometric tables, and a pencil in case we needed to plot a new course. We each strapped a portable message board to our right forearm; these had tight, membranous covers over the sand that allowed just enough give for writing. They were small and balky, but good enough to send a couple words to each other or the State Office. In the mudroom, I collected my harness: a heavy leather vest with straps running over the shoulders and across at the waist, plus leg straps that fit around the upper thigh. Four heavy steel carabiners were mounted on the back to clip into a passenger's harness, with four more carabiners on the front for securing a second passenger.

We kept several powder bags filled for emergency calls. They looked like oversized pastry bags made of waxed canvas and filled with premixed corn powder and sand. I grabbed an extra-large forty-pound bag, plus a ten-pounder as a backup, and strapped them to my harness. Mother, who needed extra powder to haul me on the first leg of the trip, attached three bags to her harness. She was puffing under the weight of ninety pounds of powder by the time she clipped the last one on.

On the pointy end of each bag, we attached a regulator—a small clock-work device the size of a child's fist, which used a thumb lever and a series of baffles to ensure that the corn powder trickled out at a consistent rate while we were in the air. Last, I clipped the carabiners on the back of my harness into the rear of Mother's and we staggered out of the house, back-to-back, into the driving rain.

"Tell me when you're ready," Mother said.

"Go!" I called.

Mother thumbed her regulator open and, holding the tip like a pencil between her fingers, used the stream of powder that flowed out to trace a hover sigil in the air. As she drew, she heaved against the weight of her pow-der bags and me. Her sigil took and we floated up to ten feet.

We immediately felt lighter. If you've never flown before—and I don't mean in a hot air balloon or an aeroplane—if you've never *hovered*, then the only comparison to make is that of buoyancy in water, of flotation. You can saddle up on the ground with six hundred pounds of cargo, but once you push off into the air, it feels like almost nothing.

"Everything in order?" Mother called over her shoulder to me.

"Fine!" I answered.

She opened her regulator wider and drew a fresh sigil. We rocketed straight up. It was all I could do to keep from whooping. Ma hadn't carried me in years, not since I'd learned to fly myself.

Every few seconds, Mother redrew the sigil, shaping it so that our ascent flattened and we accelerated in the horizontal plane as well. After a couple minutes, we'd reached ten thousand feet. Mother could estimate her altitude by intuition—the thickness of the air, the bite of the breeze on her cheek, the pressure on her eardrums.

We traveled at two hundred miles per hour, following the Yellowstone River Valley as it wound westward. Below us, the flat, scrubby land gave way to hillier terrain and then to the Rocky Mountains themselves. Mother had flown the first part of our route hundreds of times, so I didn't feel especially nervous about plowing into a mountain, which happened with frightening regularity to hoverers stupid enough to be out at night in bad weather. What I was feeling, however, were the seven biscuits, three bowls of stew, mug of cocoa, and ham sandwich I'd consumed during my night watch. That, combined with the persistent, irregular sway as I hung from Mother's harness, was conspiring to churn my stomach.

I tried breathing through my nose and closing my eyes, but that only made things worse. I had the sensation of running down a flight of stairs and missing the last step endlessly, stuck perpetually in the first two inches of a six-inch fall. My cheeks flushed hot. Rivulets of water streamed down my face and into my mouth.

I turned my head and upchucked, managing simultaneously to get vomit down the neck of my rain slicker and spin us off course. Mother drew sigils furiously, trying to point us back in the right direction. If we missed Bozeman, it was going to be a very dark night on which to be lost. Mother leaned forward to fly more headfirst, which caused my harness to dig into my armpits till my fingers went numb. I tried to reposition myself.

"Quit it!" Mother barked. Many a flier has been knocked off the level by a fidgety passenger—a poorly timed squirm followed by a long plunge.

I resigned myself to holding as still as I could. But it was cold at our high altitude and the wind buffeted me fiercely, though not half so badly as it must have my mother. I tried to tense my body to avoid shivering, but I shook all the same. Every movement nudged us farther off course.

After a miserable hour of flying, Mother broke through the cloud cover and descended over what we presumed to be Bozeman. We couldn't see a damn thing. Ma began a series of gradually widening turns, searching for the city lights or the church steeple, which was lit at night with a handful of cold chemical flares, partially for the glory of God, but more practically so that hoverers would have a fixed navigation point. We needed twenty minutes before Mother spotted the steeple's distant blue glow and took us to it.

"Look sharp," Mother called. "You're navigating."

Mother was perfectly capable of keeping time and watching the compass herself but it never hurts to give an airsick passenger something to occupy his mind.

"Come about to 284 degrees," I called. She began a slow yawing turn, the sort of maneuver that looks as if it ought to be one of the first lessons a hoverer learns, but is fantastically difficult without setting your body spinning in a second plane of motion. When the needle hit 284 I yelled for a stop, though trying to read a compass to within one degree of accuracy was questionable even under the best of conditions. Mother leveled and adjusted until we were both satisfied, then pulled above the clouds to get us out of the rain.

"Set your speed to two hundred miles per hour and we'll fly for 395 seconds," I said.

Mother charged forward again. She flew crisply, but I was worried we might never find our destination. We'd nearly missed an entire town—spotting a single house, based on rough coordinates from the State Office, in the dark, in the rain, would be almost impossible.

As we raced through the darkness, I squinted at my wristwatch and compass in the starlight. A couple of times I instructed Mother to ease back a degree or two when we started to drift. When I called time, Mother put us into a turn to bleed off speed and dove beneath the clouds. We couldn't see anything promising. Mother circled wider and lower. By the time we'd come down to eight hundred feet, we were losing hope that the folks who'd originated the call had bothered to light a signal for us.

"I swear to God," Mother said. "If these idiots didn't mark a landing field . . ."

"Do you smell smoke?" I asked.

We blundered lower still. Ma caught sight of something burning with writhing, flickering green flashes.

"Looks like a sheet of smokecarved insulation," Mother said. "It burns that color for hours. But that's an odd choice for a marker."

She flew us closer. The piece of insulation was pinned under a collapsed roof beam. We could make out embers hissing in the rain. The house had burned nearly to its foundation.

"How does a smokecarver's home burn down?" I asked. A good smoke-carver could throw blankets of anoxic smoke over a burning building to smother the flames—there was no one you'd rather have at a fire. Unless she'd never made it out.

"I don't like this," Ma muttered.

She found an open area behind the house and tossed flares onto the grass below to light a landing field. I pulled my knees to my chest and Ma set us down.

I unclipped from her and we shucked our bags. Mother drew her gun, a big army-surplus revolver.

"County philosopher!" Mother shouted.

No one answered.

"They ran?" I suggested. "Or they flew for help?"

"Evelyn doesn't fly," Ma said. "She always said it was too dangerous."

I took a cold chemical flare from my pocket and cracked it so that the two vials of smokecarved chemicals inside mixed together. The tip of the flare glowed faintly at first, then more strongly, until it was brighter than a lantern. I played the light over the ground. An outbuilding lay in a smoldering heap fifty feet from the ruins of the house.

"That was her lab over there, maybe?" I said to Mother. "How'd that burn, too?"

"Stay close," Ma whispered.

We went toward the front of the house. Something moved in the grass. Mother froze.

"Hello?" she cried. She leveled her pistol at the noise. "Evelyn?"

Something rushed toward us. Mother fired twice—but it was only a rabbit bounding away into the night.

I'd never seen her so trigger-happy.

"It's okay, Ma," I said. "The fire was an accident, right? A smokecarver keeps a million powders that can burn. Something exploded in the lab and the house caught."

"Maybe," she said.

We continued walking.

"They went for the neighbors," I suggested. "Nearest house is probably a couple miles away. I'll get on the board with the State Office and ask them to figure out where—"

I tripped over something and went down in a heap.

It was a body, lying facedown in the high grass. A big man, three hundred pounds.

"Oh, God!" I said. "Ma!"

We rolled him on his back. I couldn't find a pulse on his neck, but saw him take a breath. He was bleeding from four or five bullet wounds in the chest and belly.

"That's her husband!" snapped Mother. "Move!"

Ma ripped his shirt open and dug several tubes out of her workbag, preparing to put the man into stasis. She pulled an inch-long strip of indicator paper from one vial, wet it with her tongue, and stuck it to his neck.

"Hold the light for me," she said, while she perched her reading glasses on the tip of her nose.

"Clear?" she asked me.

"Clear!" I said. If you were touching a body as it went into stasis, the sigil could spread and freeze you, too.

Ma popped the cork off a tube of silver chloride and let the powder spill out in a thin stream, with which she traced a series of interlocking loops on the man's chest. For a second, I thought her sigil had gone bad. A failed stasis can end up immobilizing just the heart, which is invariably fatal. But then the man convulsed and went stiff. Ma yanked on his arm, which didn't move.

"Looks good," she said.

A body in stasis isn't merely immobilized. It goes right on doing everything it always does—exchanging air in the lungs, bleeding from a wound, being injured when it falls—but at an infinitesimal fraction of the usual rate. So, we could fly him to the hospital in Helena and he would lose only a drop or two of blood. But we needed to know how long we had before the sigil wore off.

Mother peeled the strip of indicator paper off his neck and applied a drop of formic acid from a third vial. The strip reacted with the acid, causing it to change color. Normally, the reaction was instantaneous, but the strip, which had been placed in stasis along with the man, now reacted thousands of times more slowly.

"Check it at two minutes," she told me, and then set about wrestling the big man into a passenger harness. She struggled to get the straps under his legs. I reached to help her.

"No, watch the strip!" Ma said. She wiped the rain out of her face.

I looked at my wristwatch. When exactly two minutes had passed, I compared the indicator paper to a color chart we kept rolled up inside the vial.

"Okay, so, uhh, looks like 1.8 percent decay over two minutes," I told Mother, who had finished rigging the man to fly.

"Fifty minutes before he comes out of it," Mother said. "Shit, that's a weak glyph."

"No," I said. "We measured over two minutes, so that's . . ."

"You're right—one hundred ten minutes. Sorry."

I wrote the stasis off-time on his forehead in grease pencil.

"Let's search the rest of the way around," Ma said. "See if there are any other survivors. Robert, this must have been . . ."

"Trenchers?" I asked.

Ma nodded.

The Brotherhood of the Trenches was a secret society that had sworn to destroy sigilry—they'd been behind a spate of assassinations and arsons in the

1890s and then again around the turn of the century. But there hadn't been a Trencher attack in ten years. And certainly never one in Montana.

"Robert!" Mother called.

A few paces away in the grass was a boy, maybe fourteen years old. Hit in the neck and cool to the touch, but he murmured when I pulled his shirt open. We stasied him and got him into a harness as well.

"We need help," Ma said. "Message the State night desk. Get the sheriff, get more fliers. Anyone they can find."

I wrote on my wrist board: *RA RA RA. R Weekes for E Weekes. Multpl wounded, shot. Arson. Send backup CP & sherif.*

I tried to keep my breathing steady. Don't panic. If the Trenchers had been here, then they were long gone or they would have taken a shot at us, too.

Received, the night desk replied. *Stand by.*

I swept the light from my flare across the yard. I thought I could see something else just ahead.

I glanced down at my message board: *Notification sent to Gallatin Cty Sheriff and awaiting response. No available CPs for assistance. Tell your mom: we can scramble the volunteer rescue team from Boise or Spokane.*

Unhelpful. Given the Boise team's reputation, they would probably need rescuing themselves. And Spokane was a three-hour flight.

"Don't come back here!" Mother shouted from the other side of the house. "They shot her halfway out the window. Just a girl. Damn them!"

"Ma," I called. "Should they scramble Boise or Spokane?"

"Damn them!" I heard her say again, stifling a sob.

"Ma?" I shouted. "I'll tell them scramble Spokane, right?"

I took another step forward. There was a big oak tree in their front yard. Something was creaking in the branches.

I shined my light toward it and screamed.

A woman's body, hanged by the neck, the skin charred black.

3

Kill the right two hundred sigilrists and empirical philosophy as we know it will come to an end. And I know which ones.

Maxwell Gannet, Trencher Party presidential
candidate, May 11, 1892

"SHE'S DEAD," MOTHER SAID. "We can't help her."

"Was she still alive?" I asked, choking back tears. "When they burned her?"

"No," said Mother. "Her hands aren't bound. They shot her and then burned the body."

A comfort to think so, at least.

"Help me get the wounded attached," Mother said. "Them, we can still help. We'll fly them to the hospital in Helena."

"Okay," I said.

Ma and I heaved the large man upright then clipped his harness to the back of hers. I dragged the stasied boy over and leaned him against Mother's chest. She clipped into him, too. The stasied man behind her shifted and leaned precariously.

"I need to get in the air," Ma said. "Grab your gear. I'll meet you at fifty feet."

I looked back at the corpse hanging in the tree—her dress charred, her face charred, her hands—

"Robert!"

"Okay," I said.

Mother drew a launch sigil and climbed into the air. I went around back to retrieve my equipment. I had just buckled my powder bag into place on my right hip when I heard a creak.

"Hello!" I shouted.

I shined my flare toward the remains of the house and reached for my belt knife. I heard another noise.

There was a door to an underground storm cellar, open two inches. Someone was peeping out from under.

"Hello?" I called. "County philosopher!"

The door rose higher. It was a little girl, about four years old.

I went over and lifted the door open. She looked out at me in the flare's eerie blue light. I took a knee so that we were on eye level.

"Hi, sweetie," I said, sheathing my knife. "Come on out."

"That's not my name," she said.

"What *is* your name?"

"Carla."

"Come on out, Carla."

"I'm not supposed to. Only if it's a woman looking for me."

"It's okay," I said. "My ma's the county philosopher. I'm—her helper." She shook her head.

"Did you see us when we landed?" I asked. "That was my ma. She knew your mom a long time ago. Your mom's name is Evelyn, right?"

The girl nodded. She had a rag doll in her hands and was twisting its arms. "I have to say good-bye to Mr. B first," she said, pointing to the doll. Mr. B had braids and a gingham dress.

"Mr. B can come with us," I said.

"I'm not allowed to take it outside."

"You can, just for today."

Carla climbed out into the rain. I took a child's harness from my rigging bag and helped her into it.

"How many brothers and sisters do you have?" I asked.

"One brother," she said. "And one sister."

So no bodies that we'd missed.

"Our house burned down," she said.

"Yeah," I said. "Yeah, it did."

"There were men with guns. I heard them shooting. Mom told me to go down in the storm cellar."

I swallowed. "You did just right."

"Did everybody get shot?" she asked.

"My ma's carrying your brother and your dad. We're going to take them to the big hospital in Helena."

That seemed acceptable to her. Carla put her arms through the shoulder straps of the harness and stepped into the leg loops.

"Can you really fly?" she asked me.

"Sure," I said.

"But you're a boy."

"Some boys can fly. I can fly."

I picked her up and clipped her to my harness, snug against my chest, facing out. Safer for a child in front in the event of a hard landing. Her feet dangled in the air.

"Okay," I said, handing her the doll. "I'm going to carry you and you're going to carry Mr. B. Are you ready?" She didn't answer. "When you say *go*, we'll go up."

"Why?" she asked.

"Because that's how it's done."

"Oh," she said. "Go!"

I pushed the lever on my regulator to open it and drew a launch sigil. We sprang into the air. I redrew my sigil to pull us up to fifty feet and picked out Mother by the light of the safety flare she'd attached to one ankle.

"What the *hell* are you doing?" Mother shouted when she caught sight of me.

"She's not supposed to say that," Carla told me.

"I know," I said. I turned and called to Mother, "There was a little girl in the cellar. She's okay. I couldn't leave her!"

"Why didn't you stasis her?"

"Because *you've* got the silver chloride!"

"Shit," Ma said. "How fast can you go with a passenger? Eighty miles an hour?"

"Sure, probably," I said, though that seemed generous.

"Well, follow me," she said.

We climbed straight up through the cloud cover and set course for Helena. Within minutes, though, I was falling behind. I opened my regulator wider and redrew, bumping up a couple hundred feet in the process. I could still see what I thought was Mother's flare, but by the time I flattened out I'd lost sight of her. Not a serious problem, since we had our calculations to fly by. But better to stay close to each other.

Location? I wrote on my message board to Mother.

Nothing.

Lost visual, I wrote. Still nothing. She might be quite close by, perhaps obscured by a whiff of fog. Or she might have dropped back to make sure I was managing. I checked over both shoulders, but couldn't see her.

Something felt wrong about it. I drew the glyph for the State night desk and messaged *Board check.*

A few seconds later I got an answer: *Received message was clear. This is a test message.*

So my board wasn't the problem.

I drew my mother's glyph and sent: *Υ OK?*

Carla turned to look up at me, tipping us several degrees off course.

"What are you writing?" she asked in an accusatory voice.

"A message to my mother," I said, drawing sigils to adjust our heading.

I checked my message board again. There was something there, but it was illegible. Mother's glyph, badly drawn, was in the sender's corner. I peered at the message in the ghostly blue light of my safety flare. A moment later, something else came across. *Ctu.*

Continue. That didn't put me at ease. Mother had grown up during a time when the fidelity of messaging was so poor they'd had boards practically the size of dinner tables and had to write in letters a foot high; by necessity, she'd learned to be economical with her words. But this was terse even by her standards.

Are you ok? I wrote.

Ctu she sent again.

Confirm? I wrote, *Ctu to Helna? W/o you?*

Y came the reply. *Ctu.*

You ok?

No answer. Obviously not okay. Maybe a minor technical problem—a jammed primary regulator—that Mother was working to fix. If that was the case, she didn't need the added distraction of responding to me.

"I'm cold," Carla whined.

"I know," I said. "I'm sorry."

A few minutes later, I reached the valley leading to Helena. I'd only been there once in my life. I could see lights, but I didn't know where the hospital was.

I put us into a gentle descent and took a black book from the pouch on my belt. It contained a few hundred important message glyphs for the State of Montana, including the Department of Philosophical Medicine at St. Peter's Hospital. They were supposed to have someone watching their board around the clock so that if a county philosopher in the field had a question she could write in for advice.

Pls light lnd field for hvr evac, I wrote.

Flier and ETA? the hospital replied.

R Weekes. Immedt, I answered.

Patient status?

It was ominous that they were asking. Ma should have messaged to let them know we were on the way.

I wrote: *50yo M, 14yo M; multipl gunsht, comatose; +STASIS.*

There was no rejoinder. There were also no lights to mark my landing zone.

I still had plenty of powder, so I kept circling, hoping I might spot the hospital as a larger four-story brick blob among a landscape of slightly smaller blobs.

"What are you doing?" Carla asked.

"I'm waiting for instructions to land," I said.

"You're going to *land*? With me?"

"That's what we do at the end of a flight."

"I think you're going to crash."

"I've never crashed yet," I said, which, discounting a few hiccups while learning to take off nine years before, was even pretty strictly true.

Off my left shoulder, I saw several blue lights flicker to life—flares to mark the corners of the landing field. I made for them, descending rapidly. The ground would be soft and muddy. No obstacles that I could see. Ideal.

There were several techniques for setting down, which depended on conditions and a flier's personal style. I decided to use the simplest one: come to a dead hover a couple inches above the ground, cut my regulator, and simply drop.

I brought my altitude down to six feet and eased toward the field.

"Where's Mr. B?" asked Carla.

"You have him," I answered, as we came to three feet.

"Where is he?" she wailed, thrashing her arms.

I tried to compensate, but somehow introduced a lateral vector and started squeaking left. I couldn't correct fast enough and overshot the field.

"I don't have him!" cried Carla.

At the same moment, something mooed directly in front of me. I tried to maneuver up and over the herd of cows that had appeared out of nowhere, but my regulator jammed, cutting off the flow of powder. For a moment we hung in the air, eight feet off the ground, as my sigil faded and died. Then we dropped like a rock.

I hit hard and blind, rolling my left ankle and falling backward, clutching Carla to my chest to protect her from the impact. I bounced my head off the ground hard enough to hear bells. Or rather, I really did hear bells. The cows, which saw fliers land several times a week, plodded over to investigate.

"Flier down!" came a distant cry.

"You lost Mr. B!" Carla howled.

"Christ," I muttered. I tried to stand, but my left ankle buckled under me.

"You're not supposed to say that!" sobbed Carla.

I worked myself into a sitting position and began unclipping the girl's harness. Two women and a man hurried over from the hospital building, carrying lanterns. One was a young nurse in a starched white uniform. One was a dour, middle-aged woman wearing a smokecarver's gray apron over her dress, which would make her the hospital philosopher. The third wore a white coat that had been misbuttoned—a young physician who'd been dragged out of bed.

"Is that Angela Weekes?" the middle-aged woman asked.

"It's Robert," I said.

She nodded, as if that better accounted for what she was seeing. "Looked like an *A* in your message."

"Is that the gunshot victim?" the doctor asked.

The nurse knelt by Carla. "What did he do to you? Are you hurt?"

"Why isn't she in stasis?" the doctor demanded.

"He lost Mr. B!"

"Where are you hurt, sweetheart?"

"That's not my name!"

"Where's Emmaline?"

"Everybody shut up!" I roared. To my surprise, they did.

"We got called for an RA out past Bozeman," I said. "There were no other fliers available, so my mother brought me. We found two injured and two more—deceased. Ma took the wounded, but I lost contact with her. I think she went down. And Carla lost her dolly."

"You two, get her inside, please," the hospital philosopher said to the others. "I'll see to him."

The nurse picked up the girl, but Carla squirmed in her arms, twisting so that she could see me. "I hate you!" she screamed.

I pressed my lips together and tried to regain my composure. The hospital philosopher put her arm on my shoulder.

"Is that Evelyn Klein's girl?" she asked me. "My God, what happened?"

I tried to find my voice. "They shot her and hanged her and burned her. They shot everybody."

"Oh, Jesus!" the woman said. "Does the girl know?"

"I don't think she understands."

"Oh, Lord." She wiped her eyes. "That's a terrible thing to see. You come inside, too, Robert. I'm Bertie Synge. I'm the chief of medical philosophy."

I took her hand and shook it. "Doctor," I said. "Are you a hoverer, by any chance?"

"Good heavens, no," she said. "I do stasisry and smokecarving. I'll be the one to do the anesthesia for the gunshot cases in the operating room."

"There aren't going to *be* any cases if we can't find my mother," I said. "Does anybody here fly?"

"One or two of the nurses, but certainly no one well enough to take a passenger."

With mounting panic, I realized I was going to be searching for Mother alone. And I had no idea where she was.

4

Upward! You must be moving upward while launching. You are not flying, you are engaging in a prolonged and well-controlled ten-mile broad jump.

Amelia Tintinalli, *Hovering Emergencies and Recovery, Third Edition,* 1915

DR. SYNGE SHOWED ME into the hoverers' room, which was a sparsely furnished office. I eased into a chair, my left ankle still throbbing, and drew to receive messages on the tabletop board. Nothing new. I tried another message to Mother.

"Nothing?" Synge asked.

I shook my head. I messaged the State Office to explain the situation and beg for help.

Impossible, they replied. *There are 100+ injured or missing at the mining camp in Eureka. Have diverted volunteers from Boise, Spokane, and Calgary to assist. Cannot provide search team to you before late morning at earliest.*

The Kleins' stasis sigils only had a little more than an hour left—they were going to be dead by the time I got help.

I spread out the large Montana map on the table while Dr. Synge looked on.

"The Klein place is forty miles away," Synge said. "That's all rough country. You couldn't search that much territory alone in a *month.*"

"Right," I said. "But I lost track of Ma five minutes into the flight. It took her two or three minutes to message me. If she stayed within ten degrees of our course that leaves . . ."

I used a ruler and compass to draw a triangle on the map and did the calculations. Fifty-five hundred acres. Still impossible.

But then there it was, scrawled across the board: *RA*.

Request assistance. I heaved a huge sigh of relief. Mother was down and probably hurt, but she was together enough to send a meaningful message.

Where are you? I wrote.

This time the reply came quickly: *Dwn. On course line.*

Every hoverer who'd ever made an unplanned landing claimed she'd stayed right on course, even if she'd glided for miles in the wrong direction. But if Mother really *had*, then finding her would be as simple as retracing my route to the Kleins' house. It might really be possible to do it myself.

Cn y light flares? I wrote.

Y.

Are y hurt?

No answer to that. So, yes.

I pushed myself to my feet, grunting in pain, and began buckling my powder bag back on.

"This is *not* a good idea," Dr. Synge said. "If you try to do this alone with a bad ankle and a concussion, then we're going to be searching for you, too."

"There's barely an hour left on those stasis sigils. They're going to die if I don't try!"

Dr. Synge hissed through her teeth. "How long can you fly before philosophical fatigue sets in?"

That was a fair question.

The problem for philosophers is that you can't get something for nothing. When a philosopher's body supplies the philosophical power for an energy-intensive sigil, like hovering, it throws her blood chemistry out of kilter. Mother, who'd been flying for four decades, could go hours without feeling the effects, but if I hovered longer than an hour I wound up with a raging headache. Push beyond that, and I risked muscle cramps, confusion, and palpitations. Go further still and my heart might simply stop.

"I'll be fine to get there and back," I said. I pulled on my helmet and goggles.

"I can't allow this," said Dr. Synge. "You're an unqualified teenager, a *male*, who's never—"

"I'm Emmaline Weekes's son!" I shouted. "Either help or get out of the way."

Synge gave a half shake of the head. She pulled my arm over her shoulders and helped me limp out of the hospital and onto the landing field.

"Godspeed, Mr. Weekes," Dr. Synge said, tucking an extra stasis kit into my workbag.

I launched and accelerated hard, cleaving as closely as possible to my line of navigation. The rain had slackened and the cloud cover was beginning to break up. That was good news for the moment, but that sort of change in the weather often presaged dense banks of fog, which would be disastrous. After twenty minutes, as I neared the point where Mother had most likely lost power, I slowed and descended.

To my surprise, I found her almost immediately. The blue light of several safety flares shone around her. True to her word, she'd stayed right on course. That was experience for you.

I drew sigils to land, setting down with an overeager touch-and-crouch approach. My ankle turned under me and I nearly fell on Mother.

"Damn time," she said.

"If you'd answer your messages—" I growled, then stopped short.

Ma looked awful. She'd ended up prone with the still-paralyzed man on top of her, pinning her to the ground. One of the straps binding her to her front passenger had come loose, tangling around Mother's right arm, which looked broken.

I reached down to unhook the boy from Mother's front, but the steel carabiner was bent.

"Cut it," said Ma.

I cut the straps with my belt knife and pulled the boy's inert body free. Then I dragged the man off her and cut away the straps that Ma's arm had fouled in. Mother rolled onto her side. She grimaced and drew her wounded arm to her chest. She was breathing in short, grating pants.

"Broken ribs?" I asked.

"Can't get any air," she gasped.

"Let's get you to the hospital."

She waved me off and for a moment made as if she might climb to her feet. Her primary powder bag had burst when she hit the ground and her secondary had a large tear in it. Not fit for use, but she reached for it anyway, like she was going to attach it to her rigging, which I'd just shredded. She wasn't thinking right or breathing right. I knew what I had to do. I tried not to let the fear seep into my voice.

"I'll put you in stasis," I said. "It'll be easy. You've seen me do it a hundred times."

"On paper," she said. "Have you ever? On a person?"

"Once. Sort of. On Willard's horse when it broke its leg."

Ma winced. "How'd the horse do?"

"Well, he died. But not because of my sigil!"

Mother shut her eyes and I helped her roll on her back. I extracted one of the thin strips of indicator paper from the kit Synge had given me, wet it with my tongue, and stuck it to Ma's neck. I could see the pulse in her neck bounding.

"Fly them first," she murmured.

That made good sense. There was enough time to get the Kleins to the hospital before their stases wore off, but not enough to take Mother and then come back for them. Putting them under a second time was out of the question—the simple stasis sigil that Mother and I used didn't work on the same person twice.

I popped the cork off the tube of silver chloride and kissed Ma on the forehead.

"Don't fuck this up," she whispered.

I blew a breath out and before I had a chance to reconsider, let the powder spill out, tracing the series of arcs over her chest. She blinked and her eyelids froze half-shut. Her pulse was gone. Her breathing had stopped. Trembling, I reached for her hand and pulled on it. It didn't move. A good, strong stasis.

I peeled the indicator strip off her skin and tested it with formic acid: sixty-eight minutes before Mother woke. I didn't have a second to waste.

I wrestled the still-stasied man into an undamaged harness and rolled him so that he was facedown in the mud. Then I clipped the boy onto my back and—thank God the kid was small—lowered myself, so that I was lying on top of the big man. I attached my chest clips to the back of his harness, then heaved onto my side and got my right leg under me. I opened my regulator wide, drew to launch, and pushed off with my good foot.

I sprang into the air and the bodies came with me. After a series of sigils to level us, I shoved my passengers into positions where they weren't banging into some vital part of me, poured on speed, and made for Helena.

I pushed my regulator to six ounces per minute and then worked my way up to 9.9. I'd never had it so high. Even with all the weight I was dragging, I should be making nearly one hundred fifty miles an hour. But any slower and Mother would come to before I got her to Dr. Synge.

I spotted the landing field in the faint predawn light and prepared to land. Touching down with stasied passengers was complicated because they hit the ground before you did. I tried to make sure that the large man strapped to my chest made contact with both feet at the same time, but he struck one side before the other and toppled sideways, spinning me down to the ground with him.

"Flier down!" came the shout.

Dr. Synge, along with the same doctor and nurse, ran over and unhooked my passengers. Several orderlies came up with stretchers.

"How's your mother?" Synge asked.

"Bad," I said. "She couldn't breathe. I put her under."

"How long on her stasis?"

"She's got about fifty minutes left," I said. "It was my first time."

"That's a hell of a way to learn. Your head's okay?"

"Achy," I said. "But I hit it twice. I don't think it's philosophical fatigue, just a concussion."

"Lovely," Dr. Synge deadpanned. "Go quick."

I launched, flew twenty minutes, and found Mother without difficulty. I landed and grabbed Ma under the armpits, pulling her upright so that she was leaning back against me. I attached her to my chest harness and lifted off.

Two minutes into the return flight, the sun peeked over the horizon and I realized something was wrong with me. Faintly at first, then steadily louder, came a sound like a vast sheet of metal being cut by an endless saw blade. As the sunlight grew brighter, the shrieking in my head intensified.

I began to panic. It was philosophical fatigue, coming on me rapidly. I'd never had it so bad—it felt as if my brain were tearing itself in two. I reached to turn my regulator down but couldn't focus my eyes. My fingers didn't look real.

Did I have minutes left before my heart seized up? Another hour?

As I approached Helena, the city dissolved into a blur. Splashes of color played across the inside of my eyelids: spinning concentric circles, dumbbell shapes expanding and contracting, tangled messes of lines.

This is how I'm going to die. I couldn't banish the thought. I couldn't breathe. I couldn't move.

Then a final reserve of energy surged up. Acting on reflex, I cut speed and turned, following the same course I'd flown twice already. The hospital materialized through the haze and then the landing field. But I couldn't judge my altitude. I was approaching too fast.

Do it ugly.

I clutched Mother to my chest, aimed for a piece of ground free of cows, and shut off my regulator. My sigil sputtered out and I glided in the last few feet, legs stretched out in front of me like a ballplayer sliding. I hit the mud butt-first, knocked my head backward into the ground, and skidded to a stop.

The whine in my head slowly dropped in pitch. I was content to lie there, my eyes clamped shut, until the end of days.

Several sets of hands unhooked Mother from me.

"—hear me? Robert! Robert?"

Dr. Synge.

"Open your eyes, Robert!"

My eyes fluttered open and I got a face of the early-morning sun.

"Well," I mumbled. "That wasn't so—"

And then my heart stopped.

5

God looked down and said, "Give me the right sort of American. Give me a woman who'll tend a garden in the time-honored fashion, with watering can, long-handled hoe, and salt for the slugs. No piece of sorcerer's glass for her. No, she'll grow tomatoes as we have for six thousand years and if she picks them three months later, they're all the sweeter for it. And I'll call that woman a Trencher."

God said, "Give me a man who'll wake at dawn to feed the horses, put in a full day's work, and ride five miles into town on a Tuesday night so that he can vote in a municipal election, then ride five miles home in the dark. What use does he have for flying? Leave it for the birds, the bats, and the angels. He lives his life in the right way, the one his father would recognize—and the generations before, straight on back to Adam. And I'll call that man a Trencher, too."

Maxwell Gannet, "Sermon on the New Trencher Party," 1917

I SPENT TWENTY-EIGHT HOURS sleeping off the effects of my overexertion. When I finally woke, I saw a familiar figure sitting in a chair at the foot of my bed. I could tell she was annoyed, no less so for being focused on her knitting, which she performed with such intensity that one pitied the yarn. My littlest big sister, home from New York City.

"Angela," I called out hoarsely.

She barely looked up from her row of stitches. "Is it true you botched three landings in one night?"

"Yeah," I croaked. "At least."

"It's a good thing they forbade me to touch you, because I should give you a thrashing like you wouldn't believe. Embarrassing me like that. Folks are going to say Angie Weekes forgot to teach little Boober how to land. You made the front page of the *Billings Gazette*, by the way. It must have seemed amusing enough that the *Tattler* in Detroit picked it up, too—'Male Flier Rescues Three in "Mantana." ' The article was almost as long as the title. I've had to fend off your throngs of admirers."

"Hundreds?"

"Thousands," she said dryly.

Angela set down her knitting and came over to take my hand. "So, you lost your pulse for about a minute after you landed with Mother. Dr. Synge said you were too stupid to die and as long as you survived the first day, you'd probably make a full recovery."

"Glad to hear it," I rasped. I touched my nose. There was a rubber tube running through it and down my throat.

"Ma dislocated her arm and punctured a lung," Angela continued. "She's looking fit, all things considered. They've caught her twice trying to sneak out to take calls."

Angela kissed me on the cheek. "I have to go find Dr. Synge. If you die in the next five minutes, I'll never hear the end of it."

Synge bustled in a moment later.

"Entirely in your debt, Mr. Weekes," she said. "We so rarely get to see the effects of over-philosophizing in a male, much less with a full-blown cardiac arrest. I'll get a paper for the *Journal of Experimental Medical Philosophy* out of you for certain."

"Terrific," I said.

She tested my reflexes and grip strength and, satisfied I wasn't dying in front of her, rang for a meal tray.

"We've been running potassium chloride into you through that nasogastric tube, but I think it might be pleasanter to do it the old-fashioned way," she said.

Dr. Synge yanked the two-foot-long rubber tube out through my nose. I groaned and wiped blood from the nostril.

An orderly brought me mashed potatoes, sliced bananas, and fresh orange slices—the philosopher's classic high-potassium recovery diet. I was ravenous. I stuffed sections of the orange in my mouth and though the juices stung my throat, I asked for a second helping of everything.

"You're indecently healthy for what you've been through," Dr. Synge told me. "You'll have to forgive me if I spend too long with you. I needed a win."

"The Kleins," I said, "did they not . . . ?"

She shook her head. "The husband went quick. He'd lost too much blood. But we spent eight hours in surgery with the son. We thought we'd repaired the damage. Then his carotid artery ruptured."

She exhaled sharply.

"And little Carla," Synge continued. "She was in every hour to see you—we couldn't keep her away. She told anyone who would listen that some boys can fly. 'Did you know some boys can fly?' "

Her voice caught at the end.

"Her aunt came from San Francisco," Synge said. "She took Carla back with her. But they left you something."

She glanced toward an old rag doll on my bedside table.

"Mr. B," I said.

"The groundskeeper found it while he was mowing the grass yesterday."

I picked the doll up and held it. It smelled like smoke. I thought of the hanged woman—her face charred to the bone, her body scorched. My jaw clenched.

"It was remarkable, what you did," Dr. Synge said. "To go back out, injured, alone, into the night, and pull out three wounded."

"I did my job," I said. "I did what I had to."

"No, you don't understand, Robert. Most of our county philosophers couldn't have done that. Even back in—well, I served in the Philippines, in

'99. I'll tell you, three-quarters of Rescue and Evac couldn't have managed it solo. You would have won the White Ribbon."

That was the US Sigilry Corps' highest decoration for valor. She couldn't have paid me a more extravagant compliment.

And it boiled up within me.

"If I had my choice of any job in the world—" I began.

If I said it out loud, she would laugh me right back to Guille's Run.

"Would I have *any* chance to fly for the Corps?" I asked her. "In R&E? As a man?"

Dr. Synge took a sheet of flat black smoke from her pocket and flipped it between her fingers, weaving it into a checkerboard pattern then unweaving it.

"You'd be the first one," she said. "They'd put you through hell. Why would you ever want that?"

"They have the best fliers in the world. They save lives instead of taking them. And it sounds stupid, but all my heroes growing up were R&E—Lt. Col. Rodgers, Hatcher and Jimenez, and . . ."

"And your mother?"

I blushed and turned away. "Yeah."

Synge smiled. "After the other night, I think you get to be one of hers. Not that Emmaline would ever admit it."

"Lord, no."

"Have you told her you want to join?"

"About a thousand times when I was a kid. You can imagine how she reacted. She always said it would be impossible."

Synge shook her head. "It would be *hard* for R&E to put a man in the field with a wing of forty women, I won't argue that. But maybe not *impossible*. The Corps has always prided itself on taking sigilrists based on their skill, not their background. Half their women are dirt-poor or foreign or colored. Hell, your mama was nothing but a little half-starved Ozark girl with red clay still between her toes when she signed up in '71. Or so I've heard."

I laughed at that. "Did you know her then?"

"No, I didn't join until '98, right out of college. I was a proper

Presbyterian young lady from a fancy part of Cleveland. I got to Manila and my platoon had a Negro as a lieutenant, two Italians, and a Mexican. You should have seen the look on my face—*impossible*. They all turned out to be better smokecarvers than me. I changed my tune in a hurry."

She seemed amused by the idea. "So why not a male, too?"

Gallatin County's sheriff joined us. He was a fat, amiable little man by the name of Lew Hansen. An old friend of Mother's—when he did searches by air for lost ranchers or outlaws hiding in the countryside, he preferred Ma to be the philosopher who carried him.

"Young Boober, good to see you awake!" Sheriff Hansen said, reaching over to shake my hand.

"Thank you, sir," I said.

Hansen sat beside Dr. Synge. He was the sort of fellow you could more easily picture with a slice of plum cake in one hand and a glass of brandy in the other, carrying on at the social hall.

"There's no other way to say it," Hansen told me. "You saw a hell of an evil thing night before last. Four murders and an arson."

"Yeah," I said.

"I already talked to your mom. Heard her account. I've been out there myself, looked the Kleins' place over. But I wonder if you could tell me what happened as you recall it."

I described for him at what time we'd arrived, the state of the house and the outbuildings, the position of the dead and the wounded.

"So, I think it might have been the Trenchers," I concluded.

Hansen and Synge shared a look.

"Well, yes," Sheriff Hansen said. "I'd say it's about the most clear-cut—"

Then he stopped and pushed his glasses up his nose.

"So, Boober, your mom . . ." he said. "Has she told you much about what she did the last time the Trenchers rose up? During the Disturbances? Who she did it with?"

Growing up, that had been a delicate topic, even with family friends.

It was common knowledge that Ma had fought in the smoldering conflicts between the Trenchers and ordinary philosophers, called the First and Second Disturbances—or the Trencher Wars, if you were feeling provocative. In 1891 and then again in 1901, the Trenchers had embarked on campaigns of intimidation and assassination, killing prominent sigilrists across Missouri and Kansas. Mother had joined several of the philosophical "societies for mutual aid and defense" that had opposed them. They'd named themselves the Jayhawks and had had no compunction about retaliating with violence of their own. It had been a dangerous time to be an outspoken Trencher. A masked flying woman might pluck you off the street in broad daylight, castrate you, and hang you naked by your ankles from the steeple of the highest church in town. With or without a bullet in your head.

As children, Angela and I had whispered about that sort of thing after bedtime. Whether Mother had been responsible for any of those "liquidations." Whether she was a killer. But we knew never to talk about it in polite company.

"Oh, everyone says she was involved some," I said.

"You recall anything from, say, 1904?" Hansen asked.

"Not really," I said. "I would have been five years old. Things got a little hot, I guess. Ma moved Angela and me down to St. Louis for a few months with a friend of hers—Aunt Nelson, we called her, though I don't think she was anyone's aunt. Ma was gone for a week or two at a time, doing I don't know what. Fighting, I'd suppose."

"You'd be right," said Dr. Synge.

"Then your ma would come back to the Nelson place in the middle of the night," Sheriff Hansen said. "And you'd sit in her lap while everyone drank coffee and went over maps. You measured distances for us—Emmaline's little navigator."

"Oh my God!" I said. "Were the two of you there?"

"As a lawman, Lew shouldn't answer that," Dr. Synge said. "But I can say that I was there. So was Mrs. Klein. About half the women who are Montana county philosophers now were, too. You ever run into Mrs. Yzerman in Missoula or Mrs. O'Malley in Butte, they could tell you some stories."

I'd met them both several times. They'd struck me as pleasant, unexceptional women.

"But, yes, Robert you're right," said Sheriff Hansen. "Evelyn Klein shot and her body hanged and burned doesn't leave any doubt. It's classic Trencher methods."

"How is that possible?" I asked. "There aren't any Trenchers in Montana."

I imagined Trenchers as most young people of my generation did: a lot of rabid, vicious old men. The first Trenchers had taken their name from the Confederate soldiers who'd survived the Battle of Petersburg, Virginia, the ones who'd crawled out of the trenches, blind and with their lungs already starting to scar, the skin sloughing from their faces and hands—the Brotherhood of the Trenches. Many of them had lived for decades afterward and had become outspoken advocates for removing sigilry from warfare. Some of the Northerners who'd endured attacks by Wainwright's Legion had joined them.

But Trencherism had gradually spilled over into trying to keep philosophy out of everyday life. They'd admitted as members all kinds of men who hated common sigilry: farmhands forced out of work by the gangs of women brought over from Poland and Romania to do agricultural philosophy; railroad men who'd lost their jobs when the National Transporter Chain opened; men who thought the country had been emasculated when Lincoln gave the vote to women by executive order in '64 and who longed for a return to a world in which the weaker sex knew their place. Those newer ones could be harder to spot. A few of my classmates in high school had inclined in that direction, not that they'd usually dared talk about it around me.

"We have Trenchers aplenty in Montana," Dr. Synge said. "They don't build meetinghouses and put a sign out front. But they're here."

"It's more like religious enthusiasm for some of them," Hansen said. "You've got Maxwell Gannet sitting in Boston, preaching that Jesus weeps every time a philosopher draws a sigil. Go back to the good old days of self-reliance and work in the traditional ways. No electricity, no sigilry. Don't send your children to school; educate them at home. Don't educate your daughters at all beyond keeping house."

I recognized the last bit. "Yeah," I said. "Those are the ones that call themselves the Hand of the Righteous. A bunch of them built a settlement near here a few years back."

"Yessir," said Hansen. "Down in the Hillcock Valley. It's a neat, clean little village that just keeps growing. Some of them are from out of state, some are local converts. Eleven hundred of them now. So, I'll put it to you, Robert—you've always been good with a map—what else is close to Hillcock?"

"The Kleins lived three miles from there," I said.

"Exactly. So, the other night was not one of the great mysteries to me. I got a few deputies and we had Mrs. Yzerman and her girls fly us out to Hillcock. On the ground, the men were running for cover like we were the angels of the Second Coming. I didn't even have my shotgun out yet and the ones who did it had given themselves up. Ten of them. All just boys. Sixteen or seventeen years old."

"Oh, Lord," I said.

"It's sad as hell," Hansen said. "Because four counts of murder? And Hap Wilhelm as the circuit judge who'll hear the case? Better for them if the Angel of Death *had* come. They're as good as hanged."

"Max Gannet was already preaching on it in Boston," Synge said. "He called them martyrs for the cause. Said they'll see heaven for what they've done."

"That whole settlement's going to be up in arms," I said.

"It's going to be a long summer, all right," Sheriff Hansen agreed. "It's going to be bad on both sides."

It was a lot to ponder—Trenchers and dead philosophers and orphans and vigilantes. And that a woman as smart as Synge thought I might be material for the Corps. That was the part I couldn't get out of my mind. The Corps. Rescue and Evacuation. R&E.

But, of course, Mother, too.

Ma came in to see me after Synge and Hansen had finished. She had her right arm in a sling and she walked gingerly, taking care not to upset her broken ribs. She looked at me, opened her mouth, shut it, and sat down in the chair beside my bed. If I didn't know better, I would have thought she was going to apologize and didn't know how. Instead, she just looked me up and down as though she barely knew me.

"Would you care for a couple hands of jiggery?" she asked.

"Sure," I said.

She took a deck of playing cards from her workbag and then realized she couldn't shuffle with only one good arm. She pushed the deck across the bedside table to me.

It seemed to me that the order of the universe had been upset.

I had seen my mother, whom I'd considered invincible, the veteran of four wars and a thousand night landings, an incomparable artist and technician, smashed against the ground. No less upsetting was that I'd been the one to save her. Boober Weekes: famous all over Yellowstone County for neat penmanship and pretty hands, stubborn, persistent, a perfectly good sigilrist for a man, but nothing special. Nothing compared to his sisters or his mother. Just a male philosopher. Emmaline's son.

"I'm glad you were with me, Rob," Ma said. "There's not too many who could have done what you . . ." She trailed off and picked up her cards. "Well, you're not quite ordinary, are you?"

And I was right back to thinking about R&E. All through the afternoon, as I lost one game of cards after another. As I forced more banana slices down my gullet. As I sat up in the night, unable to sleep.

R&E had been the subject of a thousand bedtime stories. The finest fliers in the world, saving lives instead of taking them. Lt. Col. Rodgers and Capt. Jimenez and Mrs. Hatcher. And Maj. Weekes. I'd wanted it as long as I could remember.

Some boys can fly.

I won't say I swore to four dead philosophers and one orphan and a rag doll that I'd be the first one to do it. But I swore to just about everything else I could think of.

Sigilwoman Robert A. Weekes. Was it really so absurd?

6

APRIL–AUGUST 1917

Some have asked what business a male has leading a legion of sigilrists. To them I reply, was not Jesus Christ himself a philosopher? Did he not hover above the waves? Did he not have philosophy by which he fed the masses, raised the dead, and preserved himself for three days in a state indistinguishable from death? Tell me why I ought not follow the example of my Lord and Savior.

Galen Wainwright, *Confessions of a Confederate Smokecarver*, 1875

MY MANIA HADN'T YET faded when Angela returned the next morning. I wanted to tell her all about trying to join R&E, but she got the first word in.

"We need to talk about Mother," Angela said. "We can't let her stay on as a county philosopher. She's going to end up dead."

"Now, Angie," I replied, "that seems like an overreaction."

"No, it's not! She screwed up the other night and she's not admitting it. When you told me about how you found her—front passenger latched tight on one side, but swinging loose on the other, with the strap wrapped around Ma's arm—I knew it could only be one thing."

It had crossed my mind as well.

"The strap didn't break," Angela said, "the buckle didn't give way. She must have been adjusting her harness in the air and pulled the emergency release tab by mistake."

"That's impossible," I said. "The very first thing she taught me about flying a stasied passenger was—"

"Don't pull your release tab by mistake," Angela finished. "But if you do, pull both sides to dump your passenger. Otherwise everyone is going down together. Boober, she messed up bad and then she panicked. She made two mistakes so basic that any nine-year-old hoverer could have told her what went wrong."

"How could that happen?" I asked.

"She ran ten emergency calls during the day. Then she got woken up in the middle of the night, hauled your heavy-as-rocks carcass out past Bozeman, and picked up four hundred pounds of passenger. In terrible weather. She was exhausted."

"So what?" I said. "It was an accident. It could have happened to anybody."

"This is too many times now! You remember in January when she was lifting roof joists for that barn and lost power? She dropped twenty feet and crushed that carpenter's leg. Then right after that she had a hard landing with six hundred pounds of apples outside the general store. And the chest cold she caught after she ditched in the water while she was dredging the Hanover Banks. And—"

"There's always been accidents," I said. "Even when she was young. She talks about them all the time. She's a sharper flier now than ever."

"It's not her flying, Boober," said Angela. "It's pure, dumb, brute strength. She's sixty years old. Her body can't take it."

I fluffed one of my pillows and set it under my head. "So, she's supposed to retire?"

"Yes! The State Office should have demanded it by now, but they're short experienced fliers with the war on. She asked them about probationary credentials for you again—after everything you did the other night, whether they'd let you come on as her apprentice."

"I heard," I said. The State Board had laughed so hard at the notion that they'd woken the neighbors.

"They're idiots," Angela said. "You'd be perfect. And Ma always wanted that job to stay in the family."

I had two half sisters besides Angela. Vivian was my middle big sister, fourteen years older than me; she'd been as much substitute mother to me as sister, before getting married and moving to Washington State. Susan, my eldest half sister, was six years older than Viv and lived in Texas, where she had children and a grandchild of her own.

"Sure," I said, "but neither Sue nor Viv is moving back to Guille's Run so they can run emergency calls for thirty dollars a month plus commissions. And you're in New York."

Angela was twisting at one of the buttons on her sweater as if she would rip it off.

"It was supposed to be *me*!" she snarled. "The good daughter. Ma offered it to me again this morning—she wants me to come back. Take over as Yellowstone County CP from her."

"Lord," I said. "I'm sorry."

"When I left, I thought she was going to take a couple apprentices, not try to do everything herself! She took ten emergency calls in one day. Nobody can do that much alone! Ten calls. If I'd been here . . ."

"Angela—it's not your fault."

She buried her head in my shoulder.

"I *could* do it," she sobbed, "but I don't *want* to do it. I want a feather-bed, and good martinis, and tickets to the theater, and lace curtains. I do *not* want to wake up in the night to some farmer pounding on my door. I don't want the wind, the cold, or the rain. I don't want to smell like cow shit at three in the morning because I have to rescue cattle in a blizzard. I am *not* coming back! I don't care how badly it disappoints her."

I held her and let her cry a minute. Growing up, the positions had always been reversed.

"Angie," I whispered. "Ma's so goddamn proud of you. Every errand in town, she won't shut up about the Upper East Side and Forty-Second Street and the Astors. She's put in for subscriptions to all sorts of fashionable catalogues and wants to discuss the latest progressive women's undergarments with me. We own six volumes of classical music for the phonograph, not because either of us likes it, but because it was recorded at Carnegie Hall."

She laughed through her tears. "Sorry."

"We never listen to it. But Angela, in all seriousness, she couldn't be prouder or happier for you."

Angela took out her handkerchief and blew her nose. "Would it kill her to tell me that?"

That was Mother for you.

"So what about you?" Angela asked, dabbing at her eyes and resuming her duties as big sister. "If Mother retired tomorrow, what would you want to do?"

If I couldn't admit it to my own sister . . .

"The Corps," I said. "Rescue and Evac."

Angela snorted. "Oh, be serious."

It only dulled the sting a little that I would have reacted the same way a few days before.

"It's an adventure," I said. "See the world—"

"If you want to get out of Billings, there are easier ways than the Corps. You're a better sigilrist than half the girls I work with and most of them have a degree in empirical philosophy. You could get one, too. You're smart enough."

I hadn't ever really considered that.

"I wasn't much of a student," I said.

"You were when you weren't bored. You got As in every chemistry and math class you ever took."

"Well, that's different. That's how you do your powder and navigation. It's life and death."

"So study something practical."

"How would I ever pay for it?"

"Sign up under the Contingency Act."

The Act had been passed in response to the shortage of philosophers caused by the Great War. The Corps had deployed ten thousand women overseas to make sure the European powers adhered to the Rouen Conventions, which forbade the use of empirical philosophy in armed conflict, except for humanitarian endeavors, like evacuating the wounded. The Act would pay your college tuition, provided you agreed to serve an equal number of years in an area in the States that was short on philosophers.

"Just do it for one year and see if you like it," Angela suggested. "You've got to do a year of service afterward, but you could request to do that anywhere. Hell, the whole state of Montana is classified as under-resourced. If you got the right reviewers, they could post you here as Mother's apprentice. Then you watch the State Office lose their minds over it. Or request an assignment somewhere you'd want to live. New York. Denver. Hawaii."

Or in the Corps. Contingency Act students could volunteer for the Sigilry Corps, too.

"That's pretty good," I said.

"Of course it's good!" Angela replied. "We just need a university dumb enough to take a male philosopher."

Dr. Synge was passing the door and caught the end of the conversation.

"Radcliffe College," she suggested.

"A *male* philosopher," Angela repeated. "They're a women's school."

"They've made a few exceptions for Contingency students," Dr. Synge said.

"Radcliffe's no place to study philosophy," Angela scoffed. "It's a lot of rich New England snobs. Do they even *have* professors of sigilry?"

"They have some excellent ones," Synge said. "I went there."

"Oh," said Angela.

"My old lieutenant from the Philippine-American War became one of their deans," Synge offered. "She'd be interested in you, Robert."

Being educated alongside a couple thousand women sounded not unattractive.

"Boston's nice enough, I suppose," Angela said, "but it's about the

Trencheriest city outside of Atlanta. You've got Maxwell Gannet sitting in his castle, giving sermons on how philosophy will bring about the end of the world."

"There's *one* Trencher meetinghouse downtown," Synge reassured me. "You stay clear of there, you'll never so much as see an anti-philosopher."

I shook my head. "But what do we do about Ma?"

"Oh, get poor Emmaline a couple proper apprentices!" Dr. Synge said. "It's long past time and she knows it. Mrs. Yzerman's youngest girl is sixteen. She's very capable, but she'll never get the experience she needs at home—she has four older sisters."

"Ma and Mrs. Yzerman go way back," Angela said. "They'll both like that idea. I'll talk to Ma about it tonight. Shit, I'll talk to her about it right now."

Angela ducked out.

"And then," Dr. Synge said quietly to me, "you use your connections at Radcliffe to find a general crazy enough to put a man in R&E."

Over the next day, I composed a letter to Radcliffe's admissions committee in which I laid out my good points, talked a bit about my practical experience, explained that I wanted to work someday serving the public interest (which Angela said they'd like), and wouldn't they please admit me under the Contingency Act? Dr. Synge wrote her friend the dean on my behalf, too.

We mailed off the letters. Dr. Synge discharged me home to convalesce with a stack of books on smokecarving and stasis sigilry, which I slogged through (in between rereading *Life and Death on San Juan Hill* for the thousandth time). When that grew dull, I played cards with Mother or Angela. I wrote letters to my friends who'd enlisted and were already away in basic training. (*I am worried*, Willard Gunch wrote in reply. *What if the war ends before I get there?*)

Three weeks passed. Gradually, I realized how little interest a women's college in New England must have for a male philosopher from out West, even if he'd recently had his picture on the front page of the *Billings Gazette*.

"Don't take it too hard," Mother said. "I can always use your help around the house. Show young Miss Yzerman the ropes."

If the thought of helping to train my sixteen-year-old replacement put me in a funk, I tried not to show it.

But the deans at Radcliffe must have been in a whimsical mood the day they reviewed my application. Deciding there couldn't be too much harm in admitting one simpleton from Montana, they offered me a spot. We got the letter a few hours before Angela was to head back to New York.

I was stupefied.

"I knew it!" Angela shrieked. "My idiot brother, the college man! I should have made you do this ages ago."

Ma was more skeptical.

"What are they going to teach you about philosophy in a classroom?" she complained. "The proper place to learn sigilry is in the field."

"Mother!" said Angela in a warning tone.

"Well," Ma said. "Maybe he'll find himself a rich wife out there and support me in my old age. At any rate, it sounds like a grand adventure."

The next morning, Ma woke me at five o'clock.

"If you want to learn sigilry out of a book, that's your business," she said, while I was still rubbing the sleep from my eyes. "But I'm not sending you clear across the country so you can horrify a lot of overbred princesses with that preposterous landing vector you favor. We're going to put you in the air and you're going to angle and tuck until you get it right."

In late May, Radcliffe messaged that they'd arranged housing for me in an apartment a few blocks from campus along with another male empirical philosopher, Karl Friedrich Unger. The college provided his postal address, but oddly not his personal glyph. I mailed him a letter asking him to message me, but never heard back. I had visions of some urbane sophisticate sitting in an overstuffed leather chair in the oak-paneled library of his family's mansion, opening my dust-stained envelope, reading my inelegant prose, and

remarking, "How ghastly! I'm to room with a primitive from the Wild West."
But there was nothing to be done about it.

By June, the youngest Yzerman daughter had moved in to act as Mother's assistant; she was joined a few days later by a pair of sisters from a philosophically minded family in Butte, who were to replace me as the "essential support personnel." I'd expected to need several weeks to train them, but one was quieter and more serious than the next, and it took them all of three days to render me superfluous. They had, after all, been raised from infancy to do that sort of work.

So I spent my last weeks at home flying, training under Mother's critical eye and building up my resistance to philosophical fatigue until I could spend two, then three hours in the air. When my temples began to throb, I drank gallons of mint tea and read Mother's library of philosophical guides and manuals, trying to fill in the sizable gaps in my knowledge.

It should have been as languid and happy and peaceful a stretch as you could ever imagine. But, as Sheriff Hansen had predicted, the summer was a bad one.

The trials of the young men who'd murdered the Kleins ended with all ten of them convicted. They were hanged. And all across Wyoming, North Dakota, and Montana, philosophers' houses burned. I could see Ma itching to do something about it, but she put her energy into her apprentices and me instead.

Then, three days before I was supposed to go east, a gang of Trenchers lured County Philosopher O'Malley into an ambush a few miles outside Butte. Shot her twenty-eight times. They dumped her body on Main Street and fled into the hills. In retaliation, a band of Jayhawks attacked the Hand of the Righteous church in Hillcock with incendiary smoke during a prayer meeting. The building erupted into an inferno—thirty-one dead, mostly women and children.

"I doubt the Hand were even the ones who killed Erin," Ma said, shaking her head. "But now we're going to see them hit back, too."

"It's getting out of control," I said. "Maybe I should stay here."

"And do what?" Ma asked. "Sit up all night on the porch with your rifle in your lap?"

"If I have to," I said. "Or . . ."

"Or you're going to go hunt Trenchers? Fly into Hillcock and shoot the place up?"

The thought had occurred to me. "You used to," I said. "Or something like it."

To my surprise, Mother looked at me with an expression of tenderness. She took me by the hand and led me outside, where we sat on the porch swing together, looking out into the darkness.

"Robert," Mother said. "This isn't a new war. Since the first woman lifted a finger to send a message, since Cadwallader carved the first piece of smoke, since I learned to fly, people have tried to destroy us. I spent years fighting. So did Lew and Bertie. We fought the wrong way. We always thought that if we killed enough of them—killed the right ones—that they would leave us in peace. All that got us was one cycle of violence after another. And now it's come back on us again."

Mother pushed the hair out of my face. "Yes, I want the ones who killed Mrs. O'Malley hung from a church steeple. But I want better, too. I want your generation to be the one that wins. It'll be a different kind of reckoning, slower and deeper. Go to school. Show average people the value of philosophy. The ones who can barely work a message board or have no sigils at all—let them see it and live among it and respect it. That's the only strategy that will endure. It took me sixty years to understand that. Don't let it take you that long."

"So, I'm just supposed to abandon you?" I said, near tears. "What kind of man does that make me?"

"A good one. If you stay home this year, you'll never leave. And then the Trenchers will have succeeded beyond their wildest dreams. Because you were meant for something bigger. And they made you too scared to do it."

PART 2

THE RADCLIFFE MAN

7

SEPTEMBER 1917

Our beautiful transcontinental railroad, constructed at a cost of fifty million dollars and hundreds of lives, its tunnels blasted through the mighty
Sierra Nevadas, its bridges constructed over perilous gorges and raging
rivers, seventeen hundred miles of track laid through dogged, indefatiga-
ble manly effort—all this and you would allow it to be run out of business
in a month by a pack of colored women who can travel by sleight of hand.
It goes against the natural order.

> Transcribed message from Sidney Dillon, president of Union
> Pacific Railroad, to President Ulysses S. Grant, May 1, 1875

TWO DAYS LATER, I flew from Guille's Run to Denver on a warm, clear
morning. Even the sweetness of hovering under such perfect conditions
didn't ease my mind: flitting off to live the easy life of a college man while
Ma fought off the Trenchers alone. Disgraceful. I would have to be wor-
thy of it—it was the only answer. I would work twice as hard as those soft
Easterners. Not merely a good philosopher for a man, but a damn good
philosopher.

If I'd been in a more reflective mood, I might also have admitted that I
was nervous over leaving the only home I'd ever known, worried over what a
bunch of sophisticated New England girls would think of me, and dreading

that my trip to Boston meant putting myself at the mercy of a form of philosophy that unnerved me: transporting.

The transport sigil worked by instantly exchanging a bubble of space surrounding the philosopher who drew it with an equal volume at the destination—one chunk of the world simply switched places with another. An expert transporter could move a huge chunk of ground and the passengers standing on it several hundred miles in a fraction of a second. The only problem was that if she drew her lines wrong and the edge of the transport bubble came up short, it might cut you in half.

Those sorts of accidents had been horrifyingly common sixty years earlier, when the sigil first came into use. Only the foolish or desperate had relied on it as a means of travel, though a few cargo routes for hauling cotton had been developed in the Southern states, using slaves as sigilrists. Those transports had been made at gunpoint, just in case the philosopher had gotten hold of an alternative destination glyph and decided to make a break for freedom.

Denver's transporter arena was a far cry from those early transporter tracks. It was a vast, warehouse-like building with a hard-packed sand floor on which dozens of sets of concentric circles had been marked with chalk, each one with a destination glyph drawn in the center. I waited along with several other travelers on a raised platform separated from the main arena floor by fifty yards. I kept checking my wristwatch and edging back from the railing.

"First time?" asked the woman waiting next to me.

"Yup," I answered. "Down from Billings."

"They ought to build a branch line up that direction. Save you the flight."

I couldn't help but feel it would probably take a gun pointed at the more sensible philosophers in Montana to get them on a transport as passengers. But I tried to remind myself about the metallurgical breakthroughs in the 1870s that had allowed aluminum to be refined to a much higher standard— the sigil was infinitely more reliable than it used to be. In fact, conventional wisdom held that it was now safer to travel across the country by transporter than by hovering.

I took another step back and then stifled a gasp.

A thousand people had appeared in the largest circle on the floor—no noise, no flash of light, no warning. They were simply there. At the center of the crowd stood a stout black woman—the transporter who'd made the swap. She had an exhausted, wild-eyed look. She staggered a few steps toward the waiting area and collapsed.

"Jesus!" I said.

The passengers waiting around me cried out with dismay, too. A pair of stretcher bearers, who'd been standing at the ready, trotted out to retrieve her.

"All's well, all's well!" called out a uniformed conductor. "Happens every now and again. A few days' rest and she'll be right as rain. Follow me, folks. All aboard for Colby, Kansas, continuing down the line to St. Louis!"

I swallowed down my nerves and followed the conductor as he wound his way across the transporter floor, giving the other sets of circles a wide berth. There were no other transporters due in for another hour, but so long as the destination glyphs had been drawn on the ground—even if they were years old—anyone who knew them could appear, including any lunatic wildcatter or amateur coming in from the field. They were supposed to message ahead for permission, but every once in a while someone arrived unannounced. If a pedestrian was in the wrong place, it made a terrible mess.

The conductor packed us shoulder to shoulder inside the huge green circle for the main east-west route. Porters arranged our luggage inside the yellow circle—if the transporter's sigils came up short, better to lose a suitcase than an arm—and everyone stayed well clear of the red line, which marked the anticipated edge of the transportation field.

A few minutes later, a fresh transporter made her way out onto the floor and to the middle of our circle. She took a tape measure out of her workbag and double-checked the distance from the center point of the circle, where she would be standing, to the green circle, drawn forty paces out, then the yellow circle twenty paces beyond that, and the red line farther out still. She returned to the center.

Our woman looked bright and competent. Well-fed, certainly, which was important: a transport burned the same amount of body mass as covering the same distance on foot. Thirty-five miles for a pound of flesh, according to conventional wisdom, with the weight loss happening instantaneously. A long enough jump would consume a sigilrist's entire body, though even repeated shorter jumps put a horrible strain on the internal organs. The first generation of transporters, the slaves who'd been put through hundreds of rounds of fattening and reduction, had suffered from that kind of overexertion; most of them had died by the age of thirty. Today, however, the union transporters on the national chain had a strict upper limit of three hundred miles per day, time off after every jump, and weekly doctor's checkups. They made a fine living working only a few hours a month, retired after twenty-five years, and had a life expectancy nearly as long as anyone else's.

But on one jump out of ten the transporter might faint, as we'd just witnessed. And a couple times a year, the radius on a bubble came up wrong and dismembered a bunch of people.

"All quiet, please!" our transporter sang out in a well-practiced cadence. "Destination status?"

One of the attendants on the platform sent and received messages. "Colby reports ready and clear at the number seven destination sigil," she called.

I knew that accidents almost never happened on the national chain's main lines—one of their best women would be running this hop. It was the little branch lines where trouble usually struck. But my hands were shaking.

The transporter flipped through a book of destination glyphs. She studied one for a moment then took a tube of aluminum the size of a milk bottle from her workbag.

"All quiet, please!" she called. "Clear the edge!"

I decided I didn't want to go through with it after all. Denver to Boston was only a couple thousand miles—I could fly it myself. It would only take a few days. I'd just be a little late for the start of classes.

"Edge is clear!" replied the attendant.

I tried to push my way forward.

"Clear the edge!" our sigilrist repeated.

Before I had a chance to holler that I wanted off, we'd already jumped to an arena two hundred fifty miles away. The only physical sensation was of the ground shifting slightly, as the ten feet of sand beneath our feet that the transporter had moved along with us settled into its new surroundings.

I let my breath out. First jump ever—nothing to be ashamed of. Just a little jittery.

Our sigilrist tossed her head as if it were nothing and walked off under her own power. A new transporter took her place and we moved in like fashion to Junction City, Kansas City, and eventually St. Louis. I changed lines and after six more hops arrived in Boston in time for a late lunch.

The scene at the Boston transporter arena was overwhelming. Hundreds of people scurried to and fro, rushing to line up for jumps or climb aboard the horse-drawn trams that provided local service. Oddly, I saw no hoverers launching or setting down. Perhaps they came and went from a particular spot—it would be safer than trying to land amid such chaos.

I stood beside my belongings on the platform. I'd consulted some maps in the Billings public library and felt confident I could find my new apartment by air. I dug my harness out of my satchel and pulled it on over my summer-weight skysuit. I stepped through the leg loops and cinched the thigh straps, buckled my shoulder bands, and attached my bag holster. I was rummaging through my regulator box, looking for a clean tip, when a tiny young woman stepped in front of me, hands on her hips. She was blond, pink-cheeked, and quite pretty.

"What the hell do you think you're doing?" she demanded.

Several of Billings' leading minds, including Willard Gunch and Blind Doyle, who'd once been all the way to Carson City, had warned me that devastatingly handsome men such as myself had to be on guard against city women, who were known to be brazenly forward in their attempts to corrupt the flower of American youth. I'd often considered how I'd reply to one of them upon my first encounter, but faced with this young lady I couldn't do more than stammer.

"I'm, uh, flying to my lodgings," I managed. I bowed and she looked at me as if I were the stupidest buffoon she'd ever met.

"Flying to your *lodgings*?" she asked. "How do you propose to do that?"

The young woman wore a gray poppy in the lapel of her jacket that rippled strangely when the wind caught it. Not a flower at all, but rather smoke pressed into the shape of one. Along with the glass tubes of powder stowed in compartments on the exterior of her handbag, it marked her out quite boldly as a fellow philosopher. I felt more comfortable at once.

"Now madam," I said, "I realize you must be concerned about the cross breeze and that there clock tower with the pointy top. But I'm going to take a hyperbolic vertical course to two hundred feet and make my turn there."

Now it was her turn to stare at me gape-mouthed. "You're a Contingency student," she said.

"Yes," I said.

"Straight off the farm from Fumblemuck, Arkansas."

"More of a country home than a farm. And Guille's Run, which is twelve miles southeast of Billings."

"I haven't the faintest idea what a Billings is," she said. "But the train station is a no-fly zone. You're not permitted to hover here."

That was the most perfectly unreasonable rule I'd ever heard—how was a person supposed to get home after a trip if not by hovering?

"The hack drivers bribed a lot of city councilmen to protect their livelihood," the young woman explained. "What college?"

"Radcliffe," I said.

She groaned. "Just my luck. Come on. We'll share a wagon."

She set off down the platform and I scrambled to keep up.

"I'm Gloxinia Jacobi," she said, extending a hand, which I shook. "You call me Jake, under pain of having your pants set on fire when you have your back turned."

"An old family name?" I asked sympathetically.

"No. Gloxinia is a showy Brazilian flower with petals in the shape of slippers. My parents saw it in a garden catalogue."

"I'm Robert Weekes," I said. "Folks call me . . . uhh . . . rather, they call me Robert."

"Yours must be a literal people, twelve miles southeast of Billings."

She led me past the streetcar line, past the row of coaches and hacks for hire, past the cheap wagons with their tough-looking drivers and broken-down horses, and past the post office carts. The only thing left before a railway siding filled with coal hoppers was the depot for Harnemon's Philosophical Supplies. Jake walked around back to the loading dock and sauntered up to one of the enormous delivery wagons. The driver was lashing down a pile of canvas bags filled with fine-milled quartz.

"Jasper!" she yelled up at him.

The man turned around. His hair was white, as was his bushy mustache, but he was spry and barrel-chested—he looked just like the Harnemon's driver back home. I wondered if they might be cousins.

"Little Jake!" he said, delighted. He leaned over the tailgate of the wagon and she kissed him on the cheek, between his mustache and sideburns. "Your daddy wrote to say we should expect you."

"I'm not inconveniencing you, am I?" she asked.

"Not at all. Big deliveries for the Gray Box, the aerodrome, and half the girls in your dorm. I'll come around and pick up your things. How many trunks is it this year?"

Jake smiled sweetly. "Eight."

"You're cutting back then! And the gentleman?"

I pulled the hand-drawn map from my pocket and read, "6A Story Street, apartment three. I believe if you come up the street that extends from the footbridge about three miles from—"

"I know where you'll be living, son," Jasper said. "I meant what have you got for luggage?"

"A duffel, two suitcases, and my rucksack."

"Fine," he said. "I'll grab my logbook and find the pair of you."

Jake led me back to the platform, which had largely emptied out except for my baggage and eight identical steamer trunks.

"I'll explain how this works," she said. "That nice big man loads your things into the wagon. Don't lift anything. Don't offer him money. You sit in back with me and make pleasant conversation. We stop in front of your apartment and Jasper carries your bags up the stairs. You say, 'Geegaw gosh, Jasper, I'm so terribly obliged,' or whatever people say where you're from. He'll be getting a lot of big tips from rich, pretty girls today, so even if you try to give him a dollar, he'll refuse. Understand?"

I did. While we waited for Jasper to bring around the wagon, Jake lit a cigarillo, which she smoked with well-practiced authority. I stepped behind her pile of trunks to remove and stow my harness.

While I was working, three young men, nattily dressed in sport coats and straw boaters, ambled up the platform toward us. Jake's trunks partially blocked my view of them, but I saw one of the boys point at Jake and whisper to his chums. He moseyed up behind her, threw an arm around her shoulder, and tried to pluck the smokecarved flower from her lapel. Jake startled visibly. The flower disintegrated.

"Hey love!" the young man said. "Is it true you philosophical gals have a sigil to make a man go all night long?"

Jake ducked out from under his arm and twisted away. "Don't touch me, you ratfuck bastard!" she shouted.

He grinned. "Oh, come on and—"

In a fluid motion, Jake dropped her cigarillo and pulled a tube of powder from her handbag. She popped the cork and pointed it at the young man, who recoiled in terror.

"I'm going to count to three. And all of you better be running," Jake shouted. "One."

They hit a dead sprint before she even uttered *two*.

Belatedly, I stepped out from around the trunks with the intent of defending her.

"Oh, don't bother," Jake sneered. "Their sort always runs at the slightest provocation."

She tried to secure her tube in one of the pockets on her handbag but her hands were trembling and she missed, spilling white powder. I picked up the cork and handed it to her.

"Welcome to Boston!" she fumed. "We've got Trenchers marching in the streets and college boys fondling strangers."

"What did those three think you were going to do with an ounce of talc?" I asked.

"Make their manhoods shrivel up, probably. Men are all the same."

"Not all of us," I said.

"You don't count, you're a philosopher. Maybe." She narrowed her eyes. "Can you really fly a hyperbolic vertical course?"

I raised my palms: guilty as charged. "Not unless I check a chart beforehand," I admitted.

"Well, aren't you a puzzle. Let me see that harness."

I handed it to her. Jake ran her hands over it, testing the thickness of the leather of one of the straps between her fingers.

"Or, rather, you're not a mystery at all," she decided. "I can tell you everything about you."

"A mind reader?"

"There are two marks on the straps four notches apart," she pronounced. "So it's secondhand, given to you pretty recently by the depth of the divot. You've used it heavily, as did the person before you. She was quite a bit smaller, which isn't a shock. A woman, certainly, somewhat taller than me. Probably your mother. It's a Springfield 1896 getup; the ink has faded, but you can still see the die stamp on the left rib guard. An original, not one of the Harnemon's reproductions, because the canvas on the shoulder pads is olive drab instead of black. Hand-stitched leather, which means it wasn't actually made in Springfield. Probably one of the special editions from Laredo issued to the most experienced officers in Cuba."

She inspected the chest plate. "No piping or unit insignia," she pronounced. "I'd say your mother went over in '97, a command officer, a captain at least. She must have been quite old already. We are talking about your mother, yes?"

I nodded.

"Old because the haul clamps are knotted with Swicker twists, which I haven't heard of anyone using since . . . Christ, since the Franco-Prussian Intervention. But if she fought in France the first time she must be—sixty-five? Is that right?"

"Sixty," I said.

"Lied about her age to join up, then. She probably taught you the same way she learned. Solid, if terribly, terribly old-fashioned. You're rigged fore and aft, so you're versatile and do mixed passengers and cargo. Double-D drop-forged rings, new ones, you've added those. Expecting to do heavy lifting."

She handed my harness back. "On the balance, you're sensible and well trained, but not overly set in your ways. More used to short hops than long hauls. You land poorly—"

"You can tell that from my harness?" I asked.

"No, because you're favoring your left ankle. Inquisitive, willing to experiment, brash in order to hide a conservative streak, and you've got sore balls."

I flushed bright red. "Excuse me?"

"Your privates must be chafed from the leg straps digging into your groin."

"Every time I bank past fifteen degrees with a load," I admitted.

"We ought to find you a solution for that," said Jake. "Dunwick Consolidated used to make a sort of codpiece, but they didn't sell any. I haven't seen one in ages. You could try a rig that puts more weight on the chest and less on the legs, or one with a wide, stable band mid-thigh. One of the new McCoules might work, but I doubt it would be long enough. You're one for custom fabrication, if ever there was."

I stared at her, stupefied. "How do you know all of those—"

"Daddy used to drive for Harnemon's in Baltimore," she said. "I rode with him for deliveries. They called us Big Jake and Little Jake. He's a part owner now."

Big Jake's business partners had adored Gloxinia and had given her every last demonstration harness, discontinued regulator, exotic tip, and prototype gizmo that had come through the depot. She'd created a minor scandal her freshman year by arriving at school with ten steamer trunks in tow. However, by year's end, she'd given away the contents of nine of them. Contingency girls who had planned on studying message sigilry or the reduplicatory arts because they didn't have money enough for supplies were able to study stasis or transport thanks to Jake's endless supply of silver chloride and refined aluminum. Anything that anyone had asked for, even beyond the bounds of reason, she'd been able to pull from her trunks. In the rare case she didn't have it, a Harnemon's man would be at their door the next morning, tipping his gold and gray cap, handing over a package containing a dozen live tarantulas or Romanian walnuts.

As a result, Jake had a great many admirers. And, as Jasper carried my trunk up three flights of stairs an hour later, I decided I was one of them.

She was the first of two exceptional, lifelong friends I made that day. I met the second only a few minutes later.

8

Do not choose a figure that may be easily guessed. Not your name nor a too-familiar image. Yet do not choose one so ornate or fussy that you or your friends will struggle to re-create it.

Miss Goodbody's Book for Girls, 1899

MY APARTMENT HAD SEEN heavy use over the years, but it was clean and serviceable. There were two small bedrooms and a shared living room with a fireplace, table, and two chairs. Several suitcases and boxes of books were stacked neatly to one side of the door—clearly my roommate had arrived, but had been considerate enough not to claim a bedroom without discussion. I liked him already.

We had our own bathroom, too. Of all the city luxuries that Angie prattled on about, she spoke most enthusiastically about unlimited hot water at the turn of a knob. I sat on the edge of the bathtub and turned the handle marked *H.* The faucet spluttered and spat out a thin stream of cold, yellow water.

Well, that was too bad. We did have the fireplace, so as long as we found some big tin buckets we could always heat the water there and . . . but then the water cleared and poured into the tub steaming hot.

"Fantastic," I murmured.

"Yes, it is," said a nervous voice behind me. A plump, bespectacled young man stood in the doorway. He looked all of fourteen. And he'd just caught me ogling the plumbing. Perfect.

"My name's Freddy Unger and I own one hundred and thirty-eight bow ties," he said by way of greeting, pointing at the forest-green bow tie with pink polka dots that he was wearing. I looked at him, agog.

"My name's Robert Weekes and I'm a-heading straight back to Guille's Run, Montana," I replied.

For a moment, it could have gone either way. Then we both burst out laughing and we were safe. Unger was eighteen, not fourteen, and he'd been raised in Jamaica Plain, in Boston.

"I wanted to send you a message, but the college didn't include your glyph," I said.

"I'll need to invent one," said Unger. "How exciting!"

I supposed he meant that he was between message glyphs at the moment, which made sense. Start college, use a fresh glyph. (Or, if you have three sisters, sometimes one of them discovers the figure you've been using for private messages and then you have to contact your confidential correspondents and switch them over to a new one.)

"I mean, you do know *how* to send a message, right?" I asked good-naturedly.

"Certainly!" said Unger. "We spent an ungodly number of hours studying message sigilry in school, even though we weren't permitted to practice it on campus."

I nodded. "We went through the same thing in high school after somebody set Mrs. Spurgeon's wig on fire with an ignite glyph—no sigils for nobody all year."

"How awful," said Unger. "But that means you can help me with the practical side of things? Because I'm an abject failure when I try to put sigils into practice."

"Oh, you'll pick them up with a little practice," I said. "I'm just glad to have someone who knows his way around the city. I wasn't here two minutes and I almost launched in the middle of a no-fly zone."

"Where was this?"

"At the transporter arena."

Unger looked confused. "Was there . . . you tried to hire a passenger hoverer? But they're not allowed to . . . or are *you* the hoverer?"

"Yes," I said.

"Oh, good for you! It looks thrilling."

"If it's thrilling, you're doing it wrong. Have you ever? Flown?"

"No, never."

As we moved on to the important business of deciding who got which room and unpacking, I had Unger pegged as an excessively modest philosopher who simply needed to build his confidence. The problem with his whole routine was that it could convince a less discriminating mind than mine that he didn't know the first thing about the actual practice of philosophy. Men especially had to be careful about that—everyone already assumed anything more complicated than message sigilry was beyond you.

"Why did you introduce yourself that way?" I asked, while hanging my shirts in my closet. "With the bow ties and all?"

"That's a strategy I adopted just this morning so that people will remember me," Unger explained. "For the duration of my studies here, every time I introduce myself, I'll mention the bow ties. Just think of it—twenty years down the road at a reunion, someone turns to the other and says, 'Remember old Freddy Unger?' and she says, 'I do so remember him: one hundred and thirty-eight bow ties!' And it's perfectly true. I adore bow ties."

It seemed to me there had to be better ways of getting people to remember you. Then, when Unger led me a few blocks up the street to the dining hall on Radcliffe's main quad for dinner, I realized that for the two of us, *not* being remembered, even at our fiftieth reunion, would be the more noteworthy accomplishment: in that entire room, there were no other men.

As Unger and I moved along the buffet line, filling our plates with meat and vegetables, I could feel the eyes of twenty-four hundred women on us. The hostility was palpable. We sat at the end of a long table with ten empty chairs between us and a group of girls who stopped their conversation long enough to stare then glare openly.

"Bit of a cold shoulder, I'm afraid," said Unger. "Though from what I hear from the other fellow, though, it improves with time."

"Only one other man?" I asked. I'd hoped Radcliffe had taken a few more of us than that.

"Yes. He's in the apartment one floor below us, a very decent sort. You'll like him. Everyone seems to. He's planning to study Eupheus."

"Wind sigilry?" I asked around a mouthful of green beans. "What's he want to learn that for?"

"I gather he's going to drop out of school, dodge the Contingency Act, and live a life of luxury drawing sigils for clipper ships, visiting every exotic corner of the globe."

"He wants to be an engine for a cargo ship?"

"That's what I gather," said Unger. "Though he may have just been saying that to impress—"

An expertly lobbed frankfurter coated in mustard struck me on the neck and rolled down my brand-new shirt into my lap. The women at the table behind me made a poor attempt at hiding their laughter.

As I tried to unclench my fists, I asked Freddy if he'd seen who threw it.

"Not which one of them, no."

That was just as well. I couldn't imagine what I might have said to her that wouldn't have made me look like an even bigger ass.

"You were saying about the other man?" I asked Freddy.

"Go home, Galen Wainwright!" someone shouted from the other side of the hall.

"Go back to Harvard, you poofs!" someone else shouted. "You oily sodomites!" This time the laughter was widespread.

I ran my thumb over my teeth hard enough to leave a mark. It was just talk. It was juvenile and galling and ultimately harmless.

"I should possibly have mentioned that there was a fourth man as recently as yesterday," Unger added. "I'm told he crudely propositioned one of the ladies while assembling his breakfast. It took one of the more talented smokecarvers three minutes to snake a cloud of vaporized resin of *T. radicans* right up the leg of his pants."

"Poison ivy smoke?"

"Indeed," said Unger. "He's quite allergic as it turns out. He decided to continue his education elsewhere."

"So, maybe the best thing is to finish eating quickly and get out of here?" I suggested. "Before they decide to do us the same way."

A carrot zipped past me and hit Freddy's glasses, partially dislodging them.

"Or right now would be fine," he said.

Unger weathered the whole incident with such equanimity that it was contagious. By the time I'd changed out of my mustard-spattered shirt and pants I'd nearly calmed down, too.

"Whenever something like that happens," Unger said, "I think of my little sister, who, when I got my acceptance letter, said, 'If you're going to Radcliffe, then I'm going to Harvard.' If you imagine what it'll be like for the first woman—well, the nastiness here will seem mild by comparison."

I could hardly disagree.

"She's only twelve years old," Unger reflected. "Maybe she won't have to be the *very* first."

He plucked a deck of cards from his desk and sat at the table in our common room, practicing his one-handed shuffle. "Do you play mudge, by chance?" he asked.

"Do I what?" I asked.

"Or double mudge?"

As Unger laid out his deck of cards and explained the rules, I recognized the game. "We call that jiggery back home," I said. "But we booted on jacks instead of tens."

"And you would have played to eighty-eight points, not one hundred," Unger added, "with queens worth half a point."

I was a decent card player, but Freddy was a master. After playing a dozen hands, he could pick out with uncanny accuracy whether I was holding a three or a five and he always knew when I had a queen.

"You should play with Grandpa Unger," he said, after finishing me off with jigs on three successive turns. "He can't even see the cards and he still wins." Unger began talking wistfully about how the real art of double mudge was playing in pairs, setting up your partner and playing out complicated defenses.

"Well, I met a young lady at the transporter arena today," I said. "Maybe she plays."

"Oh, but men aren't allowed in the women's dormitory after eight," said Unger.

"Are they allowed to visit us here?" I asked. Not that after our dinner debacle I imagined many women would be racing to befriend us.

"It's not *explicitly* forbidden," Unger temporized. "Technically, our apartment isn't on university grounds. But how would you get word to her?"

"We exchanged glyphs."

"You what?" asked Unger.

Rather than try to explain, I retrieved my message board. Even under ordinary circumstances I would have felt nervous sending a message to a pretty girl I'd just met; after Unger's suggestion that there was something indecorous about proposing a meeting, I adopted a formal, written-out style: *My roommate and I are looking for a pair for double mudge. Any chance you might be interested?*

Her reply came inside a minute: *Y. Arr 2145 w/2. Nd tlk to y nway.*

"Astonishing!" said Unger. "But it doesn't seem to have quite worked. Half the letters are missing."

Hoverers were bad about shorthand—every second you spent writing while in the air meant your arm was out of position—though Jake's language was simple enough: Yes, she would come at a quarter to ten, would bring a partner, and was glad I'd written, since she needed to talk to me anyway. Not that she'd said *glad*.

Unger was pleased at the prospect of a real game. But his amazement at the simplest of practical sigils surprised me.

"Freddy," I asked, hoping I was being tactful. "Yes or no: Can you send a message?"

"I've studied them a great deal."

"That's not a yes or a no."

He cleared his throat. "No."

"Have you ever even *tried*?"

"No, never." He sounded relieved.

"I'll teach you right now! It's the simplest thing in the world. Why, back in Billings, we even have a dog that can send messages. Name of Barney." (The last was a lie, of course.)

An hour later, I regretted my flippancy. Unger designed his glyph with aplomb—he'd spent the last twelve years thinking about it—a stylized version of his initials, with a double bar on the U. That was an embarrassingly literal choice, but no one else in her right mind would ever use it, which was the point of a personal glyph. If you chose a figure that someone else in, say, Florida had already laid claim to, then you got each other's mail for a few days, apologized, and switched to a different one.

But Unger couldn't get it to work. He was a little inconsistent with his counting and a bit sloppy with his form, though not so much that I would have expected his sigil not to take. Yet after an hour of labor, he could neither send a message nor retrieve one.

I've been asked countless times whether I think skill with empirical philosophy is inborn or learned. In 1917, I would have come down on the side of nurture. My mother and sisters had instilled in me the notion I was capable of any sigil they were—just not with the same strength as a woman, of course. If I couldn't get a glyph to work, I had nothing to blame but my own laziness. But I've since learned that a few people really have no aptitude for empirical philosophy. They can practice all they want, study with the finest teachers, read the most authoritative books, and still fail to perform even the simplest sigil. It's no different than one fellow who's born with perfect pitch and another who can't carry a tune, one who's a natural artist and another who can't so much as draw a straight line.

Unger was one of the tone-deaf ones.

It came as a relief for both of us when Jake arrived and we could put away the message board. She'd brought her roommate, Delores Isadora Gutierrez, or simply Dizzy to anyone who'd known her for more than a minute. Dizzy was a third-generation practitioner of Eupheus sigilry. She was the product of one of those stereotypical romances between a kite jockey, who drove one of the last sail-powered stagecoaches through the deserts of the Southwest, and his philosophical counterpart, who summoned the wind. Dizzy was tall, dark, and carelessly good-looking, with flyaway strands of long black hair that formed a perpetual halo around her head.

Unger was smitten. "Welcome, welcome to our humble abode," he said. "May I offer you a seat?"

Dizzy accepted. Unger plopped into the chair opposite her.

Jake stood in the doorway, hands on her hips. "Did you seriously invite us over with only two chairs in the whole place?"

"Looks that way," I admitted.

"And nothing to drink?"

"Not a drop," I said.

"You'll have to correct that. I'm only here because nobody bothered to mail instructions to the prospective fliers. That's typical—the college would rather not allow flying at all, since they're responsible for our safety and not all the girls are bright enough to avoid a sudden introduction to the ground."

Jake looked at me as if I likely fell into the accident-prone group.

"There are check-out flights tomorrow morning at six, eight, and ten—to make sure you won't dig a ditch the moment the instructors turn their backs." She handed me a sheet of paper with the testing requirements printed on it. "The serious fliers check out at six. Now if you'll excuse me, I have one more hoverer left on my list."

Unger was demonstrating his shuffle for Dizzy, who seemed enchanted. Jake coughed.

"Oh, let's play just one game," Dizzy said. Her voice had a delightful lilt. "Who is it you have left? Yancey? She knows when to come."

"Well, I'm not playing standing up," Jake said.

Unger gave up his seat and we played standing men against sitting women. Unger played magnificently, Jake played indifferently, I played badly, and Dizzy appeared never to have held a card before. We stopped one or two thousand times so that Unger could re-explain the rules. Dizzy was inquisitive and charming and Unger was patient and gentlemanly. By the third time Dizzy stopped the game to ask what the name of the card with the *J* on it was, Jake and I were openly rolling our eyes—she was putting on a show.

Unger and I won by forty-two points, a colossal victory. Unger explained that traditionally this would mean they owed us forty-two cents, but that teaching the game was reward enough and he would never imagine playing for money with a novice.

"But surely *some* sort of reward is in order for so marvelous a triumph," Dizzy purred. "A kiss perhaps?"

Jake rolled her eyes so hard I was afraid she would injure herself.

"Madam," said Unger, "I would like nothing better, but under the circumstances it hardly seems right. I barely know you."

Dizzy nodded seriously. "When you know me better, then."

"Robert from Billings can get his twenty-one cents from me tomorrow morning," Jake replied. "Six o'clock. Bring your own harness."

9

Hovering is a dangerous, useless pastime for tinkerers and rogues. It has no future in the Corps nor anywhere.

Mrs. Lucretia Cadwallader, quoted in "Chippewa Woman Flies Across Lake Ontario!" *Detroit Defender*, May 3, 1870

I ROLLED OUT OF bed at five thirty in a foul mood. The noise from the street, unfamiliar and vaguely sinister, had kept me up all night. Shops being opened and closed, wagons making deliveries or dropping off passengers. Dogs barking. Conversations. All of it quotidian, but compressed and layered so closely as to seem threatening.

I dressed in a light skysuit and packed my harness, then walked down to the Charles River and across a footbridge to the far side, where Radcliffe's hovering building was located—the aerodrome, the girls called it, in the French fashion. It was surrounded by a large grassy field for practicing launches and landings. Unfortunately, the city of Cambridge, in its wisdom, had zoned the area between the college and the field "no fly" out of concern that a student hoverer might fall out of the air and kill a bystander on the ground. That meant a twenty-minute walk, instead of a two-minute flight.

A young lady a block ahead of me turned down the path toward the aerodrome, but found her way blocked by a group of middle-aged women holding handbills. They reached out to stop her, thrusting papers at her. The girl put her head down and pushed her way through, making for the aerodrome at a run.

I reached the same group a minute later, though they behaved more civilly with me, perhaps not recognizing a man as a hoverer despite my skysuit.

"Sir, do you have a moment?" one of them called to me. "Do you know about the Philosophical Corps?"

"Sure, yeah," I said, committing the tactical error of making eye contact.

"They've forced the country into war—they're the ones responsible for the draft! They've as good as taken President Wilson hostage."

"Listen," I said. "I'm running late for—"

"They have whole warehouses packed full of plague! They could release it at any moment. They wouldn't hesitate to kill you, to kill your family."

It was a lot of typical Trencher nonsense. One of the women shoved a piece of paper into my face.

"Not interested," I said, plowing past them.

"That Radcliffe lot is a pack of common whores!" one of them shouted after me. "They'll corrupt you, body and soul."

"Have a pleasant morning," I replied in a voice better suited for saying, "Go back to the hell that spawned you!"

But the Trenchers' wives, or whichever concerned organization the women represented, didn't dare come closer to the aerodrome.

Roughly two dozen young ladies had queued up in front of the building. A handful looked like veteran fliers—their broken-in skysuits and looks of sleepy assurance gave them away. The rest were a much chattier, more stylish group. I spotted a pair of gold-rimmed touring goggles more appropriate for a costume party than field use and a set of divided skirts that would have made it impossible to fly faster than ten miles per hour. There was no sign of Jake.

"Are you lost?" one of the well-dressed fliers asked me.

"It's the man with the wiener in his lap!" observed a second.

"He can't be here," insisted another. "He's not allowed to be here, is he?"

No one was willing to try and drag a 210-pound male philosopher off the field, however.

At six, an instructor in a sharply pressed red-and-black skysuit marched out of the building. She was barely older than me. A few of the more experienced fliers snickered.

"Uh-oh! Uh-oh!" one of them called out in a voice like a parrot's.

"Where's your parachute, Rachael?" another yelled.

The instructor blushed as red as her uniform.

"Who's the rescue flier?" a third woman shouted.

"Ladies, that's quite enough," the instructor said. "For those of you I've not met, my name is Rachael Rodgers. I'm the senior flight instructor. Professor Brock will be along shortly to fly point. If you encounter any difficulties, she will assist, including catch and carry if necessary."

Rachael launched into a dry description of Radcliffe's grades of hoverers, which I suspected she'd memorized from the same sheet Jake had given me: Zeds were novices, allowed to fly only under direct supervision. Ones were provisional; they could draw up to ten pounds of powder a week from the supply room and fly below two hundred feet when an instructor was on duty. Twos were proficient; they were allowed twenty pounds a week and could fly in fair weather during daylight hours within a two-mile radius of the aerodrome. Threes were expert; they were given a key to the storeroom, asked to log whatever supplies they took, and permitted all-weather, day or night flight on any flyway. You had to pass a flight test for each level.

Those with no experience whatsoever signed their names in a logbook as Zeds. That took care of a dozen girls.

The qualification for a One was to climb to ten feet, fly the length of the field, and set down without injuring yourself. We lined up and the instructor handed out harnesses and prefilled bags fitted with late-model regulators. I took one of the standard-issue harnesses and slid the shoulder straps out as far as they would go, but there was no way it was going to fit me. "Ma'am?" I said, calling the instructor over.

"Is this a joke?" she asked. "Who put you up to this?"

"May I use my own?" I asked. "I brought my gear."

She waved disgustedly for me to go get it. I put on my harness and rejoined the others. One of the regular faculty came out of the aerodrome and, after a word with Rachael, launched to spot us.

We proceeded in alphabetical order.

Despite the minimal requirements for a One, two girls failed. The first tried and tried to draw a launch sigil but couldn't get it to take. After her twentieth attempt, she broke down in tears and was led off by Rachael to stand with the Zeds. The second managed to launch and wobble along for a few seconds, before warping her glyph and veering right. Somehow she maintained her altitude, but couldn't recover directional control. She was headed right for the river.

"Put down!" shrieked the instructor. "Land!"

For all the snide remarks during the other flights, the group fell silent now. Above us, the rescue flier noticed something was wrong and dove toward the struggling girl, who had the good sense to simply turn off her regulator when she was over the river. She flopped into the water with a huge splash, bobbed to the surface, waved, and swam to shore. The rescue flier swooped in, too late to do any good.

"Well done, Professor!" one of the more experienced women yelled. "Quick as ever." The rescue flier yelled something back, but the wind took it.

The girl climbed out of the water covered in muck, gave us a curtsy, and went to stand with the Zeds.

I was last in line, but in the fifteen minutes I'd had to look over my gear, I still couldn't figure out the regulator.

"Psst," I said to the woman in front of me. She was a rail-thin, anxious-looking dishwater blonde. "Where's the regulator lever?"

"What?" she whispered back.

"Where's the lever?"

"What lever?"

"How do I set the regulator to four ounces per minute?" I asked.

"Oh," she said, looking at me skeptically. "It's a double-dial system. Turn the outer one clockwise four clicks. The inner ring sets tenths."

I turned the dial. A thin, steady stream of powder spilled out of the tip. I turned it off again. Less precise than the lever regulators I'd grown up using, but much more forgiving. No risk of bumping the lever with your thumb and becoming the first man to land on the moon.

"Thank you," I said.

"You're sure you've done this before?" the woman asked.

I flew my course without incident.

For a Two, we had to climb to one hundred feet, spin in a complete circle while stationary, then roll to forty-five degrees and make one banked turn in each direction. Two girls got to about twenty feet, decided they couldn't go on, and put right back down. Another got snarled in her starboard turn and had to be righted by Professor Brock. A fourth lost her sigil entirely and started to fall. Brock had been staying very close to her; she reached out, caught the falling girl's shoulder strap, and clipped onto her harness almost before we'd realized anything was wrong. She returned the girl to the ground to a warm round of applause. Brock smiled politely and climbed back to her station.

"She's only smiling because she got to touch Jamie's bosom," whispered one of the jokers. "Brock's the biggest Sapphist in the whole college."

My own flight was uneventful, though my thigh straps rode up during my turns and stuck. I winced when I landed.

"How are your balls, Ace?" Jake yelled. She'd appeared out of nowhere, having skipped both of the qualifying rounds that were supposedly mandatory.

There were six fliers left. Rachael lined us back up.

"Is anyone here attempting to qualify as a Three?" she asked. No one answered. Someone at the end of the line cracked a joke that I couldn't hear. A couple of the fliers tittered. Rachael reddened. "Is anyone attempting to qualify as a Three?" she snapped.

"I am," I said. Someone down the line hissed.

"Very well," Rachael said. "Those wishing to attain the grade of Three must undertake one of the following."

We had the option of performing two approved aerobatic maneuvers;

or, climbing to five thousand feet and returning to the ground in under a minute (which would require a difficult, diving descent); or, picking up a hundred-pound sack, lifting it to two hundred feet, and setting it down in a five-foot-by-five-foot landing zone. I'd essentially done the last one every day since I was ten, only with sacks not as nice as the ones supplied by the college.

"Ladies," said the instructor. "I will not tolerate showboating. If you try something flashy, you will *not* receive a Three. Let's set a good example for the younger women. You're first." She pointed to the nervous sophomore who'd showed me how to use my regulator.

"*I'm* first," said Jake, and pushed off the ground. She came up hard to two hundred feet and did a beautiful inverted pike flip-spin—flying upside down and backward, kicking into a somersault and cartwheel at the same time, tumbling and whirling, before snapping back into perfectly controlled level flight. She followed that with a Rappaport loop in *trois-point* stance, a maneuver so complicated that my mother had once assured me it was impossible. On her landing, Jake bowed in midair and set down doing a handstand.

"Jacobi!" Rachael shouted. "Those were not approved maneuvers!"

"Then add them to your little list," retorted Jake. "Let me spell it for you: it's R-A-P-P—"

"Enough!" barked Rachael. She motioned for the next woman in line to proceed.

The next flier did a death spiral, leveled out, then did a second death spiral, pulling out inches above the ground to screams of terror from the Zeds and Rachael.

"That was only one maneuver!" objected Rachael, after she'd regained her voice.

"The regulations don't say two *different* maneuvers," the young woman said, "only two maneuvers."

Rachael squinted at the paper and looked as if she would tear it in half. The third flier rigged the sandbag on an extra-long line, took it to altitude, and came hurtling down, hammering the bag into the ground right in the middle of the square so that it split open and sent up a shower of sand. The flier landed lightly next to it.

"It says I have to put the bag in the square, not that it has to be intact," she said, before anyone could object. There was a delay as Rachael went into the building and wheeled out a fresh hundred-pound bag on a dolly.

The next woman rocketed up to five thousand feet and then disappeared. Was it possible we'd lost her in the sun? I scanned the sky but couldn't find her.

Beside me Rachael was frantically doing the same. "Uh oh, uh oh!" she squawked.

"Uh oh, uh oh!" said someone standing behind me in the same parrot voice as before. It was the missing hoverer. Rachael went from sickly gray to bright red.

"The regulations say I have to be back on the ground in under a minute," said the flier. "There's nothing against transporting down."

The instructor looked like she was ready to explode. "You," she hissed, pointing at me. "Go."

I thought I had it pretty well figured out: if you wanted to impress the other experts, you did something flashy. Rachael wasn't *really* going to fail any of the experienced fliers—she just had to put on a good show in front of the new girls.

I ran a twenty-foot line from my back clips to the sandbag, then launched and climbed hard. I accelerated full-out in the horizontal plane before pulling back sharply, sending the bag shooting upward in an arc with me at the center somersaulting backward. I took the bag through one full orbit. Pendulum flip—I'd spent all of July practicing it. I flipped the bag a second time for good measure, then twisted out, brought my line back under control, and set it neatly in the landing square.

Rachael was white as chalk.

I sauntered over to Jake and the other experts. One looked more shocked than the next.

"That's not something freshmen do," Jake said. Not reproachful, exactly, but with a warning tone.

The last woman did a forward somersault followed by a reverse somersault, only she came straight down and landed quietly.

"Very nice," said Rachael. "Now, Ones through Threes line up for the
safety quiz. If you answer incorrectly you will automatically receive a rating
of Zed."

She had a list of questions that she read off the sheet as she moved down
the line. Each of us answered one. They were simple and practical. *Why do
hoverers never wear metal buttons?* (Spark hazards.) *What amount of powder
does a hoverer use per one hundred pounds of ground weight flying average
high-efficiency?* (Two ounces per minute.) *When loading two passengers, where
should the heavier one go and why?* (On the back due to improved in-flight
balance.) No one missed.

When she got to me, Rachael asked, "What would you do if your regulator tip jammed due to wet powder during a lengthy flight?"

"Switch to my secondary bag," I said without hesitation. There were a
few snorts up the line from people who knew the textbook answer. The examiner made a note on her clipboard.

"What would you do if you didn't have a secondary?" she asked.

My mother had taught me the answer to that one, too: "Then I wouldn't
fly cross-country." Rachael made another note.

"That concludes today's assessment," she said. "I will now assign you a
grade from Zed to Three. Stand together according to grade, please." She
went down the line giving each woman a rank. Despite her threats about
showboating, the experts all got Threes. Then Rachael stopped in front of
me. She looked at me with contempt, straight in the face.

"Zed," she spat.

The water around my eyeballs went hot. I damned myself for not having
been on my best behavior. One thing to do a reckless maneuver if you were
a woman, but quite another if you were the solitary man. I tried to steady
myself. If I broke down in front of everyone, I could only imagine what they
would say.

A couple of Zeds whispered and shook their heads.

"Three!" shouted Jake.

I swallowed and tried to keep my face a flat mask.

The other Threes shouted "Three" as well.

Rachael smiled icily. "Zed," she repeated. She turned to Professor Brock, who had landed behind her, for confirmation. Brock—stout, broad-shouldered, double-chinned, and topped by a mess of thinning hair—shook her head and held up three fingers. I'd never seen someone more beautiful.

"Three," Rachael said, seething.

Still dazed, I walked over toward the women who'd qualified as experts ahead of me. They'd all lit up Cuban cigars. The biggest, the stolid blonde who'd smashed the sandbag, was nearly as tall as me. She held the cigar box tucked under her arm.

"The correct answer," she said, "is pump the manual discharge valve on your regulator three times to clear the jam and land immediately."

"The correct answer," said the girl next to her, who had high cheekbones and straight black hair like the Salish Indians I'd known in Billings, "is skip the hundred-dollar regulator and fly in the old style."

"The correct answer," said a middle-aged redhead who was missing several teeth and looked like she'd recently had her nose broken, "is curse out that bastard of a nozzle until its jaw drops and it opens back up."

"The correct answer," said Jake, "is that Rachael didn't get her Three until the fifth try and only an idiot would hire her as an examiner. And might I add that the correct question is whether bold Mr. Weekes gets a cigar."

"Hey von Viking," said the redhead, "do men get to smoke?"

The big one shrugged. "Do you smoke?"

I didn't. I debated whether I'd cause myself greater embarrassment declining or taking one and smoking it badly.

"We've never let freshmen smoke," Jake supplied. "And Astrid, might I observe that the point of the cigars is that they're supposed to get nicer over the course of the year. Setting the bar with a forty-dollar box makes life hard for the rest of us."

"Astrid can afford it," said the black-haired girl. "She'll go home and pump the manual discharge valve on dear old Liam and he'll give her whatever she wants."

"Yes," said Astrid, "but I'll have to pump it more than three times to clear it."

That got a raucous laugh from the other women and a tentative one from me.

It took us a moment to notice that one more girl had joined us—the polite, conservative flier. She looked terrified.

"Essie!" shrieked Jake, running to hug the new girl. "Congratulations." Essie hugged her back stiffly.

Astrid trimmed a cigar, lit it, and handed it to Essie, who took a tiny puff and spat out a mouthful of smoke. Jake drew deeply on her own cigar and blew a series of smoke rings. Essie tried to do the same, but ended in a fit of coughing.

"Honey, stop," said Jake, taking the cigar away. "You're turning green."

The Zeds, Ones, and Twos were each led inside the aerodrome in turn. Jake and company recollected which of the novices they had coached and in what areas they needed further work. After a couple of attempts to get a word in edgewise, Essie fell silent. I was pleased to see that her color was coming back, but she was looking at me with unsettling intensity.

"I thought you were going to crash when you did that flip—all of us did. But you were really good," Essie said, as if such a thing ought to be impossible.

"Thanks," I said. "I'm the fifth best hoverer in my family."

"Why did you learn that trick?" she asked me. "It's not very pretty and I can't imagine it has any practical use."

"Drogue landing," I said at the same time as the woman holding the box of cigars.

"And demolition," I said.

"And it's good practice if you ever have to fly a stringer," the big woman said. It would seem we flew much in the same style. She smiled kindly and shook my hand. "I'm Astrid van Dyke."

"You mean Astrid Bonner," the redhead cut in.

Astrid punched her in the shoulder, not gently. "I'm *not* taking his name. We've talked about this."

It was as motley a group as I could have asked for. Astrid had come from a village in central Pennsylvania as a four-year Contingency student—take a Bachelor of Empirical Philosophy degree and then do four years of service. She was getting married in the spring.

The redhead's name was Francine Dubois. She hailed from Lowell, Massachusetts, a tough mill town where she'd worked as the municipal equivalent of a county philosopher. Thirty-five years old, divorced, with two children back home in the care of their grandmother. She'd come as a four-year Contingency, too, the oldest in the class of 1918. She was largely self-taught in her book learning, but had a vicious intelligence when she decided a subject was worth the bother.

The lean, dark-haired woman was Tillie Blackroot, another Contingency, out of Oklahoma City. Five-eighths Cherokee and a fourth-generation flier. Her family was the sort that painted their address on their roof rather than beside the door, operating on the assumption that visitors were more likely to drop out of the sky than come by foot. She had the tightest, most efficient lines of anyone I'd ever met and could blaze past even Jake on a long enough straight line.

And the polite nonsmoker was Essie Stewart, a sophomore from the staid Boston neighborhood of Back Bay.

"Essie isn't Contingency, but we like her anyway," said Tillie.

"Couldn't fly at all until we got hold of her," said Francine.

Rachael called the Threes into the aerodrome. There was a locker room down the hall in one direction; in the other was a large classroom lined with pegboard panels on which were hung all manner of tackle, lines, and harnesses. Straight ahead was a counter with a storeroom behind, filled with hundreds of barrels, boxes, and sacks. In the middle of the counter was the sort of bell you'd ring at a hotel to summon the desk clerk.

Rachael recorded each of our names in a logbook, then printed them on certification cards and signed her name. Professor Brock stood next to her and countersigned each. When she came to me, Brock tried to put on a serious face.

"Weekes, is it?" said Brock. "You almost decapitated me with your flip."

"Almost," I said politely.

Brock shook her head, suppressing a smile. "You may fit in *too* well here. All I ask is that you warn me next time before you try to give me a stroke."

"Okay," I said. "I'll warn you right now: I want to join R&E."

"And I want a pretty French maid to cook me dinner," Brock answered. She signed the card and pushed it across the table.

"I'm not joking," I said.

"Oh Mother of God," Brock said. "Do you have any idea how difficult it would be—"

Brock was cut short by the sound of Jake furiously ringing the bell on the counter beside us and crying out, "Quartermaster! Quartermaster! Where's the damn quartermaster of the day?"

Rachael slammed the logbook shut and took the bell away. "You know very well I'm in charge of supplies today. What do you want?"

"Six forty-pound powder bags," said Jake.

"That's not reasonable!"

"I don't have to be reasonable, I just have to sign for it!" retorted Jake. "Besides, I'm saving you paperwork by ordering all of them myself."

"You haven't even filed a flight plan!"

"Bring me the powder and I'll file."

Rachael weighed out measures of sand and corn powder on the spring scales in the storeroom, then dumped the powder into a large hand-cranked mixer, which combined them with a set of rotating paddles and discharged the mixture into a bag. It was work I'd done thousands of times and knew to be physically taxing and unpleasant under the best of circumstances. By the time Rachael had heaved the sixth forty-pound sack onto the counter I almost felt sorry for her.

"Miss Jacobi, I need a flight plan before I hand any of this over," she insisted, indicating a clipboard holding a stack of forms.

"Improvisatory aerobatics," said Jake, writing the same on the topmost form.

"That's not a flight plan! I need anticipated range, accompanying fliers, estimated time of return—"

"It means I'll fly where I like, with whom I like, and come back when I damn well please," said Jake. She tossed the form over the counter, handed the clipboard to Francine, and helped herself to one of the forty-pounders.

"Same for me," said Francine, scrawling on another form. "I can't spell it, but 'improvisatory aerobatics.' " Astrid and Tillie agreed heartily. Essie agreed meekly then filled in the rest of the information. I wrote "improvisatory aerobatics" like the rest.

"Just stop a moment and I'll show you how," said Rachael. "You won't last a minute around here if you don't pay attention to paperwork. Besides, you're not really interested in aerobatics, are you?"

"I am now," I said. I took the sixth bag off the counter and left her fuming in my wake.

The morning having turned warm and Jake being in the mood for a swim, she settled on Sagamore Beach as our destination. We launched and formed a loose line abreast. It was a beautiful day for hovering, calm and mild, with the sun off our left shoulders. Jake set her speed at two hundred miles an hour, which was quite a relaxed pace for everyone except me. I flew full-out, head down, streamlining as tightly as I could, but fell farther and farther behind. Jake took pity on me and backed off the group to half speed.

Can't keep up with the girls, not even on the first day.

Not that it had been any different with my sisters. Or with most of Montana's better amateur fliers.

In a half hour's time, we reached our destination. The sandy beach made an easy landing for everyone but Essie, who made an unusually tentative approach. She had her jaw clenched and was panting so hard through her nose I thought she would hyperventilate. When she touched down, she closed her eyes and swallowed, looking as if she had stepped in front of the firing squad.

"You made your first Three," Jake said solemnly, taking a step toward Essie. "First Three drinks first." The others repeated the mantra as they closed in on her, reaching to pull several different types of liquor from beneath their harnesses. Jake had rum in a metal flask; Francine, gin in a glass bottle; Astrid, vodka in an ornately carved ivory flagon; and Tillie, bourbon in a canteen. Essie couldn't open her eyes.

It was too much to watch.

"Well, it was my first Three, too," I said, as if I knew the rules as well as they did. "And Essie must be senior to me. So, shouldn't I drink first?"

No one objected. I went down the line, knocking back a belt from each of the containers. The world took on a pinkish, misty glow.

I'd given Essie just enough time to regain her composure. She stepped up to Jake and wiped the top of the flask with her sleeve before lifting it to her lips.

Jake snorted. "It's strong enough to kill whatever Mr. Weekes may have brought with him from Montana."

"A duffel bag, two suitcases, and my rucksack," I said unsteadily, having heard a question where none had been posed. I sat down before I lost track of the ground.

Essie drank as little from each container as her honor would allow, but still ended up retching into the sea.

With the ordeal over, we lay down in a row, took off our boots, and commenced imbibing at a more sociable pace, passing the flasks back and forth. Tillie rolled up the legs and sleeves of her skysuit, enjoying the warmth of the sun. Francine put on a pair of spectacles with smoked-glass lenses and a floppy, wide-brimmed hat.

"Protects against freckles," she explained.

"Too late," said Astrid.

"I'll lay a beating on you for that, even if you are twice my size!" Francine threatened.

"Three times your size," quipped Jake.

Two thrown boots and four death threats followed before Jake turned the conversation to the subject of Rachael Rodgers.

"We have to break her before she hurts someone," Astrid said. "The only question is how."

"Pick the lock on her cubby and dye her skysuits purple," suggested Tillie.

"Millipedes in the corn powder," said Essie, almost getting into the spirit of things.

"Place a personal ad on her behalf in the *Koru Cooperative Newsletter*," Francine offered. " 'Bad flier seeks good loving.' "

That met with a roar of approval from everyone except me, since I wasn't sure what they were talking about.

Jake sighed and rolled on her side to look at me. "We're not always this bad," she said, "but Rachael had to be rescued twice during her first check-out flight, to say nothing of how many times the instructors carried her down when she froze. She flew all last year carrying a parachute."

"Pardon?" I said.

"It's like a . . . oh God!" said Jake. "Somebody make him understand."

Tillie took over. "The aeroplane pilots just started using them in France. It's like a giant folded silk parasol you stuff into a bag and strap to your back. You pull a cord, the parachute flies out, forms a canopy overhead, and slows your descent to a manageable speed."

I'd never heard of such a thing. "This is a philosophical device?"

"No! It's attached with lines. You only use it if everything goes tits up—your powder flow fails at a thousand feet and you can't clear your regulator."

"Or in Mr. Weekes's case," said Jake, "if he suffers a failure in both his primary and secondary bags."

Tillie nodded. "Now the hell of it is, one time Rachael actually used it. She was way up at cloud level trying to do a banked turn and she just froze. She kept her altitude but she was too scared to come down. The flight instructor was helping someone having a real problem, so Rachael just floated there for half an hour until her powder ran out and she started to fall. So, she pulls the rip cord and out pops the parachute. But there's a problem. It's a windy day and she can't control which direction she's traveling."

Astrid and Francine were holding each other and laughing so hard they could barely breathe.

"Right smack in the middle of the river?" I said.

"No, better," said Tillie. "She gets blown clear across the river into Harvard Yard and the parachute hangs up on the University Hall weather vane. In two seconds, there's a hundred Harvard men gathered round, catcalling her. Because this is a warm day, too, and our Rachael has never been one to fly in a skysuit if she can help it. She's wearing a light skirt, which keeps blowing up around her ears, and purple underwear. Not bloomers, either, but a pair of real sleek, stylish, French-cut panties, a fact recorded with great precision in the *Harvard Crimson* the following morning. The president of the university, who has his office on the third floor, hears the commotion and sticks his head out the window. He sees Rachael's feet hanging there. But he's so polite, he doesn't know what to do other than tip his hat and say, 'Madam.' Then he closes the window and goes back to his books."

"Who fetched her down?" I asked.

"No one," said Tillie. "The fire department had to cut her lines and carry her down a ladder. She was up there an hour."

Tillie, who had been remarkably straight-faced throughout, broke up in hysterical giggles, too. All the girls—even Essie—were laughing and wiping away tears.

Now, I suppose if it had been a hoverer I'd known, and it had been the steeple of St. Mark's Church in Billings on a Sunday morning, and if it had been old Father Valentine who had to call out the volunteer fire company, that would have been about the funniest thing in all creation. But hearing that story, try as I did to laugh along, I mostly felt sick that such a thing should happen to another flier.

Jake seemed to sense my mood. She blew her nose and said, "You know how the story really ends, though? Rachael broke her arm when she hit. We had two instructors fired for carelessness and Brock nearly lost tenure. Someone broke all the windows on the aerodrome and smeared the door with human excrement. And then after Detroit drubbed us at the General's Cup, they threw purple panties at us. I don't bear Rachael ill will over it. She got back up a week later and checked out for her Two with a cast still on her arm. She's as strong-willed as any. But she never should have made Three. And hiring her as instructor is absurd. Someone is going to plummet out of the sky, and instead of catch and carry, it'll be 'Uh-oh, uh-oh,' splat!"

"We petitioned the department," said Francine. "But they don't want students weighing in on hiring and firing. So, we'll ride her till she cracks. Trust me, she'll crack. We nearly had her in tears today and she only had to survive fifteen minutes with us."

"Why'd they hire her?" I asked.

"Her auntie is Lt. Col. Rodgers," said Francine, naming the most famous R&E flier of the Spanish-American War.

"Shit," I said. "I read all her books growing up."

"We had so many better women," lamented Tillie. "We graduated fifteen Threes last year. Five took good jobs. I mean really good ones, eight thousand dollars a year for high lifting or passenger flights in New York, they're so short on competent hoverers. The other ten are flying in France."

"*Three* are flying in France," Jake corrected. "Trish, Xu, and Tammy couldn't stomach the gore. They're working the message boards now. Gomez is missing. Clara bought it. The Germans shot down Sue the Sioux. And Ruby's still in the hospital."

"You've heard from her?" asked Francine.

"She told me," said Jake, trying not to let her voice waver, "that she doesn't much feel like sending messages, so stop writing. She thinks she'll recover enough to walk a few steps at a time. And she says . . ." Here Jake abandoned any pretense of composure. "She says she doesn't have to be able to walk to be able to fly."

Jake was half-drunk and weeping.

"And she says she saw a horse at Passchendaele that looked just like Detroit's number two long-courser."

Everyone went silent. There was no sound but the gentle wash-wash of the waves.

"You have to understand," said Jake at last, "Ruby was our queen bee. When she was good, she was very, very good, and when she was bad—when all of us were bad—no one talked about anything else for days. That's important. Radcliffe's board of directors keeps threatening to cut empirical philosophy as a field of study. They hate having a bunch of common sigilrists mixed in with their upper-crust Yankees. We're not genteel enough, not pretty enough, fated to do common labor when we graduate. Responsible for attracting 'a dangerous element.' Well, sometimes the higher-ups need a good shaking. So it falls to the hoverers. The stases are too serious, because they deal in matters of life and death. The transporters are too busy stuffing themselves. The smokecarvers burned up their sense of humor. The message specialists have to be good because they're trying to land husbands."

"Not that there's anything wrong with that," interjected Astrid.

"The koruists are all Sapphists and they're too busy kissing each other to raise hell," Jake continued. "The synthesists are synthesizing because they can't do anything else right. And I'm sure the theorists come up with all sorts of good ideas for trouble, but they can't actually put them into practice. Did I leave anyone out?"

"Cartogramancers," I said.

"We only have one of those and he's the dean," said Jake. "So it's our job to shake things up."

The lapping of the waves had a soporific effect on me and that, combined with the early start to the day and the warmth of the sand, caused me to drift off. I awoke an hour later, disoriented and groggy. Beside me, the other Threes were stirring, too.

Tillie produced a thin wooden flute from her pocket and launched into one of the popular tunes of the day. We all sang along:

Oh, Mama's gone off to the war.
She went and joined up with the Corps.
Daddy is sad, cuz his cooking's so bad,

And Mama's gone off to the war.

Oh, Mama's in Gay Paree.

I hope she remembers me.

She'll scrap with the Hun, but when the fighting's all done,

I hope she remembers me.

When Ma marches into Berlin

Daddy will tuck me in.

No kiss on the cheek, and my eyes will leak

When Ma marches into Berlin.

Francine shuddered. "Don't play the rest. That's such a terrible song. I'd hate to think of my children singing the last couple verses."

"Aw, my ma remembered me when she got back from the war," I said.

"Which one was she in?" asked Francine.

"All of them."

Jake dragged herself to her feet and the rest of us followed. I shook my head to clear the spinning sensation.

"I think I'm missing freshman orientation," I said hazily.

"Up," said Francine, pointing at the sky. "That's all the orientation you need."

But Jake wasn't in a joking mood. "Seeing as how Mr. Weekes has well and truly fouled up our tradition of nude bathing, and whereas we do have a responsibility not to contribute overmuch to his delinquency so early in the semester, I propose an immediate return home. And we'll divvy up the new girls."

We found the aerodrome deserted. Posted outside the door were lists of the fliers who had checked out that morning, organized by number grade.

"Oh my God!" said Jake as she perused the lists. "This is a disaster."

"How so?" I asked.

There were three hundred twenty-four Zeds, a hundred fifty Ones, twenty-seven Twos, and exactly six Threes: the six of us. To train the five hundred four student hoverers, Professor Brock was scheduled to spend sixteen hours per week doing practical instruction and Rachael Rodgers was on for forty. Ordinarily, volunteer instructors drawn from the ranks of the Threes made up the rest of the time. We would have to work dawn to midnight to provide enough hours for the trainees.

"All the little ladies must have decided this was the year they were going to learn to fly," Tillie said.

"They've been watching too many news reels," Francine said. "They make it look glamorous."

"Rachael's got to be having a conniption!" Astrid gloated.

"But who do you think she's going to take it out on?" Jake asked.

10

No, all my students will be women. It's impossible for men to fly—they lack the philosophical strength to so much as get off the ground.

Mary Grinning Fox, quoted in "Hovering to Become Field
of Study at the U," *Detroit Defender*, January 8, 1871

I STUMBLED BACK TO my room, shed my gear, and took a brief but re-nvigorating bath. I would have to hurry to make the end of orientation.

Unger returned, carrying an armload of books and fliers, while I was getting dressed.

"I'm sorry to have missed you," he said. "I looked for you everywhere."

I filled Unger in on my morning's activities. "So we ended up holding, erm, an administrative meeting," I concluded. "Among the student hover instructors. Of which I'm now one."

"Are you, then?" he said, looking genuinely pleased. "Oh, splendid! Well done. I'm sure you didn't miss anything of value."

As it turned out, I'd missed quite a lot, including the card that contained my schedule and the name of my advisor, with whom I was supposed to meet. I hurried to Moss Hall, where a couple of elderly ladies were packing up the last of the paperwork. After only a little abject begging, they dug my card out.

My advisor was listed as *L. Murchison, Garden Hall 448*. We were sched-uled to meet at noon. I was already late. I set off at a run and by twelve thirty had found the office in question. But the door was labeled DEAN OF EMPIRICAL PHILOSOPHY. That hardly seemed possible for the likes of me—perhaps my card was in error. Much as I hated to disturb one of the bosses, I needed to ask someone directions. I knocked and a firm female voice told me to enter.

The anteroom was large, but felt claustrophobic due to the stacks of paper piled on every available surface—filing cabinets, bookshelves, small tables, even the thickly carpeted floor. Seated in the middle of the storm was a black woman of about forty-five, with steel-rimmed glasses and a severe expression. She was working her way through a pile of forms.

"I'm terribly sorry," I said. "I'm looking for Ms. Murchison?"

"You're looking for whom?" she asked. She signed a piece of paper and pulled the next one off the nearest stack.

"Mrs. Murchison? Professor Murchison? My advisor." I extended my card toward her. Paperwork being something she was apparently more comfortable with than social niceties, she snatched the schedule from my hand and took in its contents in a glance.

"That's *Mister* Murchison you're looking for," she said. "Dean Murchison. Unless he got married this morning, there's no Mrs. Murchison." Her hand twitched, as if it didn't know what to do without a pen.

"I'm sorry I'm late," I said.

The woman sighed and looked up at me bleakly. "The dean is not having a day on which he wishes to speak to other human beings. I don't suppose you brought any interesting rocks?"

I hadn't. She waved for me to sit.

"I'm Ms. Addams. I'm the Special Assistant Dean of Empirical Philosophy—it means I do whatever Dean Murchison can't. Come to me if you need to drop a class, resolve a scheduling conflict, or report a death threat."

She didn't sound like she was joking with the last.

"I'll act as your advisor today. You're Contingency, so your course of study is mostly set. Theoretical Empirical Philosophy is required; all the freshmen take it. Lecture hall with two hundred people. Dr. Yu covers the theoretical part in ten minutes, which means she spends the next eighteen weeks speculating. Stay awake and you'll pass. Empirical Chemistry is also required—laboratory in groups of twenty. If you don't ignite your partner, you'll pass. Essential Sigils is required, too, groups of twelve. Most of the sigils are useless, but some committee put them on the Contingency Exam, so for you they really will be essential. German fulfills your liberal arts requirement. It's a good language for a practical sigilrist—lots of articles were coming out of Berlin on new smokecarving techniques before the war."

Ms. Addams drummed her long, immaculately polished fingernails against the desk and gave me a look of concern. "Introduction to Hovering puts you at twenty credits, which is ambitious. If you find yourself overwhelmed, you might ask whether you really want to learn to fly."

"I do fly," I said.

I could hear the schedule cards reshuffle in her mind. "Oh, you're the one from Montana! Capt. Synge raved about you—and she was the meanest son of a bitch I ever had the pleasure to serve with. If half of what she said is true, you'll find Intro Hover far too elementary. But it puts you in a strong position for your Contingency Exam in the spring. Have you thought about what kind of position you want for your service year?"

"Would it be absurd if I said the Corps?" I asked.

"Yes," she replied, nothing cruel about it, just a cold statement of fact. "Though maybe not impossible. They have two dozen cartogramancers, all of whom are men, naturally, to make maps. Aside from that, another ten or so males in clerical capacities. They go into the field to train the army board technicians who direct medical flights. Would you have interest in that sort of position?"

"No," I said. "Rescue and Evac."

Ms. Addams set down her pen. "That's so far past impossible that you'd need at least three separate miracles. You have family in the Corps? Someone pressuring you to go out for R&E?"

"I've always wanted to. Since I was a boy. I read *Life and Death on San Juan Hill* every night. And all the other books for kids that Lt. Col. Rodgers wrote."

Addams looked at me with amusement. "Those books aren't meant for children."

As I mentally tallied up the number of deaths in the opening chapter, I realized she might be right.

"Everyone ought to have a dream, Mr. Weekes," Addams said. "But the time comes when you have to put childish things away and face the world as it is."

The world as it is.

No fewer than three women speculated as to which anatomical parts I might or might not have as Unger escorted me through the dining hall. I stacked my plate with a couple of ham sandwiches and macaroni salad, but he didn't take a thing.

"Not hungry?" I asked him.

"From what I hear of the freshman social this evening, you don't want to fill up now," Unger replied. He went on to describe the lavish food and swank decor that made the welcome soiree one of the year's premier events.

It all sounded nice, but I'd heard Willard Gunch describe the barn dance during my last year of high school in similarly glowing terms. The promised decorations, which were to have rivaled those in the Palace of Versailles, had ended up consisting of one roll of purple crepe paper streamers donated by Mr. Lupkin from the general store.

At seven in the evening, I threw on my new summer suit, the one that Billings' finest clothier had promised would be the height of fashion anywhere on earth, what with its splendid taupe color and the hems that didn't quite reach my ankles. Then I watched Unger dress, slowly and meticulously, in his sharply pressed cream-colored three-piece with matching cuff links and pocket watch. Unger was not particularly handsome—average height, chubby, matted black hair—and his family was of modest means. But he'd had the advantage of an excellent Boston tailor. By comparison, I looked perfectly country.

Unger picked through the wooden box holding his collection of 139 bow ties (he'd bought one just that afternoon, couldn't resist) and decided on one striped in black and red, Radcliffe's colors. "You're sure I can't interest you?" he asked.

"I wouldn't want to confuse folks," I said. "You having that introductory line that you like so well."

We walked five minutes up Brattle Street to Radcliffe's main campus. Moss Hall had been reserved for the social, as it had the only room large enough to comfortably accommodate the entire freshman class.

Like all of Radcliffe's newest buildings, it was part of the college's fortunate legacy of empirical philosophers. Bertha Moss, who'd discovered the koru sigil when her six-year-old daughter drew a design in the steam on the frosted glass screen of her bathtub and caused a nearby philodendron to grow to enormous size, had been in the college's first graduating class. Barbara Polstonetto, the developer of glyphs for flat-bottomed transport fields, had earned her degree from Radcliffe a decade later. Both women had made millions off their discoveries and donated generously to the study of empirical philosophy at their alma mater. That meant the labs and lecture halls devoted to sigilry were plush and modern, while much of the rest of the school was crammed into a few older, ramshackle buildings. The lay students resented us for it.

A pair of burly men stood on either side of Moss Hall's entrance. They wore vests emblazoned with the college's crest and had the unmistakable look of well-seasoned men of action.

Three women reached the door ahead of us. Each flashed an invitation at the guards, who gave them a perfunctory look and waved the young ladies through with much laughter and a fatherly warning about not imbibing too much punch.

When Freddy and I approached, the men were still jovial but I could see the straightening in posture, the instant tension around the eyes, their right hands drifting toward the holsters on their hips.

"Good evening gentlemen," one of them said. "How can we be of service?"

"Good evening," I said.

I handed over my invitation and the guard checked my name against his list, then held the card up to a lantern, scrutinizing the watermark on the paper. He took a notebook from his pocket and flipped through it. On one page, a photograph of Freddy was pasted in. On the next was the picture of me that the *Billings Gazette* had run after I'd rescued Mother. The guard studied the picture and then me.

"Very good, Mr. Weekes," the guard said. "You wouldn't mind if I helped you straighten your jacket, would you?"

He patted me down—arms, back, chest—then legs and ankles, which neither of us could pretend was anything but him searching me for a weapon. The other guard was doing the same to Freddy.

"Expecting trouble?" I asked my guard quietly.

"Never trouble, young sir," he said, his smile becoming colder, but more genuine. "*Preparedness* is the watchword here. You just keep hold of your invitation. In case we have to prepare anyone off the premises. Wouldn't want you caught up in the confusion and prepared out by mistake."

He put his stage grin back on for the group of girls closing in on the entrance.

"What helpful doormen!" Unger said to me in the foyer. "I didn't even realize my pants cuffs were crooked."

"Hmm," I said. I straightened my tie and followed him inside.

From the moment I crossed the threshold, I realized that the freshman social more than deserved its reputation. The ballroom's wood paneling glowed faintly in the gaslights, which were turned down low. Two rows of tables running the length of the room held thousands of tiny candles, each thinner than a strand of hair, all burning in different colors. I picked up one of the tapers and examined it. Not a candle at all, but a twist of solidified smoke treated with a pinch of luminescent powder on the tip. Smokecarver work, hastily done, but still impressive. It was the sort of detail that even folks who hadn't a single kind word to say about sigilrists still wanted for their fancier parties.

A giant ice sculpture of the Radcliffe seal dominated the center table on one side of the room. On the opposite side, blushing orange in the candle-light, was an even larger ice sculpture of a winged woman wearing only a crown of leaves and a strip of cloth that hid one shoulder and her netherparts. An inscription on the base read VICTORY FOR THE CLASS OF '21!

Unger plunged into the crowd, but I hung back, uncertain of what was expected of me. Should I introduce myself around, or did only a bumpkin approach a stranger? Was it improper to chat up a woman if she was alone? Could I simply graze my way through the platters of food scattered across the tables and sneak out the back?

After observing for a minute, I better understood the scene before me. The best-dressed girls, decked out in fine jewelry and ball gowns, tended toward the side of the room with the Radcliffe seal. I'd always thought women ought to look like my sisters—sturdy and intense, a bit exasperated, favoring gray in dress because it hid smoke marks and wool because they could brush the sand out of it. But these creatures were draped in silk, ankles and arms bare, their shoulders wrapped in scarves so light they might disintegrate if you stared too hard. They fluttered from one person to the next, never making more than a few steps of progress—I didn't suppose their footwear permitted it. Those would be the rich, upper-crust Easterners, the ones Jake had warned didn't appreciate common sigilrists invading their exclusive college.

On the opposite side of the hall, I spotted what had to be my fellow Contingency students. They'd retreated to the tables surrounding the statue of Winged Victory, eyes downcast, waiting for the ordeal to end. Here there were rough hands, faces with the odd scar or chipped tooth, skin toughened by the sun and wind. Their dresses would not have looked out of place at Sunday services in Butte or Bozeman. I suspected that out of all the women in the room, they would least appreciate my company. I would mean atten-tion and most of them seemed to want to avoid that at any cost. Put in their year of study plus their service time then go back home.

But ultimately, I drifted toward the Contingencies and the massive ice sculpture. Who could have imagined such a curious thing as that block of ice in the shape of a nude? Captivating, really, as the droplets collected and ran down the long, curved flanks and jutting hips, scattering the smokecarved light when they fell.

"It's dreadful, isn't it?" said a young man who'd sidled up next to me. "Every year the Contingency Society donates something more outrageous and this has to be the absolute worst. The Fultons can give a million dollars, but it doesn't buy good taste." There was an appreciative titter from the cadre of fancy young women who'd followed him.

I realized that he must be Radcliffe's third male philosopher. He was lithe and jaunty, his suit cut elegantly, blond hair oiled and combed into a flawless helmet atop his head.

"The proportions are ghastly," he continued, appraising the sculpture. "She's . . ." He took a moment to consider how to put it without upsetting his delicate female companions. "Top heavy."

There was more appreciative laughter.

"She looks like Donna," said the horse-faced girl standing next to him. "I bet she modeled for it."

"Oh don't," said another of the young ladies. "Donna's sweet."

"Of course she is," said the young man chivalrously. "But we should hear the opinion of this fine gentleman. Is our *dame de glacé* a deformed monstrosity or hidden beauty?"

I considered the ice statue and plucked at my chin. "I'd say she favors Hazel Louise."

"Really?" he asked with interest. "I don't think I've met her."

"She's the innkeeper in Billings," I said. "Four dead husbands, ten kids, and the nastiest dog you ever saw. That cur will take your arm off as soon as look at you."

That got a laugh from the flock of chirpy girls. The young man looked annoyed—upstaged by a country rube.

"I haven't even introduced myself," he said, extending his hand and smiling with sickly warmth. "Brian Fenwick Mayweather." Intoned as if that should mean something.

"Pleasure to meetcha," I said. "Robert Weekes."

"Oh-ho!" said Mayweather. "The man from the Wild West! Robert is from Montana."

"How lovely!" exclaimed the girl who'd come to Donna's defense. "Do you ride?"

I nodded, since that question could only mean one thing to a flier. "I ride a Springfield harness with a one-and-three-quarters canvas double weave and a rib guard," I said. "What do you ride?"

She looked at me, confused. "Well, Safie, mostly. She's an Arabian." Her lip quivered. Possibly she thought I was mocking her.

"Robert means that he hovers," supplied Mayweather. "He's the one who flew in from the transporter arena."

"Very nearly," I said.

"A real male sigilrist?" observed the first girl. "Every one of those I've ever met wanted to play dress-up in his mother's skirts. Though a transvestite might be preferable to some of the atrocities on display tonight. Did you see that dark-skinned girl in the yellow gingham dress? It's one thing for Radcliffe to take a few scholarship cases, but they find the most appallingly vulgar women. The blacker the better."

She was so awful that I couldn't find the words to reply.

"Collette is having second thoughts," Mayweather cooed. "What was it you called Boston? 'A squalid backwater?'"

"I called it a crude little town full of ignorant rabble," she replied.

"Though I imagine the city must seem frightfully strange to poor Robert," Mayweather said. "You'll have to share with us your impressions of it."

I had the overwhelming urge to get away from them. "I haven't seen enough to decide," I answered. "I'll report back when I have a firmer opinion."

I put my hand out, Mayweather shook it, and I all but ran for the opposite side of the hall. The man had to be the most colossally foppish ass in existence.

I wanted to snag one of the flutes of champagne that an army of waiters was carrying on silver platters, but they seemed to be forever orbiting away from me and toward the center of the room, as if pulled in by Mayweather's gravity. Indeed, the room seemed to surge and ebb in waves around the man, the twinkling necklaces and bracelets and hair combs spiraling about him like the spray above a whirlpool.

The whole event stank of the worst sort of decadence. Half of Europe was starving, soldiers and corpswomen wading up to their necks in mud in the trenches, Mother probably fighting off assassins with her boot knife, and here I stood in the midst of the rankest superficial frippery.

I might have spent the rest of the evening in similar reverie, but young women kept pushing their way toward the table behind me. It held something remarkable: a smokecarved chocolate soufflé that really was lighter than air, contained in an upside-down cut glass bowl anchored to the table with wires. Serving it required two girls to work together; one to scoop the chocolate foam with a long-handled ladle, the other to hold an upside-down cup at the ready. Even the most adept young women lost a little soufflé over the edges of their cups and blobs of it drifted up to spatter against the ceiling. The girls who managed to get it from their cups into their mouths giggled as they ate; whatever gas was inside the dessert made them tipsy and caused their voices to squeak.

Contingency students and staid Radcliffe ladies who ordinarily never would have spoken to one another stood side by side, scooping soufflé and laughing.

"Try it!" a woman in a ball gown said, pressing a cup into my hands.

I managed to suck a mouthful out of the cup without spilling too much. It was rich and oily, as insubstantial as a soap bubble.

"Thank you!" I said to the young lady who'd given me the cup, my voice sounding like a drunken soprano duck.

Then I realized that all the tables surrounding the ice statue of Winged Victory contained similarly extraordinary smokecarver-prepared dishes. I sampled scoops of vanilla ice cream with an inner layer of insulated chocolate that protected a hot, molten caramel core. There was a ham smoked to taste like peaches accompanied by peaches smoked to taste like ham—more clever than delicious, but that didn't prevent me from taking seconds. Corn kernels that popped when they touched your tongue, lemon bubbles that rolled across their dish in choreographed patterns, deadly hot jalapeño peppermints, fresh steamed Wail-a-Duke, and piles of coconut fizzysnaps.

Contingency students and unphilosophical Radcliffe ladies alike wandered among the delicacies, pointing out to one another this outstanding treat or explaining how you ate that one. Some of the iciness between the two groups began to thaw.

I located Unger, who'd paired off with an expensive-looking young woman with thick glasses and a brown velvet hair bow. They were carrying on an animated discussion about double mudge.

"I don't see why you'd give up six percent on a pair to open with a jack," the young woman said.

"It's 5.7 percent," said Unger. "And I'd only do it if I were certain my partner could jig it. I could do it with Robert here. I played with him last night—he's the flattest partner I've ever had."

"I'm what?" I asked.

"It's a compliment," said the girl. "Sort of. He means you're literal when you play cards. You don't go in for psychology."

"I'm very tricky!" I objected.

Unger patted me on the back. "A few more weeks and we could hit the Beacon Hill Sunday game. We'd win seventy games out of a hundred."

"You would not," the girl said. "They'd throw you out after you won the first one. The regulars always come out ahead. What you need to do is . . . Oh! That one right there!" She pointed at a tiny fish tied to a cracker with a celery thread.

Before I could reach for one, I heard a crash outside the hall, followed by a series of dull thumps. At least I *thought* I heard, because no one else seemed to. Unger blathered on about cards, young ladies worked to corral the soufflé, the statue of Winged Victory glowed contentedly. But then I caught a glimpse of Mayweather. He, too, had noticed something amiss and was shooing his group of admirers away from the main entrance. I set down my plate and walked toward it.

A moment later the doors flung open and a man staggered in. His skin was painted with purple and yellow makeup to look like putrefied flesh. He had a wooden framework mounted on his shoulders, across which a large sheet of fabric had been stretched. THEY MURDER THE INNOCENT was written across it in dripping red paint, as if drawn with blood. He had more red paint in a bucket, which he splashed toward the Contingency students.

"Murder!" screamed the man. "Philosophers have driven the country to war. They kill babes still unborn. Their very touch is corruption!"

My classmates, many of them paint-spattered, shrieked and ran.

"Murder and ruination!" he shouted toward a group of wealthy girls. "Stay away from those harlot sigilrists. Remember the righteous cause!"

He threw the last of his paint and looked frantically about the room. His gaze fixed on Winged Victory, the smashing of which would have made the perfect finale to his performance. He made a run for it a moment too late.

One of the doormen, real blood streaming down his face from a cut on his cheek, barreled in. He was still smiling. He continued smiling as he hit the wet paint and skidded, recovering to launch himself with balletic grace at the interloper. He knocked the Trencher to the ground and there was a sharp snap as the wooden framework holding his sign broke.

Even pinned to the ground, the little man kept struggling. The guard twisted the man's arm high into the air and drove his knee into the small of his back. The Trencher went limp. Another doorman pushed his way through the crowd, bringing a set of manacles. He was not as practiced in the art of smiling. The guards handcuffed the intruder and pulled him to his feet.

"Sigilrists hate real Americans!" the man screamed. "Whores and warmongers, all of them!"

The first guard wrenched the man's arms backward and the second punched him in the gut. He fell to his knees with no breath left to spew further abuse. The guards dragged him out.

The young ladies streamed for the doors, too, leaving in packs of eight or ten, no one walking alone. Many girls were in tears, their dresses ruined, in a few cases their *only* good dress, which was supposed to last the entire year. The remaining Contingency students retreated to their side of the room, the gentlewomen to theirs.

"Leave it to the Trenchers to break up a perfectly good party," Unger muttered when I recovered him. The young woman with whom he'd been speaking so animatedly just a minute before had taken up a position on the opposite side of the hall and was now eyeing the Contingencies with disdain.

Sounds lik Bostn, all right, Mother replied when I messaged home with a summary of my day. *Trnchrs under evry rock. If y see Max Gannet on the street, tell him the Montna Jyhwks ar srry they didn't remove him in '04 whn they had the chnce.*

I chuckled at that. Gannet was one of the original Trenchers, a drummer boy at the Battle of Petersburg who'd escaped unscathed. He'd been one of the masterminds behind the First Disturbance, the man who'd planned the assassinations but always found a way for the blood to end up on someone else's hands. In his latter days, he'd run for president four times as the nominee of the Trencher Party. He'd been so hateful that even the most vociferous anti-philosophical bigots had been scared to vote for him. The Trenchers in Boston had taken him in after the Gray Hats—the Eastern sisters of the Jayhawks—burned down his house in Virginia. Not the kind of person I'd be rubbing shoulders with.

Any more troubl by y? I asked.

N. Quiet last coupl days. Mybe Trnchrs scared.

Or waiting for the right moment to hit back.

11

You will find him a trial, I fear, for he spends his days as if lost in a waking dream. Yet Captain Clark's maps are so incomparably detailed that they shall repay you many times over for the trouble he causes.

President Thomas Jefferson, Letter to Meriwether Lewis, 1803

EVEN TODAY, I CAN recall a few moments from the opening weeks of classes with perfect clarity.

I remember sitting in Theoretical Empirical Philosophy beside Unger, who took voluminous notes and turned to punch me in the shoulder whenever I drifted off to the sound of Professor Yu's monotone. I remember working at a battered large-format message board on a bench table in Essential Sigils, delighted by the improved Huk method for sending images, only to learn with horror that the sand cost forty dollars per ounce. And I remember the first time I saw the Hero of the Hellespont, the Darling of the Dardanelles, the greatest American hero of the Great War, our classmate, Danielle Hardin.

On the day I met her, I was in the Gray Box, as we called Cadwallader Memorial Library, working through a difficult problem from my hovering textbook. It involved a pair of fliers clipped to each other who alternated as flier and passenger. Given certain constraints for powder type and glyph efficiency, what was their maximum range and flight duration? It would have seemed a ridiculous question had I not known that Jimenez and Hatcher had solved it while planning the first nonstop transatlantic flight in '93.

Someone touched my shoulder. "Robert?" she said.

I jumped a mile.

It was Essie. She looked terrified. "Jake said to come get you. Rachael froze up a couple minutes ago. She was at five hundred feet helping a One with a turn. The One was so frightened she nearly crashed. A Two went up and brought Rachael in."

"Good God!" I said. "Who was the Two?"

"Frieda," said Essie.

"I believe we'll have to promote her and give her a medal of some sort. Does Harnemon's carry—"

"Jake says we're going to the dean. Immediately." Poor Essie looked even paler than usual, but twice as determined.

"Hasn't she already tried that?" I asked.

"I don't know what she's planning," said Essie. "I don't want to lose my instructor's position."

"Why would you lose your position?"

But Essie had caught the sleeve of my shirt and was pulling me toward the stairs.

We met the other Threes, minus Jake, outside the dean's office.

"We're marching right in there and if that bitch Addams tries to stop us, I'll throw her out the window!" Francine fumed.

"This is why we're not letting you do the talking," Astrid countered.

"Well, I still think it's idiotic to bring *her* along for this," Francine said.

Tillie laughed. "She gets what she wants. And *she* knows how to threaten the administration without cussing."

Francine turned as red as her hair.

I wanted to ask who they were talking about, but right then Jake joined us accompanied by a large, unsmiling figure. I recognized her from her pictures in the newspapers: the deep brown skin, the curly black hair that hung to her shoulders, and the rings around her eyes just as dark: Danielle Hardin.

To write about Miss Hardin, especially in the current age, is to invite every sort of intense feeling and prejudice. I would invite you to think of her as you might have in the early fall of 1917—as a young woman well known but not yet famous, viewed by the general public not as a philosophical radical or a revolutionary, but as a soldier who had acted with exemplary valor.

The US Sigilry Corps, which counted Miss Hardin among its officers, had been in France from the opening days of the Great War to ensure that the belligerents observed the Rouen Conventions and abstained from using sigilry for military ends. The British and French were hopeless philosophers, so there was little risk there; the Germans, on the other hand, had concluded the Franco-Prussian War four decades before with a display of smokecarving so overwhelming that it had nearly smothered Paris. Popular opinion held that the Huns were likely to try it again unless the Corps kept them in check. But as the Great War dragged on into its second and third years without serious philosophical misconduct, the Corps had nothing to do but pick daisies.

So, in late 1916 when the British Army inquired about borrowing a few transporters for a mission in the Dardanelles Strait, the Corps was happy to oblige. The British Commonwealth had some sixteen divisions, mostly Australians and New Zealanders, trapped at Gallipoli, where the Anglos had advanced a scant mile from the beaches during two years of bloody fighting against the Turks. The British had decided to abandon the campaign, but withdrawing their forces would be tricky. If they massed on the beaches for evacuation by sea, the Turks would rain artillery on the exposed soldiers. On the other hand, if they pulled out gradually, their rearguard was likely to be overrun.

Instead, the British generals had decided to transport their entire army out in one night. The Greek-held island of Imbros lay only fifteen miles west in the Aegean Sea; with appropriately placed destination sigils, a few experienced American transporters would be able to evacuate all quarter of a million men in a few hours, moving entire divisions at once.

On a moonless February night, the generals gave the order to proceed. The Commonwealth soldiers abandoned their positions to muster at the evacuation sites. The five American transporters on Imbros drew their sigils and vanished. But only one of them appeared on the beach in Turkey. No one could understand it. The British staff discussed aborting the mission, but the Turks had realized the trenches opposite them were empty and were already advancing. It was retreat or be slaughtered.

The only remaining philosopher, Sigilwoman Second Class Hardin, agreed to take as many men as she could. She began running transports back to the island, moving thousands of troops with each jump. She continued even as the evacuation sites came under fire, past the point of exhaustion, then past the point where the strain should have killed her two or three times over. By morning, she'd saved nearly the entire Commonwealth army. She'd made forty-eight jumps—720 miles—and lost twenty-one pounds. Somehow she'd survived.

The Germans had been furious—they'd called Gallipoli a flagrant violation of international law, one that had freed 250,000 men to oppose them on the Western Front. They'd threatened to pull out of the Rouen Conventions and use their Korps des Philosophs to obliterate France.

But the Sigilry Corps had been delighted. Here was the unlikely hero they'd been waiting for, a quiet Rhode Island lass, the daughter of a Congregationalist minister. "Dardanelles" they'd dubbed her, and that was the name by which she became known throughout America, her serious visage plastered across a hundred front pages.

In person, though, Dardanelles looked terrible. Her face was haggard and blotchy, as if she'd been dragged out of bed two hours into a ten-year nap, an impression reinforced by the wrinkled khaki skirt and tattered blue cardigan she was wearing. Her eyes were sunken and her gait shambling. She wasn't fat, exactly, but she'd more than regained the weight she'd lost seven months earlier.

Hardin nodded to a couple of my colleagues, straightened her posture, and got down to business. "Jake's explained about Rachael Rodgers," she said, her voice a quiet alto. "There's more than enough evidence of incompetence. I'll lay the facts out to Belle Addams. If she asks for one of you to corroborate, we should choose—well, which of you have had run-ins with our special assistant dean in the past week?"

Francine's lip curled into a half snarl. She raised her hand. So did all the others, including Essie, who to my knowledge had never even met Addams.

"She seems to like *me*," I offered.

Dardanelles rolled her eyes. "That about figures. If she wants to hear from one of you, then that one speaks," she said, pointing at me.

We entered the office to find Addams sitting placidly at her desk.

"No," Addams said. "Whatever you're here for, the answer is no."

"Ma'am," replied Danielle. "We would like your assistance."

"You of all people have no right to do this," Addams said. "I went to the chair of Romance Languages last week on your behalf. Do you have any idea how poorly it reflects on this office to have to beg for an exception for a young lady who has failed introductory French twice?"

Danielle looked needled, but she persevered. "I'm not here about French," she said. She summarized the events of the morning cogently and pointedly, with an earnestness that Jake, even on her best days, couldn't have approached.

"We're aware of the situation," said Addams. "It's being handled."

"Really?" Francine cut in. "Because that's what you said last week when I told you Rachael needed five tries to launch herself while teaching the Ones basic maneuvers. It's what you said when I reported we'll need *two years* at the rate we're going to get the Zeds their individual instruction time—"

Addams cleared her message board with a swipe that sent sand skittering across the floor. "That's enough!" she roared. "This is not Sunday school. There are no gold stars for tattling. If you're so concerned for the well-being of your fellow fliers, then you should spend more time instructing and less time undermining the efforts of your senior instructor. And Miss Hardin, I hardly understand your interest. If these young ladies"—and here Addams seemed to include me—"are so concerned, then why don't they speak for themselves?"

Danielle looked pleased to be asked. "Because they're going to strike if Rachael isn't removed. That's the sort of message that ought to be delivered by a neutral intermediary. Besides, I'm the one with standing invitations from the *Globe* and the *New York Post* to contribute columns on whatever subject I like. Dean Murchison's indifference on this matter could make a very interesting story."

Addams was apoplectic. "The Corps may treat you like their Princess Sergeant Major, but around here you're nothing more than a second-rate student who comes into my office sniveling for special treatment one day and making threats the next. Get out!"

"You told me the dean was available to me at any hour," said Danielle without so much as raising her voice. "I want him right now."

Danielle started toward the dean's office flanked by Astrid and Francine. Addams leaped to her feet as if to block the much larger women.

"Out!" Addams cried. "All of you, out!"

Danielle slid past Addams and opened the door to the dean's office. The rest of us followed her in. Only, there was no sign of the dean. Just a faint, rhythmic thumping.

Addams found Dean Murchison squatting under his desk, his fist pressed to his mouth. He rocked on his heels, bumping the back of his head against his chair, staring at the carpet. He was barefoot, having abandoned his shoes and socks on his desk blotter.

"Lennox," said Addams. "Come out from under there."

"The warp and the weft, you see," the dean said, still rocking. "If paper were woven in such a fashion, the ink . . . If paper were made . . . If paper . . . If . . ."

"Sit in your chair, Lennox," Ms. Addams said in a voice that brooked no disagreement. The dean took his seat.

Lennox Murchison was a grizzled old man from Peoria who happened to be the world's leading cartogramancer—a philosophical mapmaker. He'd spent twenty years on loan from the Corps to the Royal Geographical Society, during which time he'd created intricate maps of New Zealand's South Island and all but accidentally invented a sigil for determining the depth and movement of snowpack. He'd devoted the next twenty years to charting the glaciers of Alaska, where he'd also developed a glyph that accurately predicted earthquakes. Hoping that he might make his next breakthrough in less than two decades, the Corps had reassigned him to administrative duty. During his first month, Murchison had created the two-ink system for identifying metal deposits, devised a method for recognizing the microscopic depressions in the earth caused by human beings standing in a particular location, and suffered a nervous breakdown from being back in polite society after forty years of solitude.

Radcliffe, which prided itself on always having a theoretician as its Dean of Empirical Philosophy, had offered Murchison the position in '14, when his predecessor resigned to take a commission in France. Murchison had proven a capable enough administrator, largely because he delegated all issues of tenure, staffing, and discipline to Ms. Addams.

"I'm sorry about the disturbance," Addams said. "These people wanted to talk to you."

"What disturbance?" asked the dean. "What people?"

Seeing what was likely to be their only opportunity, Jake and Francine began speaking as loudly as possible. Addams talked right over them. Tillie and Astrid joined in for the sake of completeness.

The dean didn't notice any of it. He disassembled his fountain pen, laying out the pieces in a row on his desk. He removed a sheet of paper from a drawer, tapped a single drop of ink onto it from the barrel of the pen, and traced his finger through, so quickly and finely that I couldn't make out his glyphs. The ink danced across the page, resolving itself into a floor plan of Murchison's office.

My hackles rose. That was *not* how cartogramancers worked. They needed hours, days even, to make a map.

"Oh!" the dean exclaimed, delighted. Everyone went silent. "The fliers are here! You can tell by the corn dust on their shoes. And one transporter.

Aluminum on hers." He looked up at us for the first time. "Welcome! The situation has been made known to me. A decision has been made. Good day!"

He seemed surprised when no one moved. "They will leave now?" Murchison suggested to Ms. Addams.

It was pointless to get angry at someone so obviously mad. You might shout at him all day and he wouldn't so much as blink. Any sort of intercession would have to happen through Addams and we'd just destroyed that option. She pointed to the antechamber and we filed out.

"Excepting Miss Hardin and Mr. Weekes," Murchison added.

I thought I'd imagined the last and took two steps for the door before Addams spun me around.

Murchison tapped his paper and the blueprint faded, coalescing into a drop of ink, which he squeezed back into his pen.

"Cartogramancy is more than the making of maps," he said to us. "It is seeing the world as it really is."

He observed us with a pair of deep-set eyes. His light-brown irises looked as if they had faded in the sun, but as he gazed at us, they darkened and intensified in hue, backed by a fierce, alien intelligence.

"Do you dream of them?" he asked. Though he did not look away from me, he meant the question for Dardanelles.

She went whiter than bones. "Do I what?"

"How are your dreams?" he asked.

"They're fine," she said hoarsely. "I don't dream."

Murchison shook his head and gave a tut. "They'll improve in time," he said, and folded his hands. "The Corps asked that an investigation into Gallipoli be conducted by me. The results may interest you. The destination glyphs on the beach were placed by a cartogramancer. A Canadian."

"Yes," said Dardanelles. "I saw him do it. He drew the sigils himself to ensure they were in the right places."

"He chose incorrect figures," Murchison said. "Designed for higher angular velocities nearer to the equator. They warped. They deposited your colleagues one mile northwest of where they were drawn."

Danielle frowned. "I never knew that. But a mile northwest would have been—that would be right in the middle of the Aegean. With forty pounds of gear."

"Presumably they drowned," said Murchison.

"Presumably," agreed Dardanelles. Her face darkened. "Even my glyph was wrong. It put me half a mile too far down the beach. So, I was just lucky, is that it?"

Murchison realized he was looking at the wrong one of us and switched his gaze to Dardanelles. He tried to contort his face into a sympathetic shape.

"Lucky," Murchison agreed. "Or perhaps unlucky, given what lies ahead. The Great War will end, by one means or another. Then the real war will begin. That's the struggle that you're meant for."

Murchison stood and reached across the desk to pat Danielle awkwardly on the shoulder. She shrank back at his touch. He didn't seem to mind.

"Now," he said. "Because you could not save your comrades last winter, you've come today to assist your classmates."

Danielle opened her mouth to object, but the dean waved for silence. "Do you believe yourself qualified to judge Miss Rodgers's expertise based on direct observation?"

"What?" said Dardanelles. "No, I've never met her."

"Do you believe Mr. Weekes to be a qualified judge?"

She looked at me derisively. "I haven't the faintest idea."

Murchison began reassembling his fountain pen. "Mr. Weekes, your assessment of Miss Rodgers?"

"Rachael Rodgers is neither expert nor even proficient," I said. "If she's allowed to continue as an instructor, she will injure or kill herself or a student."

"Thank you," Murchison said. He screwed the nib of the pen back on. "You will not be permitted to take Introduction to Hovering. Please sign to withdraw." He slid a form across his desk and passed me his pen.

I was stunned. He'd asked for an honest opinion. I'd given one. Now he was punishing me?

"Sir, I came here to fly," I managed. "I've flown near every day for the last ten years."

"Naturally," he said. "The introductory course is insufficiently challenging. You will learn more by devoting that time to instructing. More relevant to Rescue and Evacuation as well. Please sign."

It was too much to absorb. Why now? Why not on the first day when he was supposed to act as my advisor? But I signed all the same.

"A second matter," he said, watching the drying ink with hungry eyes. "If the Cocks offer you membership, it would be prudent to decline."

"If *what* happens?" I asked.

Murchison ignored me. "However, it would be educational to accept. Now for both of you: the situation regarding Miss Rodgers has been resolved. It would be most appreciated if you waited one full day before taking further action."

"Okay," said Danielle. I echoed my agreement.

We waited for an indication that our audience had come to an end, but instead Murchison began removing the screws from the drawer handles on his desk with his thumbnail. Dardanelles and I backed out of the room then left Addams's office at as close to a run as we could decently manage.

"Jesus Christ!" Dardanelles burst out when we reached the hall.

"Not exactly Santa Claus, is he?" I said.

She shuddered. "Shut up. Just shut up!"

We walked down the stairs together and out into the bright September sunshine. The day was warm; the air smelled of cut grass. Across the quad groups of women called out to one another and laughed. In the distance a church bell pealed.

Dardanelles thrust her hands into the pockets of her cardigan and assumed the look of sour indifference she wore for public occasions. "He's right about the Cocks, you know," she said.

"He's right about *what*?" I asked.

But she was already marching down the sidewalk away from me, the soles of her heavy shoes thudding on the pavement.

12

Take the student to altitude and make her turn somersaults. Stop her at intervals to ask which way is up. If she cannot point it out immediately and without fail, she is not yet ready for unsupervised flight.

Mary Grinning Fox, "Instructions for Instructors," 1872

THE FOLLOWING WEEK I found a plain black postcard pinned to the door of my apartment. On the reverse was a stylized rooster, printed in red and yellow. In gilt lettering was written: THE COCK CAN FLY, BUT CAN HE FIGHT?

"That's strange," I muttered. I decided I'd have to ask Freddy about it when I got the chance.

The next day another card, same as the first: THE COCK PERSISTS, BUT WILL HE ENDURE? I stuck it in my pocket and went down to the dining hall for lunch.

On the day following, a third card: TONIGHT THE COCK MUST CROW AT MID-NIGHT OR GO SILENT FOR ALL TIME.

If I was less inquisitive about the cards than I should have been, then surely the lack of hours in the day was to blame. I was teaching more than full-time at the aerodrome, laboring with the other Threes to prevent our five hundred trainees from performing accidental face-first landings now that Rachael Rodgers had been grounded.

Not that Addams and Brock were calling it that. No, Rachael had been *promoted* to Senior Flight Instructor for Education, responsible for creating curriculums and doing ground instruction. Every day Rachael sat in the aerodrome's classroom teaching sigil form and flight posture to groups of Zeds, theory of maneuver to the Ones, rigging strategies to the Twos, and advanced continuing education for the Threes (not that she ever deigned to put on a class for us—and not that any of us would have attended).

So, the Threes took up the slack teaching in the air, but Rachael seemed determined to make our lives as difficult as possible. Mine especially.

She'd assigned me two hundred Zeds—nearly twice as many as the rest of the instructors put together—and a good measure of the Ones besides. Not a single class of Twos. Always the classes at six in the morning and six in the evening, which required me to perform the opening and closing regulator inventories. No locker in the locker room ("Could you imagine the uproar?" Rachael had asked when I suggested it. "You wouldn't want a man barging in on your sister in a state of undress, would you?"), which meant I had to carry my personal tackle to and fro every day.

The teaching, though, I didn't mind. On a good day, I might coax two or three Zeds off the ground for their very first flights. By contrast, my classes with the Ones were wild mob scenes, with a dozen fliers cutting one another off, swooping and whooping, and learning how to bank and turn in the process.

On the same day that I received the third rooster card, however, a contingent of Twos asked me to lead an extra session in night landing, which really *was* excessive. It was also unwise: I didn't know the girls asking, didn't know their strong points of flying, or who was most likely to punch a hole in the ground. And of the Threes, I was the weakest night lander and the worst lander in general.

"Francine is too screamy, Jake is too sarcastic, and Essie is too nervous," the girls complained.

"And Astrid? Tillie?" I suggested.

Astrid would have been a superb choice, but she was just as overworked as me and had had the good sense to say no. Her nights, especially, she held sacred. She and her beau, Liam, as good as lived together. And Tillie, well, she was in love, too, with Florence, a sophomore from Long Island. They were both lean, long-limbed, raven-haired raconteurs, perfectly suited for each other—the Indian and the Italian. It was the first time I'd ever seen two women kiss, though they made it look like the most ordinary thing in the world. But many of the girls felt uncomfortable around an outspoken Sapphist and Tillie *did* like to flirt.

In any event, I should have begged off leading the night-landing session, but the truth was I was flattered to be asked. Not infrequently the novices refused to fly with me. *Wouldn't it be possible to have a real hoverer*, they would ask, *a more expert sigilrist, someone a little more . . . female?* Rachael took a perverse delight in obliging them.

So, at nine o'clock on the night in question, the Twos assembled on the field. I passed out chemical flares and reviewed low-velocity vectored landings, the old touch-and-crouch technique. Inelegant but safe. The Twos were a good group, loose and relaxed, though I knew nerves must be running high. I double-checked everyone's rigging, which proved unnecessary and led to whispering about Mr. Weekes wanting to cop a feel. I marked a landing zone with flares and made sure all my charges had theirs lit and attached at the ankle. Then my students climbed as a group to one thousand feet, while I took up station just above the ground to spot. One by one, the girls approached, low and slow, and set down. There were some tuck and rolls and a few muddy knees, but overall they acquitted themselves well.

With two left in the air, I saw the incoming flier's blue light veer way off course. Maybe she was following the reflection of the moon off the river, maybe simple panic.

"Stop!" I shouted. She continued toward the water. I pulled out my red flare, yanked the tab, and waved energetically to signal "abort."

She went straight in.

I opened my regulator wide and sped toward her, but not fast enough to see her go under. Safety flares were supposed to glow even underwater, but I couldn't see hers. I homed in on the sound of her splashing and came to a dead stop inches above the water.

"Grab on!" I called.

She thrashed wildly.

"Grab my feet!"

I slid lower, so that my legs were actually in the water. My sigil sputtered and threatened to fail as I fought to hold position. Still the girl couldn't catch hold. She was struggling with her bag, only a ten-pounder, but enough to pull her to the bottom now that it was soaked.

"Pull your bag release!" I shouted. She couldn't. Exasperated, I pulled my own release cord and my bags fell away. I splashed down beside her. She grabbed me about the head and shoulders, forcing me under.

I was a good swimmer, but not a great one. I managed to twist free of her, but the weight of my skysuit and rigging dragged me down. My boots filled with water. I kicked for the surface, my lungs burning. At last I broke through.

I shouted for help. No one came. I tried to catch the girl around the waist, but she was thrashing madly.

"Help!" I screamed again.

Desperate, I pulled my belt knife, ducked under the water, and grabbed hold of the young woman's powder bag. I stabbed it. Corn dust and sand swirled away in a dark cloud. She floated higher in the water and I got an arm around her.

One of the Twos had gotten herself launched and was in a slow turn twenty feet above us. It was Frieda, who'd rescued Rachael Rodgers only a few days before.

"Drop me a line!" I shouted.

"A what?" she yelled back.

"A line! A rope."

"I haven't got one!"

Which made sense, since I'd been carrying the rescue gear.

"Come down and give me a leg," I called.

She lowered herself carefully, stopping four feet above the surface.

"Closer!"

I was nearly spent.

Frieda, who was smart enough to be terrified, slowly, excruciatingly, dipped in a straight hover until I could grab her foot.

"Now go!" I yelled.

She began to pull up using the same deliberate style.

"No!" I shouted. If Frieda pulled straight up, there was no way I could hang on to her with one arm and to the half-drowned girl with the other.

"Flat!" I bellowed. "Fly flat to the shore."

She flew flat and level, towing us behind. A minute later, we were in shallow water and I let go. Frieda went shooting off with the sudden reduction in weight, nearly crashing, but recovering at the last moment. I got my feet under me.

"Stand up!" I said to the girl I'd rescued. She couldn't and I had to drag her onto shore.

The rest of the Twos had come to investigate—on foot!—like the pack of mewling children they were. "She's not breathing!" one of them wailed. Several of the girls were in hysterics, crying, screaming that she needed a doctor.

The girl I had pulled from the water was, in fact, loudly choking, so she was moving air. I sat her down, thumped her on the back, and, with the assistance of a bottle of smelling salts from the aerodrome's first aid kit, had her back to herself in three minutes.

"Very serviceable landings all around," I said, trying to keep things light, "but when you're assisting at an emergency, fly, don't walk. Check your harnesses in and sign the book. After that, you're dismissed."

All the girls except Frieda trouped dutifully back toward the aerodrome.

"Sir," said Frieda. She pointed to the sky, where there was a light circling at one thousand feet. "Laura's still up."

"Shit!" I said. I'd forgotten about my last trainee. Frieda gave me her powder bag and I went up and landed the final girl without further disaster.

I held myself together until I got back to my apartment. Then I began shaking. A near miss—two near misses. Two girls had nearly died and it was my fault. I tried to imagine what I would say to Brock in the morning or to Jake. Or the lecture Rachael was certain to give me.

Though hadn't I redeemed myself in some small measure? An hour before, I never would have believed I was capable of such a rescue, not until the moment I'd attempted it. My success was just as upsetting to me as my carelessness.

Any landng y can wlk away frm is a good one, Mother reassured me by message. *If y nvr splashd a trainee, all it means is your still new.*

I smiled at that. It would take another thirty years before Ma considered me experienced.

How are things? I asked.

Im fit. Busness brisk. Town quiet.

I could translate that easily enough: *Nothing else has burned down, so stop worrying.*

Grades good? she inquired.

Rather than answer that, I started work on an essay for Philosophical Theory that was due the next morning. I hated the class—it was a lot of vague notions and statistics, nothing practical. I concocted an ever more confused paper, crossing out one line after another. By midnight, I was on the verge of wadding it up and going to bed, when there was a knock at the door.

I opened it to find three young men in black sport coats, standing with arms crossed, their faces stony. I thought for a moment they were policemen come to arrest me, but they were wearing outrageous yellow ties and tall cylindrical caps that would have looked more at home on the trombone section of an eighth-rate marching band. They had red plumes stuck in their hatbands—two men wore a single feather and one wore three.

"May I help you?" I asked.

The three-feathered man bowed and intoned, "To you, oh unplucked one, we extend membership in the Most Ancient and Noble Order of the Chanticleer, the rooster who rules the roost, the cock of the walk, the bantam blooded in battle. Do you accept, with all the rights and perils thus pertaining?"

I looked at them dumbly. "*Who* are you looking for?"

"Do you accept?" the man repeated.

Well, this seemed to be what I got for not asking Unger about the rooster cards pinned to the door. I was exhausted, hopelessly behind on my essay, and my socks were still wet. I had no idea what this ludicrousness was about, but my night couldn't possibly get any worse.

"Sure!" I said, throwing my hands up. "Why not?"

The men erupted in a cheer. They stepped forward to shake my hand.

"Splendid!"

"We knew you were the one!"

"Never doubted it!"

They had an extra black jacket, which they slipped on me. Too long in the sleeves and too narrow across the shoulders.

"No matter!" said one of the boys. "We'll get you kitted out properly in no time." They had a spare hat without a plume too, which they placed on my head.

"Well, we have our card set," said their leader. "I say that calls for a drink. In fact, I say it calls for a *bottle*."

"Do we dare?" asked the second.

"We must!" said the third. "And the thirsty future generations be damned. Besides, that 1908 is starting to turn." They ushered me toward the door.

"Is this going to take long?" I asked. But they ignored my question, and by the time they had spirited me out of the building I was more than a little curious.

They led me several blocks to a tumbledown old clubhouse. A young lady was on the way out, locking the front door behind her. Each of the men dropped to one knee and pressed his knuckles to his forehead.

"Hail to the victor!" the first man said.

"Hail to the queen of the roost!" said the second.

"Hail to the scourge and terror!" said the third.

"Good evening," I said.

The girl smiled at me toothily, like a wolf eyeing a lamb. Or, for that matter, a wolf eyeing a rooster. "You took a Radcliffer?" she asked. "That's hilarious! It must be getting harder and harder to find a Harvard man willing to have his face smashed in. Well, cheerio until Saturday, boys!"

The men climbed to their feet. Instead of using the front door, as the woman had done, they led me around to a low side entrance that we had to duck to pass through. We descended to the basement. A wine cellar with a stripe painted down the center dominated the space. One side, marked HENS, was well stocked with many different types of bottles. On the other, marked COCKERELS, a single shelf held two dusty bottles of champagne.

We took a bottle upstairs to a kitchen that lacked any sort of cookware or eating utensils, but was equipped with glasses of every shape and size. The triple-feathered man opened the bottle and poured four generous coupes.

He raised his glass. "To victory!"

"To a better showing than last year!" said the second man.

"To keeping all our teeth!" said the third.

They looked to me. "Umm," I said, spilling a little champagne on myself. The only toast I knew was the old Halloween invocation, but it seemed appropriate: "By the ashes of Cadwallader, may she obscure us by day and strike with us by night!"

"Hear, hear!" they called out. We drank. The warm sparkling wine tasted terrible.

Their leader pulled out a card on which there were four lines labeled

1. The Beak _____
2. The Wing _____
3. The Spur _____
4. The Tail _____

On the third line he wrote *Krillgoe Hosawither.*

"Only one drink and you've misspelled your own name," exclaimed the second man.

The third examined the card carefully. "No, he's got it right," he reported. "Poor chap got hit so hard last year it scrambled his letters."

"Killgore, is it?" I asked.

"No, no," he said, smiling. "It really is Krillgoe. Terribly traditional Belgian parents, I'm afraid." The others chuckled knowingly.

He passed the card to his right. The second man sucked at the pen, then signed *Osgood Fletcher* on the first line.

"Brave man!" the third one said.

"Not at all," Osgood replied. "Patrice is sure to claim top billing for herself. I, at least, know who I'm up against."

He passed the card to the third man, who sighed and gave me a long look, sizing me up. "Quite a lot of practical philosophical experience you've got?" he asked.

"I suppose," I said.

"You don't frighten too easily?"

That was unsettling. "Not terribly."

"Oh, and you're a hoverer! It works on so many levels." He wrote *Dmitri Ivanovich* on the fourth line.

"Seems ungenerous to put the new fellow in the two slot," said Osgood.

"Hmm?" said Dmitri. "I don't understand English." That got a round of laughter from everyone but me. "Besides, I donated three teeth to the cause last year." He ran his tongue over his gums and popped out a piece of bridgework.

He passed me the sheet. The remaining blank was on the second line, next to *The Wing*. I took up the pen and unscrewed the cap, but couldn't quite bring myself to sign.

"Gentlemen," I said, "this is perhaps the wrong moment to mention it, but I haven't the faintest notion what any of this is about."

Krillgoe nodded sympathetically. "Very sensible of you. The wager this year is for cognac and we've got a line on a good deal. It will only run one hundred dollars each."

"Better make it one fifty and we can keep a few bottles for ourselves," Osgood suggested.

"Plus dues," added Krillgoe. "But there's no rush. We know you're Contingency, so you'll be good for it in May when you get your bonus check. If you get killed, we'll let you off scot-free. You get ten tickets. I suppose we'll have to allow you to give them to your lady friends at Radcliffe, though God knows the crowd will already be on their side—"

"On account of them having so many more ex-Hens who come back each year and all of them with their ten, too," added Osgood, not altogether helpfully.

"You wouldn't mind explaining the specifics of . . . I mean, what it is actually that I'm signing up to *do*?" I asked.

"The less you know, the better," said Krillgoe. The others heartily seconded the sentiment.

"Can you draw a push?" asked Dmitri, referring to the sigil that did exactly what the name implied.

"Of course," I said.

"Then you're in! All you need to do is sign."

I recalled the moment in *Fresh Gale on the High Sonora* when Edwin Fitzenhalter joins the US Kite Marshalry after walking into the wrong building on his first visit to San Antonio—the slow, burning feeling in his gut as he realizes he doesn't know what kind of work he's signing on for, countered by the notion that the chaps around him seem to be men of quality. I couldn't say that those three in the yellow ties resembled the deadeye sharpshooters and wild ex-mariners with whom Fitzenhalter had served; they looked instead like mildly spoiled Harvard College boys. But they were so excited and expectant. And after all, what was life without a little adventure?

I signed.

"Bravo!" shouted my compatriots. We drank a second round to finish the bottle.

On my walk home, however, the fizz of the preceding hours leaked away. I'd just stayed out until two in the morning with a paper unwritten and a full schedule of Zeds to teach at six. That was sheer stupidity. I hadn't come halfway across the country in search of adventure, I'd come for an education! Contingency students could ill afford adventures, not unless they wanted to lose their scholarships.

As I approached my building, a light came on in the room below mine and a silhouette paced before the window. Mayweather. No rest for the wicked, it seemed, though a wicked gossip might be just the man I needed.

I climbed a flight of stairs and knocked. I heard the thud of footsteps and then the door crashed open. Mayweather and a young woman answered it together, both laughing uproariously, completely drunk, neither wearing a stitch of clothing, a fact which they had ineffectually attempted to hide by wrapping themselves in the same blanket. My instinct was to run, but I was too plum shocked.

"Robert!" cried Mayweather. "Lucille, do you know Robert? This man is a hero! He swam the Charles to save Norah's life. Nancy's life. He'll tell you all about it. He shot a man in Abilene! Isn't that right? Come in, come in! Do you know Lucille?"

As it happened, I did: she was one of the Zeds I was supposed to teach in roughly four hours.

"Did you tell him to come?" asked Lucille, whose feet had become tangled in the blanket. "You told him to come!" she said and tripped, sending both of them tumbling to the floor, paralyzed in hilarity, and doing a poor job of protecting their modesty.

"I don't know why you told him to come," complained Lucille, climbing to her feet and yanking the blanket away from Mayweather, who rolled over onto his belly and grinned stupidly.

Lucille wobbled toward the bedroom, stopping to collect several articles of clothing, hurl an expensive pair of trousers at Mayweather, and lose track of her blanket entirely.

"I was just going!" she shouted from the bedroom.

"I'm so sorry," I said.

I began backing out of the room, but Mayweather, drunk or not, was quick and surprisingly strong. With one hand clamped around my arm and the other clutching his trousers to him, he dragged me over to a plush lounge chair.

"We are going to have a drink, Robert! A man like you, you'll go places.

A man worth knowing. You should hear what everyone says about you—a goddamned saint." He reached for a bottle of Scotch and upended it over a glass. The bottle was empty.

"I should go," I said, but Mayweather restrained me.

"Robert, Robert, Robert. You're out in the middle of the night. There's only one reason at this hour. They're so *easy*, these philosophical girls. You want to defend them from all that slander, but it's true—they fall over one another to give it up. A man can hardly choose! So who was yours? You saw mine, you have to tell me yours!"

"I was coming for advice," I blurted. "Three men dressed in feathered hats came to initiate me into some sort of society. They have a rickety clubhouse four hundred yards northwest of Harvard Square."

Mayweather looked at me, stupefied. Then he gasped. "Your problem isn't your *cock*, it's the *Cocks*," he said, delighted by his own wit.

"What *are* the Cocks?" I asked. "What do they do?"

"It's the best party of the year. You have to give me a ticket. So I can come watch you. Two tickets."

"What happens at the party?"

"Blood sports. They try to kill you."

"The other men try to kill me?"

"No! The Hens. Each one of them tries to mash one of you."

That made sense. Almost. Four women and four men—an empirical prizefight. I'd suffered through plenty of those as a child without any opportunity to win liquor.

"I thought long and hard when they invited me," said Mayweather. "I want to see it, but I'm not suicidal."

"They asked you?"

"Ages ago."

That didn't raise my opinion of the Cocks. Mayweather knew his way around a message board—during the day he didn't seem to go longer than twelve or thirteen seconds without checking his portable—but he was no practical philosopher.

"Do you know who the Hens put in the two slot?" I asked. "Who their Wing is?"

Mayweather nodded, and rattled off a list of names, none of which I recognized as Radcliffe students unless Mrs. Woodrow Wilson and Queen Victoria had recently enrolled.

I was saved from further conjecture by Lucille, who reentered fully dressed. Despite wearing three-inch pumps, she seemed to be having far less trouble maneuvering than she'd had barefoot.

"I was just leaving," she said.

"No, no," I said, rising. "*I* was just leaving."

"No!" said Mayweather. "You can't go. This man is a hero! He's a prince. Let me pour you a drink."

"You did pour me a drink," I said. "It was delicious. But I have to be off—there's someone waiting up for me."

"Oh-ho!" said Mayweather, winking. "Well give her one from me." Then he turned to Lucille. "Where are *you* going?"

"I was just leaving."

"You can't leave now!" objected Mayweather.

He tugged at her hands and she sat down hard in his lap, both of them laughing. I heard thrilled-sounding shrieks as I climbed the last flight of stairs to my room, where, to my surprise, someone really was waiting up for me.

13

Energy comes in a packet
That can't be further divided—
Moving, it interferes with magnets—
Measure finely enough and you will see
The spark in your glyph—that moves the world.

Maria Trestor, "5th Precept," *200 Precepts*, 1848

I FOUND UNGER PACING the living room, mouthing along as he read through a sheaf of papers.

"Late night?" I asked him.

He looked up at me in surprise. "I heard you nearly drowned rescuing Nancy Durstman. Are you quite all right?"

"Yeah," I said, feeling embarrassed that he'd thought it necessary to wait up. "It wasn't as dramatic as all that."

"Robert, three different people told me you dove in after her and she pushed you under. They kept repeating what you said, that you have to fly instead of run at an emergency."

"I didn't come up with that, my mother used to—"

"It put me in mind of a classic calculus problem," Unger continued, his eyes bright and distant, "about saving a drowning man who's down the beach a few hundred yards and some distance out to sea—you can run faster than you can swim and how far should you go before entering the water? It's really a metaphor for the refractive index of optical media. That gave me the most intriguing idea about Trestor's eighty-eighth precept."

"About what?" I asked.

"There's a way to put it to the test! It's not practical, it would take a thousand years—but I simply had to rewrite my paper. I ought to have you read it over, Robert. You have the most original notions about empiricism."

He thrust his paper into my hands. "Tell me if it's coherent. And would you mind terribly if I had a look at yours? I won't alter a word, I just want to see what you've come up with."

So, I read Unger's essay. The parts I could understand dealt with one of the precepts written down by Maria Trestor, who was either the greatest theorist sigilry had ever seen or its greatest madwoman. Trestor had spent her brief life shut away in a garret apartment in her parents' house in Connecticut, writing on the theoretical underpinnings of glyphs. When she'd died at age twenty-nine, her last wish was that all her papers be burned. Instead, her family published the more comprehensible ones. Several of her precepts had provided invaluable insights into empirical philosophy, though no one knew how she'd formulated them—experiments or mathematics or intuition.

Unger had applied Trestor's principles of inversion to the problem of creating a Zephyrus glyph—a sigil that would summon the west wind—by reversing the Eupheus glyph, which could only call winds from the east. That much I understood. But the rest was so technical that I could barely follow. Unger seemed to believe that a simple inversion *did* work, but so slowly and inefficiently that by the time your west wind finally arrived it wouldn't blow with any discernable force and you'd have been dead for four hundred years. It struck me as a typical theorist's solution.

Unger had read my essay as well—all six lines of it. He couldn't help himself and had penciled in several improvements to my grammar.

"A bit of work left, then," he said.

"A bit," I said morosely.

"What were you doing all night? Weren't you in the library?"

I explained my diversion at the hands of the Order of the Chanticleer.

"Dear heavens!" Unger exclaimed. "I saw the cards pinned to the door. I thought you knew."

"Knew what?"

"That if you want to decline, you slide your card under the door of their clubhouse. I know I never ran so fast as I did last week when I returned mine."

They'd asked *Unger* ahead of me? Krillgoe Hosawither and his brethren must be even bigger fools than I'd thought—there wasn't a man on earth less well suited for an empirical duel than Freddy.

"Do you know the logistics of it?" I asked. "How it actually plays out?"

"Oh, they go to tremendous lengths to keep the whole thing secret," he said. "It's supposed to be great fun to watch, just—well, perhaps hazardous for the participants."

He came over to shake my hand. "In all seriousness, congratulations. The Cocks don't ask just anyone."

"No," I said. "Apparently they asked *everyone* and I was the only male sigilrist left."

Unger didn't know what to say to that. In fact he looked a little hurt. Well, why shouldn't they ask the local boy before me? It wasn't his fault.

"You're coming, of course," I said. "And you'd better cheer louder than anyone."

"Bully!" said Unger. "It would be an honor." Then a thought flashed across his face. He cleared his throat. "This is going to sound terribly selfish . . ."

"You want a second ticket so you can ask Dizzy."

"You needn't give *me* the ticket, you could give it to her."

"You're trying to invent a sigil that'll let her call the west wind, right?"

"For everyone," Unger murmured, embarrassed. "But yes."

"Then have two tickets and ask her yourself," I said.

Unger looked apprehensive over the prospect but also pleased.

I stayed up the rest of the night working on my essay, which became ever more nonsensical as morning drew nigh. At five thirty, I hid my paper in my desk, lest Unger read it out of curiosity and die of heart failure, and dragged myself to the aerodrome.

(I earned a richly deserved D– on that essay. Unger got his paper back without a grade. Professor Yu had been so excited that she'd forgotten to mark it. After several lunches with the best theoretical minds at Radcliffe, Yu and Unger concluded that he'd made a mistake in his mathematical model and that the actual time to run his experiment would be on the order of twenty thousand years. Unger published his work the following spring in *The Annals of Theoretical Empirical Philosophy*, to overwhelming disinterest. But I never saw Unger prouder than the day he got his copy of that journal in the mail.)

Exhausted as I was, I couldn't beg off teaching my classes. I did uneventful individual sessions with two Zeds. Mayweather's lady friend, Lucille, should have been my third student, but didn't show—probably still hungover at his place. I took advantage of the break to make a cup of coffee at the little perpetual heat stove we kept in the aerodrome's storeroom.

I emerged a few minutes later to find Rachael Rodgers blocking the aerodrome's main door. She held a leather harness strap in one hand, a prop for the class she was about to teach. When she saw me, she pressed her lips into a nasty smile and thrust her chin in the air.

"You stupid son of a bitch!" she sneered. "You thought I wouldn't find out? You nearly kill a girl in an unauthorized session and don't say a word?"

"I logged it," I said, trying to keep my face steady. "It was a supervised self-study class. Nobody had to authorize it."

At the sound of our voices, thirty or so heads popped around the corner from the classroom. Rachael looked pleased to have an audience.

"You've been an insolent, incompetent distraction from the very first day," she raged. "I want you gone. Now!"

"I'm going outside to teach my next Zed," I said.

"Don't you *dare* contradict me! You're through. You're fired!"

"You don't have the authority."

Probably that was true—I'd heard Jake claim so. But Rachael seemed to sense my uncertainty and it emboldened her.

"You're nothing more than a whining little brat who wishes he'd been born a girl. You ought to be taken out back and paddled."

A couple of the Ones giggled at the thought. "Do it, Rachael!" one of them called. "Put him over your knee and spank him!"

If there was further laughter, neither Rachael nor I heard it. I knew what she was going to do almost before she did. It didn't matter that I was twice her size; she'd just made a half-serious threat in front of thirty novices and she either had to follow through or lose face.

She raised her strap and stepped toward me.

"Don't touch me," I growled.

Rachael caught hold of my skysuit and swung at me. I shoved her arm down and away. She lost her grip, took a step backward, and sat down hard.

"Don't touch me!" I shouted.

I walked around her and out the door without looking back.

It was liberating in the way a death sentence must be. The worst had happened: I'd knocked down a girl and she would see to it I was fired as an instructor and probably expelled. Nothing I could do would change that. In the meantime, I had complete freedom.

A woman waved to me from the hover field. Undoubtedly my seven thirty—the brand-new tailored skysuit and cream-colored kid gloves gave her away as a particular sort of Zed.

"Halloo!" she called. "Over here."

I walked over. She'd been waiting outside and had missed my exchange with Rachael.

"Good morning," I said. "I'm afraid I shouldn't—"

"Oh, I do get the famous Mr. Weekes after all!"

"Yes," I said. "I'm sorry, but—"

"I saw Nancy last night and she is just *so* impressed with you. 'The very epitome of alacrity and sangfroid,' she called you."

I had to take it on faith that was a compliment, as it would have sent me to the dictionary three times in the space of five words.

"I shouldn't say this, but Nancy's *thrilled* to be the center of attention. A good, modest girl all her life but now with a frisson of danger, too! She won't stop talking about you. She's going to eat her liver when she finds out I got you to myself for a whole lesson."

"About that," I said. "I should really—" And then I thought to myself, *What's the harm?*

"Well, show me your launch sigil with good body position, if you'd be so kind," I said.

"Good body position," she tittered. "I'm sure if I actually tried it, I'd end up in the river, too. Though I might not mind the dunking if I were certain of being rescued. Would you tell me how it happened?"

I gave an account of the previous night's rescue and then tried to keep up with her questions about my sisters and the native flora and fauna of Montana and, yes, really, poor Nancy had gone straight in. I persuaded her to draw a few glyphs, but she was no more a practical philosopher than I was a deep-sea diver. I'd had girls like that now and again, more interested in flirtation than flying. Usually, I resented them for taking time away from the more dedicated students, but the way the day was going, I didn't care.

"I'm glad you tried a sigil, at least," I said at our session's end. "You're probably my last student. I believe Miss Rodgers fired me as I was on my way out to meet you."

"Oh, Rachael's insufferable! Don't pay her any mind. Besides, Nancy comes from money—her father would never allow you to be let go, not after last night."

That was something I'd never considered.

"For what it's worth, I thought you were brilliant. You're so *unusual!* I mean, everyone always says any boy who can do philosophy must like other boys—romantically, I mean. But you're such a man's man! All business. You don't seem like one of *those.*"

I'd heard endless versions of that line over the years—"Hey, philosopher—you a pansy? A shirt lifter? A little witch, just like your mama?" I'd beat the tar out of half my male high school classmates over quips like that.

"No, I like women romantically," I answered, trying to maintain a veneer of politeness.

"Do you have someone back home? I hope I'm not prying. I just never heard of you with anyone here, is all."

"No one back home."

"Well, you're going to make someone happy with those big hands of yours. A few of the girls were saying they thought you and Miss Jacobi—well, it's very silly."

"Very."

Ridiculous to imagine the two of us together. No time, no privacy, no interest on Jake's part, she'd made that clear from the day I met her. And yet the thought stirred something in me. If I were to be tossed out of the aerodrome, then *that* was the affair I wanted—not this tactless little rich girl. Gloxinia was too beautiful, too fearsome for me not to chance it. Find yourself chained to a bedframe falling out of the sky at ten thousand feet if you ever crossed her. Though that might be preferable to whatever method Cocks and Hens would find for staving in my head. And Jake just might be able to shed some light on that, too.

Shitty chain of commnd if nonsuprior officr threatns to flog you, Mother sympathized. *Hit hr hardr nxt time. And, Y, agree discuss w/ yr lead flyr ASAP.*

So I messaged Jake, asking for an audience; she said to come by that evening. *Dn't wrry—I only spank men wh ask nicely.*

Which was intriguing. Perhaps my well-dressed Zed knew something I didn't.

I tried out my sharpest shirt and tie, with a brown fedora supplied by Unger, and headed to the Women's Philosophical Dormitory with a gait pretty well approximating a swagger. But when I strolled into the women's dorm, a wide, matronly woman intercepted me.

"May I help you?" she said.

"Here to see Jake," I answered.

The woman frowned. "Who?"

"Gloxinia Jacobi."

"Just a moment," she said, and retreated to a desk next to the door. She took out a slip of paper. "Whom shall I say is calling?"

"She's expecting me," I explained. "I'll just go up."

"Certainly not!"

So, twenty minutes later, after a note had been sent up to Jake and she'd sent one back, as was required protocol, my sense of derring-do had diminished.

Jake came down the stairs, grabbed my arm—though not in the way I'd been hoping—and led me outside.

"Holy hell, Weekes, you've had a day for the ages!" she said. "You don't have any idea who Nancy Durstman is, do you?"

"No, but everyone keeps—"

"Her daddy is president of the fourth-largest insurance company in America. Then you went and goaded Rachael into a fight? And slugged her? Did you also set the aerial speed record while you were at it?"

"No," I said. "But I do seem to have joined the Most Ancient and Noble Order of the Chanticleer."

Jake smirked. "Of course you did! Well, they picked the right man—you'll put up quite a fight."

"Provided I don't get expelled first."

"Nobody's expelling you," Jake said, laughing. "It's not the first time Rachael's started a fracas. No, you just go into Brock's office first thing tomorrow morning for confession and she'll tell you say ten Hail Marys and sin no more. It'll blow over."

The relief must have been spelled out all over my face.

"Better for you that you *had* been expelled," Jake snickered. "Joined the Cocks. No wonder you're living recklessly. You're not going to survive the weekend."

A good joke, I hoped. "It's like a pyramid scheme, right?" I asked. "There's no actual violence involved?"

She looked at me with mock solemnity and shook her head.

"Could you enlighten me on . . . I mean, what actually happens?"

"It's a secret," she said, and winked. "I've been twice as a guest and we're made to swear a bunch of very bloody oaths never to reveal it."

Her wink emboldened me. I gazed at her with enough smoldering intensity that she frowned and looked away.

"Tell me anyway?" I asked.

"Yeah, sure," she said. "You sit on stools ten paces apart. You get a belt with four vials of bronze on one side and four of talc on the other. There's a referee and a surgeon standing by. When the referee says go, you both draw dissipate glyphs to shield yourselves. Ten seconds later, the referee blows her whistle. Draw another dissipate, draw push, or jump for your life—whatever you choose. The first one to get knocked off their stool loses."

Only moderate potential for remodeling your skull in a game like that. "So it's like Queen of the Hill," I said. "But that's all about brute philosophical force. How do the men ever win?"

"They don't," Jake said. "They did, once, in '08. They cheated. But the Hens have been more careful since. They haven't so much as lost a round."

We turned for a second lap around the quadrangle and Jake retook my arm.

"Out of sheer morbid curiosity, which piece of the rooster will you be representing?" she asked.

"The Wing," I said.

"Oh, poor Robert. Write your last will and testament now."

"Why, who's the Wing for the Hens?"

"Hmm-mmm."

"Mayweather will tell me."

"He doesn't know."

"If I give you one of my invitations?"

"You're going to do that anyway."

Her golden hair glistened in the sun. I could feel the heat of her palm on the crook of my arm.

"If I took you to dinner beforehand?" I asked.

"No," said Jake.

"If I took you out another time?"

"No!" She dropped my arm and looked up at me in annoyance. "Stop it! I'm not kidding."

"I just thought—"

"Stop looking at me like you want to rip my shirt off. I'm not interested and I'm not your type. You need somebody who's as goddamned serious as you are."

"And that's not you?" I asked, trying my damned most serious to sound light.

"No!" she said. "You may think I'm a hell-raiser, but I'm daddy's little princess who's six credits short of a degree in accounting. You need an Amazon warrior queen. We're fresh out of those."

She stood on tiptoes to adjust my hat to a more rakish angle. "You just worry about putting on a good show at Cocks and Hens. If you manage that, you'll have no shortage of interested parties offering to take you over their knee in the bedroom. I'll pick the right one for you, I promise."

I visited Professor Brock in her office in the fifth sub-basement of the Gray Box the following morning. It smelled of mildew and machine oil. She had a foot-powered lathe and crates of regulators in various states of disassembly, as well as books and journals stacked high enough to kill someone if they toppled over.

"Sit," Brock said. "Every time I hear the story it gets bigger. Please tell me Rachael didn't actually order you to strip naked or threaten to sodomize you. And tell me that *you* didn't slap her in the face or threaten to retain a lawyer and sue for battery."

"No ma'am," I said. "She laid hands on me, I pushed her away, and she fell down."

"Fine. Apologize when you see her next. I've told her to do the same. You're not fired unless you want to be. I can't afford to lose you, not with as many girls as you've taken on, and I can't afford to lose her—her ground instruction is the reason most of your Zeds pass on the first try."

"She came up to me carrying a—"

"I don't want to hear any more about it. Yesterday's fight is small potatoes. You know what your real sin was?"

"Splashing a young lady?"

"Splashing the richest girl in the sophomore class. She's too stupid to understand how close she came to drowning. Her father's no brighter. He wrote to express his gratitude at the amazing instruction his daughter's receiving—if even our male can effect such an effortless rescue, then we must be the most extraordinary group of hoverers in the world. He wondered if he might do something nice for us. I suggested a set of spiral-cut regulators from Denver Custom Instruments for our General's Cup team."

I whistled at that. I wasn't going to resign if I had the chance to fly with one of *those*.

"I personally don't mind what you did," Brock said. "I trained at Detroit in the '90s and we splashed a couple girls a week off Belle Isle. That was the culture. But eight years ago—right before they hired me—Radcliffe had a novice die in a crash. If we ever lose another one, that'll be the end of flying at Radcliffe, maybe the end of empirical philosophy entirely. So, you *cannot* turn your lessons into an audition for Rescue and Evac."

"Understood," I said.

"Good. I should add that if you're still serious about R&E, I think I've found someone to train you. It'll be a couple of weeks before we can finalize the arrangements. We'll bring in a bunch of other instructors at the same time—we can't have the six of you trying to cover five hundred trainees all year."

"That sounds terrific," I said. "I'm on the schedule for eight Zeds this afternoon."

Brock grimaced. "Ouch."

Then she laughed. "Is it true you're sitting for the Cocks?"

It startled me that even she knew.

"I'll clear the schedule for Monday," Brock said. "It'll give us time to attend your funeral."

14

By obliterating a sigil, one begins to see its edges.

Dr. Jenny Yu, *Toward a Unified Theory of Empirical Philosophy*, 1926

RACHAEL AND I SHOUTED apologies at each other from across the landing field that afternoon. Then I turned my full attention to not being mashed into a pulp during Cocks and Hens.

The fundamental problem was that I didn't have the raw philosophical strength to overcome a woman. We would begin the match by drawing dissipate glyphs—shields that could soak up a limited amount of philosophical energy—and then attack on the count of ten with push sigils. Unfortunately, a good woman would have a shield stronger than my best push and a push that was much, much stronger than my best shield.

If my opponent drew faster, she'd win, period: her push would burn out her shield, burn out mine, and hit hard enough to knock me to the ground. If I beat her to the draw, I would burn out my own dissipate, only to watch my push die against her shield. She'd be able to flatten me with a counter-attack.

Guess y hav to cheat to win, Mother advised.

How? I asked her.

Dunno. Y need smbody smarter thn me.

I should hv said no. Its a stupid distraction. Time away fr aerodrom & fr studyng.

So? Ma answered. *Snds lik fun.*

As if I'd ever seen Mother take a couple days off work in the name of fun.

Any mor Trnchr trbl? I asked her.

Oh for Christ's sake, Boober! Go enjoy yourself for a whole ten minutes. Trencher situation is much imprvd. Lew Hansen sat dwn w/ Hand and Trnchr leaders. Negotiatd a ceasefir—they would only tlk to a man. So, put Trnchrs out of yr mind and giv thm a good show.

I met with the Cocks on Friday morning, the day before the event itself, for our final planning session. They seemed more concerned with the catering arrangements than with winning any of our matches.

So, I found someone smarter than me.

"What a fascinating problem!" said Unger, when I put the scenario to him. "You do realize that the men haven't actually tried to win a bout in years. You're supposed to do something amusing and then your opposite number knocks you off your stool as gently as possible."

"What if I want to try?" I asked.

Unger sighed. "Robert, that's unwise. If the Hens put up a true brute force philosopher—a precision wide-field transporter, say, a woman the caliber of Danielle Hardin—her push could hit hard enough to kill you where you sit."

"Well, do you have any good joke books then? If I make her laugh, maybe she won't break me in half."

"Hah, joke books!" laughed Unger. And then his face settled into a wild, distant expression. "Though, you know, there was a funny bit in that paper on constituent quanta of vectored sigils in the *Annals of the Société* in . . . ohh, was it '97 or '98? The one with the red cover . . . Breaking in half, that's not a bad way of putting it . . ."

Unger wandered off to his room and shut the door. I wondered if I'd said something to offend him. But he emerged five hours later equipped with an armload of books.

"It *could* work!" he said, with a manic gleam in his eyes. "It's possible. It's theoretically sound!"

"What are you talking about?" I asked.

"Come with me!"

We went down to the sixth sub-basement of the Gray Box, where Unger requisitioned several pieces of equipment and signed out a room for us to use. It was a bare ten-by-ten-foot cube. Unger stood me along one wall and set a sturdy chair opposite us. In the middle of the room, he positioned a battered contraption that looked like a metal suitcase with a hose and showerhead attached to the top.

"What have you got there?" I asked.

"This?" Unger said, looking shocked that I didn't recognize it. "Why, it's a Trestor device. You can't mean to tell me you haven't seen one before?"

I hadn't, though I understood roughly how it worked. The Trestor device had been invented two decades earlier by Thomas Edison, who, fresh off the motion picture camera, had decided there was good money to be made in inventing sigils. As his first order of business, Edison had wanted to measure philosophical energy. He'd read the bits of Maria Trestor in which she claimed philosophical effects were transmitted by discrete packets of energy called quanta; he'd become convinced she must have built a detector. After three years of maddening failures, Edison had cobbled together a functioning machine, which he'd named in her honor. (The great irony, of course, is that Edison never managed to invent a single new sigil, though he described the characteristics of dozens of existing ones in minute detail.) The Trestor device in front of me was not much changed from Edison's early models— heavy, awkward, and balky.

Unger handed me a tube of talc and aimed the detector in my direction.

"All right now, sport," he said. "I want to take a couple of readings before we try the tricky part. Would you be so kind as to draw one push at that chair?"

I took aim and let the talc trickle from the tube, drawing a push sigil in the air. The chair flew backward and slammed into the wall. I expected someone to come running at the commotion, but apparently loud, abrupt noises were common at these depths.

Unger's eyes went wide. "Is that typical for you?"

"Why, what'd I get?" I asked.

"Thirty-four hundred milli-Trestors."

"Is that good?" It had felt good. I hadn't hit anything as hard as I could in ages.

"If that's accurate, it would put you—maybe four standard deviations above the average male for philosophical power," he said, consulting one of his books. "Let me recalibrate the coils."

He fiddled with some knobs and had me draw three more times. I moved 3,900, 4,200, and zero milli-Trestors, missing entirely on my last attempt.

"Remarkable," Unger said. "Four standard deviations, indeed!"

"What does that mean?" I asked.

"It makes you one male out of thirty thousand. There would be, perhaps, two or three thousand men in America who have that much power."

I blinked at that. "Huh," I said. "A couple thousand of us. I guess I just never met one."

"Well, raw power doesn't mean anything unless you develop it," Freddy offered. "How old were you when you started philosophizing?"

"Oh, three or four," I said. "I learned a few sigils before I could write my name—my sister used to tell me that."

"So, exceptional power and fifteen years of intensive instruction. That would explain how you do what you do."

A second question leaped to mind, but I was almost afraid to ask it. I'd wondered my whole life. One answer was as frightening as the other.

"Fred, where would that put me against . . ."

"Compared to a woman? Quite a lot above the median."

I rubbed my forehead. "Are you sure?" I asked. "Everybody always said I was pretty good for a boy, but that I'd never be able to—"

"You're very good for anybody."

I let that wash over me for a second. Certainly, I'd been a better philosopher than many of the girls in Billings and I could out-fly most of Radcliffe. But I'd never really considered what that meant.

"Sure," I said. "But the Hens are going to have the best women at Radcliffe. Even if my opponent's a lady about it and lets me hit her first, I would need two, maybe three shots to burn out her shield. She's not going to sit back and let me hit her that many times."

"Oh, that shouldn't be necessary," Unger said. "We'll want her to hit *you*. Here's the secret: you're going to layer your shields."

"No," I said, "that's impossible. Dissipate dissipates dissipate."

After drawing a dissipate sigil, it absorbed the energy of whatever sigil you drew next, including another dissipate. So, if you drew your first dissipate at three thousand milli-Trestors, followed by a second one at two thousand, then you had a total net dissipate of one thousand, not five thousand.

Unger waved away my complaints and gave me a pad of paper. "Show me how you draw your dissipate," he said.

I drew the glyph and Unger compared it to a large reference book. He frowned. "That can't be right," he said, flipping through several pages of line drawings. "What text did you learn it from?"

"My mother."

"Or, no, here it is . . . version originating in the Philippines. Quite obscure. Splendid." He handed me the book. "Now choose one of the others. Any of them."

I picked a second dissipate sigil that had only a few lines—the Reverse Pearl Standard—and practiced it ten, twenty, three hundred times, until its shape ingrained itself in my memory. Unger watched with fascination.

"You draw it the exact same way every time," he remarked.

"That's the idea," I said.

When I was satisfied I knew the figure, I drew one on the chair and Unger measured: three hundred milli-Trestors. Not even strong enough to ward off one of my own pushes.

"That's useless," I said.

"No, it's perfect," Unger reassured me. "I want you to sit on the chair and lay down four overlapping dissipates. The first should be a wide, weak Reverse Pearl Standard. Then a tighter, stronger Philippine style. A Reverse

Pearl, narrower still. Then a Philippine, very, very narrow and as strong as you can—just enough to cover your body and the chair."

I was dubious. I'd fiddled around with dissipate glyphs plenty as a kid and what Unger was describing simply wasn't going to work. But I drew the sigils according to his instructions. Then I stepped back and fired off a push at the chair.

Nothing happened.

Unger shouted in delight as he watched the gauge on the Trestor device.

"Did I miss?" I asked.

"No, you hit it dead on at full strength. Do it again!"

I couldn't figure it. I checked my powder tube—no sign of impurities contaminating the talc. I unloaded twice more on the chair, drawing as hard as I could. It didn't move. It was the damnedest thing.

"What did you do?" I asked Unger.

"Nothing!" he cried. "Once more."

I fired off one more push and knocked down the chair. I was dumbfounded.

"That's impossible," I said. "Every one of those pushes had ten times more energy than the shield could soak up!"

"No, that's *philosophy*," Unger said. "The strength of your dissipate sigils doesn't matter. It's the interfaces."

"The what?"

"When you lay down two different styles of dissipate on top of each other, they leave an interface—a layer—along the border of their overlap. That layer refracts a quantal-minimum-dependent vectored sigil, like a push."

"So, what—it bounces off?"

"Not precisely," said Unger. "As I said, it's a refractive effect—"

He saw my expression.

"Yes, it bounces. But when it bounces, the sigil breaks apart into many pieces, none of which constitutes a push on its own. It also destroys the interface."

I thought that over.

"So it doesn't matter how hard she hits me," I said. "The layers will deflect anything."

"Oh, no, not *anything*!" Unger said. "If she had sufficient powder mass—roughly twelve pounds of talc—she could overcome—"

"She's only going to have four tubes with one ounce each," I said.

I picked up the book he'd found his strategy in. Twenty years old and written in French.

"All of that was in here?" I asked.

"It was mathematically described," said Unger. "I doubt it's ever been demonstrated practically. How often do you try to protect a fixed point from a push?"

"Never," I said. "But it's going to make Saturday night a lot more interesting."

15

Look at Brother, big and strong—he's always in a rush.
Until Sister breaks his leg when she's careless with a push.

Miss Goodbody's Book for Girls, 1899

ON THE NIGHT OF the tourney, I arrived at ten and sequestered myself in the basement. Krillgoe and Osgood were upstairs seeing that the caterers had everything they needed. Dmitri, who had not yet changed into his uniform, wore a singlet and shorts. He spent a long time stretching, followed by calisthenics and one-handed push-ups.

"Why do all this?" I asked him. "Two years in the tourney, I mean."

"It's good fun," he answered. He bent himself in a way that looked like it should have broken his spine in two, held it for a ten count, then straightened.

"Did you want something more contemplative?" he asked.

I shrugged in the affirmative.

"I'm not philosophical myself, I didn't grow up with it," he said. "But my family knows what it's like to be made outcasts in your own country. So, when I saw the abuse the lady philosophers take around here—the slurs and threats and beatings, the men with signs in the street—I knew whose side I was on. I appreciate that one night each year the common order gets stood on its head. You can take the most intractable anti-philosopher at Harvard, one who says he can't come within ten paces of an empiricist without going faint from the stench, but offer him a ticket to Cocks and Hens and he'll be the first one through the door. There's good in that."

He wiped his face with a towel. "Of course that's a lot of high-handed sentiment for what amounts to a clown show." He changed into his black jacket, loud tie, and ridiculous hat. Osgood and Krillgoe joined us.

At eleven, the doors opened to spectators: eighty onlookers invited by this year's combatants, plus another ninety as the guests of former partici-pants, who were entitled to tickets in exchange for a small donation. I'd disposed of my ten passes easily—Jake, Francine, Tillie, Astrid, and Essie. One for Frieda, in appreciation for having pulled me out of the river. Two for Unger, who really was bringing Dizzy. And two for Mayweather for the simple reason that, though he seemed to have forgotten the rest of the details of my late-night visit, he remembered having asked.

At a quarter to midnight, Patrice Magoren, who was heading up the Hen side, snuck down from the second story where the girls had their changing room.

"Not even dressed yet?" asked Osgood, shaking his head.

"Don't I know it," she answered. "Just wanted to check one last time to make sure there were no other special requests for the bouts."

"Yes," said Dmitri, "tell whoever's your Spur to bloody well line up her shot."

"Of course, of course," said Patrice. "She's aware. None of us wants a repeat of last year." She turned to Krillgoe. "She'll get you in the middle of the third one?" He nodded. To Osgood: "You'll signal me about four min-utes into yours?"

"Precisely," said Osgood.

"And I don't believe I've spoken with Robert. Planning a swimming exhibition, perhaps?"

"Not tonight," I said.

"A surprise, then?"

I wondered if Unger had been talking. "I hope so."

"Well, we can't wait to see."

Soon enough, the clock struck midnight. The Cockerels lined up and, with a great adjusting of plumes and ties, we were off, tramping up the stairs to shouts and applause.

At the same time, the Hens paraded down from the second story. They were dressed in identical brown-and-white-spotted dresses, as well as black masks that covered their faces from eyebrow to cheekbone, like carnival-goers in Venice. Patrice's mask was adorned with two feathers; the others had no plumage at all. Being a Hen had some degree of prestige among the Radcliffe women, so they usually did one stint and passed the honor on. Only the Cocks had trouble finding volunteers.

The referee was an illustrious old Radcliffe alum equipped with a tiara and scepter. With a flourish of her hand, the referee silenced the crowd and made a few grandiose pronouncements, interspersed with lines of Latin. A space was cleared and two stools set opposite each other. The Hens lined up on the far side of the room. With the crush of people between us, I couldn't get a clear look at their Wing. Tall, certainly.

Then Dmitri was walking forward to shake hands with his opponent. I heard mutters that it was Alvina Williams, a senior I'd never met. Regular Radcliffe, not Contingency. Dmitri whispered something in her ear and she said something back, looking offended.

They took their seats to great cheering.

"Draw!" shouted the referee.

Both of them pulled tubes of bronze from their belts and drew dissipates. Dmitri's technique was sloppy, so much so that I wondered whether his sigil would take at all. Then again, it could have been one of the variants from Unger's book. The referee blew her whistle to start the match.

Alvina crossed her arms.

"Point of clarification!" Dmitri sang out. "So long as the contestant *does not break contact with the stool or touch the ground*, he is not disqualified?"

The referee seemed to be expecting this. "Correct!" she called back.

The audience buzzed.

Dmitri took his hat off and tossed it on the ground. Then he removed his tie and jacket, followed by his shirt and undershirt. Every woman present whistled and screamed—and not in horror. I'd never seen a more perfectly formed male figure. He might have been drawn by one of the Old Masters; the muscles in his arms and torso stood out in perfect relief. He unbuckled his belt, took one tube of talc, and dropped the rest on the floor. Alvina cracked her knuckles and took up a tube of talc, too.

Dmitri spilled the powder onto his hands, slapped them together, and took a firm grip on the stool's seat. Winking, he lifted himself into the air. He extended his legs outward, parallel to the ground, and then flipped them up so that he was doing a handstand on top of the stool. He walked his hands around the seat until he'd made a full revolution. Then he swung his feet down, catching himself an inch above the ground. He did a few dips and steadied his legs in front of him. Slowly, then with increasing speed, he swept his legs about the stool, lifting one arm and then the other, as if he were on a pommel horse. After a few passes, he reversed direction, split his legs wide, and continued his rotations spinning on one hand. The stool wobbled beneath him.

Eventually, he brought himself to a stop and returned to a sitting position. The crowd roared in approval. Dmitri nodded in acknowledgment, then held up his index finger. He removed his shoes and socks and climbed on top of the stool. With his back to us he raised his arms so that he was shaped like a T. He flexed his knees once. Twice.

Alvina had extended her left arm and was sighting along her thumb. She was being extraordinarily careful, despite the sigil having to carry only twenty feet. She had the tube in her right hand and brought it halfway down, then back up in time with Dmitri.

On the third bounce, she tipped the tube over and drew. Dmitri leaped a moment before her push sigil struck his stool, spinning it across the floor. He managed his backward somersault half twist without difficulty, landing facing the audience.

He bowed to enormous cheers.

"Last year the stool rebounded off the wall and caught him in the face," Krillgoe whispered to me.

"Point to the Hens!" cried the referee.

It had been the most superlative display of physical agility I'd ever seen. The man would be a natural flier if only I could get him in the air. Alvina rose and curtseyed to more cheers.

The stage was reset and Krillgoe took his seat, carrying a guitar strapped across his back. His opposite number was Maria Valdez, a junior, a transporter. She'd tried to join the Corps with everyone else the previous spring, but even after twenty years, the Corps still had hard feelings toward Spaniards. She'd been denied on "medical" grounds.

They drew their dissipates. On the whistle, they both quick-drew pushes, obviously underpowered glyphs that their own shields easily absorbed. But the crowd gasped. Most of the onlookers could barely see and nine-tenths of those who could were too drunk or unphilosophical to recognize the attacks as feints. Both redrew dissipates and made second attacks, just as weak as the first. But the crowd was on tiptoe, yelling encouragement. They might love a gymnastics routine, but they were mad for a real fight.

Then Krillgoe unslung his guitar and struck a couple dramatic minor chords to bring the shouting down to a more moderate level.

"Now we fully intend to finish this bout," he announced. "And the third time's the charm. But I think not nearly so charming as 'The Charming Lily Brown.' "

With that, Krillgoe's clear, warm tenor filled the room. His song concerned a highwayman on the gallows, looking back regretfully on a life of crime undertaken in a failed attempt to win the affections of a lass named Lily Brown. It was a sad, tuneful piece. If our audience had adored Dmitri, they melted for Krillgoe. I could understand how he'd survived three previous bouts. There was hardly a dry eye when he finished.

"Madam," Krillgoe said to Maria, "if I may in your honor?"

She nodded, grinning.

Krillgoe launched into an a cappella arrangement of Schubert's "Ave Maria," hitting and holding several impossibly high notes. The applause when he finished was genuine and sustained.

"One final song, by your leave?" Krillgoe asked. Maria smiled and waved as if to say "by all means."

"Ladies and gentlemen, my closing number this evening will be 'One Thousand Bloody Tigers.' "

"I say!" called someone from the crowd, sounding a little too well rehearsed. "Isn't that supposed to be 'One *Hundred* Bloody Tigers'?"

"Not tonight," deadpanned Krillgoe. He strummed a few chords and began an up-tempo rendition:

One thousand bloody tigers,
They're right outside the door.
One thousand bloody tigers,
I wouldn't wish for more.
I box 'em 'round the whiskers,
I drag 'em 'cross the floor.
That's one less bloody tiger
That's right outside my door.

Everyone stomped and sang along. Maria yawned and stretched.

"Nine hundred ninety-nine bloody tigers," sang Krillgoe, as the audience got tangled in the unwieldy line.

Across from him, Maria readied her talc.

"They're right outside the door—"

Maria loosed her first sigil, knocking the guitar out of Krillgoe's hands with a sour note. She had uncanny precision with the sigil, and the instrument went spinning through the air in a high arc, right into Dmitri's hands.

"Nine hundred ninety-nine bloody tigers . . ." sang Krillgoe, tucking his chin, like the veteran of three bouts that he was, *"I wouldn't wish for—"*

The push took him straight on, knocking him to the floor flat on his back, but sparing the stool entirely.

"—*more,*" he wheezed. Maria fired off a third push with her last half tube, just enough to topple the stool so that it fell on Krillgoe to laughter and applause.

Dmitri had to help Krillgoe to his feet. Another point to the Hens.

"Took the wind right out of me," said Krillgoe as Dmitri half carried him back to our side. "Go get her, Robert."

The crowd parted and my opponent stepped out to cheers that exceeded even Krillgoe's: it was the Hero of the Hellespont. My heart squeezed itself so hard that it stuck. She could hit me hard enough to kill me where I sat. Dazedly I moved to shake her hand. The crowd roared its approval for Radcliffe's war hero.

"So are you a juggler?" Dardanelles whispered into my ear. "Sketch artist? What do you want me to do?"

She waited for my reply, caught up in the moment. But I could only shake my head.

"Hit me," I whispered.

I stumbled back to my corner and took my seat. The referee called for silence and then for sigils. I fumbled for a tube of bronze. I couldn't remember how to draw the Reverse Pearl. Five, six, seven seconds ticked away. Finally, my hands, unwilling to accept further inaction, drew from muscle memory.

Then came the whistle. As quickly as I could, I tore the three remaining bronze tubes from my belt and drew: Philippine, Pearl, Philippine. And my shields were in place with three interfaces that should deflect whatever Dardanelles threw at me.

Across the room, Hardin was looking at me quizzically. My entire strategy had hinged upon the assumption that she would strike first. I didn't dare try to attack *her*; I had no idea how the refractive effect worked from inside the shield—maybe the push would bounce right back at me. While Unger would certainly be interested, I preferred not to potentially go out in a self-inflicted philosophical explosion.

The crowd grew restless. They had expected a talent, then some sort of joke.

"One hundred bloody tigers . . ." sang a drunken man, before his neighbors shushed him.

I had to make a move. Every second that went by, my dissipate sigils faded. They didn't have to be at full strength for the scattering effect to work, but I didn't know how weak was too weak. If the sigils wore out, I wouldn't get a second chance—I'd used up all my bronze. How much time had passed? Thirty seconds? As long as two minutes?

A few boos broke out. The Darling of the Dardanelles glared daggers.

"Hit me!" I shouted in desperation.

Dardanelles rolled her eyes and obliged, drawing a huge push. It was a big, fat, serves-you-right that should have meant *good night, Robert*. But nothing happened.

There was a look of disbelief on Hardin's face. She drew another heavy one, then another. Still nothing.

I could see her mutter "Son of a bitch!" as she reached to check her last tube. I knew what she was thinking. *Did my powder get wet? Did I use bronze instead of talc? Is someone playing a prank on me?*

But it was no joke. And I had my own talc at the ready. Hardin saw me, realized she was completely exposed, and at the last moment switched to bronze. She got an awkwardly drawn dissipate done a second before I finished my own draw.

I'd aimed low and away. My push brushed the bottom edge of her dissipate and squeaked through to the unshielded part of her stool. It struck with enough force to lift the front legs two inches off the ground, but not quite enough to tip her over. The legs clacked against the floor as they touched back down.

Dardanelles had a look of panic.

I reached for another tube of talc and so did she. Rattled though she might be, Hardin was impossibly fast. She—

•   •   •

"—one of these idiots with the feathers every year," a distant voice said.

"What?" I croaked.

I opened my eyes. A female figure dressed all in white was bent over me, applying a compress to my head.

"One of them ends up on my ward," said the nurse.

"What?" I said again.

"Easy there, old Robert," said Krillgoe, who was sitting beside my bed with Patrice.

"What happened?" I asked.

Dardanelles had fired off two half-strength pushes with her final tube. Her first had burned out her shield with enough energy left over to toss me into the air; her second had caught me a moment later, driving me across the room and slamming my head into the wall. The crowd had realized it was a real fight the moment before it ended and had gone wild; the consensus was that I'd lost my mind, attacked without regard to my own safety, and gotten the whupping I deserved.

I'd been knocked out cold before I'd even hit the ground. Krillgoe, Jake, and Dardanelles had dragged me off to a back room where neither smelling salts nor concentrate of bitterroot smoke had brought me around. Dardanelles had put me in stasis and Jake had flown me to the hospital. (It was the only time in my life I'd heard of Jake hauling a two-hundred-pound load.) Patrice and Osgood had gone out and told the audience that I'd popped right back up, demanding a second round; Osgood had done his comedy routine to uproarious laughter.

"The crack you took," Patrice said, shaking her head. "I thought you were dead."

"Thick skull," I replied. "You might have warned me that trying to win is bad manners."

"Not at all," Patrice said. "Someone tries every few years. Rarely that spectacularly. Actually, it's good form—they'll come next year not knowing whether to expect a prizefight or a serenade."

"Oh, they'll expect a prizefight when old Robert sits down," said

Krillgoe. He laid a long red feather on the pillow next to my head. "This is yours. You earned it."

It is a truism I've relearned many times, that the quality of one's hospital stay is directly proportional to the quality of one's visitors. And I've never had such a busy social schedule as I had during the next twenty-four hours.

Among my well-wishers were Jake and Francine, who visited to complain about having to teach my class of Ones. A few minutes later, the Ones hovered over en masse to complain about having to be taught by Jake and Francine. Dmitri and Osgood dropped by to pay their respects. Unger visited, too, curious to learn whether his stratagem had worked.

"Did you not see her first three pushes go bust?" I said.

"They did?"

Leave it to Unger, who'd been in the front row. The only way the man ever would notice a sigil being drawn was through the gauge of a Trestor device.

Stories of my prowess made it even as far as New York City, where Angela felt compelled to message her regards: *Sluggd it out w/ Danielle Hardin? New stupidest.*

By Sunday evening, my stream of visitors had left me with a throbbing headache behind the eyes. I was exhausted but couldn't sleep and still saw double when I tried to read. So when Danielle Hardin appeared in my room out of nowhere, I took it as a sign of further brain damage.

"Hi," she said. "Sorry. Don't be startled. There's a destination glyph in this room. It's on the city register. The originator must have decided it was easier to transport in, rather than climb five flights of stairs. Not that I wouldn't have climbed five flights to visit, but . . . well, there were an awful lot of people around and it makes me panicky, sometimes. I—I'm so sorry about last night."

She was trembling. A few weeks later, she admitted to me that this was the longest piece she'd spoken in private conversation since returning to Radcliffe.

"Hi," I said. I couldn't believe she was nervous. She'd saved a quarter of a million men at Gallipoli. There was talk of King George V knighting her. *I ought to be the nervous one.*

"Are you feeling better?" she asked.

"No," I said. "This is the second worst I've ever felt."

"Oh?"

"When I was twelve, my friend Willard Gunch tried to teach me to ride a horse. I needed all of forty seconds to get thrown. I hit the ground so hard the sky went orange and the sun turned blue. 'Well,' I said to myself, lying there, 'this must be as bad an injury as a man can live through.' Then the horse came around for a second pass and trampled me. Willard sent for my mother and after she determined I was still breathing, she gave me the worst thrashing of my life. That was worse."

Hardin looked startled by the story. She'd expected me to be angry.

"I'm sorry about hitting you the second time," she said.

"Don't be," I replied. "Hell, if you'd been one of my sisters, you would have hit me a third time and stolen my pocket money."

She smiled wanly at that and I smiled back.

"It was just—I thought you'd played a trick on me," she said. "Replaced my talc with gypsum. Put me on display to have some fun at my expense. What *did* happen?"

I explained about Unger and layering shields and scattering vectored sigils.

"Who's Unger?" she broke in.

"My roommate," I said. "Chubby Hungarian-American fellow? Favors bow ties?"

"A hundred forty-one bow ties," Danielle said. "I knew I recognized the name. He just figured this out?"

"He read it in some journal from 1896."

"There for anyone who wanted to find it." She shook her head. "You know, you had me. When I was putting up that dissipate, I drew it like all my years of single transports, instinctively, as tight as I could. A little voice in my head was saying, 'Sister, if he goes for the bottom of the stool, you're finished.' And then you did."

"How do you get a dissipate that tight?" I asked.

Our conversation degenerated into shoptalk. We drew figures back and forth with our index fingers in the air and carried on like a couple of old sigilrists who loved nothing better in the world. I got the impression that war heroes didn't get to do much of that, people taking their opinions so seriously and all.

"You'll have to teach me your dissipate form," I said.

"Sure, if you teach me yours," she answered. "Yours were both new to me. So were the ones the other Cocks used. They weren't real sigils, were they?"

"Krillgoe's might have been real, but the rest were faking it. I'd bet money on it."

"That's funny. Do you know what *we* were betting on before we came out?"

"Whether Dmitri would take his pants off, too?"

"What your act would be. It was knife throwing, bird calls, or rope tricks."

"Which one did you say?"

"I said a man as dim-looking as you could only do an impression of President Taft stuck in the bathtub." We laughed too hard at that and heard the clack of footsteps out in the hall as my nurse approached.

"Now, I'm going to get in trouble," I whispered. "I'm not supposed to have female visitors without a chaperone."

Dardanelles pulled a double-sealed tube containing a gram of milled aluminum from her pocket.

"You never saw me," she said, moving to an unobstructed position in the center of the room. "We'll have to do that lesson another time."

"I'd like that," I said. "Let me give you my glyph."

But she was gone.

16

Have you heard the carpenter's adage "Measure twice, cut once"? Now consider that for you "cutting" may mean your death or that of your passengers. So how many times will you measure your radius? Once? Twice? The answer should be: until you are absolutely certain.

Jessica Littlejohn, *The Ten-Minute Transport*, 1912

I WAS GROUNDED TWO weeks following Cocks and Hens on account of headaches and intermittent dizzy spells. Instead of teaching, I worked in the aerodrome's supply room, filling bags and mending harnesses.

A few of the novices took to sneaking in to visit me, asking to see my bruises and pumping me for details on the secret plan that had nearly beaten Danielle Hardin. Jake chased them out time and again.

"Stop encouraging them!" Jake scolded me.

"She had a question about her rigging," I replied, looking regretfully at the pretty young Two headed back to the classroom.

" 'Oh, Mr. Weekes, could you put your hand right *here* and tell me if my thigh strap seems tight enough?' " Jake said in a simpering little girl voice.

"It was a reasonable—"

"Not one from the aerodrome! There are plenty of respectable Cliffes who wouldn't mind a male philosopher with a few dents."

Not that Jake seemed to be putting much effort into finding me one.

I trudged fifteen minutes back to campus, my harness and a half-filled powder bag slung over one shoulder—I would be back on regular duty the next morning. The sunset was huge and orange. The chill of the first week of October hung in the air.

As I passed the Gray Box, I saw a group of women gathered by the west side of the building, pointing at something.

"She's going to jump," said a young lady.

"No, she's not," scoffed another. "She's having a pout and wants us to notice."

A three-foot-high brick lip ran around the edge of the library's roof. Someone was sitting on it, her legs dangling over the edge.

"It's Ida," said the first woman. "That Harvard boy she's been seeing proposed to a society girl from South Carolina. She said if she couldn't be with her one true love—"

"Don't be ridiculous," the second broke in. "It's the Hero of the Hellespont."

"What's she got to sulk about?" asked the first.

"Maybe the pastry shop ran out of doughnuts," retorted the second, to a general titter of laughter.

If it were a young lady contemplating ending her life, I might be able to talk her down, or barring that, grab her before she jumped. If it were Dardanelles—well, she'd suggested she might not mind seeing me again. Of course, if she decided she wanted a rematch, *I'd* probably end up as the body hurtling off the roof.

I walked around to the opposite side of the building, put on my gear, and took a short, low-angle hop up top, setting down as quietly as I could.

The whole building had a golden sheen to it, as if the trace of bronze powder that had been mixed into the concrete—intended to prevent any philosophical accidents from leaking out of the building—was catching the light. On the far side, silhouetted against the setting sun, sat the young lady. I stole toward her in a crouch.

She glanced over her shoulder at me. It was the Hero of the Hellespont indeed.

I smiled inwardly.

"Hi," I said. "Don't be startled. There's an old—"

"Don't," she said. "There are people watching."

"I know," I said.

"They talk. They see me together with anyone, they talk. You don't need that sort of trouble."

Far be it from me to go looking for trouble. Still crouching, I duck-walked up to the ledge, screened from view by the wall. Not a bad place to meditate, other than the drop. And the occasional shouts, alternately concerned and sarcastic, from the ground.

"It doesn't look the same," Dardanelles said, her back to me.

"Pardon?"

"The sun. It was bigger over there. Redder."

"At Gallipoli?"

"On the island," she said. "On Imbros. The generals brought us over and then they got cold feet about the evacuation. They needed four months to decide. We sat there the whole time."

"That's a long wait," I said.

"It was excruciating. We played five-handed mudge all day long, endless games that we were too exhausted to finish. Then the sun would finally set over the Aegean and we would all go out to watch. One hundred twenty-eight times."

"That's why you're up here?" I asked. "To see the sunset?"

"Yes. And to be alone. And to think. I've come up a few times and no one ever noticed. But now I've made a spectacle of myself."

She swung her legs around, climbed down, and sat beside me. The scent of crushed jasmine and lavender clung to her. A smokecarved perfume, perhaps. Those could be dangerous—under the influence of some of the heavier fragrances, you might have to be forcibly removed from the wearer's bosom. And Dardanelles had quite a nice one, I couldn't help but notice, as her blouse's collar flapped in the wind, revealing a lacy undergarment beneath.

She put a hand over her chest.

"People keep paying me the nicest compliments for thumping you," she said. "I've thumped a few men in my day, but never anyone coming up to me on the street and saying, 'Oh, well done!'"

"I must have had it coming," I said. "My sisters always told me I had it coming when they thumped me."

She smiled at that. "I can scarcely imagine. That must be what made you so brave—a lot of women beating courage into you."

Her hair rippled in the wind. A few strands stuck in my mouth when I opened it to reply.

"You mean Cocks and Hens?" I asked.

"Yes," she said. "And pulling Nancy out of the river. And just going to the aerodrome every day knowing that some of the women will hate you for doing it."

Nobody had ever said the last to me in as many words.

"Thank you," I said.

"I wondered if you might—" Danielle began. "Well, do you know about the march tomorrow?"

I didn't.

Danielle and a small delegation of Radcliffe women were headed to Washington to march in protest of the Zoning Act. The Trencher sympathizers in Congress reintroduced it every year: a bill to make the practice of philosophy illegal, except in explicitly defined zones that each state legislature would choose and only then for philosophers licensed in each glyph. Sending a message might be prohibited on one side of the street, but legal on the other. You would have to carry one card in your wallet to transport, another to fly, more for ignite glyphs and stases and korus. Absurd. But plenty of people liked the idea and each time it came closer to passing.

"The Corps always organized against it in the past," Danielle explained, "but this year, with so many women overseas, the professional sigilrists' unions had to step up in their place. They asked me to be one of the grand marshals."

"That's terrific," I said.

Dardanelles shook her head. "I went to one a few years ago and there were fifteen thousand women. It really impressed me. But we'll be lucky to have a tenth of that tomorrow. Plus, no trained killers in uniform to scare off the counter-protestors. It's going to be ugly."

"You think it'll turn violent?" I asked.

"It might. The threats have been . . . graphic."

I narrowed my eyes at that. "Trenchers?"

"Of course. And Maxwell Gannet is sending his disciples down to Washington in droves."

"Lord," I said. "I used to think he was a boogeyman that my sister made up to scare me. 'Behave yourself or Max Gannet will chop off your fingers and stew them for his supper.' "

"Oh, he's real," Danielle assured me. "He's never the one to throw the rocks, never the one to tell his followers to do it in as many words. It's all innuendo and insinuation from him—until one of his fanatics comes out shooting. Though, you're from Montana, right? You probably know all about that. All those attacks last summer. Were any of them close to you?"

"One of them was," I said. "I saw . . ."

I hadn't told anyone about it since coming out East. Not that I didn't trust my classmates, but Radcliffe felt like a different life sometimes.

"What did you see?" Danielle asked.

"My ma's a county philosopher," I said. "She got called for an evacuation. She didn't know what she was flying into and brought me to help. It was four philosophers murdered. Two of them were children."

"Oh my God," Dar breathed.

"Yeah," I said. "Then all summer long, one side behaved worse than the other. I think it's settled down, finally."

She nodded.

"You'd understand better than most, then," she said. "I came up here to worry about tomorrow."

"I can imagine," I said.

"I was wondering, too—well, whether you might like to come with me. You'd confuse a lot of people, which I would enjoy. And God knows we could use more bodies."

I tried to decide whether she'd just asked me on a date.

"I'm supposed to teach tomorrow morning," I said. "A bunch of Zeds, all hopeless cases. But maybe when you get back, you could tell me how it went? Over a cup of tea or a dish of ice cream or . . ."

"Are you asking me out?" she said, a smile tugging at the corner of her mouth.

"No, just—" And then I sat up straighter. "Yes."

Danielle looked amused, but her eyes blazed with an unexpected warmth, too.

"I'll probably be in a terrible mood when I get back. But, yes, you can buy me a glass of beer and I'll tell you about it."

She smoothed her hands over her trousers. "May I offer you a lift down?" She pulled a double-sealed tube of powdered aluminum from her handbag, opened the outer container, and snapped off the top of the inner ampoule.

"Well, now," I said, flinching away from her. "I don't want to say I'm a nervous transportee, but . . ."

"Don't move," she said.

Danielle drew a complicated sigil and then we were simply in one of the basement cubicles in the Gray Box. On the floor beneath me there was a film of sand.

I was too shocked to be terrified. Usually a transporter making a short hop extended her bubble an extra foot or two to ensure the edge didn't injure her passengers. Danielle hadn't bothered—if she had, she would have taken a chunk of the roof along for the ride, plus a good-sized piece of the wall we'd been leaning against. All she'd brought for a safety margin was a fraction of a fraction of an inch. She was either damn reckless or the finest transporter alive.

I inspected the seat of my pants and the soles of my shoes. They were intact.

"You don't have to count your toes," Dardanelles said archly. "I *am* a professional."

Outside the room a sign read: TRANSPORT DESTINATION ZONE. KEEP AWAY! EXTREME DANGER!

That was as prescient a warning about Danielle Hardin as anyone could have ever offered.

17

While smokescreens had often been used to cover retreats or annoy the enemy, Mrs. Cadwallader took the unusual step of veiling her own force during its advance on the Korps des Philosophs regiments besieging Paris in 1871. She kept the screen in place throughout the ensuing twenty-one-minute battle, even as the fighting temporarily became desperate, with her women unable to see the enemy. But Cadwallader's strategy succeeded in hiding her numbers: not until hours after the Prussian surrender did Field Marshal von Moltke realize that his ten thousand rauchbauers had been defeated by only two hundred corpswomen.

Victoria Ferris-Smythe, *Empirical Philosophy: An American History*, 1938

MY ZEDS THE NEXT morning flew better than I'd expected, but one of Tillie's Ones wandered off into the clouds. It took Tillie, Essie, and me two hours to find her and coax her down. She landed with a scant ounce of powder left in her bag. Even Essie was yelling by the end.

"Damn it!" Tillie said to me once everyone was back on the ground. "Brock's going to kill me for almost losing another one."

"How the hell did she get all the way up there?" I asked, pointing at the cloud cover. "That's eight thousand feet!"

"I don't know," said Tillie. "I don't want to know. If I have to say one more word to her, I'm going to stab her."

"Okay," I said, "so how about I check your girls back in and you can take a few minutes to—"

A large group of women materialized on the landing field fifty yards away from us.

There were several hundred of them, shouting and screaming. Many held signs on sticks. One read: NO ZONE, NO WAY. Another: A VETERAN IS A VETERAN. A few wore Corps uniforms; others were in long, modest dresses that had been ripped and muddied. Nearly all had cuts or scrapes on their arms and faces. One lay on the ground naked and sobbing, with several women trying to wrap a coat around her shoulders. Near her, four or five other bodies were sprawled out, motionless. Beside them, a man was screaming out the most terrible insults, while a group of women brandished walking sticks and cudgels at him. A riderless horse climbed to its feet and went galloping away.

"What in God's name . . . ?" Tillie said.

We ran over to investigate. I spotted Danielle, pushing her way out from the center of the crowd, looking thin and shaky. Her worst fears about the march seemed to have come true.

"Danielle!" I shouted to her. "How can we help?"

Her eyes fluttered as she staggered toward me. "Get the wounded to the hospital," she said. "And could you possibly do something about *him*?"

The Trencher, who didn't seem to care that he was outnumbered several hundred to one, was right back at it. "Whores!" he shouted. "If you were my wife I'd whip you till you knew your place. Prostituting yourself with those effeminate French, spreading your legs for those bloody German butchers—"

I walked up to the man and tapped him on the shoulder. He turned toward me and I punched him in the side of the face, my full weight behind the blow. He crumpled like his string of life had been cut. The man was about sixty, thin as a stork. He'd been wearing glasses that were now lying in pieces beside him on the ground.

"Shit," I muttered. But too late to take it back.

I had a look at the most gravely wounded women. Three were unconscious. They looked like they'd been attacked—bruised, trampled, beaten.

Another with a bullet wound in her abdomen, writhing in pain. One with a hole in her chest, blood bubbling out every time she breathed. Plus two with legs broken too severely to walk, one head wound so bad that most of her scalp had peeled back from her skull, and one broken nose with fragments of bone pushing through the skin. So, nine bad enough to evacuate by air. Plus the old man, who hadn't moved since I'd hit him.

"Let's get silver chloride over here!" I called.

Between purses and workbags, we found five tubes; I used half measures to stasis the worst off. My indicator strips returned at twenty minutes of stasis time.

"Harnesses!" I shouted to Essie. "We're taking ten to the hospital by air."

"We're doing *what*?" Essie answered. But she got the Ones out of their harnesses and they began putting them on the stasied women.

"Robert, there's three of us and ten of them," Essie said.

"Get me the rope bag!" I yelled to one of Tillie's novices.

I daisy-chained four of the stasied women together with straps, one to the next to the next. I would carry them as what we called a stringer. It was a dangerous configuration—the passengers would stream out forty feet behind me and swing like a pendulum every time I maneuvered. But I didn't see an alternative. I would have taken more, but four passengers put me right up against my weight limit.

"Have you ever flown a stringer before?" Essie asked.

"Sure," I said. "A couple times. With sandbags instead of people."

I clipped the last stasied woman into place. I could hear Tillie yelling at Danielle.

"You come blasting right in!" Tillie shouted. "No warning. No check. You could have ripped apart my girls! I know that's not how they teach transporting in the Corps."

Dardanelles was in tears. "I'm sorry," she kept saying.

"Why didn't you take them straight to the hospital?" Tillie asked.

Dardanelles tried to compose herself. "If you have a tube of aluminum . . .

I'll try." She was barely on her feet. It was only a few miles to Massachusetts General Hospital, but in her condition another transport could kill her.

"No tube!" I barked. "Tillie, two to fly."

Tillie nodded—she'd never in her life not flown someone who needed it. We rigged Essie with two of the stasied casualties and then I helped Tillie buckle into the next pair.

"I'll take the last two," said Dardanelles, who looked a bit steadier now. She was putting on one of the extra harnesses. "I know how to fly. I've had passengers before."

Well, if she was willing, a few minutes of hovering shouldn't harm her, not like even a short transport could. That just left the other eight dozen less critically injured. I dashed off a message to Boston's general police response glyph, so that they could arrange rides.

"Okay," I called out. "Miss Blackroot, as the senior flier, we're on you."

"Up as you will," Tillie said. "We'll keep above two hundred feet so Robert doesn't hit anything with that line. Mass General. Let's go!" She launched and the rest of us followed.

I got off the ground without too much difficulty, but when I turned to match course with Tillie, my stringer, with six hundred pounds of passengers and rigging on it, swung wildly. It pulled me off the level and I slipped back toward the ground. I slammed my regulator on full and redrew.

"Come on," I grunted.

My sigil took and I began to climb again. I followed, flying full out to keep up. The hospital was barely a two-minute trip by air, right in the middle of the crowded downtown streets. The landing field was marked on the roof instead of the ground.

"You've got to be kidding," I whispered.

A rooftop landing zone saved space, but it exposed incoming hoverers to all kinds of cross breezes. And if you missed . . .

Tillie, Essie, and Dardanelles landed ahead of me—though Danielle flinched on her approach and had to do a double dip to get down. I braked hard to give her room.

My stringer twisted and swung, yanking me forward and then back. I redrew and my sigil failed entirely.

I began to fall as the sigil's residual power faded.

"Come on!" I growled, redrawing again.

I was dropping straight toward the apartment building next to the hospital.

"Come on!"

I drew a third time. It didn't work. The last stasied body in line smashed into the apartment building's roof, punching through it and sending a shower of slate shingles into the street below. The second body hit, followed by the third.

I drew a final time at maximum power. Somehow, the glyph took and we inched upward. I tried to catch my breath. Well, it wouldn't hurt my passengers, though I saw a shocked-looking face staring up at me through the hole I'd knocked in the ceiling of his sixth-floor apartment.

I brought us down on the hospital ceiling, settling my four wounded into a twisted heap and myself beside them. Essie, Tillie, and Danielle were all watching me, their faces white as talc.

After we'd gotten the stasied on stretchers, after the police had arrived with nine vanloads of minor injuries, after too many doctors and nurses to count had berated me on some violation of protocol in running a mass-casualty evacuation, and after I had been interviewed by a detective baffled as to how a man could possibly fly, I found Dardanelles still on the hospital roof, slumped beside the door. She had her face in her hands.

"I thought you were dead when you went down," she said to me.

"Yeah, well, I've been told I'm too stupid to die," I replied.

I sat beside her. "Are you okay?" I asked.

"I'll live," she said. "Some of the ones we brought won't."

"What happened?" I asked her. "The march?"

"Everything went wrong. There were only six hundred of us, against every last diehard Trencher in the mid-Atlantic—plus railroad men, sailors on leave, millworkers. Anyone interested in shaking up a few girls. Thousands of them."

"Jesus," I said.

"The public safety commissioner had told us outright that if you provoke the Trenchers, you deserve the consequences. So, there were barely any police along the route. Most of the ones who did turn out watched from the sidelines and cheered. We didn't even get lined up before the crowd started throwing beer bottles. They were yelling about what they would do to us. I thought it was just to scare us, but then some of them started exposing themselves. They got hold of a couple of women. They ripped their clothes off."

"My God," I whispered.

"I was on a float right in the middle of our group. I could see everything, but I couldn't do anything to stop it. I was just standing there, screaming and praying that good sense would break out, that twenty men weren't going to rape a woman in the street with a thousand witnesses looking on. But they only egged one another on. The women who had walking sticks or clubs tried to beat them back. And then it was just a brawl everywhere."

She looked at me with a flat expression of hopelessness. She was so far beyond tears or reassurance that I couldn't think of what to say.

"How did you get out?" I asked.

"The smokecarvers came prepared. Some of them had canisters in their purses with smokescreens. They threw them out at the perimeter. You never saw men run so fast, climbing right over one another. Some had stronger stuff—stink gas or tear gas—and they streamed that out, too. It threw the Trenchers into an even bigger panic. A few of them fired into the middle of us with guns. Then I heard shouting for transporters to measure lines. Anna Blackwell—you've heard of her, right?"

"No."

"One of the organizers. She pulled me down off the float and told me to evacuate the first group because I could draw the widest field. Take as many as I could. Our other transporters would move the rest. I had string and a stick of chalk in my handbag, so I walked off a twenty-foot radius. I was combining tubes that people had in their handbags or stuck in their brassieres to get enough powder. We packed in as many women as we could. We were in pretty good order. The other transporters were setting up their bubbles, too. And then the cavalry came crashing through."

"*What* happened?"

"Blackwell's a veteran. She saved a man's life in Cuba. He's a general now at Fort Myer, just across the river in Virginia. She warned him that there might be trouble, so he took two hundred cavalrymen and camped in one of the parks in Washington. In case something went wrong. Blackwell was messaging him the whole time."

I winced. "And he showed up at the wrong moment?"

"They charged the Trenchers with swords drawn. But that drove them right back across the smokescreen and into us. I was yelling to clear the edge and suddenly I had another hundred women scrambling over the red line with Trenchers right behind them. I eyeballed it. I wasn't sure I would have enough range. But the Trenchers were yanking cavalrymen off their horses. So I did it."

"And thank God you did."

"No!" Danielle sobbed. "I didn't dress my lines. I didn't check for a clear destination. If I didn't kill anyone or take off somebody's arm, that's sheer dumb luck."

"I didn't see any loose arms. Or heads."

"I cratered the street to a depth of thirty feet. I left behind two hundred people. I left behind Patrice—she and I went together and promised we'd each make sure the other got home safe."

"Danielle—"

"I was so stupid." She was slurring her words. "We had destination sigils set up in Washington, but I couldn't find my black book. I drew the first destination I could remember. I practiced down there on the field by the aerodrome every day my freshman year. Back and forth, across the river. The day I die, my corpse will still be able to shape those glyphs. So, I jumped us from Washington to Boston because it was the only place I could think of."

"That's four hundred miles," I said.

"I lost twelve pounds. It's too much at once."

And suddenly it all made sense—the odd greenish pallor to her skin, the breathlessness, the look of hopeless exhaustion. Not hysteria or anger, not even philosophical fatigue of the sort I'd suffered on the night I evacuated the Kleins. Rather, acute transporting toxicity.

"You need a doctor, too, then!" I said. "Let me get you down—"

"No!" Danielle pleaded. "No more hospitals. You can't force me. If I didn't collapse already, it's not going to kill me."

She would know best, but she looked dreadful. I thought of the old cures: foods rich in potassium and calcium and dense with calories.

"Stay here a minute," I said.

I flew down to a market on the street below and tore out the lining of my skysuit's sleeve where I kept a ten-dollar bill sewn in case of emergency. I bought a chocolate cake, a sack of oranges, a bunch of bananas, a couple quarts of mineral water, and a pint of milk.

"What's all this?" Dardanelles asked when I returned. She looked like she was dying.

"You have to eat," I said. "Isn't that how it works?"

"I can't," she said. "I feel sick."

I peeled an orange for her. I wasn't even hungry and the smell was marvelous. "Just a couple pieces and I'll fly you home."

I handed her a section, which she bit into and chewed mechanically. Once she'd started, she wolfed down the rest of the orange, then a couple more and most of the bananas. I cut the cake with my belt knife and she ate three slices, washing it down with the milk and both bottles of water. By that time she looked much improved, but was nodding off midbite.

"I hate eating like that so much," she muttered. "I know I should do it, but I hate it."

"I'll take you home," I said.

"I'll take myself," she murmured, but didn't complain when I stood her up and attached her to my chest. "You don't have to put me—it's better if I ride in back, right?"

"No, it's not," I said. I wasn't going to have her develop a case of rear-facing motion sickness and throw up all over me.

I made the flight back a gentle one and Danielle fell asleep from the slow rocking motion. I had to wake her as I came in low over Cambridge to ask directions to her apartment. We set down in the street and the neighbors appeared at their windows to stare.

Danielle could barely stand. "Let me guess, twelfth floor," I said.

"Second," she said. "My window's shut though."

I smiled at that—it was a very dramatic idea of how a hoverer preferred to get into a building.

"Flying through a window is a stupid, stupid risk," I said. "You can hit your head or catch your bag on the sash. But, if you'd put your arm around my neck . . ."

I picked her up and carried her.

"You're going to hurt yourself," she said as I staggered up the stairs and around the corner on the landing between floors.

"Am not," I said between gritted teeth. "You're just . . . a little . . . slip of a thing."

A little slip who weighed almost as much as I did. And I'd been living the easy life, lifting a few powder bags, but nothing like the sort of work I'd been used to at home. I was getting soft.

I set her down and she unlocked the door, holding on to the knob for support. "I never even thanked you," she said.

"Let me take you out to dinner," I suggested.

"I have to eat dinner twice. You want to take me out the first time or the second?"

"Both."

18

The coach swerves back in the other direction. "Give me a good strong Eupheus," I shout to our sigilrist, "and overlay a powerful burst each three seconds!"

"What good will that do?" she cries.

"It will buffet us until we travel straight!" I answer. Or it will buffet her right out of the cockpit, which seems not a bad result, either.

Edwin Fitzenhalter, *Fresh Gale on the High Sonora*, 1888

"I GOT A MESSAGE that the Trencher you knocked out woke up," Danielle remarked between spoonfuls of banana pudding. "He spit at Mass General's medical philosopher and demanded a transfer to a different hospital."

Danielle took a long drink from a glass of milk and began dismantling a slice of apple pie. She'd recovered well from the morning's ordeal and had chosen the dining hall for her first dinner, a bold decision for a woman who'd traveled four hundred miles under her own power in a single day and had to eat like it. Sitting alone with me would only worsen the gossip. She didn't seem to care.

"May I express my gratitude again for the way you dealt with him?" she said.

I examined my right hand, on which I'd split open two knuckles. I didn't regret hitting the frail little man, only that I hadn't struck him a little more gently.

"I was afraid I'd killed him," I said.

"Nasty old men like him live to two hundred," said Danielle with a shake of her head. "What kind of punch was it?"

"What?"

"Like a cross or a jab or what? I'm going to have to describe the whole thing to my dad. He loves boxing and it's the kind of detail—"

"A wild punch like that is a haymaker," I said.

Danielle tipped her head to one side and practiced the line: "A dark, handsome man came out of nowhere and flattened him with a haymaker."

"Nobody's going to believe the handsome part," I said.

"Oh, please. You have quite the collection of young ladies who fan themselves at the mention of your name. If Rachael Rodgers had made you perform that striptease, you would have had a big audience."

The incident still made me seethe. "That's not how it—"

"I'm sorry," Danielle said. "It would make me mad, too, the way people talk about it."

But the idea had tickled her and she tried and failed to hide a smile behind her spoon. "It's just that I might have bought a ticket, is all."

It was an opening for a risqué rejoinder—something about a repeat performance or being available for private engagements. But I couldn't quite find the words.

Danielle yawned.

"I should thank you for running that evacuation, too," she added. "You really could try for R&E. You're the one who's always talking about it, right?"

"A couple times," I said.

"Well, what you did today—I don't think they're that efficient in France, even. Have you done that before?"

"Not really," I said. "But my mother was forever putting questions to us like that. A dozen wounded and two fliers: which ones do you take first, which ones go in stasis."

"Is your mom a veteran?" Dardanelles asked.

"Cuba and the Philippines. And Hawaii. And France, the first time, in

'71." I explained a little about my upbringing and our frequently unconventional dinner table conversations.

In return, Danielle told me about her first lessons in sigilry, in grade school. She'd shown immense talent, much to the surprise of her parents, neither of whom was philosophical. (Her mother came from a wealthy Tunisian family that had made its fortune building sailing ships; her dad was an old-money Yankee blue blood who'd become a minister largely because his father had forbidden it.) They'd told Danielle that sigilry was a gift from God, no different from mathematics or sculpture, and she should pursue it with her full energy.

From the beginning, Danielle had been fascinated by the transport sigil. A philosophical family would never have allowed her to try it until after puberty—it took an awful toll on the developing body and the chance of death or destruction if the sigils went awry was enormous. But her parents had found a series of private tutors willing to teach her. Danielle had run her first transport at the age of eight, taken her father as her first passenger a year later.

Danielle saw me cringe at that.

"Appalling, I know," she said. "But my parents understood enough to protect me. They wouldn't allow me to transport farther than I could walk in an afternoon. So, on my eighth birthday, I took my dad and hiked from Providence to Warwick, which was nine miles. And for years, nine miles was the longest I ever went. Not that it makes a difference—if you can go ten feet, you could cross the Pacific, though you'd burn up your heart doing it."

Danielle had been less interested in long-distance transportation than high-geometry. She'd learned how to shape the transport field so that it was squared off, rather than spherical, then how to make it irregular, clinging to an arm or a foot, a hair's breadth from the body. She'd practiced incessantly to extend her radius, switching acres of uninhabited woodland with each other and then putting them back. It had required huge amounts of philosophical energy to move that much territory, but, since she was covering only a few miles, very little weight.

She'd come to Radcliffe at seventeen to hone her abilities and had won a well-deserved reputation for being arrogant and hotheaded—and for being the best transporter in New England. By her junior year, she'd become fed up with the school's prim distaste for working sigilrists and had stormed out of her final exams to join the Corps, hoping that her talents might be better employed there. Instead, she'd been badly misused, moving supplies to France over the long jumps on the transatlantic chain, leaving her feeling sick and weak. When the British had inquired, she'd gladly accepted duty at Gallipoli.

"Transporting 250,000 men fifteen miles is what I was born to do," she said. "But I kept asking why we hadn't done it two years earlier, instead of letting them languish on the beaches. Or why not move them five miles beyond the Turkish lines and let them smash through from the rear? For that matter, why not move the troops straight to Constantinople? Or Berlin?"

"Why?" I asked.

"Because they're afraid of us! When they passed the Rouen Conventions in '80, they weren't forbidding military sigilry out of concern for the welfare of soldiers, or to reduce bloodshed, or promote the common good. It was a lot of old men trying to prevent philosophers from taking power."

"But even Lucretia Cadwallader argued for the Conventions," I objected. "She wrote about a thousand letters, made that famous speech to Congress—"

"Ah!" said Danielle, looking pleased that I'd disagreed. "You're right. And it came from a good place in her, a humane place—*I don't want to see my life's work used to kill.* God knows she saw it taken to the extreme in the Franco-Prussian War when the Germans tried to smother Paris. But she didn't argue to ban smokecarving from warfare, she argued to ban *all* philosophy. It was an overreach. It started the age of outlawing sigilry: can't hover at the train station, no philosophy in the Atlanta public schools, shut down the Church of Christ Philosopher for promoting immoral behavior. From there, it's a short walk to the Zoning Act."

"Now, the Act is just inconceivable to me," I said.

"Then you're being lazy. It's easy to understand."

The fervor with which she said it made it sound not insulting.

"Let me ask it like this," Danielle said. "If you could ban bonekilling, would you?"

That was a sigil that had come of age in the Philippines, a method of killing both horrible and intimate: draw the glyph on your victim's skin and her bones dissolved instantly. The resulting wet sack of blood and tissue collapsed to the ground, suffocating without ribs to expand the chest, all the body's muscles contracting into tight quivering balls that went on fasciculating for hours.

"I don't need to ban it," I said. "Murder's already illegal."

Danielle raised her palms to concede the point, but I saw her expression change, as if I'd revealed something in my answer. "Then, I'll ask the question I should have: How old were you when you learned it? And who taught you?"

I was taken aback by that. I took it for granted that every serious philosopher knew how and that no one would ever discuss it.

"I was eleven," I said. "Nobody taught me—just the opposite. It was in a book that my mother and sisters always told me never to read, it was absolutely forbidden."

"Yet they never locked it up or hid it?"

I nodded.

"I was ten," Danielle said. "Then literally the week after I saw a picture of the glyph, a girl at school said something to me and I decided to kill her. Because you can't unremember that sigil—it's only five lines. I went to the chemist's shop down the street, plunked down a silver dollar, and said, 'A tube of sulfur and bone meal, if you please,' like it was the sort of thing I did all the time. The chemist, who knew my dad, said maybe I ought to talk it over with him first. I did, and Dad said sometimes we have to suffer the little children. So I didn't kill her. But here's my question: Would you sell sulfur and bone meal to a ten-year-old?"

"He didn't have it behind the counter," I said. "He was putting you on. Harnemon's doesn't carry it, either."

Danielle was grinning. "Now you're just being literal to annoy me."

"What did she call you?" I asked.

"A name."

"What—"

"A fat, miscegenated harlot."

"I'll kill her for you now, if you like," I suggested.

"Very kind of you. But if you were the chemist behind the counter and I—"

"No," I said. "I wouldn't sell you the powder."

"See! You admit it! And you feel like a traitor to other philosophers for even suggesting that a few regulations might be a good idea."

"That really happened?"

"Exactly as I said. But now that you admit it, it's a short walk. Is it reasonable or unreasonable to prevent your neighbor, who happens to be a smoke-carver, from stockpiling a thousand cubic feet of incendiary material in her basement? And don't give me, 'Well, what kind of tank does she use to—' "

It was a good imitation of my voice at its dimmest.

"Reasonable," I said.

"And if I require paperwork from every hack driver who owns two horses and a cab, what about a license for a flier who takes passengers within the city limits? Or a transporter who runs crosstown service? Reasonable or unreasonable?"

"Reasonable."

"Then you've got common ground with the men trying to pass the Zoning Act. And so do I! It's just a matter of where you draw the line. If we want to prevent them from banning philosophy outright, then we have to engage them: editorials, debates, conversations at dinner parties, marches. That's what I want to do. It's what you ought to be doing, too."

"I think I punched the last one instead of having a debate."

"Not him! Not the Trenchers tearing the skirts off elderly ladies. Not Max Gannet's fanatics. Sometimes you have no choice but to meet force with force. But you? As a man? You'll have lots of chances to convince other men."

I must have looked uncomfortable at the prospect.

"If you don't—if you and I hang back and do what's comfortable, if philosophers wall themselves off and only associate with other philosophers, then the Zoning Act is going to sneak through and we'll all shake our heads and say, 'How did it happen?' I tell you, if we don't fight now, with every breath of air in our lungs and every ounce of powder in our hands, we'll be the last generation of philosophers."

I looked at her and I believed it. She was ready to go to war and I was ready to follow her.

"I'll have to march with you next time, then," I said.

Danielle smiled. "I hope you do."

She blinked so slow and long that I thought she might fall asleep at the table.

"Are you really up for a second dinner?" I asked.

She pressed the heels of her hands into her eyes. "Oh, don't even talk about that! I feel like I'm going to burst. I'll go home, sleep a few hours, and then run out at midnight to eat a pile of sandwiches somewhere. Don't feel obligated."

"If you'd rather not take me . . ." I suggested.

She shook her head. "I hate going out alone at that hour."

"Well, I haven't been out at all in Boston. I'd consider it a favor."

"You're doing this to be kind?" she asked.

"No."

"Because you think you're in love with me?" She said it in a way that suggested it had happened more than once.

"I barely know you," I said. "But I'd like to."

That seemed to placate her. "I'll send you a message about eleven thirty," she said. "Just say no if you're not interested. No hard feelings."

I didn't have any second thoughts, just a lot of nerves. No way around it— I was sweet on her. Worse than Unger pining over Dizzy, even. I couldn't go two minutes without checking my message board and wondering why she hadn't written yet. By midnight, I'd decided that Danielle must have forgotten about me. Or, it was a deliberate snub, she'd been so exhausted that she'd never woken up, she'd fallen and injured herself, she'd been called away on secret business for the Corps, President Wilson had needed her opinion on vital matters of national interest, or her father the minister had dropped in for a surprise visit. Probably all of them. At 12:02 she messaged to ask if I was still interested.

Yes, I answered. Then I damned myself for not waiting long enough to look decent. Make her sweat a little in return, not that she seemed the sweating type. She replied that I should call at her apartment building; she knew a place close by.

As it was a cool night, I put on my gray wool suit, made by the same Billings tailor who'd manufactured the tan linen calamity I'd worn to the freshman social—he'd assured me the suits were cut identically. Yet this one was long enough in the legs and wide enough in the shoulders so that I didn't look like I was wearing a younger cousin's church clothes.

It was all I could do not to put on my harness, too, and fly over, or, barring that, to run. But some degree of self-control was called for. Brisk walk, ten minutes. I rang up to her apartment and Danielle came down wearing a light coat over a black dress, which, while modestly long, swooped down at the neckline, exposing a great scoop of chest.

"Hi," I said, trying not to stare.

"Hi, yourself," she said. "You didn't have to dress up."

"You did," I said. "You look beautiful."

Danielle grimaced. "It's all wrong. I don't have a thing to wear when I'm this chicken-necked."

She buttoned her coat and took my arm. "Besides, that means a lot coming from you. You look like you're dressed for a funeral."

That rankled. Some of us didn't have two family fortunes to spend on our wardrobe.

We set out, arriving a few minutes later at the Widow's Waggle, a nightclub named for a kite jockey maneuver. The place was decorated in a pseudo-Western style, with wagon wheels on the walls and lifter sails on the ceiling. The bar itself was made of doors taken from kite coaches, which had been nailed together and coated in a thick layer of shellac.

The hostess recognized Dardanelles and led us to a table in a secluded nook beside the bandstand, where a sextet played a slow, reflective tune. It was music for listening, not dancing.

I couldn't help but notice that all the musicians were black. Having grown up in one of the whitest states in the Union, this struck me as extraordinary.

"Don't think I've ever sat this close to a bunch of colored folk before," I remarked.

Danielle glared at me, livid. "You must *really* be country to say that in front of me. Now you get to tell the boys back home that you stepped out with a colored girl and she took you to a bar full of Negroes, is that it?"

"No, but you're not—"

"I was born in Africa. My mother is half Arab. You're going to tell me what I am?"

Neither of us breathed for a second.

"I'm sorry," I said. "I didn't mean anything by it."

She set her jaw. "Well, I don't suppose *you'll* mind when I tell the girls back at the country club that I went out with a dumb hick with his head so far up his ass that he doesn't need a pillow. Because most people who make remarks like that *do* mean something by it."

We regarded each other for a long moment. I wondered if it might not be safer to press forward than retreat.

"Could I ask you—how'd your parents meet?"

Somehow, that was a good question, a right question.

"Well, that's complicated," Dardanelles answered. "My dad comes from old New England stock—the Puritans threw one of his forebears out of Plymouth for heresy. After Dad finished divinity school, he went on a grand tour of Europe and got it into his head he wanted to see the site where the city of Carthage used to be. So, he visited Tunis and fell in love with the place. He met my mother and fell in love with her, too."

She took a sip from her water glass.

"Mom's from a venerable Arab family on her mother's side—not that they've had any real power in two hundred years—and a French count on her father's. Mom was his illegitimate daughter. That was a whole different scandal."

I was duly impressed.

"So, Mom and Dad got married and lived in Tunisia for five years," Danielle continued. "That's where I was born. Then Dad inherited a lot of property back in Providence and the three of us moved to the States. Even in a church as progressive as Dad's, there was no end to the innuendos. The society ladies whispering behind their gloves when they didn't think I could hear. They had lots of names for me. You're going to sit there and tell me I'm not colored, then what would you call me?"

"Sophisticated as hell," I said.

That surprised her just enough to win a faint smile.

"French counts and inheritances and ancient cities," I went on. "I never knew my pa—he died when I was two. I never really lived anywhere but Montana. Probably on account of my head being so far up my ass."

That got me a real smile.

"Well, I didn't mean anything by that, either, then," Danielle said.

Our waiter came. Danielle ordered cheese toasts, eight watercress sandwiches, a chicken salad, an ice cream sundae, and a glass of porter. The waiter was unperturbed—either they got a lot of transporters or he was well trained.

"And you, sir?" he asked me.

"I'll have the same," I said.

"Oh, for God's sake!" Danielle said.

"What?" I said. "My sister told me if I'm ever in a restaurant and I'm not sure what to order, especially if the menu is in a foreign language, just say 'I'll have the same.' "

"You couldn't ask for a plainer menu! Or don't you have chicken salad in Montana?"

"Touché," I said.

"Hah! You can play the rube, but your French is better than mine!"

Was it possible I hadn't ruined the night after all?

"My real concern," I explained, "is that they might have a smokecarver in the kitchen. No telling what you'll get—ice cream that tastes like a snake egg omelet."

"There isn't a smokecarver in the kitchen here, I promise," she said. "We'll be lucky if there's so much as a cook."

The glasses of porter arrived and we both took a long drink. I had a little experience with whiskey, but almost none with beer. The stuff was bitter and thick enough to stand a spoon up in.

"Tell me you've never really eaten a snake egg omelet," Danielle said. She wiped foam from her lip with the back of her hand.

"Not me," I said. "It was Blind Doyle who always said he'd rather collect rattlesnake eggs enough for dinner than face up to his second wife when he came home drunk at two in the afternoon."

"It was who that said what?"

This necessitated a digression a quarter hour in length, explaining the character and wisdom of Blind Doyle, the oracle of Billings, who sat in his rocking chair in front of Billings' hardware store, sorting bags of mixed nails by touch and dispensing sage remarks.

The cheese toasts came and went and the watercress sandwiches were delivered. In following Angela's advice, I'd ordered the single item on the menu unfamiliar to me: shreds of bitter lettuce on white bread spread with soft sour cheese. I ate one to be polite, but I couldn't understand why anyone would choose such a thing. Danielle, though, tucked into hers with relish. She finished them more quickly than was decent, even for someone who'd covered four hundred miles that morning. I saw her eyeing mine.

"If I were to offer to trade you seven watercress sandwiches for—"

"No," she said. "But you could *give* them to me."

I did.

Chicken salad, bland but edible, followed, and then ice cream sundaes, which were the best part of the meal. Though the porter steadily improved in taste through second and third glasses.

We were both feeling expansive. I told her the life story of my best friend, Willard Gunch; she countered with the sad tale of her tall aunt Sandy. She recalled the time she had transported into the back row of church just in time for her father's sermon; I told her about stealing nephrite jade out of my mother's laboratory. It was her awful koru tutor versus grizzled old Mrs. Rutt, my primary school teacher; Feargus, her family's elderly sheepdog, in counterpoint to Skinner, our champion mouser; her first round of golf against my early handling of a shotgun.

"I'd like to learn," she said. "The Corps pays sharpshooters an extra three dollars a month."

"Then you don't want a shotgun. You need a rifle."

"I'm sure I couldn't tell either from a brass cannon. They installed a shooting range in the basement of the Gray Box when the war broke out. They'll let you check out a gun for target practice."

"So, let's go sometime," I suggested.

"Really?" she said. "I already almost killed you once."

"We can stop the lessons when you get good enough to hit me. Otherwise folks will say, 'Poor old Boober, shot down in his prime by the deadeye Dardan—' I mean, Danielle. I mean, what do you like to go by?"

She scraped with her spoon at the layer of fudge on the bottom of her glass dish. "Call me Bill or call me Sue, just don't call me late for supper."

"Okay, Bill," I said. "I just thought you must hate the nicknames."

"I do. But I hated them more when I was trying to get people to stop. Dar I don't mind. It was a pet name when I was a girl."

She'd caught me by the eyes and I couldn't look away. Neither of us could. "Dar," I said, trying the name on for size.

Like an incantation, the word melted the lining of my chest and it all dripped down into my belly. Nothing philosophical about it, just good old-fashioned magic.

"Do you like it better?" I whispered.

"Better than what?" she asked.

She leaned in close. I waited a long moment, afraid to speak. Afraid of what another word might do.

"Danielle," I said.

She cocked her head a fraction of an inch to the right. "First one again?" I could feel her breath, warm on my face.

"Dar."

Our lips touched. Once, twice. Hungry, curious, open.

We leaned back and for a minute there was no need to say anything.

"Robert," she said finally. But whatever cantrip had been in the air was gone; names no longer held erotic power. Or perhaps it was just *my* name. She laughed. "You were never anything but plain old Robert?"

"Weekes," I said.

"That's even worse! What did you call yourself before? When you were gunned down in your prime?"

"Robert," I lied.

At a quarter past two we paid our checks. I walked her to the door of her building.

"That was really nice," she said. "Even if it was just the Wag."

"Yup," I said.

She clasped my hands between hers. "Good night."

I said, "Good night, Dar."

And it happened again! The enchanted name working its spell. A slow, lingering kiss, our lips tentative and conversant:

Really?

Really.

Me, too.

We separated, giddy, my hands still enveloped in hers. "Good night, Robert," she said, hiccupping as she pronounced it.

"Please," I said. "Give me a new name. Anything."

She brushed her fingers down my throat and took hold of my lapel, keeping me near for a moment longer. "Plain old Robert sounds just right."

19

Imagine what it was like, back in '61: Cadwallader assembling her Corps, scouring the whole Union for its finest philosophers. And every day for three months, Comfort Tyndale went to Cadwallader's laboratory for an interview. Each day Cadwallader's secretary threw her out with the same words: "We are not enlisting Coloreds." Eighty-eight times. The eighty-ninth time, the secretary was eating lunch and Mrs. Tyndale slipped into Cadwallader's office. No one knows what Tyndale demonstrated for her, but both women came out with singed hair, covered in soot. Mrs. Cadwallader announced: "Any Negro woman who can do the work—take her."

The causes were bound together from the first days: civil rights, women's rights, and philosophical rights.

Rep. Danielle Noor Hardin, Speech on the Second
Zoning Act at Spelman College, March 1, 1926

I FLOATED THROUGH THE rest of the weekend. Then, bright and early Monday morning, the world came to an end.

I was sitting in Empirical Chemistry, reducing walnut ink over a flame and adding iron filings, when all around me the young women went quiet. Then the voice of my instructor, invoking the same warning about explosive demagnetization that I'd heard a thousand times in childhood, stopped, too.

Rachael Rodgers was standing at the door.

"That one," she snarled, pointing at me. "Now!"

Tillie and I had discussed the possibility that Radcliffe's higher-ups might be just a tad upset over our impromptu evacuation of the wounded marchers, though we'd convinced ourselves no real trouble would come from it.

A tear-streaked Essie was waiting in the hall.

"Where are we going?" I asked.

"To Professor Brock," Rachael answered. "This is the end. For all of you."

Rachael led us out of the building, toward the Gray Box and its sub-basements.

"You just don't learn," Rachael said. "Right back at it, you and Miss Priss and that lesbian squaw."

I opened my mouth, but Essie elbowed me.

"Well, you showed us just what kind of incompetent, ungrateful bastard—"

"Stop it!" Essie said. Her voice was small, but had steel behind it. "Fire us if you're going to, but don't speak to him that way."

Rachael went silent, though it didn't stop her from smirking the whole way to the library. We entered and descended five flights of stairs, each one narrower and lower ceilinged than the last. Rachael led us along the poorly lit corridor to Professor Brock's office. Tillie was standing inside, silent. Brock was sitting behind her desk. She looked drained.

"Thank you for collecting them, Miss Rodgers," Brock said. "Why don't you reduplicate those lesson plans and we'll review them in an hour."

"I wanted to stay and see that these—" Rachael began.

"This doesn't concern you. I'll see you in an hour."

We could all but hear the shriek of frustration as Rachael clamped her mouth shut and stormed out.

Brock, thick-necked and coarse-featured, dressed in a heavy, no-nonsense fisherman's sweater, watched the three of us for a long moment. A pump in the bowels of the building kicked on and chugged away. I could feel the vibrations through my feet.

"In the last thirty-six hours," Brock said, "I've had no less than the president of the college, the chief medical officer at Massachusetts General Hospital, and the New England liaison for the Department of the Interior try to tell me how to run my aerodrome: who should be fired, expelled, and charged with attempted murder. That's to say nothing of the dozens of faculty and donors and alumnae—and even the janitor—who've felt compelled to tell me what size sticks I should use to knock some sense into you."

I glanced at Tillie: she didn't even wink. We were in real trouble.

"You violated three different no-fly zones. You made a stringer flight over inhabited territory, to say nothing of a landing that almost killed a man who was sitting at his kitchen table eating breakfast. No message ahead to warn the doctors they had ten critical cases incoming. And you had an eighteen-year-old boy putting broad-spectrum stasis sigils on unconscious women in the middle of a field. Every bit of that is insanity! Except for the intervention of Ms. Addams, all three of you would be sitting in a prison cell instead of in my office."

Essie was weeping quietly.

"All of you are fired," Brock continued. "The rest of the Threes are fired. The whole aerodrome is grounded, one week, effective immediately."

Brock leaned forward in her chair, shouting. "Grounded! Without exception. Spread the word—if Mrs. Woodrow Wilson stops by to borrow a regulator, she's grounded. If the ghost of Lucretia Cadwallader requests a tour of the city by air, she's grounded. If Jesus Christ himself puts down wearing his Holy Shroud of the Skysuit and begs for a cupful of powder in return for eternal salvation, he's grounded, too!"

She wiped the sweat off her forehead.

"Now get out—except for Weekes."

Tillie and Essie filed out. Brock looked even grimmer than they did.

"Do you have any idea," Brock said after we were alone, "how much easier it would be to just expel you?"

I was not going to sit idly by and be thrown out for doing the right thing.

"For what?" I said, trying not to raise my voice. "What did I do that they didn't?"

"How can you ask that?" Brock said. "The constant insubordination toward Miss Rodgers."

"I'm not the worst! You're not threatening Jake or Francine or—"

"The physical altercation."

"Which *she* started by laying hands on me."

"Nancy Durstman in the river."

"Which could have happened to anyone."

"But it happened to *you*. And then Saturday morning. Running a mass-casualty evacuation? Robert, one of those women died yesterday!"

"What was I supposed to do?" I shouted. "Wait for a professional to show up?"

"Yes! The hospital has a team. They can hover out and do it themselves."

"How long would that have taken? Ten minutes? Some of those women were dying in front of me! You want to tell me that one died, then how many did we save?"

Brock shut her eyes and took several deep breaths. "The Board of Overseers met last night to discuss expelling you," she said. "Dean Murchison threatened to resign if they did. That's the only reason you're still here."

I was mighty short on friends if I had only a madman to protect me.

"This isn't fair," I said. "This is because I'm a man."

"No it's not!" Brock yelled. "This didn't happen with Radcliffe's Contingency man last year. It doesn't happen with Mr. Unger or Mr. Mayweather. If you want to play at being an R&E corpswoman, then this is what happens!"

"I don't want to play at it, I want to *do* it!"

Brock put her hands to her temples and looked at me in despair.

"Lord help me, but I know you do," she said. "And you're good enough."

"*What?*" I said.

"Maybe you need to hear it," she said, her tone softening. "I know what it's like to be different from the other girls, how reckless it can make you to prove yourself. So, I'll say it again: you're good enough. I know it, Addams knows it, and Murchison knows it. The dean says he doesn't care how many laws you break—you'll be useful to us, so we ought to train you for R&E.

When the aerodrome reopens, we will. But your behavior has to be beyond reproach. You *cannot* give the Overseers further cause to expel you. No flying while grounded. Don't antagonize Rachael. And for the love of God, don't save anyone else's life!"

That kicked off a dismal week, top to bottom.

Dar, after keeping up a flirtatious string of messages on Sunday, flitted off to Washington for a series of meetings. She wouldn't reply to my notes with anything more extensive than *Made me smile, pls keep writing*. Well, if I'd made her smile, she couldn't take one minute to do the same for me?

On Tuesday, the synthesis of mercury fulminate went horribly awry at the lab bench next to me in Empirical Chemistry, releasing a noxious cloud that forced us to flee the building and left me hacking up yellow phlegm. Unger sprained his ankle playing tennis on Wednesday and was pouting about being on crutches. On Thursday, I messaged Mother, who mentioned that Julie Yzerman was working out so well as an apprentice that the State Office had granted her full credentials. Reject me for a probationary license, but give an unrestricted one to a sixteen-year-old girl! I tried messaging Angela for sympathy, but she replied *Boo hoo hoo, save your tears to water the salt garden*.

Coming back from class on Friday, I had a good mope and a cup of luke-warm coffee in the dining hall. I couldn't move myself to eat a proper lunch, not even a scoop of apple crumble. As I shuffled out the door, intending to go to bed for the entire weekend, a group of women nearly knocked me over. They were walking arm in arm, laughing and singing a triumphant tune:

> *We'll march up to Heaven*
> *We'll march into Hell*
> *We'll march to Aunt Laurie's down in the dell.*
> *We'll march through the morning*
> *We'll march through the gloam*
> *But nothing compares*
> *To marching back home!*

They wore gray dresses and capes and shook out their umbrellas in time to the song.

I raised my collar, lowered my head, and skirted around them.

"Weekes!" one of them cried.

It took me a moment to recognize her—Dar. I'd never seen her so happy. She ran over and flung her arms around me.

"We won! Oh, we won and it wasn't even close."

"You won?" I asked.

"The vote! The Senate voted on the Zoning Act last night and it lost—fifty-four to forty."

I'd been too wrapped up in my own troubles to notice.

"That sounds pretty close," I said.

"Don't be absurd, it's four more votes than we thought we'd get. The Trenchers are going to eat their livers!"

"Well, congratulations," I said.

"And," Dar said, lowering her voice, "you sent me two hundred thirty-eight messages." She crinkled her nose in delight.

"I did?"

"Yes. Since Sunday morning. I've been counting."

That seemed impossible. I hadn't sent more than—well, a couple an hour for six days.

"I'd get out of a meeting with the Undersecretary of the Interior, check my board, and it would be *Senator Larson will def vote nay*, and *Pls confirm you can meet the wounded veterans tmrw at 8*, and *Unger on crutches looks like a raccoon on stilts*. I swear, I missed a luncheon with the Benevolent Society because of your series on Professor Yu lecturing through the apocalypse: *Plague of locusts has jammed slide projector.*"

"I'm sorry," I said.

"Well, from what I hear, that meeting was perfectly useless."

She tapped her umbrella on the floor to knock the water off.

"Ask me out," she said.

"What?" I said.

"You heard!"

I looked at my feet and shrugged. But nothing I could do would ruin Dar's high spirits. "My God! Is this because you're grounded this week? What's wrong?"

"I don't know," I said. "Everything. Go a whole week without transporting and see how you feel!"

"But I *have* just gone a week without transporting. I feel wonderful. I forgot how much I like walking."

"Would you like to go for a walk, then?" I asked.

"It's rainy and miserable outside. Try again."

I tried to remember the list of grand things I'd said I'd do when I got to Boston, the thousand destinations I'd dreamed up back in Guille's Run while standing my night watches. I couldn't think of a single one.

Dar took my arm. "You're blue. And why shouldn't you be? I used to fall into these awful depressions every other week when I was a freshman. Away from home and all alone in the world."

Embarrassed, I pulled away from her.

"Oh, come on. You can sit at home and brood with your pet raccoon or come out. Where do you want to go?"

"A picture palace?" my inner six-year-old answered.

It was all Danielle could do to keep from howling. "Did you say—"

"Forget it."

"No! I'll take you to the picture show. Leave it to me. Come by about eight."

"I didn't mean to ruin your day," I said.

She grinned. "You haven't. Though you still have time."

20

The modern prophylactic sigil emerged from discussions and comparisons of forerunners used by thousands of corpswomen during the Civil War. In May 1865, Katie Flynn published it in a broadside titled "A Sigil for the Female Complaint," which sold for one cent in New York City. By August, committees for public decency throughout the country were burning similar pamphlets alongside "immoral" books containing sigils for ensuring female babies and smokecarving techniques for ending pregnancies.

Victoria Ferris-Smythe, *Empirical Philosophy:
An American History*, 1938

I SHOULD HAVE BEEN elated. Instead, I sulked back to my room, napped away the afternoon, and got up at six, groggy and even crankier than before. I found Unger sitting in the common room, trimming his toenails with a penknife.

"Howdy," I said.

"Howdy yourself," he replied. He'd caught my mood earlier in the week, or I'd caught his. Not that we were being any nastier to each other than to the rest of the world.

"Suppose one were going on a date this evening," I said.

"Suppose one were."

"What's the etiquette for accompanying someone to the movie theater?"

"Is it Jake?" he asked.

"No."

"Because if it is, maybe you could have her say something to—"

"It's not. Besides, if you're so wild about Dizzy, go over there yourself."

"I have. It doesn't do any good."

"Well, there are a few hundred other birds in the sky."

"I've noticed," retorted Unger. He pared a thumbnail. "So, who asked whom?"

"She asked me to ask her. What am I supposed to do?"

He sighed. "How the hell should I know? You could ask Mayweather. Probably you screw at her place instead of yours. Christ, did you hear him last night?"

"No."

"All night long. There's a pipe that carries the sound right into my room. It's obscene." Unger almost said something else, but stopped himself.

"What?" I asked.

Unger scraped a grain of sand from beneath the nail on his ring finger. "Mayweather was in my group in Essential Sigils today. He came completely unprepared. Not the slightest notion of the red-green sigil's design or the nuances of its amplification. He tried a couple of draws and even with his damned casual attitude he got it to take forty or fifty percent of the time."

"And you didn't?"

"No," said Unger. "I studied that sigil forward and back, all the variants. Worked it beforehand until I reeked of pine shavings. And he just picked it up in twenty minutes."

"Freddy—have you gotten anything to work all semester?"

He looked at me with full dark eyes. They said, *No. Nothing. Not a thing.*

"I'm going to wash out, aren't I?" he said. "I could be a historian, a theorist, a synthesist. Never a practitioner. But I'm a Contingency and that means come April, I'm either a practical sigilrist or I pay up. I should leave now and save myself the tuition."

"Don't say that. Half the trick to sigilry is self-delusion. There's no reason that if you put a doodle on a man's chest that he should stop breathing. You stop to think about it and it sounds insane."

"It sounds perfectly reasonable to me," Unger said. He finished with his nails and put his knife away. "If she asked you to ask her, take flowers."

"Okay," I said. "How might I do that?"

Unger recommended a florist a few blocks away. "How many flowers?" I asked. "And what sort would be appropriate?"

"Who is it?" asked Unger.

"It's . . . umm . . . would you mind very much if I didn't say?"

Unger threw up his hands. "God! Figure it out yourself then!"

I located Unger's florist, who'd seen his share of lost farm boys over the years and sold me a bouquet of pink and white roses. The fragrance of those hothouse flowers on a chill October evening cheered me and by the time I'd carried them to Dar's, I was smiling.

"They're lovely," said Danielle.

She was lovely, too. Healthy and vigorous, compared to the week before. She wore a high-necked black dress embroidered with red threads like vines of fire creeping up her arms. She offered me the choice between *Cleopatra* at the Columbia Theater or *This Coincidental Life!* at the Majestic. Given my mood, she preferred the latter, as it was a comedy of mistaken identity, rather than a tragic love story. I agreed.

We ducked under our umbrellas and headed out. It would have been faster to transport or fly, but Dar was still on mandatory rest and I was grounded. Instead, we packed into a horse-drawn tram in Harvard Square with the rest of the Friday-night crowd.

"I thought you'd be out celebrating with your friends," I said to Dar, who was wedged into a seat beside me.

"We celebrated last night," she said.

Dar laid her hand on mine and I felt electricity shoot up my arm following the same pattern as the one on the sleeves of her dress.

"Patrice was in the delegation with me," Danielle said. "She kept asking if you and I were together. I told her—"

A girl of about five was standing in the aisle beside us, awestruck, reaching tentatively toward Dar. The smile fell right off Dar's face.

The waif looked back toward a middle-aged woman standing in the aisle, who nodded encouragingly. "Are you Mrs. Hardin?" the girl asked.

"I'm *Miss* Hardin," Danielle replied, looking as if she might climb over me to escape out the window.

"Miss Hardin, were you scared when you were at the war?"

"No," Danielle said. "It was too dark to be scared. I couldn't see anything to be scared of."

The girl nodded. "I'm afraid of the dark."

Dar fumbled for something to say.

"Are you going to be a philosopher when you grow up?" I asked her.

"My mother's a philosopher," the girl said.

"You should come by the aerodrome at Radcliffe," I said. "We'll teach you to fly." Then, remembering that we weren't permitting even Jesus Christ to go aloft, I added, "After Monday."

"Could she teach me?" asked the girl, pointing to Danielle.

"No," said Dar.

The girl's mother scooped her up and pulled the bell for the next stop. The girl waved to Dar, who reluctantly raised her hand.

The Hero of the Hellespont slouched down next to me. "God, I hate that. At least she didn't say she wants to be a transporter. Those ones are the worst."

We rode in silence to Boylston Street, then walked three blocks through the rain to the theater.

The Majestic was everything I could have wished for. Its marquee was lit with more electric lightbulbs than existed in the entire state of Montana. Every piece of molding on the lobby's ceiling was gilded; every ornament was brightly polished brass. The ushers wore enough gold braid on their jackets to outfit four or five lieutenant colonels each. The seats were plush velvet, thirteen hundred of them. We sat not in the very front row, but close to it. I'd seen a couple pictures projected at the social hall in Billings, but never anything to compare to this. The lights went down, the curtains parted, and the film began to roll, eleven reels in all.

Almost from the first frame, I realized we'd picked a stinker.

"He's supposed to be a prince?" I whispered to Dar. "He looks about seventy."

"His throne's made of plywood," she whispered back. "Look. They didn't even paint the back."

"Professor Yu has a mustache just like the grandfather!"

"Oh, be nice."

The fearless nobleman, after a steamship voyage on which he was lengthily seasick, reached America, lost his suitcase, and, having very little in the way of English, was mistaken for a distant cousin by a family waiting at the dock.

"Can I hold your hand?" I asked. I'd been working on saying that for the preceding twenty minutes.

"Only during the scary parts," Dar answered.

"The whole thing is frightful."

"In that case . . ."

A remarkable thing, the human hand. The infinite number of ways it fits together with another. Fingers interlaced, first with my thumb on the outside, and then rewoven so that hers was. Palm against the outside of a curled hand. Forefinger tracing thumb. Fingers teasing the edges of sleeves. Fingertips circling knuckles. Dar found the calluses along the base of my fingers from my years of holding a regulator. I tested the sharpness of her nails against my forearm.

Prince Louis the Hapless was trundled off to Laredo and put to work on the cigar assembly line. By the fifth time he got his tie stuck in the conveyer belt, the runs of comic notes from the three-man band providing accompaniment had taken on a sarcastic tone. By the tenth time, the musicians gave up any pretense of supplying a soundtrack and struck up "Alexander's Ragtime Band" to widespread applause.

I turned to whisper to Dar at the same moment she was leaning in to whisper to me and the tip of my ear caught in her mouth. Her tongue brushed against my flesh and I let out a sigh that must have been heard three rows away.

"They changed actors," Dar said. "The innkeeper had short hair in the last scene."

"That's not the innkeeper. It looks like the palace again . . ."

"And that's the Arc de Triomphe. How'd he get back to France?"

The projectionist, as bored as everyone else, had spliced in the final reel two reels early. The one person in the theater riveted by the story got up from his seat to complain and the film was halted as the projectionist attempted to correct the error.

"Someone should give him a medal for trying to cut it short," I said.

"We should all be decorated for sitting through this," Dar answered.

While he worked, the projectionist put up a newsreel. The band broke into a well-rehearsed patriotic tune. Beside me, Dar stiffened.

The film concerned "our boys," the first boatloads of whom had just begun to arrive in France. They marched past in full field gear, smiling and waving for the camera. Some stock footage of artillery blasting away. A map of Europe. Title cards praising their fighting spirit. Then a group of rescue hoverers flying in formation at a speed and altitude that suggested they weren't within a hundred miles of someone who might shoot at them. *Our bold, beautiful girls rush to the front to rescue the wounded!* A pyrotechnic explosion, followed by an artfully positioned man with a blood-soaked dressing on his head. A hoverer set down beside him. Most definitely not a regulation skysuit—long skirt, a silken sash from shoulder to waist, boots with heels much too high to be stable. She wasn't even wearing a harness. Or carrying a powder bag. *In seconds, the brave soldier is whisked to safety. (Ain't he lucky, lads!)* The wounded man in a hospital bed, his leg in a cast, getting a kiss on the cheek from the angel who had rescued him.

Then, ranks of women standing at attention in a neatly kept barracks, rows of carefully made cots behind them. *It may not be Home, but it's an Adventure!*

"I need to go," Dar snarled. She rose and pushed her way toward the aisle.

I caught up with her in the lobby. She was pale, eyes shut, lips pressed together, breathing rapidly.

"I'm sorry," I said. "You probably don't want to see that again."

"No, *I'm* sorry," she said, opening her eyes and trying to smile. "It's not seeing it. I'm not a neurasthenic case. I didn't even see anything when I was over there. I didn't see a battle. I didn't see a corpse. I didn't see so much as a rat. Just a lot of friendly Australian soldiers delighted to be guarding a tent full of ladies rather than getting murdered in the trenches. I didn't get gassed. I didn't get shelled. Other than the one night, nobody ever shot at me, and even then there were a thousand men standing between me and the bullets. No, it just makes me mad. It makes me *furious*."

"That they faked the bits with the fliers?"

"That they put a pretty face on it. And that they put *me* in one of those newsreels when I came back. They called Gallipoli 'a bloodless miracle.' No mention that the supply officer miscalculated my powder and I ran out with one group left to take—eleven hundred New Zealanders slaughtered on the beach for want of aluminum. Nothing about the four corpswomen we lost. And God forbid they admit that half a million men died there over two years. Or that ten million soldiers have died since the start of the war—for *what?*"

She balled up her fists and for a moment I thought she was going to strike me.

"It's not the war to end all wars—we're sending Americans over there to die so that the munitions factories can make a fortune and our allies can grab a few square miles of extra territory. It's criminal. And the Corps used me to sell it. *'It's an Adventure!'* I can't tell you how many women wrote to say I'd inspired them to do their part for the welfare of humankind. 'You'll be pleased to know I left my daughter in the care of my elderly mother and went straight down to the recruiting office.' "

"Dar—"

"And while I was getting their letters, the generals were marching me through that ghastly goodwill tour. One hospital after another, all the philosophical wards. Smashed legs, mangled arms, bullet holes, burns. They were all R&E fliers. I saw a lieutenant, blind, all her hair burned away. Her scalp was just a mass of twisted pink scars. She said Rescue and Evac suffers fifty percent casualties, but the Corps won't let them tell anyone at home. Or they'd never get another volunteer."

"Fifty percent *killed?*"

"No, not killed. But injured badly enough that they can't return to duty. They're professionals, too, cargo fliers or passenger carriers. If they lose a leg, that's their livelihood. Hundreds of them."

"That's horrible."

"The generals told me don't dwell on it, don't speak out about it—it'll only hurt the cause. So, I shut up like a coward. But I couldn't stop thinking: *How many women did I put in one of those beds?*"

If I'd known Danielle only a little better, I would have taken her in my arms and she would have wept.

"Well," she said bitterly, "now I've gone and ruined *your* evening. Let's go back in."

"Let's not," I said. "We should have left one minute into that film."

We headed out into the drear. The first streetcar to come past was packed, so we waited for the next. As I watched her, Danielle seemed to withdraw deeper and deeper, remote and forlorn. I didn't know how to reach her.

We'd been waiting several minutes when a man in a shabby overcoat came up beside us. He peered at Danielle. He had no hat or umbrella and his thick black hair dripped with the rain. He was about forty, stooped and poorly shaven, but with a thick neck and shoulders. He looked at Danielle again, wiping the water from his face.

"You're her, aren't you?" he asked.

"Excuse me?" said Danielle.

"You could save so many." He said it with extraordinary calmness and mildness. Danielle was too taken aback to answer.

"You've been given a gift," he said. "I pray every night for your soul—and the souls of your sisters. You must intercede with them."

"Okay, listen—" I broke in.

But he wasn't interested in me. He continued addressing Dar, who had shrunk even farther under her umbrella.

"Babies smothered in the womb. Their mothers hear their screams as they die, unbaptized and unsaved."

"Stop it," I said. "Just stop—"

"And yet every month they draw the Devil's sign on their bellies again. Trapped in an endless cycle of sin and lust. Help them break free. Take this—"

He reached into his pocket and lurched toward her.

Danielle whipped her hand into her purse and seized something. The man froze.

"Robert!" Dar screamed.

I was right between them.

"Don't touch her!" I shouted. I shoved the man in the chest and found him to be quite solid. My shoes slid on the wet pavement and he caught my arm to prevent me from falling.

He pressed a cheap wooden rosary into my hand.

"Tell her the souls of—"

"Robert!" Danielle screamed again. She had me by the belt of my raincoat, yanking me toward her.

She pulled me close with her left hand; with her right she popped a tube of aluminum and drew.

And we were back in her apartment.

Danielle was shaking with anger. "What did you do that for?" she demanded. "Don't ever do that!"

"Do what?"

"You have no idea what he might be carrying! Just walk away. Or run!"

I was amazed by her reaction. Before I'd come out East I'd been warned against every kind of lunatic, confidence man, leper, grifter, drifter, pimp, and stickup artist. But he'd seemed a harmless blowhard.

"Did you think he had a gun?" I asked.

"Yes! Or God knows what."

"He wasn't going to hurt you," I said, trying to calm her, "he was just—"

"Don't you *dare* tell me that."

She seized an expandable accordion folder off her desk and all but threw it at me.

"You think I'm paranoid? I'm crazy? Just a hysterical female?"

I recognized Ms. Addams's precise, angular script: *Hardin. File #5. September 4–October 10, 1917.*

It was filled with newspaper clippings and letters, meticulously organized and dated. The clipping on top was a political cartoon, featuring three women, all of them dead. One was a thin old lady with prominent ears who had been hung from a noose made of smoke; one was wearing hip waders and frowning severely, folded backward over a chair, her body limp as a rag; and the last was a heavy, dark-skinned young woman with wavy black hair, who'd been sliced neatly in half and was lying in a puddle of her own blood. I recognized the first two: Lucretia Cadwallader and Gen. Yeates (who'd led the police action in the Philippines). And with my heartbeat echoing loudly in my skull, I realized the third looked a little like Dar. *A fitting end for war criminals*, read the caption. Penciled at the top was *Trencher Times, Sept 4, 1917.*

Beneath that was a letter, signed by four Radcliffe professors who had resigned in protest when Dar had been allowed to reenroll:

> She represents the worst sort of militant feminism, atheism, and anti-Americanism; her influence would pollute the moral fabric of her classmates and pervert the dignity of this institution. Indeed, her very presence will inspire disharmony and outright violence.

Then letters from the general public, hundreds, with threats more or less explicit:

You ever come to Wichita, I've got an axe I'll use to break every bone in your
body, then shove it up your arse and gut you from the inside out.

And typewritten:

Do you remember how Comfort Tyndale died? We'll do you the same way.

Another, in a more tremulous hand:

Already we see fire and hail mingled with blood cast upon the earth, the
seas turned to blood, smoke rising as if from a great furnace, and the sun
and the air darkened. You are the herald of end times, the original whore of
Babylon, with your murders, sorceries, fornications, thefts, and heresies. You
are beyond repentance.

Maxwell Gannet

I looked up at Dar.

"You think I'm crazy?" she asked.

It had taken me perhaps two minutes to read that much. I would have needed hours to read them all.

"This one," I said. "The one from—"

"Don't say another word! I know all of Gannet's by heart. I don't even get to open my own mail. Addams keeps the worst ones from me."

"Dar, I never thought—"

"Well, now you know. And either you run out of here as fast as you can or you stay and you don't say a word."

I stayed.

Dar threw her coat on the floor and went about fixing a pot of mint tea. Her apartment was a tiny studio, the bed against one wall, a couch against the other, with a minuscule galley kitchen containing a single gas burner.

I picked up her coat and hung it to dry.

"Do you know, ten minutes before all that happened, what I was think-ing?" Dar asked. "I was hoping you'd kiss me goodnight."

The roof of my mouth went dry to hear her say it.

"I'll tell you what I want," she said. "I want you to stay and drink tea and not say anything. I don't want to talk and I don't want to be alone. And later, when you leave, I want you to kiss me."

I nodded. I sat.

She poured boiling water over a strainer of dried mint leaves.

"God, I'm glad you were there," Danielle said, concentrating on the teapot. "The other times, I've been alone. It's terrifying."

What followed was the longest cup of tea of my life. Dar wouldn't look at me but did sit across from me and take my hand. I watched her as she studied her mug—she was so serious, the wrinkles that would deepen into crow's feet already creasing the corners of her eyes. Yet when she did look up at me, her eyes were filled with heat.

I leaned forward and pressed my lips against hers.

Her tongue was scalding hot from the tea. I didn't have much idea what I was doing, but our mouths negotiated. Our kiss became deeper, less tenta-tive. I wondered if it was too much, but there was the palm of Dar's hand against my jaw, holding me fast.

After some minutes, we disengaged. I was amazed and terrified to look at her. Frightened of the "Please don't take this the wrong way . . ." or the "We mustn't ever . . ." that was sure to follow.

"Stay," Dar whispered. "Stay a little longer."

21

Brock, Janet Simone (University of Detroit, 1889). Only competitor to ever sweep the gold medals in the short course, efficiency flight, team pull, and long course in a single year. Coached Radcliffe's Cup team 1910–24, including notable fliers Pilar Desoto, Gloxinia Jacobi, Michael Nakamura, S. E. Stewart, and Robert Canderelli Weekes. Her development of novel flight glyphs with Jenny Yu, as well as construction of all-metal flight enclosures, axial thrust couplers, and pressurized powder tanks ushered in the modern age of blended philosophico-mechanical aviation. With her brother, Steven, a founding partner of Brock-Sudeste Aerospace.

Who's Who in the General's Cup, 1939

THE FOLLOWING WEEK BROUGHT with it further miracles and wonders.

Brock reopened the aerodrome and unveiled our new hovering instructors: ten Corps veterans who'd been pensioned off due to age. All the Radcliffe women who were still interested in flying assembled on the landing field to be divided up among the old crones. One after the next, the instructors stepped forward to call out the names of their trainees and lead them into the aerodrome.

But my name wasn't on any of the lists. I would have thought I was being singled out again, but Essie was left unassigned, too. We stood alone on the field, looking for some indication of what we were supposed to do.

"Bookkeeping error?" I suggested. Essie chewed at her lip.

An ancient lady, leaning heavily on a cane, hobbled out of the aerodrome. She wore thick spectacles and had a pair of field glasses on a leather strap around her neck. She hadn't been introduced with the other instructors.

She stopped in front of us and straightened painfully.

"Well, this is a sorry state of affairs," she drawled. "Out of this entire aerodrome, only two hoverers have dared mewl the phrase 'Rescue and Evacuation' in connection with their own names. One has fewer flight hours than any of my great-grandchildren and the other has a phallus."

Essie blushed to hear such coarse language.

The old woman pointed at her. "You're Sarah Stewart?"

"Ma'am, I go by Essie, if—"

"That's a weak name. A child's name. Stop using it. Now, get kitted out and scout me three different landing approaches to Harvard Square."

"Ma'am, we're not permitted to hover between—"

"The Cambridge Police Department has no way to catch you. I want you to land and then record on paper three approaches with compass headings and lists of potential obstructions for each. Give it to me in one hour. Get a bag and get up!"

If Essie was torn about committing a technically illegal act, she overcame her doubts quickly. She trotted toward the aerodrome.

"Run!" the woman bellowed.

Essie accelerated to a sprint.

"And *you*," the old lady said. "Let me see if I have this right. Conducted a solo search and rescue mission over rough country in Montana and lifted out three souls. Dove into the river to save a drowning hoverer. Ran a mass-casualty evacuation on zero minute's notice and flew a goddamn forty-foot stringer. I would say that just about makes you the best male flier in the world, doesn't it?"

"No, ma'am," I said.

"Mother Mary, but he doesn't understand! Child, I was in the Corps fifty-five years—that's since before modern hovering was invented, to save you the math. Back in '11 they said to me, 'Gertrude, you're too old to fly.' So, I instructed at Fort McConnell. Then this year they said, 'Gertrude, you're too mean to teach. We've got a war on and we don't want every third girl quitting.' So they retired me. Janet Brock, with all her gold medals and monographs and professor of such and such, said she had a man worth training. A man for the Corps. For R&E. What better revenge for invaliding me out than to dump on them a man who's too good to refuse. So—do you think a woman of my prodigious experience would waste her golden years on anything less than the finest male flier on earth?"

"Uh, no ma'am," I said.

"Good! I want you to believe it. I want you to train like it. And if you choose to not boast about it, then that's your business."

As if I would dare say such a thing aloud in the aerodrome!

"Show me your hands," Gertrude said.

I extended my hands for her. Dirt under my nails and my calluses all rough and yellowed. But she wasn't checking for cleanliness. She produced a tape measure from the workbag at her hip and measured my thumb and index finger, then across my palm in several different dimensions.

"You have lovely long, girlish fingers," she said, nodding her approval. "Do you know how to fly a lever regulator?"

"Grew up with them," I answered.

"Then no more of the dial reg trash they favor here. You'll fly a Chesapeake Mark-20 lever regulator with a two-inch conical tip, three-twist burr, bored to eighty mil."

"I don't think we have—"

"Janet found a used one. She ground the tips herself. Now, kneel or I won't be able to reach."

I knelt and she made further measurements across my neck, chest, hips, thighs, belly, and shoulders, recording each with a stub of a pencil in a little book.

"Beg your pardon," she murmured. She put the field glasses to her eyes in time to see Essie dash out of the aerodrome in full harness.

"Run, *run, RUN!*" the woman bellowed.

Essie flung herself into the air. The old lady checked her wrist chronometer. "Six minutes forty seconds to kit out and then a three-step launch. Christ in a fish barrel! And she flies pretty! God*damn* it."

She turned back to me.

"Brown or black?" she asked.

"Excuse me?"

"You're riding a Springfield harness with a lot of homemade improvements?"

"Yes," I said.

"Not anymore. We're bringing you into the twentieth century. Janet should have had you in custom tackle from the day you came in."

"I can't afford—"

"You're not paying for it. Brown leather or black?"

"Brown."

She noted that, too, and put her book away. "What do you weigh, first thing in the morning, naked, after you've voided?"

She didn't mean anything untoward by it and I didn't take it that way. "I'm not sure," I said. "I don't have a—"

"Then buy a scale later today. Give me an estimate."

"Two eleven."

She winced. "You stand seventy-two and a half inches high. I don't want to fly you above a hundred eighty-six pounds. You going to faint on me at that weight?"

"Probably not," I said.

"Then you're on a diet starting this morning, unless you care to dabble in transporting to improve your figure. I don't judge. Powder flow for your current weight will be 8.9 ounces per minute."

I was aghast—at the powder expenditure, not her comment regarding weight loss, which was simple physics.

"A little more cornmeal than you used back home?" she asked.

"Four times more," I said. I would be burning through powder like mad.

"You're not paying for that, either."

Then she laid herself down on the ground. "Prove you're worth the effort. I'll play the role of your casualty. As fast as you can, I want you to run into that building, kit out, and grab whatever style of harness you intend to fly me in. Then launch, take me two miles out to sea, turn, and land back here. And, oh shoot, you happen to be out of silver chloride this morning, so fly me awake. Clear?"

"Perfectly."

"Then run!" she bellowed.

I grabbed my harness and sprinted for the aerodrome.

"And if you can't do this in half the time it took that little daddy's girl, I'm sending you straight back to the farm!"

I sprinted harder.

There was a line of women snaking out the door, waiting to draw powder and equipment. One of the other old sigilwomen watched my approach.

"Clear the way for a hot evac!" she yelled. The girls stepped aside to let me through.

Professor Brock was behind the counter.

"Twelve-pound general purpose bag," I panted. "Chesapeake twenty-ounce regulator with a two-inch—"

"Fine, fine," Brock said, and handed over the items that she'd had waiting right beside her. I'd already slipped into my harness and was cinching down the leg straps.

"I hope you're enjoying yourself," Brock said. "I had to message every—"

"And a twenty-foot loop of one-inch cotton webbing."

Brock looked flummoxed.

"Oh, come on!" I said. I attached my bag to my hip as Brock pulled out the aerodrome's catalogue to see where we stocked such a piece of rigging.

The old lady at the door laughed. She took a cloth bag from her belt and tossed it underhand to me.

"Gertrude's seventy-four years old," the only slightly younger woman said. "Be gentle."

"Yes, ma'am," I answered, and ran back out.

I shook the webbing out of its bag. It was nothing more than a single long strap with the ends sewn together, but it made the world's quickest harness.

I skidded to a stop next to Gertrude, who was lying flat on her back, and laid out the webbing in a circle around her.

"Oh, for the love of St. Jude, are you serious? A web harness?"

"You said as fast as I could," I gasped.

"So do it."

I yanked a loop of webbing beneath her feet and up between her legs, then reached through it to pull the strap up from under her armpits. I hauled her to her feet and clipped her to my harness so that we were chest-to-chest—the old "lover's clinch" position. Undignified but fast.

"Go!" she barked.

I launched, trying to make it gentle, then poured on speed as I rushed toward the Atlantic. I was unbalanced, my regulator was unfamiliar, and the powder flow rate was absurd. I struggled to keep us on the level. We reached the ocean in three minutes; I turned and reversed course.

"You okay?" I asked.

"Had worse," she replied. "Mind me asking—ever land like this?"

"Nope."

Over the field I descended briskly.

"I have bad hips!" Gertrude warned. "Bad ankles. Bad knees."

I cut our vertical speed and splayed my feet wide so that she touched first. This had the unintended consequence of thrusting my pelvis right into her bosom. I brought my legs down, crumpling into a crouch to support her. I had to grab her rump to keep us from toppling over.

Some bright young thing gave us a wolf whistle.

"Quiet on the field!" Gertrude bellowed.

I unclipped her and retrieved her cane. She polished her glasses and set them back on her nose.

"Wonderful that at my age I should experience something new," she proclaimed. "Are you married, Mr. Weekes?"

I blushed crimson. "No, ma'am. I'm terribly sorry that I touched—"

"Sorry, nothing! I've grabbed every last piece of wounded soldiers to get them up and down. No, Mr. Weekes, you misunderstand: Better for you if you were married. Go pick one of those pretty girls, make lots of babies—girl babies, if you please—and teach them to fly. Your daughters will be brilliant."

"Was I that bad?" I asked.

"No, you dumbass! You're adequate! A woman who flew like that could get a test at Fort Putnam tomorrow and she'd be in France by Christmas. If you were shorter, I'd suggest a wig and a set of bosom pads, but you'd never pass for a lady. So, for you, a man, to join R&E, you're going to have to fly perfect. And that's a *miserable* existence. I wouldn't wish it on you. Go settle down instead."

I had a brief vision of Dar and me with a brood of daughters, all of them with dark, wavy hair and perpetual frowns, scolding me on some point of politics and then flying rings around me. I rather liked it. But not just yet.

"I came to fly," I said.

Gertrude nodded, as if it would have been impossible for me to answer differently. "Then fly it again, unladen, at best speed, and show me your hottest landing."

I did a one-step launch and might have touched two hundred miles per hour on my return leg. I blistered in for a direct approach and landed with a smart angle and tuck.

"No!" Gertrude screamed. "What was that?"

"It was an angle and—"

"A hot landing! Hot! Do you know what that means?"

"Like a flashy—"

"Hot! Hot landing field. Like I'm drawing a bead on you with a rifle. Quick to the ground! If I can hit you six times with a flintlock musket, that's not hot. Do you know a flare and settle landing?"

"Of course."

"Then show it to me! I have a machine gun. I'm trying to kill you. So fast, fast, fast to the ground!"

The flare and settle, which involved flipping upside down to speed up the approach, was my least favorite landing—too much potential for hitting the ground face-first if you didn't flip back upright quickly enough. But I climbed to four hundred feet, pitched head-down, and dove. I could see Gertrude leveling her cane at me like it was a gun. At one hundred feet, I began frantically back-drawing my sigil for counterthrust. A few feet above the ground, I kicked upright, leveled out, and hit the ground hard enough to jostle my teeth.

"No!" Gertrude screamed. "That was an upside-down angle and tuck with a terrible touch. Who taught you that horror?"

I flushed with anger and humiliation. "My sister."

The old woman softened, as if she understood me for the first time. "And she was twelve years old."

"Umm—sixteen, I think."

"Babies teaching babies to fly. It's the worst kind of sin and one we'll never stop repeating. But you've got to learn it right. You own a copy of Tintinalli's *Hovering Emergencies and Recovery?*"

"Yes."

"They shot a beautiful series of photographs with a high-speed camera. The body in each position of the flare and settle. Learn it. Know it cold for tomorrow. It's a landing that can kill you or save your— oh, for heaven's sake!"

Essie was running up to us. In her hand she had a piece of paper, rolled and tied with a hair ribbon, which she pressed into Gertrude's hand.

"I'm so sorry to interrupt," Essie said.

"Sweet Jesus in his bedroom slippers, what did you . . ." Gertrude unrolled the paper to find a charming little hand-drawn map of Harvard Square, the buildings crosshatched with contrasting blue and black ink, the approaches labeled with Essie's immaculate copperplate script.

"You made it *pretty*! What'd you do that for? You won't have two fountain pens on the front lines. You won't have time to blot it and wait for the ink to dry. Redo it in pencil. Make it ugly. Then land all three approaches."

"Ma'am," said Essie, "it's the middle of rush hour. It's going to be—"

"They'll get out of the way for you. Go!"

Essie launched without further objection.

Gertrude returned her attention to me. "Tomorrow, nine o'clock, flare and settle. Until you learn it, you're rated a Two. You don't fly without my personal supervision."

"That's not how—"

"It's how it works starting today. Now go stow your gear in your locker."

"I don't have a locker," I said. "Most of the women felt—"

"I don't care how they feel. I count eight souls evacuated in your life. That makes you the ranking member of the aerodrome. So, you're assigned locker number one."

"There's going to be an uproar."

"It won't be any better in France."

We walked into the aerodrome and paused outside the locker room.

"Man on deck!" Gertrude roared in her Sigilwoman First Class's voice. "Two minutes! Make yourselves decent."

There were a few shrieks and incredulous shouts, much laughter. A stream of women hurried out, but quite a few seemed willing to stand and protect their territory.

"Each morning, sing out and then two minutes later claim your locker," said Gertrude. "I don't care what you use it for—keep your chewing gum there—but use it every day."

She glanced at her wrist chronometer. "They give you problems, take it to your senior instructor."

Which was no solution at all.

"Begging your pardon, ma'am," I said. "But that's Miss Rodgers and she's likely to be the one instigating the problem."

Gertrude scoffed. "Her aunt was a sniveling little pissant, so I can't imagine the niece is much different. Learn to manage it."

She reached into her workbag and handed me a key.

"First locker on the left. If some ladies have chosen to remain in a state of undress, don't tell tales."

She put her hand between my shoulder blades and pushed.

•   •   •

Dnt think I evr met yr Gertie, Mother wrote after a series of messages in which I detailed the morning's events. *She snds like crap if sh liks flar and settl for landng. Bad cmmndr who sends y to hot field in frst place.*

My fellow ex-Threes agreed with the "crap" part. We convened in the dining hall and one tale of woe was worse than the next—all of us had been demoted and set different challenges to earn back our ranks.

"A lot of disrespectful old biddies," Francine sniffed. "Treating us like children. Robert's told him he's fat and to learn a flare and settle out of a book. What kind of shit is that?"

"I thought Gertrude was great," I said. "She told me—"

"You're just excited because you get to see a lot of young ladies in their underwear," Astrid said, laughing.

"I didn't see anybody's—"

"Knock it off," said Jake.

She'd come back changed, too. After her preceptor had thrown her flight plan back in her face and called her "honey," she'd taken Jake up to thirty-five thousand feet, where the old lady had demonstrated the Ostebee Loop, named for the famous aerialist who'd died during her third attempt at completing the maneuver.

"Your old lady didn't *really* do it, though, right?" Tillie asked her. "At that altitude, it's thirty, maybe forty seconds before you black out?"

"She says if I want my Three back, it's my turn to do it next week," Jake answered. And then said nothing else during the remainder of her lunch.

"What's the matter with you, anyway?" Astrid said to Jake. "Just because you don't get to be queen bee and lord it over—"

"Shut up," Jake said, and stood. "Weekes, walk me home."

I'd never seen her so quiet. There was no companionable hand on my arm, no gossipy banter.

"You've been running your mouth about the Corps," Jake said. "You and Essie."

"Sure, but we've talked about that plenty of times since—"

"The girls are going to start believing that you can. They saw you this morning. And they're not wrong—you're better than some of the women R&E took last year. It's just politics whether they commission a man."

"Then what's the problem?"

"All sorts of girls who have no business in R&E are going to decide if you can do it, then they can, too. The ones who see it at the movies or those posters of Winged Victory at the library. 'Why not a little adventure before Daddy and Mum marry me off?' A story to tell at cocktail parties. Then they'll get slaughtered."

"No they wouldn't."

Jake looked down at her boots. "How many of your pals from back home have died in the war?" she asked.

"A lot of my friends volunteered in April," I offered. "They're still in the States, finishing training or waiting for their boat over."

"So, none of them, right?" Jake said.

"Yeah," I said. "Even the Americans who *are* in France aren't seeing much fighting. Gen. Pershing doesn't want them in combat until he has enough men to launch a real offensive. Next summer, probably."

"How nice for them. Let's not risk American soldiers, but if we run a few hundred R&E fliers into the ground pulling out the French wounded, no harm done."

She looked up at me. "Most of my friends volunteered in April, too. Congress declared war and Ruby, the queen bee of the aerodrome before me, said, 'This is it, ladies!' Nine of them joined R&E with her. They came back from Fort Putnam with their commissions, and I had the Harvard marching band waiting to strike up 'Yankee Doodle.' But even then, I realized that R&E must be getting desperate. Three of ours barely rated a Two. They had no business in a war zone. I should have spoken up. But they were my friends and they desperately wanted to go. Then last summer, in the course of a month, they ended up dead, dead, and missing. And then Ruby crashed."

"That's awful."

"That's what happens in a war! It happens to people you love. Do you know how Ruby got it? Somebody told you the story?"

"No."

"She was my best friend. She was very successful when she went over, promoted twice, squadron leader. Then she took a group out to pick up casualties at night with bad coordinates—set down right in front of a German machine gun. All the women were hit, Ruby, too, but she picked up two wingmates and flew out as fast as she could. No time for stasis, she just scooped and ran."

Jake coughed and steadied her voice.

"Halfway back, so much blood had soaked into her powder bag that it failed. She tried to set down in a British trench, got shot by a panicky sentry, and crashed. Both her passengers died on impact. The Tommies thought she must be dead, too, lying out there for hours, tangled up with the bodies. They didn't go out to check until just before dawn. She'd shattered both legs and broken her back."

"Jesus."

Jake trudged on toward the ladies' dorm. "Now imagine you're the one who gets word first and you have to tell the rest of the girls. I know it's petty of me—my burden is nothing compared to the ones who are actually over there—but I had to do it *four* times last summer. Weekes, I don't believe in God and I was on my knees every night praying there wouldn't be a fifth. So, don't act so shocked that I don't want you to go. Or Essie. Or whichever little Zeds those veterans sweet-talk into signing up."

"They may not win too many hearts," I said.

Jake shook her head. "*Your* heart's easy to win. A girl just has to be mean to you. You and Danielle Hardin?"

"No, you can't go around saying—"

"Everybody knows. I said you needed serious, Robert, but *damn*. You'd be safer in France than you are here. You so much as look at another woman, she'll castrate you."

· · ·

"Man on deck!" I announced the next morning. "Two minutes, please!"

"Don't you dare!" someone yelled back.

"Two minutes, please!" I repeated.

There was no recurrence of the previous day's mass exodus, which seemed ominous. But there were fewer women in the locker room at this hour and they likely understood I wasn't trying to cause mischief. After all, no one had been turned into a pillar of salt.

I debated giving them an extra minute, but decided that was a dangerous precedent.

"Coming in!" I called.

I walked in to a chorus of enraged shouts. I kept my head down and didn't look at anything but my locker. Only ten feet to cover.

"Get out!"

"Pervert!"

"We're calling the police!"

Several towels came flying my way. A rock clunked off a locker next to my head hard enough to leave a dent. I grabbed my regulator and harness and got out before anyone with a more accurate throwing arm had time to take aim.

Gertrude was on the landing field, sitting in a camp chair with a flannel jacket buttoned to her chin. She was eating a croissant.

"Ma'am," I said, "I think the locker idea—"

"Sit," she said. "I don't want to hear it."

I took a knee beside her.

"You've studied the flare and settle," Gertrude said. "What do you think?"

"I liked the pictures," I said, trying to be diplomatic.

"The *pictures?*" She frowned. "Well, spit it out. You're not going to hurt my feelings."

"My ma called it a crap landing and said it's a bad commander who sends you to a hot landing field."

Gertrude threw her head back and howled. "His mama! A corpswoman,

I'll wager—I probably trained her. You tell your mama that your war is going to be different from hers. She flew in Cuba? Or the Philippines?"

"Both," I said.

"They didn't use trench warfare there. Your mama had nice big landing fields well back from the fighting. Under those circumstances, a flare and settle is reckless. But for you, it's essential."

Gertrude ate the last bit of croissant and brushed the crumbs from her jacket.

"Imagine how a busy morning plays out in France," she said. "They ring the bell for a hundred wounded at the forward aid station and your squadron of twelve women goes to evacuate it. You have a ten-foot-by-ten-foot landing field and the Germans are shooting at incoming fliers. How many women will you land at a time?"

"One," I said. "She's got to approach fast and hard so she doesn't get hit."

"Exactly. And how long does it take to get to the ground doing a tuck and angle, like you favor? We'll say the gunfire has driven you up to a thousand feet."

"A minute or two."

"Twelve of you. The last woman in line is circling *twenty minutes* before she ever sets down. The women coming back from the hospital run right into the caboose and now they're circling, too, before they can make a second run. That's unforgivable. With a flare and settle, you can bring a flier in at full speed at one hundred feet and have her on the ground in fifteen seconds. Space your fliers properly and the whole squadron runs continuously—a hundred and ninety souls evacuated each hour instead of forty. If you fail to learn it, wounded who were supposed to live will die."

"Okay," I said.

Gertrude picked up a rag doll outfitted with a harness and used it to demonstrate each step.

"From level flight, you perform a half somersault."

She flipped the doll upside down, so that it was flying upside down and backward.

"You draw sigils for full thrust until you've killed your forward momentum."

She stopped the doll, still facing head-down.

"Now, you never want to be hanging motionless in the air, so at the same time you're braking, you're also accelerating toward the ground. At the last moment, you flare back upright, get your legs up, draw for maximum upward thrust, and settle to a stop right above the earth."

She flipped the doll right-side up, lifted its legs into an L shape, and halted it an inch above the ground. "It's a very simple maneuver."

"Yeah," I said. "But if you take a half second too long to stop, you dig your own grave."

"It saves me digging it for you. We'll practice your timing tomorrow. Bring a towel, a change of clothing, your warmest coat, and your lightest skysuit."

"Man on deck!" I shouted the following morning. "Two minutes."

I didn't hear a sound from inside the locker room. Had the novices been so offended they were simply changing at home?

When the time was up, I found the door blocked by six women standing with their arms linked.

"Absolutely not," one of them said. "This is a gross invasion. If you touch any of us, that's battery."

"I'll be thirty seconds," I said. "I'm not undressing, I just want my equipment."

"We'll get it for you. Give us your key."

Lord knew what kind of mischief they might cause if they got hold of my regulator.

"It wasn't my decision, I—"

"Let him in," said Essie, who'd come up behind me.

"They taught you how to strip for men at that fancy finishing school of yours?" one of the young ladies jeered.

Essie appeared unflustered. "He has a right to be here, too."

"He has *no* right. It's disgusting."

"Then let me fetch his gear," Essie suggested.

They were willing to yield for that.

Essie collected my regulator and we walked down to the field. She was wearing a black pea coat over her winter-weight skysuit and had a lifting harness slung over her shoulder.

"They're terrible," Essie said. "Doing that to you. And I hate . . ." She swallowed. "I hate that last year I would have agreed with them."

Gertrude was waiting for us on the riverbank. The morning's exercise was straightforward enough: I would put on a pair of ankle shackles connected to a long line and Essie would haul me up to one hundred feet, with me dangling upside down. Then she would cut me loose and I would drop headfirst toward the river, just like in a flare and settle. All I had to do was flip upright, get my legs up into an L position, and brake as hard as I could.

"Time it right and you'll just get your toes wet," Gertrude said. "Time it wrong and the water temperature this morning is a balmy sixty-seven degrees. Professor Brock has a life preserver and will be spotting."

I sat and removed my boots. Brock fitted the shackles around my ankles.

"Robert, tuck your chin and put your arms across your chest on the launch," Brock reminded me. "Engage your glyph before Essie drops you—just minimal force—so that you have directional control when you start to fall. Both of you, be very, *very* careful."

Essie launched gently, pulling me behind her upside down. The blood rushed to my head. At a hundred feet, Essie came to a stop. I drew my hover sigil to initiate thrust. Essie counted down from three and pulled the release strap. The shackles popped open and I fell away.

I let myself plummet for half a second, trying to get used to the sensation before kicking my legs forward and rolling my shoulders back. I over-rotated and ended up tumbling back-first toward the river. No chance to land it—safer to abort. I added power and flew off.

"What the hell was that?" Gertrude said as I angle and tucked down beside her.

"I missed."

"You weren't even close! Show me the motions."

I showed her.

"Slower!" she said, putting her hands on my body to guide me. "Slow. Roll the shoulders back. In the same moment, thrust the chest forward, then the hips, and then swing the legs up and hold. Elbows in tight so that you don't flail with your off arm. Slower!"

I practiced on the ground, slow, over and over, as Gertrude made minute corrections to my body position.

"How many times did you rehearse the motions last night?" she asked.

"Ten or twenty," I said.

"You should have done it two or three hundred."

I ran through the motions once more.

"Better," Gertrude allowed. "Now, go up and do it right."

Essie lifted me again. I dropped, somersaulted into my L, then spun out of position while I was trying to brake. I barely pulled up and away in time.

"Terrible!" Gertrude said on the ground. "Sustain your L. Do it again!"

I dropped another half dozen times without better success.

"That's enough!" Gertrude said. "You're practicing failure. You're weak right here." She poked a finger into my belly. "The really embarrassing part is that you ought to do this better than any woman. A more powerful shoulder roll, a stronger chest-forward move, a harder kick. Take a month and work your abdominal muscles, then come back and try again. Twenty-five pounds lighter wouldn't hurt, either."

Laughter broke out among the girls who had come down to watch me. The old ladies had brought three full classes of Ones to observe. On the Cambridge side of the river, several dozen private citizens had also stopped to watch.

I reddened. "I can do it!" I insisted. "Give me one more. One more!"

"Last one, Robert," Brock said. "I have a meeting."

Essie lifted me a final time. I put too sharp an edge into my sigil while I was dangling, causing Essie to balk and twist on the release. I slammed my regulator on full to stabilize and then left it there a moment. A little extra speed ought to make the somersault easier. I flipped upright and kicked into my first good-looking L of the day. Maximum power and I should just about—

I got a clear look at the river a fraction of a second before I hit. I struck butt-first and went under.

A stinging jolt, tail to head. Water up my nose. Stunned, but all my limbs still worked. As I broke the surface, a whistle blast pierced the air. I blinked.

"Are you okay?" Brock shouted from above me.

I didn't have my wind back.

"Wave if you're okay!"

I tried to wave my arm, but it was more a fling of the sort a drowning man might make.

Brock hurled her ring buoy. It hit me in the face, the rope slicing across my brow. I went under and bobbed back up. I grabbed hold of it.

"Damn you, Weekes!" Brock shouted. She commenced towing.

Blood was streaming from my right eye. I couldn't see out of it. Once I was in the shallows, Brock let go of the rope and I tried to stand. Only two feet of water, but I slipped in the muck and went right back down, crawling toward the shore. Several of the veterans splashed in to grab me.

"Help him up!"

"Christ, do you see that eye?"

"Call for the doctor!"

"Quiet on the field!"

"Did it get the eyeball? Or just the lid?"

"Here, pry it open."

I groaned out an objection but they pulled my eye open. I shut my good one and squinted out of the injured one.

"Only a little blurry," I said.

One of the veterans brought my towel and change of clothes, which were sopping wet.

"One of your lady friends kicked them in the river," she said. "Some dissatisfaction over your locker, perhaps?"

"For God's sake, get him out of those clothes before he catches his death. I don't care who's watching."

"No," I said. "No!"

"Robert!" Essie screamed as she raced up with her coat. She laid it over my shoulders. "I'm so sorry! If I'd dropped you straight—"

"No," said Brock, who'd landed nearby. "If I hadn't hit him in the face—"

"Enough, the both of you," said Gertrude, as she hobbled up. "It's his fault. He wasn't ready and he knew it. And it's my fault—I should have grounded him after the first one, ugly as it was. I'll remedy that now. Weekes: Grounded, one month. Reclassified Zed."

"You can't—" I objected.

"Lift barbells. Do sit-ups. And don't show your face around here until you're ready to flare and settle for real."

22

NOVEMBER–DECEMBER 1917

During our first runs with the new glyphs, one of my test fliers confided that she felt a malevolent presence as she approached seven hundred miles per hour. Something evil and monstrous, sitting just off her shoulder, waiting to destroy her. I told her it was hypoxia affecting her peripheral vision. But the first time Mr. Weekes used the new sigil, I swear I saw something following him—I could describe for you its teeth and talons. We are fortunate that he is not even a little superstitious, perhaps because he and that devil are so well acquainted. I think it's been chasing him his whole life.

> Dr. Janet Brock, Lecture to the Scientific Assembly of the
> Société Internationale de la Philosophie Appliquée, 1927

MS. ADDAMS DID A local nerve stasis to numb up my brow and put in twelve stitches to close the wound.

"Never a dull moment with you," she said, as she taped a bandage in place. "If you're not too concussed, we also need to discuss a somewhat delicate matter."

"The locker room?" I asked.

"I have a letter from one hundred and ten women threatening to take legal action against the college for promoting gross indecency," Addams said.

"They're also worried this may be a first step toward unisex toilets and bathing facilities."

"I really, really don't want that," I said. Though with only one men's bathroom in the Gray Box—on the fifth floor, no less—the idea might have something to recommend it.

"I could arrange an area reserved for your use in the storage room," Addams suggested.

As much as the idea of integrating the locker room hadn't been mine, I hated the thought of abandoning it.

"You'll stretch a sheet across a couple powder barrels and write *Men's* on it?" I asked. "You want me to call that fair?"

"Call it unjust, but the locker room is a losing battle. And by the looks of your face, you have some other fights that need your attention."

I sought out Dmitri before Addams's stasis glyph had even worn off.

"You bit it in front of *how* many people?" he asked.

"At least a hundred," I said.

"Sprained your pride, then, but I've done worse, I promise."

We went to Harvard's gymnasium, where Dmitri led me to a set of hanging rings.

"Show me the position, as best you can," Dmitri said.

I needed two tries to jump and catch the rings. Without the weight of a bag and harness and minus the thrust of a hover sigil, my body felt unfamiliar in the air. I struggled with my balance before getting my legs up into the necessary L shape. I held it only a few seconds before I started to waver.

I dropped off and Dmitri took my place, springing up with such ease I couldn't help feeling shamed.

"Like this?" he said, assuming a rough copy of my position.

"No, the hips have to swing forward so the bag—yeah, like that."

Gertrude would have loved him. Dmitri froze in position and held it, the muscles in his arms rippling as he adjusted to cancel out the sway of the ropes. He got bored before he got tired. He swung his legs until his body was describing long arcs through the air. He let go, pulled in his knees, did a double somersault, and landed on the balls of his feet.

"Give me an hour a day and you'll flare and stick every landing," he said.

"An hour?" I objected. "I just have to make my belly muscles stronger is what she said."

Dmitri shook his head. "It's not just the abdominals. It's the lateral muscles in the back, pectorals in the chest, everything in the upper legs, the shoulders. An hour a day."

Over the next month, my Russian taskmaster supervised my workouts. On Mondays, I ran three, then five miles along the river for conditioning. Tuesdays, I wore boxing gloves and hit a heavy bag. Wednesdays, I ran up and down the steps in the football stadium until my legs burned. Thursdays, rope climbing. Friday, the parallel bars and rings. Saturday, swimming. And to conclude each session, a regimen of barbells, dumbbells, sit-ups, calisthenics, stretching, and tumbling.

Snds like th quintessence of yuck, Angela wrote when I described my routine.

But by the third week, I was turning somersaults more easily, I could hold the L position on the rings longer, I could do a hundred sit-ups without suffering cramps. There was something to it.

Unger caught wind of "an hour a day," and decided to inflict his own brand of cruelty on me for precisely that length of time, too. Given my grades in a couple of classes, I could hardly refuse.

Unger had learned German as a child and he still spoke it at home. So it was an hour a day of grammar, vocabulary, and conversation.

"You're going to have me with an accent like a Hungarian," I complained.

"It's at least getting recognizable as something other than very confused Dutch," he replied.

Then an hour a day of philosophical theory. I hated it, but it was only an hour. I could endure anything for an hour. Unger, much as he wanted to lecture on the intricacies of glyph design and differential equations, instead pared Professor Yu's lectures down to the essentials. I scored an eighty-three on the midterm and Unger was delighted.

"You went from the worst essay in history to a low B!" he said.

"It wasn't actually the worst—"

"You're going to pass that class whether you like it or not," he said. "Now get your book out. We are most certainly *not* taking the day off."

That still left plenty of hours to spend with Danielle. Her schedule was packed— she might have to travel to Washington for a meeting with the Deputy Secretary of Philosophy, or write an article for a women's magazine on top of her schoolwork, or fly out to Fort Putnam to review a fresh batch of cadets. But she always had Sunday mornings free and we always spent them together.

"When the Corps made me a reservist this past summer, I requested no duty on Sundays so that I could attend services," Dar told me.

We were strolling through the streets of Cambridge and the churchgoers were out in droves, bundled up in their hats and scarves against a November cold snap. Danielle took my arm to pull me closer as we made our way down to the river.

"I haven't so much as set foot in a church, though," she said. "Dad says he doesn't care as long as I'm there for his Christmas sermon. I told him that's not church, it's entertainment."

"Hmm," I said.

I liked it when she fell into this mood, open and chatty, even when the conversation veered into dangerous territory. She found me easy to talk to, she said. Most of her friends and confidantes had graduated during her time overseas. She'd found Radcliffe a changed place upon her return, its ablest philosophers and brightest students in the Corps and the remainder a little lost without them.

"Or maybe it's just me," she said. "Feeling lost."

"You do a good job of hiding it," I said.

We stopped under a bridge and Dar looked out over the water.

"May I tell you something I've only told two other people?" she said.

"Yeah."

She stuck her hands in her pockets. "I wake up some mornings and I have this feeling like I'm not supposed to be alive. Not like I *want* to be dead, but that I was supposed to die over there. And it didn't happen."

She stood in front of me and pressed her head back against my chest. I wrapped my arms around her.

"That night in Gallipoli, twenty jumps in, when I hit three hundred miles—that was my do-not-exceed number—I didn't even have half of them out. I knew I was going to keep going until it killed me. Ten thousand of them with each jump, how could I not? So thirty times in a row I said, 'This will be the one that kills me. And I'm ready to die.' "

A flock of geese launched themselves from the water, honking and coming about to a southerly course.

"I was delirious by the end. I spent three weeks in the hospital. I kept telling the doctors I was supposed to be dead. I stopped eating and they shoved a feeding tube down my nose. The neurologist they made me talk to—she said I survived because I started transporting at such a young age. It conditioned me. My dad said God had kept me alive for some purpose. I told him I couldn't bear to think that."

Danielle turned and wiped the tears off my face.

"Fuck, I'm sorry," I muttered.

She kissed me.

"Robert, all your training for R&E—" she said. "I admire the hell out of you, it's just—it makes me feel like a coward. Because if I could do it over again, if I knew what I know now—I wouldn't. Never. I would stay home and let them die."

I held her tighter. "But you didn't."

After a few minutes, we walked on, arm in arm.

"This is why I'm going to teach you to shoot," I said. "Take your worries out on a paper target. It's therapeutic."

Danielle laughed. "And a sharpshooter's pin for my uniform—don't forget the pin!"

So, we made our way to the musty sixth sub-basement of the Gray Box, where Radcliffe had installed a shooting range during the previous spring's war fever. There was nobody else in the big echoing room but us. We lay there on our bellies on dusty mats, side by side, with battered Springfield rifles that we checked out from the circulation desk. I put my hands over hers to help her aim. Dar turned out to be a terrible markswoman; she flinched every time she fired.

But it became part of the routine: Sunday walks followed by shooting followed by lunch followed by studying followed by dinner followed by reading or paper writing or sending messages to our families from Dar's apartment while playing footsie under the table. We began spending Thursday afternoons in like fashion. Wednesdays, too, and Saturdays and any other day we were able. When we were snowed under with work, I took my books and we read nestled opposite each other on her couch, lying head to toe.

Even now, when I look over the final chapter of *Hovering Emergencies and Recovery*, I recall the first time I read it, lying on my back with Dar's feet in my lap, the book propped up in the crook of my left arm, my right hand tracing sigils over her toes.

And so my month of exile passed. Training sessions with Dmitri, lessons with Unger, evenings with Dar. I decided there was no reason to rush back. Get stronger. Wait until next semester to return to the aerodrome.

But the Threes, all of whom had earned back their ranks, noticed my tardiness. They descended on the dining hall to call me out.

"You're going to let that bitch bust you back to Zed and just walk away?" asked Francine.

"Dmitri is sweet, but we're sweeter," said Jake.

"Stop pouting," said Astrid.

"It's boring with you gone," complained Tillie.

"I'm taking a second month," I insisted.

"He needs time for his secret slimming plan to work," Jake said. "He's shaking the sheets four times a day with the Hero of the Hellespont."

The air went out of me. Dar and I had been discreet about our first few dates, but Radcliffe was a small place and we'd eventually given up the pretense.

"Does she lecture you during the act of carnal knowledge, Weekes?" asked Tillie.

"If you move the mattress to the floor, there's no risk of the bedframe collapsing," Astrid suggested.

"There are species of spiders that bite off the male's head and consume the body after mating," Francine offered. "So, if she had a long transport that day, be careful."

Essie looked mortified. "You have to come back," she whispered to me. "The river will freeze by the end of December and then you won't be able to fly until spring."

Which was sound advice—and from someone who'd done a perfect flare and settle on her fourth try, too. (Essie had credited it to years of ballet lessons.)

"Tell Gertrude I want another month," I said. "Second Monday of December. Nine o'clock."

"What did you think they would say?" Danielle asked that night over mugs of cocoa prepared in her little kitchen.

"I don't know," I said. "But it's your reputation. And mine. Maybe we shouldn't—"

"Because Gloxinia Jacobi made you blush? One of the ordinary Cliffes in my political science class told me she was *shocked* to hear your name and mine together, because she'd always assumed I was a committed Sapphist. 'Though, I shouldn't suppose a deviant man is very different from an ugly woman.'"

"Well ain't she a perfect lady to say so!"

"That Sapphism line is everywhere right now. You heard the latest from our friend Max Gannet?"

"Lord, don't even—"

"Look at it, at least. You should know what he's saying."

Dar read the *Trencher Times* and the *Boston Informer* and the several other leading anti-philosophical periodicals to monitor the opposition.

I looked at the page, torn from a magazine:

The discovery of a new sigil to induce pregnancy without sexual congress represents the most vile and unnatural development ever to challenge mankind. Used in concert with the glyph that murders unborn boy children, these harlots can, within five generations, eradicate the entire male sex. This was the goal of the female Antichrist Cadwallader from her earliest days.

"God," I said. "That's wrong in every possible way! There's no sigil to—"

"Now, now," said Dar. "If you were smarter, you'd worry about convincing me to include you in the small harem of men we're building for our own pleasure once we render you superfluous."

"There's no such sigil! Does he think the women in the philosophers' communes get pregnant by magic?"

Dar laughed. "Your mistake is thinking the Trenchers want to know the truth. They've been doing variations on this line for forty years—something about it thrills them. You'll never reason it away."

"I don't think it's funny," I said.

"Neither do I," sighed Danielle. "Not even a little. Did you know the State of Kentucky is launching an investigation? They want all philosophical clinics closed until they can guarantee there's no conspiracy to make men go extinct."

"How do they plan to investigate something that's imaginary?"

"They won't. But it's all part and parcel—their governor's trying to get back to the good old days when women knew their place. Ten years ago, he told the county clerks to start dropping women from the voting rolls. Any who complain or try to register, come up with an excuse. Keep delaying. And it worked. Only nine hundred thirty-eight women in Kentucky voted in the presidential election last year."

"For the entire state?" I asked. "That's outrageous! That's *illegal*."

"Who's going to stop it? You think President Wilson is lining up a blue-ribbon committee to investigate? He's a Democrat, too—he doesn't want a million Republican voters back on the books. No, what we need is a national movement for philosophers."

"The Jayhawks," I suggested.

"With fewer murders. Something mainstream. I got this—oh, I don't even want to—"

"What?" I said.

"I got a letter about a conference in Syracuse over Christmas. Blackwell will be there and Polidori and Senator Cadwallader-Fulton," she said, naming several of the better-known philosophical agitators of the age. "Trying to get organizers from different states talking to one another. Cadwallader-Fulton wrote me a note after the march in Washington, said I seemed like the sort of woman who ought to be involved. But I don't really want to go."

"You got a letter from *Josephine Cadwallader-Fulton* and you don't want to go?"

Old Josie was the senior senator from Wisconsin, the daughter of the famous smokecarver and an exceedingly capable sigilrist in her own right. She'd served as her mother's board girl during the Civil War—only eleven years old when she marched out of Detroit at Lucretia's side—before running for office in middle age. She was the sole woman in the US Senate and its only outspoken philosopher.

"You're not the one who has to explain it to my mom," Dar said. " 'I'll only be gone a few days—and I think I've developed a taste for politics.' She'll lock me up, Robert."

"She'll have a hard time holding you."

The rest of November and the first week of December passed in a similar blur of calisthenics and tutoring and politics. And then it was time to fly.

"Do you want me to come tomorrow?" Dar asked.

"There's nothing to see if I do it right," I said.

"Put the kettle on and wait at home with warm blankets?" she suggested.

"God, if I splash in front of everybody again . . ."

"It wouldn't be so bad. Bring you up here, half-frozen, strip you out of your wet clothes and . . . well, isn't body heat how you save someone dying from the cold? Bare skin on skin?"

I nodded, wide-eyed.

"Are you scared to say it?" she asked.

"Yeah," I said.

"May I say it, then?" she asked. "You want it. And I want it. And I want it even if you're not freezing to death."

23

The town's entire population had lined up to receive us: the council-women, the shop mistresses, the professional philosophers, all in their Sunday best. The children, too, the sweetest little girls you could ever imagine, row upon row, all in matching pearl-gray dresses. Everywhere, a sense of peace pervaded, of feminine order and solidarity. One could begin to see why women might choose to live apart (and visit a man with sterling references when it came time for children).

Anna Blackwell, *Travels Among the Women's Settlements of Upstate New York*, 1916

"MR. WEEKES," GERTRUDE SAID the following morning, as she surveyed the gray water of the Charles River, "if I have to go swimming, it'll be with the intent of drowning you. It's too cold to mess about. On the first drop, rotate clear and brake immediately."

I was in my sleeveless summer-weight skysuit with no boots. I wedged my hands under my armpits, trying to keep them warm enough to draw. If I landed in the water, there really was a chance of hypothermia.

Essie launched and carried me to one hundred feet. I flexed my fingers to keep the blood flowing, then drew my sigil for down thrust, keeping it as small as I could.

"Dropping!" Essie announced. "In three, two—"

I consciously stopped listening. Just the position of the body. Shoulders, chest, belly, hips, legs. The cold metal of the regulator biting the skin between thumb and forefinger.

I felt the vibration of the strap about my ankles releasing rather than hearing it.

Shoulders, chest, belly, hips, legs.

And with no more than that, I'd somersaulted backward and snapped into the L position, falling fast.

Right hand.

The largest glyph for upward thrust I could manage, followed by another hard glyph and another.

And I was sitting motionless in the air thirty feet above the river. I held my position a moment then drew for forward flight and a landing.

"He doesn't want to get wet!" Gertrude crowed as I set down. "That was serviceable. Next one, dive under full power. You'll flip after one and a half seconds."

Essie towed me back to altitude. I drew to initiate. Essie counted down.

Don't listen. Don't anticipate. Only the position of the body. Where were my upper arms in relation to my pelvis relative to my feet?

The shackles came away. I was diving headfirst. I drew hard and harder still to push toward the ground. No counting. Brake at fifty feet. Wait for it. I knew fifty feet. Had known it for years and years.

I snapped upright into L position—shoulders back, chest out, belly tense, hips forward, legs up. Sigil to brake, brake, *brake*, BRAKE.

I came to a stop two feet above the water in a dead hover.

I straightened my legs to brush the surface with my big toe and made for the shore. I had no feeling of triumph, no joy. More like exhaling a breath I'd been holding for two months. I was now competent a single time in performing half a maneuver that I should have mastered years before.

I didn't realize until I landed how many people had come to watch me. They were cheering.

"Christ, but that was an ugly swan dive!" Dmitri shouted, pushing his way forward to thump me on the back. "We'll have to find a ten-meter platform and fix that, too!"

"Congratulations, then?" asked Unger. "Did you do it right?"

"Like he was born to!" proclaimed Jake.

"Robert!" shouted Danielle. She was running toward me, unbuttoning her coat to pull out a blanket that she'd kept tucked against her body. She wrapped it around my shoulders. I'd never felt anything so warm.

"I'm taking you out to celebrate!" Danielle said. "You and your whole army. We're going to drink up all the—"

Essie was in front of me, too, holding my parka. She handed it to Dar, who helped me into it.

"I'm sure that's more sensible," Dar said. "So we'll go to—"

"Begging your pardon, Sigilwoman Hardin," Gertrude said as she forced her way up to me. "But you're not taking him anywhere. He hasn't been up in two months. I need to fly him."

Gertrude turned to me. "Change into weather-appropriate gear and start working on the first half of the flare—flipping inverted to brake against your forward momentum and start your dive. As many repeats as you can manage in an hour."

"Well, after that—" Dar said.

"I reserved the boxing ring for this afternoon," Dmitri broke in.

"And the final exam for Theory?" Unger added. "You said I could take you through—"

I did an hour of flares with Gertrude critiquing my form. Then to the classroom for Essential Sigils and Chemistry, to the gym with Dmitri, back home for Unger's tutoring in German and a cram session for Theory.

Splndid, as expctd! Mother messaged when I sent word to her. *Hope th big dustup here ddnt wrry y. We're all wll.*

What dustup? I asked.

Tell y all abt it when y gt home.

Which was classic Mother. *Don't worry about the thing I won't tell you about.*

I'm rentng an apt in Billings, she continued. *More busness in town. We'll have Chrstms there. I'll send y addrss.*

That was unexpected. When it had been just the two of us, Ma had contemplated selling the house and moving into town. But with three apprentices, the big old place seemed sensible enough.

I tried pumping Angela for information.

Ma wont tell me nthing eithr, Angela wrote. *I say, good fr her if sh wants to be in town. Mor social. Speakng of whch—y hav girlfrnd? Whn wr y going to fess up!*

I'd asked a few too many offhanded questions: What was the style of dress on an outing to the botanical gardens? Should one split the tab at a dinner suggested by the woman but planned by the man? Would a phonograph record be an appropriate gift for your one true love? I'd prefaced all my queries with "I'm advising a friend on . . ." or "Willard Gunch was on leave and messaged to ask . . ." She'd seen right through me.

Dnt knw wht yr talkng abt, I tried. I could hear my sister's laughter through the sand.

Liar. Tattler *had 2 lines in gossp column—Hardin w/ a Radcliffe Man. Mrs. Pasczek askd Julie Yzermn and she askd me. I said had to be y.*

"Damn it, damn it, damn it!" I sang out. Everybody back home as good as knew.

"Popular man," Dar said, when I made it to her place quite late that evening. She was sitting at her table, answering her mail. I pulled up a chair beside her.

"Is your mom okay?" she asked.

"I think so," I said. "I still don't know what kind of dustup. Maybe a disagreement with a client. Folks get upset when you can't resurrect their sheep or bore a two-hundred-foot well in an afternoon. Or angry when the bill comes and it's high as the doctor's. Collecting used to be my job."

"Poor Robert. Well, shall we round up whoever we can find and drop in on the Wag?"

"Unger's writing a paper," I said. "Jake has a study group. Essie's a tee-totaler. Dmitri doesn't keep a message board."

"God, you have boring friends," she said. "Just the two of us, then? Or would I have to carry you home?"

I stifled a yawn. "Yeah, you might."

"Cup of tea?"

"No thanks."

"You bring a book?"

"No," I said.

"Well," Dar said. She was standing, looking at me with intensity. "What *do* you want, then?"

The question boomed out across the room. My heart rebounded from sternum to spine.

She came to me and took a double handful of my hair. My hands went around her waist. I kissed her.

"Come to bed with me," she whispered.

My scalp was on fire and my shins were sweating.

"I'm not going to be any good at it," I said.

"I don't care."

The top button of Dar's blouse was a little pearl thing girded round by a thin loop of fabric. My hands were trembling so badly I could barely keep hold of it.

And then, after a minute, we were standing naked in each other's arms, her flesh—warm, smooth, ample—pressed against mine, my mouth against hers. The room spun. Or perhaps we spun, rocking back and forth, turning barefoot circles on the cold wooden floor. Then we were in bed, our hands and lips searching out the full length of each other's bodies.

I wanted so desperately to please her. The only thing I could think of was a piece of advice Willard had given me once in Billings—a foolproof method for inspiring supreme ecstasy in any woman. I took Danielle's buttocks in my hands and commenced rubbing. I tried gently at first, then with more vigor.

Dar seized my hands. "*What* are you doing?"

She looked at me for a moment as if I must harbor some sort of bizarre perversion. I stared right back at her, burning with desire.

"Anything," I said. "Tell me."

She stroked my cheek and kissed me hard and long. Then she took my right hand and guided it between her legs. "Tiny circles, like that, with your finger," she said. "For ten minutes or an hour, I don't know. Afterward, anything you want."

I lay against her, caressing the spot like she'd asked. My other hand followed the angles of her face, her shoulder, her collarbone. Cupping the curves of her breasts and flanks.

After hours or days I felt Dar stiffen, clutch me to her, and convulse, letting out a long, husky sigh in a register I'd never heard her voice reach. Her face was slick with perspiration.

"Stop," she gasped.

She looked at me, and her eyes shone. "Anything."

I whispered four words, one of which I'd never before uttered aloud, much less in the presence of a woman.

Ninety seconds later, we lay in a heap, our sweat intermingling, my forehead pressed against her neck. I was gasping for air.

I drew back to look at her.

"Hi," I said stupidly.

"Hi yourself," she said, so flushed that I could feel the heat from her cheek radiating to mine. She adjusted the pillow beneath her head and gazed at me.

"You're shy," she said.

"Yeah," I said. "A little."

"Don't be. You're going to be wonderful. Was that—well, it wasn't your *very* first time, was it?"

I fumbled for a reply, unsure what she wanted to hear. I tried to explain about Daisy, a high school classmate for whom I'd provided flights to and from Billings' two-room schoolhouse. It had been a chance for me to make a few dollars and for her to avoid walking an hour each way—I'd done the same for a few different families over the years. Daisy had been stolid and provincial, unphilosophical, not the sort of girl I usually noticed. But carrying a passenger regularly creates a strange kind of intimacy. Yoked together, her rump brushing across your thighs each time you maneuver, the pressing together of bodies during a landing.

One spring day during our last year of schooling—I was seventeen, she was eighteen—Daisy asked if I could help her with a philosophical matter. She'd just gotten engaged to a bachelor farmer from out past Dolph's Rock and wanted to know how to draw a particular glyph. I took her by the house, but Mother was out. "Don't *you* know how to do it?" she asked. I did. I got a bottle of saline, she pulled up her shirt, and I showed her how to draw the glyph on her belly. "Don't you want to make sure it works?" she asked. And so we did, on a blanket spread out in the root cellar, where it was cool and dark and the air smelled of onions. I spent the whole time too terrified that Mother would come home to think about her pleasure or mine. I'd felt like the worst kind of cad for months afterward.

"But that's the most innocent story I've ever heard!" Dar objected.

"No it's not," I said. "Stealing another man's fiancée."

"Don't say it like that—like he owned her. Besides, you think she didn't know your mom was away?"

I'd never considered the possibility.

"I hope she was paying attention," I said. "I barely knew the glyph myself." Then I looked at Dar in a panic. "Did you—"

"Of course," Dar said. "I've drawn it the last two months, just in case."

Perhaps I was an innocent after all.

I closed my eyes.

"You'll keep me?" I asked.

She nipped me on my chest.

"Yeah," she said.

I stumbled home the following afternoon to find Unger at work with his dish of walnut ink and a ream of paper, having failed four hundred consecutive times to get the manual reduplication sigil to take.

"Did you spend the night with Danielle?" he asked. He was so genial about it that I almost slipped. But surely better to be discreet, even with Unger.

"I was out late," I said vaguely. I pulled off my boots and tried to organize my thoughts. If I slept three hours, I could study a bit of German, eat an early dinner, and then work on my vocabulary until I dropped. My final exam was the following morning.

Unger sat smiling, still watching me. "The two of you radiate it when you're together. I could set up a detector and discover the wavelength of happiness."

"I always look happy," I grumbled.

I bludgeoned my German exam into submission and took a B for the course. Empirical Chemistry and Essential Sigils were easy As, while Freddy's genius was enough to steer me through my Theory final so I could escape with a C.

Dar and I lingered for a couple of days after the end of exams. We flew out to Harvard's arboretum to hike, just us and the trees. We ice-skated on the pond at the Boston Common. Dar bought me a new pair of gloves at the counter of one of Boston's finer department stores. ("Close your eyes! It's supposed to be a surprise! Just let me borrow your hands to see if they fit.")

We spent our nights at her place, no pretense at all.

"What'll you do at home?" I asked her.

I was wearing the gloves and nothing else.

"Be spoiled rotten by my aunts," she said. "Spend hours upon hours baking with my mom. Watch my dad fuss over his Christmas sermon for days and then rewrite it at the last minute."

She pulled the quilt over us and nestled closer to me.

"You never talk about your dad," she said. "Did you know him at all?"

"No," I said. "He passed away when I was little."

"Tell me something about him?"

"Sure," I said. "Ma brought him back from Cuba. He was an American by the name of Beau Canderelli. He used to work for the Société as a field officer. They sent him to war zones to look for violations of the Rouen

Conventions. He could fly some. He spotted Angela when she was learning—Angie still talks about that. Then when I was two, he died from septicemia. Ma was pretty broken up over it. She didn't like to talk about him when I was little, didn't like to hear him talked over. That's pretty much it. Vivian could probably tell me more."

"Your middle sister?" Dar asked.

"Yeah. She's going to visit Billings for Christmas. I haven't seen her in a couple of years. Angie will be home, too."

Danielle sighed. "That sounds nice. It's going to be all yelling at our house. I wrote back tonight and said I'd do the meeting in Syracuse. My mom will be furious, but you said it yourself—when Senator Cadwallader-Fulton comes calling, you can't say no."

I ducked my head and looked away.

"What?" she said.

"Nothing," I said. "A country boy who thinks he's going to court a big important person."

Danielle laughed at that. "*I'm* the one who should be worried." She swatted me on the bottom. "Fancy college man. All the milkmaids paying you visits."

"It's sheep and cattle ranching by us, not dairy farming."

"What?"

"We don't have milkmaids."

"Cattlemaids, then," she said. "I ought to be the one making sure you remember *me*. Oh, I could ruin you."

She popped her head under the covers.

"Wait," I said, "what are you—"

By the next morning, I'd strained my voice from begging for more.

We rode the streetcar to the transporter arena together. We were a couple of dull young people in love, besotted, barely conscious of the hubbub around us.

But that's just the sort of moment when the gods decide they ought to lay you low.

24

Sherm's gang comes at us, guns ablazing. We run for the cabin to take cover. "Don't worry, boys!" cries Mrs. Gower. "I'll put a watchman sigil upon it!" We pile in and Gower does just that. The glyph makes those bandits look straight past the place, though they ain't ten feet away. But it does its work on Gower, too. After she's drawn the glyph she can't find her way back in, neither.

Edwin Fitzenhalter, *Fresh Gale on the High Sonora*, 1888

THE TRIP HOME WAS rough. A freelance transporter coming in from the field mistimed her jump and cut two attendants in half on the floor of the Kansas City arena, causing a twelve-hour delay. I didn't arrive in Denver until four thirty in the morning.

The temperature was ten below. I packed away the kidskin gloves Dar had given me in favor of my old rawhide mitts for the flight back to Billings. I made town shortly after dawn and orbited, blearily searching for the building where Mother had settled. Anticipating my difficulty, she'd written *Weekes* on the roof with coal dust in the fresh white snow, so I was spared the indignity of having to ask directions to my own home. It turned out to be the apartment above the dentist's office.

I staggered into the building and up a flight of stairs in my gear, which was covered in a thick rime of frost. Mother was waiting in the kitchen.

"Good God, we'll need till Easter to chip the ice off you!" she clucked, as I struggled out of my coat.

"I've had colder," I tried to say, but my face was so numb that the words came out slurred.

It wasn't until she pulled off my fogged-over goggles that I got a clear look at her.

Ma looked appallingly old. Not merely gray, but white around the temples. Her shoulders were stooped; there was a moment of hesitation as she maneuvered to sit in her chair, the barest hint of a tremor in her hand. How could she have aged so in only four months?

But Ma went on the offensive, pouring coffee into me as she fired off one fusillade of questions after another: Boston, classes, foodstuffs, entertainment. She was kind—jolly, almost—and perhaps in my increasingly excited answers, she saw something of the young girl who had left rural Missouri for Paris, St. Louis, and Kansas City, before settling down in Guille's Run.

"And there's a lady friend, I hear?"

No way to escape it.

"The corpswoman who led the evacuation at Gallipoli, no less!" Ma said. "God, but we could have used one like her in '97. You have to tell me *something*."

"Tall and dark," I said. "Political type. Her dad's a minister. Not much else to tell. Rich Eastern girl, Ma. Sorry."

She waved as if to say it couldn't be helped. "Are you silly for her or serious?"

"Both, maybe."

"You don't have a silly bone in your body."

She was right. And now that my serious bones had begun to thaw, they were insisting that this was not the Emmaline Weekes I knew—sitting at home at eight o'clock on a weekday, gossiping with her son. I had the overwhelming sense of wrongness, of something big and awful.

"What aren't you telling me?" I asked. "What happened?"

"Oh, lots has happened since—"

"Ma!"

She grimaced.

"There are a few things we ought to talk about," she allowed. "First, I've had trouble with my arm. The shoulder's come out of joint a few times. Twice while I was in the air. Once with a client."

"But you didn't get hurt," I said. "Not worse."

"I got down to the ground in a hurry—not my most graceful landings. I asked Bertie Synge if she knew anything for it, a brace or exercises. She says the more often it's popped out the more often it will. Told me to ground myself before I kill someone. Indefinitely."

Grounded. Half my childhood memories involved Ma throwing on a skysuit and charging out to intervene in a disaster or coming home afterward with tales that made us wide-eyed. Even quiet nights she'd devoted to instruction on some technical point of regulator maintenance. Mother was so inextricably bound up with hovering—I couldn't imagine her not doing it. To say nothing of her livelihood.

"Will the State Office let you stay on as a county philosopher?" I asked.

Mother stood and went to the sink to wash dishes.

"They expressed their thanks over my having trained Julie Yzerman," Ma said. "Said if a doctor ever cleared me, they'd be happy to take me back."

"No!" I said.

Ma rinsed the coffee percolator. "Truth is, I would take the chance and fly again. But it's not right to risk a passenger that way. I have lots of clients in town and lots more close enough to walk or ride to—they're keeping me plenty busy. It's been a more regular schedule, which I like. And Julie's done a fine job as Yellowstone County CP. For a little over a month now. Took the younger apprentices with her."

I looked at her, incredulous. "A *month*? Why didn't you tell me?"

"What were you going to do other than worry about it?" Ma said. "Vivian said it would be worse if I waited, but I wanted to tell you face-to-face."

She reached for a dish towel and dried a mug.

"And that's why you moved to town?" I asked. "Closer to business?"

"In large part," Ma said.

She was being too careful with her words.

"What's the other part, then?"

"Well, I've had more free time," she said. "Some friends from the old days got in touch. They'd figured out which men shot Erin O'Malley last summer. They wanted someone local as a guide. So, we went together and fixed things."

"God, Ma!" I said. "You told me that killing Trenchers was the wrong way. You said it only caused more—"

"I know. But Erin and I fought in the Disturbances together. She would have done the same for me."

She wiped her hands.

"Afterward there was some talk in town: 'Emmaline's back at it.' Then a couple nights at home I woke up and—well, I don't know what. There aren't many Trencher-sorts near Guille's Run and they aren't very brave. But one woman, alone, in a big old house in the country? It doesn't take brave and it doesn't take many. So I moved in here."

"And you feel safer now?" I asked.

She nodded. "Can you imagine someone dumb enough to try to shoot his way in? Doc Haley downstairs don't but drink, pull teeth, and pop-pop-pop."

And indeed, Doc was probably a better marksman than dentist.

"No, I'm plenty safe," Ma said. "It's you I'm worried about. You and your lady friend."

She ducked into her office and came back with a piece of paper.

"It was three men who killed Erin," Ma said. "One, she'd given evidence against in a burglary trial. Another owed her a lot of money. But the third— he was a different kind. He had this."

"A list of names?" I asked, as I looked it over. They were all famous philosophers, numbered one to two hundred. In the first column, I recognized Josephine Cadwallader-Fulton, Anna Blackwell, Apollonia Polidori, and Josofea Jimenez. Number 28 was Annabelle Addams. Number 141 was Erin O'Malley. Number 198 was Danielle Hardin.

"Oh, hell!" I breathed. "Is this Maxwell Gannet's list? 'Kill the right two hundred sigilrists and empirical philosophy as we know it will come to an end.' "

"You say that like you worry it might be true," Ma said. "It's not. Kill those ones and you'll have a shooting war without any of the sensible voices left to oppose it. But Gannet's been plying that line for so many years that the Trenchers take it as gospel."

"Danielle," I murmured.

Mother put a hand on my shoulder. "Dr. Synge put me in touch with your Lt. Addams. She told me my list was three months out of date. She's aware."

"Lord." Getting an anonymous death threat in the mail was one thing, but being on a thinly veiled hit list was quite another.

"Danielle's in good hands," Mother said. "Addams had a reputation in the Philippines—even the other smokecarvers were afraid of her. What _I_ can't get over is that Gannet wrote it down. That's new. During the Disturbances, all the Trencher factions were paranoid as hell. They waged their little local campaigns, but they were afraid of the other sects conspiring against them. Even Gannet, as often as he went on about 'the right two hundred,' never named which philosophers, let alone wrote a list. This is something bigger, something for them to rally around all over the country."

Ma reached into her pocket and pulled out a little four-shot revolver. It was one of her treasures. Several of the women she'd commanded in Cuba had commissioned it for her, a one-of-a-kind piece designed so that she could cock and fire it left-handed while flying without the recoil knocking her out of the sky. I'd never seen her carry it. Instead, Ma had favored a big Colt .45, working from the principle she'd rather plant both feet on the ground and use a weapon that made a large hole.

Ma laid the gun on the table in front of me. It was comically small—tiny enough to fit in a change purse—with rose-colored mother-of-pearl grips and silver plating etched with a whorling design that some gunsmith must have imagined resembled sigils.

"For you," she said. "If you want it."

"Ma, I couldn't!"

"I offered it to Vivian once," Ma said, smiling. "She called it a 'pretty little girl's gun' and asked for a semiautomatic. Boober, if it's not your taste, I'll find you a—"

"It's beautiful," I said. "Thank you."

The silver glinted as I picked it up. It wasn't even as long as the palm of my hand.

"I don't think I could ever bear to do more than polish it," I said.

Ma laughed. "Neither could I, mostly."

I opened the cylinder to unload it and shook out the tiny cartridges. Ma's smile faded.

"It shoots straight enough, though," she added.

I slept and ate and worried over all of it: Mother's health and assassins in the night, but most of all Danielle being on Gannet's list. If Ma had thought it necessary to arm me, then did that mean I was supposed to take matters into my own hands?

"Have you talked to anyone from the old days about Gannet?" I asked Mother that night.

"A few people," she said. "He's a dangerous one. He's got purity of motive, purity of action. I can almost respect him."

"Why do you say that?"

"He acts as he preaches. He's not one of those hypocrite Trenchers who keeps a message board or rides the National Transporter Chain when it suits him. No, damn the inconvenience—no philosophy, not in the slightest."

And he lived not even four miles away from Radcliffe.

After Teddy Roosevelt had banned the Trenchers as an organization in '08, many of them had relocated to Boston. The city's mayor had been a famous anti-philosopher and had given them protection, going so far as to install Gannet in an apartment in the old Trencher meetinghouse, which they now called a private gentlemen's club. Gannet had been holed up there ever since, writing his screeds and making the occasional speech.

"It's about the most secure building in the world," Ma said. "It looks like a medieval fortress. He sleeps in an interior room, always, no windows. So a smash-and-grab job is out."

She'd clearly thought it through.

"His sermons," I suggested. "Someone sets up across the street on a roof with a rifle and a good scope. Or, hell, hover your markswoman in."

Mother clicked her tongue against her teeth. "No, that's how a *man* would assassinate him, not the philosophical underground. You're curious how we would have done it back in the day?"

"Educate me."

"Used to be two schools of thought on technique. One was to choose an obscene method and then display the body so there's no mistaking who's behind it. Dissolve his bones and tie the corpse in a knot. Flay off his skin and hang what's left by the heels from the highest church steeple in town. But that scares the common folk to excess. I always favored disappearing someone."

I almost laughed. "What, you had a sigil to make him—"

"Don't be ridiculous," Mother said. "No, take them quietly in the night and then dispose of the body. It terrorizes the right ones. Is he alive or dead? In hiding? Did he go over to the other side?"

"Hmm," I said.

"If you ask me, Gannet's a lousy target," Ma said. "He's old and frail—it's always unseemly when you kill those ones. Him dying would rile up the whole Trencher movement, even the ones who think he's a madman. And if they *have* started cooperating between states, it clears the way for a younger, smarter man to take command."

"So if Gannet disappears . . ." I suggested.

"Then it was someone better than me who did it," Ma said. "And someone a lot more experienced than you."

I wrote to Dar, who did her best to reassure me—Addams had warned her about the list months ago; nothing had ever come of it. Besides, if Gannet's followers hadn't made a move against her on their home turf in Boston, they were hardly going to attack her over the next week in Providence.

My mom on the other hand, Dar wrote, *might try to kill me if I go to that meeting in Syracuse. It's been one quarrel after another here. I'm miserable. I miss you.*

I couldn't sleep at night for thinking of her.

I took target practice in the backyard, I reread *Life and Death on San Juan Hill,* I cooked overly elaborate meals for Ma—anything to distract myself. Then on the morning of Christmas Eve, while I was at work in the kitchen chopping garlic and rosemary for a leg of lamb, Vivian arrived, having flown three hours through subzero temperatures from Spokane. Seeing her dug up long-buried feelings of a different kind.

My earliest memories were of having two mothers. One of them was old and cruel and had to be watched like a wounded dog, lest you get too close or play too loud and set her off, snapping and snarling at you. My other mother had been young and (to my eye) beautiful, kind, and gentle. I remembered crawling into Vivian's lap, night after night, as she sat knitting by the fire, so that she could pet my head after Ma had said something that frightened me.

I didn't remember much else about those early years—or I chose not to. I did recall Vivian lighting out for Washington when she was twenty years old and I was six. ("With the first man who would have her, homely as she is," Ma had once bitterly remarked.) I remembered what I'd said to Vivian in a screaming fit when I'd last seen her; I'd been fourteen and had used every curse word I'd ever heard. Viv had just shrugged. She'd been cordial enough by message board since. Always a note for my birthday, how proud of me she was when I'd rescued Ma, congratulations when I'd been accepted to Radcliffe. I'd usually written back a few half-hearted words.

I'd never been confused about Angela—she was my big sister, bossy and snotty and mean at times—but I knew what she was. Vivian though . . . there wasn't a name for what a fifteen-year-old who was put in charge of her kid

sister and baby brother for weeks at a time was. Or a word for how abandoned I'd felt when she left.

Mother was out shopping, so I helped Viv out of her ice-covered helmet
and belted flying coat. I always remembered her as she'd looked when she left
home—short and stringy. Now, she looked like a plumper, ruddier version of
Ma. They stood the exact same height, same dull brown hair.

"Hey, sis," I said, my voice trembling a little.

"Oh, look at this one!" Viv said, holding me at arm's length. "Baby
Boober all grown up. Harvard man."

"Radcliffe," I corrected.

"It's all the same. Welcome back!"

Viv stood there in the kitchen, warming her hands in front of the stove,
talking away about her consort and her two girls—too cold to haul them on
a stringer in this weather, much as they would have liked to come.

I stared at her and I could barely comprehend it.

"And you have a lady friend, I hear?" Viv said, with a familiar cackling
warmth. She cocked her head as she said it, just as Ma did when she joked.

I burst out crying.

"Boober—what on earth?" Vivian said. She hugged me and the buttons
of her skysuit were cold through my shirt. "What's wrong?"

"Everything," I blubbered. "You and this apartment and Ma. She can't
fly. And she's hunting Trenchers again. She's too scared they'll kill her to stay
at home. There's a list—"

"I know," Vivian said. "I know."

"I don't know what to do!" I sobbed. "I should stay here. To protect
her. But Danielle— I don't— Viv, *help!*"

"Oh, Boober."

She held me to her for a minute and I might have been six again.

"Kiddo, it's going to be okay. They've been trying to kill Ma for forty
years. Do you remember any of it from when you were little? Her and your
dad?"

"No."

"Then let's talk. We won't get six words alone once Ma comes back and Angela gets in. Let's fly out to the old place right now. I'll tell you anything you want to know."

"Okay," I said, wiping my nose.

I gathered my gear and Vivian got back into her coat. For the first time in days, I felt like I could breathe. She would know what to do. Viv always knew.

"Hey, did Ma draw a watchman sigil on the house?" Vivian asked.

"Yeah. She thought leaving it empty would be an invitation for trouble otherwise."

"Trouble for *us*. Where'd she put the directions?"

"Viv, I've flown Billings to Guille's Run a thousand times. I'm not going to get lost."

"Oh, yes you will!"

We went outside and launched, making the short flight to the home we'd grown up in. But a few miles under way, I began to feel the effects of Mother's protective sigil. Doubts overtook me. Should the sun be over my left shoulder or my right? The closer we got to the house, the more intense my disorientation became. Surely I'd gone too far—but, no, on reflection I must be well short; I should fly on another half hour at least. I shook my head and looked at the note with Mother's instructions, but they trickled out of my mind. Did it say to land after the second branch flowed into the creek or the third? Could it really be the third? Then on final approach, flickers of mounting dread—*if I land here, I'll die!* I should fly just a bit farther, another mile.

Once we'd landed, the house wasn't invisible, exactly, it wasn't camouflaged—I still had the sense of an object nearby, a large structure—but the eye slipped right over it.

"Is that the shed?" I asked. "Over there?"

"Yes." Viv consulted the instructions again. "There's a post with a rope tied to it and a second post . . ."

"Over there," I said, stringing the rope between them. Then I stopped.

"Don't we have this backward?" I said. "The shed was always on the other side of the house, wasn't it? Someone must have moved it to confuse us!"

"No, you're doing it right," Vivian said. "Close your eyes. It helps."

I held the rope in one hand and walked between the posts, reaching with my other arm. To my surprise, my hand thumped against a door. I swept it back and forth to find the knob and pushed.

With that, the front door popped open and disrupted the sigil. The house, yard, and shed looked as they always had. Drawn on the door in chalk impregnated with nephrite jade was a glyph that branched and crossed and branched again, like the roots of an ancient oak tree rendered by a mathematician.

"Ma traced it out to ten levels," Vivian said, nodding in appreciation. "Nobody was ever going to find this place unless they knew exactly where to look."

We entered the house, which was just as frigid as outside. Snow blew in around our feet. Vivian and I sat at the kitchen table, where I'd stood so many night watches.

"Ma drew that sigil lots of times when I was young," Vivian said. "She and Beau would go hustling off, she'd tell me they'd be back in two or three days—six at the outside—and don't let anyone break the spell by opening the door. It was like being jailor to you and Angela."

"*When* was this?" I asked.

"God, right at the start of the Second Disturbance, years before anyone called it that. In 1901. You were two, Angela was nine. Right when we nicknamed you Boober."

"On account of having a spot of trouble pronouncing my own name."

"On account that it suited you so well."

Vivian pulled off her helmet and set it on the table. "The sigil would hit them, too, when they came home. Ma and Beau would blunder around the yard, shouting for me, and I'd let you run out to them. Then everything would go back to normal for a while."

She ran her hand over the thick slab of scarred, stained wood.

"I don't remember any of that," I said. "Would you tell me about it? And could you tell me something about my dad?"

"Well, shit, this is ten years overdue! What do you know about Beau? He's a good place to start."

"A little. He grew up in Arkansas. Italian parents, so he had an accent his whole life."

"Mmm, not quite," Viv said. "That's the version he told around town— it's the one Angela believed, too. But the first thing I noticed about him was that he drew his message sigils upside down."

Due to a curiosity of the Earth's magnetic fields, glyphs had to be drawn inverted south of the equator. Message sigils were the only ones that worked if you drew them wrong-side up in the Northern Hemisphere.

"So, not from Arkansas?" I asked.

"Nope. He was a military philosopher in the Chilean Army. They fought their own civil war down there in '91. The rebel smokecarvers incinerated half of Santiago and the president committed suicide. Beau was on the wrong side of it."

"Jesus."

"He joined the Société in Geneva as a war zone monitor afterward. They sent him to China and Ethiopia during the uprisings there. He interviewed the local sigilrists and made sweeps with a Trestor device to look for illegal philosophy among the soldiers. He had lots of stories about exotic animals and horrifying foods. He'd teach us little phrases in Cantonese—'Sir, I admire your peonies very much!' "

"How'd he and Ma meet?" I asked.

"He lived in Kansas City between assignments. He and Ma sat with a couple of the same working groups for mutual protection—Jayhawk clubs— as early as '95. The Société deployed him to Havana in '97 to monitor the Cuban rebellion against the Spaniards. The Corps sent a few dozen women, too, as an advance force in case we decided to invade. The Spaniards didn't like that—they attacked the corpswomen without warning. Ma led the counterattack. Beau joined in, even though he wasn't supposed to. In the end,

Ma won the White Ribbon for valor, Beau quit the Société, and they came back married."

"What?" I said. "That's not the way she told it to me!"

"Ma tends to leave out the part where she violated international law and married a foreigner. Oh, let's see. You were born in January of '99. Ma was deployed to Manila and then Honolulu later that year. Afterward, she and Beau ran a lot of raids against the Trenchers. Beau came back from one of them sick. Then the next morning he was dead. That was in November of '01."

There was something in the way she'd said it.

"Sick how?" I asked.

"Shot. Ma spent the next three years looking for the Trenchers who'd ambushed them. Those were bad times. I used to put you to bed with a passenger harness over your pajamas, in case a mob came in the night and we had to escape by flying out an upstairs window. When Ma finally had a good lead, we put you and Angie in a safe house in St. Louis—"

"I remember that a little," I said. "Dr. Synge and Sheriff Hansen went with Ma."

"And me. And Winnie Yzerman, Evelyn Klein, and Erin O'Malley. We burned and shot and poisoned our way through half of Kansas. In the end, we got all the ones we were after. We're still wanted there under a bunch of false names."

"Oh my God!"

"We told ourselves we were doing it so the next generation wouldn't have to. But now Ma's whispering to you about Trenchers and Max Gannet and lists of names. Slipping a pretty little gun into your pocket."

"You know about all that, too?"

"Who do you think went with Ma on her little expedition the other week? Erin O'Malley was my friend, too."

Viv reached over and took my hand.

"Part of Ma still wants to keep you clear of it. That's why she's never told you the whole story. Told me not to tell you, either—and we've had some rows about *that* over the years. But part of her thinks that killing Trenchers is the family business."

I stared at my hands. Every strained joke the shopkeepers in Billings had told—"Tell your mother I gave you a good deal. Wouldn't want a visit from her in the middle of the night!" The rope-skipping rhyme that the girls at school had sung, with the words altered whenever I walked past—"Parsley, rosemary, thyme, and dill, how many Trenchers did the Major kill? One, two, three, four . . ." Every nightmare I'd had about her.

"Everybody knew but me," I said.

"And Angela," Viv said. "She escaped it, God bless her. But you . . ."

Viv sighed. "Come with me a minute. I'll give you a present if I can find it."

We went into her old bedroom, which still held the furniture she'd used when she was young. She removed the bottom drawer from her dresser and fished an envelope out from under it. It contained a tarnished silver chain strung with a quartz crystal that had been hollowed out into a vial. Viv unscrewed the vial and tipped out a clod of blackened powder.

"A necklace for drawing a sigil?" I asked.

She nodded. "Ma gave it to me when you were born. She filled it with bone meal and sulfur and told me if anyone ever tried to hurt you, I was supposed to use it."

"She wanted you to *kill* them?"

"Oh, yes! And it bothered me—did I have it in me to take a life? It was hardly a subject you could talk over with your friends from school: boys and sewing patterns for dresses and justifiable homicide. So, I worried on it alone. Until Beau noticed. He was a good listener. He always heard what you took pains not to say."

"What did my dad do?"

"He told me if you can get close enough to kill a man with bone meal, you can draw a stasis glyph on him. It's just as quick. Then you have time. You can run. Or you can string him up by a noose so that when he comes to, he hangs until he's dead. Beau poured out the bone meal and replaced it with silver chloride and said don't tell Mother—as if I would have dared!"

Viv fit the drawer back into place.

"I've thought on it the past few days, too," I admitted. "About what I would do if they hurt Danielle. Or even if they don't. I could get close to Gannet at one of his speeches. The Trenchers wouldn't suspect a man."

"I'd rather not see you cut down in a hail of gunfire five seconds later," Vivian said.

She took the necklace from me and blew into the vial to clear out the last grains of powder. "I wish Beau were here. He would know what to say to you."

"What do *you* say?" I asked.

Viv found a tube of silver chloride in her workbag and refilled the hollow crystal, then threaded it back onto the necklace.

"I think I ought to listen to what you're not saying. Two months practicing a flare and settle? Little Boober, who asked me to read him *Life and Death on San Juan Hill* every night? And who asked Ma every day whether he could join R&E? And then stopped asking the thousandth time she told him it was impossible, but didn't stop asking for the book? I know what it means."

I looked away in embarrassment.

"Just a dream, right?" I asked.

"No," said Vivian. "I think it's wonderful. We've got killers enough in the family. You—you're going to be the first man in R&E."

Vivian strung the chain around my neck.

"God put big sisters on Earth to keep little brothers out of trouble," she said. "But sometimes when you're trying to be good, trouble finds you anyway. So, use this when it does. And then go save lives instead of taking them."

PART 3

THE

CORPSWOMAN

25

To see this heinous piece of legislation introduced by my own party—the party of Abraham Lincoln, who gave the vote to women in '64—the party of Theodore Roosevelt, who ensured the Corps was the best-equipped, best-trained expeditionary force in the world—to see *Republicans* advocating for the Zoning Act—that is betrayal. It is cowardice. It is treachery.

Rep. Danielle Noor Hardin, Congressional
Floor Speech, October 31, 1925

TROUBLE DID FIND ME—on my first day back at Radcliffe. Not Jake or Francine or any of the garden-variety hell-raisers, but the capital-T Troublemakers: Addams, Brock, Gertrude, and Murchison.

"What could I have possibly done already?" I complained, when they summoned me to the dean's office.

"Nothing," said Addams. "I've assembled every person at the college who thinks your one-man campaign to win a spot in Rescue and Evac isn't a waste of time."

All five of us. (And Murchison seemed so intent on pulling apart the wires in a mesh tea strainer I didn't think he'd even noticed me.)

"It might be possible," Addams conceded. "We have a connection in the Corps, a brigadier general, who's interested in you. But taking a man for her wing would create huge controversy. She needs you to prove yourself in a public venue. So, at the end of May, Radcliffe will fly you in the General's Cup in the long course. It doesn't get any more public than that."

For two decades, the General's Cup had been America's premier intercollegiate flying competition. The Cup had begun as part of the University of Detroit's celebration of Lucretia Cadwallader's fiftieth birthday: a week's worth of exhibitions and competitions, to which they'd invited the country's three other leading schools for philosophers: the Sacramento Institute of Philosophy, Maria Trestor College in New Hampshire (where young women studied the theory, rather than the practice, of sigilry), and Radcliffe. The hovering events had proven so popular that they'd continued every year thereafter, with each school hosting in turn. This would be Radcliffe's year.

"The Corps sends a scout to the Cup," Addams continued. "She invites well-qualified women to test for R&E. Usually that means the medalists in the long course, but she's allowed to invite any expert hoverer. If you fly well, maybe beat one or two women, you might impress the scout enough for an invitation. Then our friend the general can work her magic."

"That's fantastic!" I said.

"It's shaky as hell," Gertrude countered. "Who do you think you're going to beat flying at two hundred and eight miles an hour?"

The answer was no one, not even the future theorists from Trestor College. Medaling would be nearly impossible—the U of D had a pool of hoverers twenty times larger than ours from which to draw and would put up some of the finest fliers in the world. Sacramento, with its own sizable population of aerialists, could field women nearly as good. Radcliffe had been shut out of the long-course medals eight years running.

"I have no doubt you'll work your fingers bloody to improve," said Addams, "and that this office will call in favors it can ill afford on your behalf. But still—still—the overwhelming likelihood is that we'll fail. You need a backup plan. If you don't win a spot in the Corps and drift into your Contingency assignment without help, you'll get stuck with the absolute dregs.

Hauling water in Death Valley or coal in Barrow, Alaska. You need an arrangement."

An arrangement. One heard the Contingencies whisper the phrase. She has *an arrangement* with a munitions factory, a foundry, a courier service. An all-but-guaranteed position with the firm asking for her by name, greasing a few palms on the Regional Contingency Boards to make sure she got the assignment.

"Mr. Weekes, you'll never have better connections than you do right now," Addams said. "Use them. That's *your* job."

She turned to Brock and Gertrude. "You pair have five months. Get him ready to fly. And you—"

She looked at Murchison, who had succeeded not only in disassembling his strainer but also in tying the wires together in a single long string.

"One to rearrange the pieces on the chessboard before it can be knocked over," he mused, "and one to escape notice. You could not offer me a better prize."

"Oh, Robert," Danielle said when we were reunited that evening. "That's not just shaky, that's—I mean, look at it from the Corps' perspective. If you were a field commander, camping with your wing in the middle of nowhere, eighteen tents and a pit latrine, running casualties around the clock, would *you* take a man? Think of the distraction! You could be the very best flier in the entire world, but—oh, it's not your fault. You just can't put a man in close quarters with thirty-five women. You can't."

Leave it to Dar to puncture my high spirits. But she was still completely buoyant herself and it pleased me to see her so. From the string of messages she'd sent, I gathered she'd made quite a splash at the conference in Syracuse. Senator Cadwallader-Fulton had offered her a job.

"I could scarcely believe it," Dar said. "I'd known her all of three minutes and she said I should be her aide. A glorified secretary, really, but—Robert, you can't tell a soul this. Nobody. The very next thing she asked is when

I intend to run for office. She said to do it soon. 'You're young, you're pretty enough—do it before public opinion on the Great War swings the other way. In ten years, the populace will have decided it was a terrible sin and anyone involved is tainted.' Besides, almost no one wins her first time out."

One thing to talk politics and quite another to throw oneself right in the thick of it.

"Would you?" I asked. "Run?"

"I've thought about it," she said. "When I was fifty years old or something. But I could try for the House of Representatives when I turn twenty-five. I could work as Josephine's aide, see if I can stand the sliminess, and then in '22 . . . Well, Rhode Island has three seats."

"I ought to move to Providence so I can vote for you."

"Yes! That'll make two votes. I'm not counting on my mom. 'Not a woman's place,' she says. But if you're talking about moving . . . God, how do I say this without sounding pushy? Would you ever consider Washington? I mean, yes, try for the Corps, but if that doesn't work? You're thinking about an arrangement, right?"

"Addams said so, too. But I don't even know how to start—"

"Nancy Durstman," Dar said. "Her father has an office in Washington. He could find a job for the flier who pulled his daughter out of the river. Not glamorous, maybe, but just for a year. And we could see each other every day. Or every night? Tell me you wouldn't want that?"

I spent the next few days trying to imagine myself as helpmeet to Congress-woman Hardin. Well, why not? When my Contingency year ended, I could find more useful work in Washington, maybe as a municipal philosopher or hospital flier. It was too soon to think about it and yet—

"Pay attention!" Gertrude shouted at me as I landed after steaming past on a speed run. "That was much too long between redraws. Even the slowest girls from Trestor College will make three hundred miles an hour. There will be eight fliers in your event and right now you're shaping up to finish last by *eight minutes*. In a thirty-minute race. That's a crushing loss. That's humiliation! A man who loses that badly I don't want for my Corps. We have to get you faster."

Gertrude was putting me up three, four, five hours a day. Almost no one else was flying, as Boston's version of January was only slightly less crippling than Montana's. But my old lady knew every trick—petroleum jelly around the edges of the goggles to prevent windburn, two layers of gloves with recirculating smoke in between, a hot water bottle in your neck protector.

As promised, Addams had put a curtain up in the storage room, giving me my own changing area. Gertrude had been incensed that I would walk away from a fight, but had nevertheless permitted me to use it, much to everyone else's relief. And the custom harness, for which she and Brock had drawn up plans, finally arrived from Northwest Aero. It was a beautiful brown leather and feather-steel piece that fit me perfectly. So, at least I was suffering in high-quality tackle.

"I need your full concentration," Gertrude insisted. "At two hundred seventy-five miles an hour, you'll be competitive. If your landings are sharp enough, you might even beat one of the girls."

"How fast was the last—"

"Two thirteen."

"That's great! That's as fast as I've ever done. Professor Brock says I can expect another twenty miles an hour from conditioning. When those spiral regulators come in, that's twenty more."

"Are you so lovestruck you can't do arithmetic? That's still too slow. If you lost just—"

"Oh, don't start with that again!"

"You came back from Christmas up four pounds! One pound a week until the Cup would buy you another twenty miles an hour. And then you'll have a chance."

I made a noise from the back of my throat.

"Think about it before you tuck into dinner tonight. In the meantime, which direction are you flying today?"

North to St. John's, west to Niagara Falls, or south to Washington—the farthest points I could reach flying full out for two hours and then return home from before dark.

"Washington," I said, and rechecked my rigging.

"Oatmeal, without milk or sugar, and one piece of fruit," Dmitri advised. "Vegetables, raw or steamed, as much as you like, but never fried. Lean fish or chicken. Water to drink, no beer or wine. Brown rice and brown bread in small quantities. No white rice, white bread, potatoes, cakes, pies, pudding, chocolates, heavy cream, red meat—"

"This sounds awful," I said.

"Finishing so far in last place that the medal ceremony is already over when you land sounds worse."

I resolved to try it for a while. By the end of the first week, I was down one pound.

"Adequate," Gertrude pronounced. "You're in it for the long haul. Looking to the future, I'm also going to start flying you left-handed."

"You're kidding," I said. "How will that make me any faster?"

"It won't. But assume for a moment that all this works and you get to test for the Corps. They're allowed to ask R&E fliers to demonstrate proficiency flying with their off hand. I've never seen it done, but if I decided to fail you, that's how I would do it."

"Jesus. I've flown left-handed about ten seconds in my whole life."

"It doesn't need to be pretty. You only need to fly a single, credible one-mile pass. So, starting today, you're a part-time lefty. You brush your teeth left-handed. Notes in class—with your left. Soup spoon—left. We'll do ten passes a day. Start real high, in case you have a hiccup."

I didn't kill myself flying southpaw, but I made a credible attempt at cutting my throat shaving left-handed.

"Darling, you're slashed to ribbons!" Danielle said when she saw my face. "This is madness! Diets and left-handed and four-hour flights. This is a bitter old lady who's hazing you."

"It's working," I said. "I'm getting faster. A little."

"To what end? When in your life, outside of the Cup, will you ever have to fly that fast?"

"I just want to— I need to do this. I need to do it as well as I'm able. And if it doesn't work, then I did the best I could and I can hold my head up."

"You can already do that, love. Before I met you, I never would have believed a man could do what you do. A thousand women here agree. I wish you'd take more pride in that instead of chasing a fantasy."

Slapping me would have stung less.

"I don't mean to nag," she said. "But Nancy? Have you talked with her? Would you? Please?"

An arrangement.

"Dar, this is the reason people say terrible things about Contingencies! The Contingency Act was supposed to send philosophers where they were needed, not to whichever insurance firms slip the regional board an envelope stuffed with cash."

"You earned it, Robert. You risked your life to save hers. I love you for wanting to come by your position cleanly, but you'd be the only Contingency playing by the rules."

So, on the first of February, I sat in an overstuffed leather chair, freshly scrubbed and suited, equipped by Unger with a navy blue bow tie shot through with silver threads, facing Michael Durstman, president of the fourth largest insurance company in America.

"Such a pleasure!" Durstman boomed. "I've heard so much about you! Nancy thinks the world of you!"

I rose to shake his hand and fell back on the briefing that Mayweather had given me. *The most vain, self-important, unphilosophical plutocrat you'll ever meet. Flatter him from the first word.* And when I'd complained that I was no good at that sort of thing, *Don't say anything that's more than half-true. Make the other half the sweetest lie you can think up—imagine the most ingratiating thing I would ever say, double it, and add ten. At the end, hit him with a "You can count on me!" and get out fast.*

"Nancy's a sharp flier, one of our best," I intoned, trying to match his bluff jollity. This about a girl I'd had the pleasure of coaching for all of seventy-five seconds as she missed a well-lit landing field and plunged into the river.

"That's a credit to you," he said. "She never showed the slightest interest in flying until she went to school. A little adventure while you're young, eh?"

"Just a little!" I agreed.

"And those fancy regulators from Denver, tell me the truth—are they any good?"

The spiral-cut regs that he'd bought us from Denver Custom Instruments were still on back order. DCI was making a fortune manufacturing rifles—less time to cast high-end philosophical equipment.

"Best in the world, sir!" I said. "We'll thrash those common women from Detroit in the General's Cup, just see if we don't."

"That's the spirit! It's good to see a man in a philosophical field. Bringing masculine discipline to the feminine art."

"Nothing to it but hard work," I tried.

Durstman had to consider that a moment too long, but decided it was an admirable sentiment. "Now, Nancy tells me you're in need of a position. Of an *arrangement*. Well, I say if Uncle Sam is willing to send me a talented young fellow and pay his wages, I'd be a fool not to accept. What job classification will you put down for?"

"Hoverer," I said.

"Yes, hmm. And which of our offices do you think just might have a terrible need for such a thing?"

"Washington, DC."

"How to make it work . . . We have quite a few dignitaries who visit, foreigners. You'd strike a very imposing figure in a company uniform. Fly them to the hotel, to the office. Very memorable."

He rubbed his chin. "*Too* memorable, perhaps," he mused.

"Have to respect that some types just don't have a modern sensibility," I ventured. "Why, I might prefer a carriage, too."

"Hah! I'm sure of it. As a courier, then! Documents between the offices. Sensitive stuff. How long for you to fly Washington to Boston by way of New York City?"

"Flew it just last week," I said, which covered the half-truth. "Two hours if I stop for a cocktail."

"If he stops for—hah! Two hours, though, splendid. You'll be a great asset. I shouldn't tell you this, but we do a lot of insurance contracts for arms shipments, vital work for the war. We need someone we can trust."

Mayweather couldn't have scripted it better. I stood and extended my hand as if Durstman had just offered me the job. "You can count on me, sir."

"Oh, thank you," Dar said, as she kissed her way up one of my shoulders, across my neck, and down the other. "Thank you, thank you. I know Durstman must have been an ass, but we're going to have so much fun in Washington. You'll love it, you just don't know it yet."

She ran her lips over a ticklish spot in the middle of my back and I sang out.

"No?" she asked.

"In a minute."

I got up and folded my suit jacket, which I'd left rumpled on the floor.

"How'd *your* meeting go?" I asked.

Senator Cadwallader-Fulton had passed along intelligence to Dar that the Trenchers were planning a national gathering in Boston. Dar had felt that Radcliffe ought to organize against it and had gone to Addams for permission.

"Really well," Dar said. "Addams says if she can't stop me, she may as well help. The Trenchers are doing a parade in all their regalia a week from Saturday. We decided that's when I should stage the counter-protest. Addams will send a few of her men to watch the crowd. If you can get Mayweather and the Cocks to turn out and maybe we get Harvard's chapter of the Benevolent Society involved . . ."

She kissed me on the back of the knee and discovered an even more ticklish spot.

"Oh, this is going to be fun!" she said.

Over the next week, Dar went to every student group, club, and professional organization she could think of, rounding up women.

"Radcliffe's branch of the Women's Home Defense League keeps going on about how they'll be ready to deploy anywhere in the country to fight the Germans within an hour," Dar complained, "but this is four meetings now to persuade them to send a few girls a couple miles down the street."

But the League, at length, would attend.

Wellesley College and Vassar arranged to send contingents. I signed up the Cocks and the Threes, while Jake threatened or cajoled most of the rest of the aerodrome into going. Astrid's fiancé would bring Harvard's chapter of the Benevolent Society. ("*Husbands, brothers, sons* is their motto," Astrid chuckled. "Really, it's Liam plus a few awkward boys who want to meet women. They're the least philosophical men you've ever seen—they're adorable.") The Greater Boston chapter of the Benevolent Society also volunteered. ("All husbands and definitely not adorable," Dar said. "We'll be glad for the extra muscle.") The Hoverers Union would send women from the docks, the Transporters Union from the arena.

All of it went through Dar.

"How did I end up in charge of this mess?" she grumbled, cycling through her various message boards. "And look at this! No, they may *not* bring signs that read DEATH TO TRENCHERS."

I would have lent more of a hand, but Gertrude kept me occupied at the aerodrome: four-hour flights, flare and settles while carrying sandbags, left-handed passes.

"If you punch someone Saturday—" Gertrude said.

"With my left," I replied.

"Can't have you breaking your good hand."

Brock was less pugnacious about it: "Your best behavior, Robert."

She and I were meeting weekly to talk strategy. Brock had flown in the Cup for Detroit in '89, winning all four events as a seventeen-year-old freshman. No one had managed it before or since.

She was plotting my top speed on a piece of graph paper.

"I would have expected at least another eleven miles per hour by now," she said. "But all my projections are for women. It's hard to know which curve to put you on."

"Do men improve slower?" I asked.

Brock shrugged. "I have no idea. At any rate, we have to think about other ways you might gain an edge."

The long course was a hundred-mile rally, loosely inspired by the flying postal carriers. Every ten miles, you landed and picked up a twenty-pound sandbag, until you were carrying nine bags at the end.

"At the first few checkpoints, everyone will secure the bags straight to her harness," Brock explained. "There's less drag and it permits faster landings. But, damn if an eighty-eight-pound little girl doesn't hate the idea of trying to land, much less walk, carrying twice her body weight in cargo. So everyone resorts to a belly bag by the last few landing zones."

Essentially, you put your cargo in a sack attached to a twenty-foot line with a pulley and dropped it to the ground before you set down. It saved your knees and back the stress of landing with the extra weight.

"But that comes with a price," Brock said. "You can't streamline as well, so you're slower in the air. You can't flare, so landings take longer. Then even more time to reel the bag in and out. But a hundred and ninety-pound flier . . ."

"You want me to carry all of them," I said. My knees ached at the thought of hitting the ground with nine twenty-pound sandbags.

"It's no worse than taking a heavy passenger," Brock said. "You'll save a couple minutes on the landings alone."

"How many did you carry when you flew in the Cup?" I asked.

"Six," she said. "If I'd taken nine—and I think I could have done it—I would still have the course record."

. . .

I asked Dmitri to adjust my gym workouts.

"How do you carry the bags?" Dmitri asked.

"You have empty sacks attached to your harness," I explained. "You pull a toggle to open the sack, drop the sandbag in, and then cinch it shut. The bags are about two foot by one foot."

"You have to reach around to your back to secure some of them?"

"Four in front, five on the back," I answered.

"That's a difficult motion. So practice it five *hundred* times."

I couldn't argue with that—it was the same as my philosophical answer for everything.

"Plus you'll have to be able to walk carrying all that weight when you land. So, squats, running up hills, weighted vest . . ." He began devising a schedule.

"You're coming to the march tomorrow, right?" I asked him.

"Oh, wouldn't miss it! There's nothing like a good protest."

"He's bringing a couple Russian friends with him," I told Dar that night.

"We'll be glad to have them," she replied, lost among her preparations: the pot of black paint, a hundred sheets of heavy cardboard, sticks, and a stapler; refinements to the list of songs to be sung to keep our spirits up; note cards in case she was called on to say some words. "They wouldn't— I mean no Communist slogans, right?"

"I believe his people were on the other side," I said. "Are you sure I can't make a few of those for you?"

"I want the lettering to be consistent. What sounds better: *Our Rights and No Less* or *No Less Than Our Rights?*"

"Umm, maybe the first one. I thought everyone was supposed to bring her own."

"Some of them will forget."

I watched her work, her brow furrowed, mouthing the words to her speech.

She sent me back to my apartment at one in the morning, still waiting for the paint on the last batch of signs to dry. I came back a few hours later with breakfast and found her slumped over her table reading a prayer book, her eyes half-closed.

"Robert, it's going to be a mess," she mumbled. "If this turns into a repeat of the last one, if people get hurt—it's half of Radcliffe. I'm putting them in harm's way. Me."

"They're choosing to go," I said.

Dar opened her eyes and shut the book.

"You really never pray?" she asked.

"No," I said. And then, to lighten her spirits: "Just Fox's Prayer."

She snorted. "Of course you would. Well, it couldn't do any harm."

She bowed her head. "Dear God," she whispered, "don't let us fuck this up."

26

Men huddled around the fire, mad with the cold. They cried out to me to give them fuel, but they were even at that moment squandering a wealth of smoke. So I did not pity them. For it is a poor flame that burns but once, a poor heat that warms but once, and a crooked soul that would freeze to death while the means of his salvation blows away on the wind.

Galen Wainwright, *Confessions of a Confederate Smokecarver*, 1875

THE TRENCHER PARADE WAS scheduled to begin at nine; by eight thirty nearly a thousand women and men had crowded the streets surrounding Boston's former Trencher meetinghouse. The "Castle Club" they called it now—eight stories of rough-hewn stone topped by a pair of crenellated turrets.

Out front, a doorman stood at attention. He was dressed in red silk hose and a bronze breastplate, the Trenchers' outfit for formal occasions, with the bronze to disrupt any untoward sigils. He finished an attempt at counting us and ducked back inside.

The toughs from the Benevolent Society had arranged themselves around our perimeter, with a handful of bats and blackjacks on display. I recognized a few of Radcliffe's guards scattered among them; they'd replaced the gaudy vests and ties that they'd worn for the freshman social with anonymous over-coats and tweed jackets. Addams herself, in her corpswoman's uniform, was attending as a member of the Philosophical Veterans Association.

Dar enlisted me to remind the latecomers that the event was supposed to be peaceful and to hand out papers with the order of the day's musical program. She'd decided that singing would keep everyone occupied, reducing the risk of a sigilrist shouting threats or throwing rocks. As soon as the Trenchers emerged, it was to be "The Battle Hymn of the Republic," followed by "Sunset on Havana Bay," and "Detroit, My Sweet Soul's Rest."

By nine, it had started sleeting. There was no sign of the Trenchers.

I was handing out flyers on the other side of the Castle Club and missed Danielle's speech. Patrice found an apple crate for her to stand on and Danielle offered a few words on the power of unity and sisterhood, asking for each woman to introduce herself to the one next to her, so that we would be able to turn to one another if we were ever in need. (It was, by Dar's later analysis, a middling effort. She'd misplaced her note cards and spoke extemporaneously. No one thought to make a transcription, so the exact wording of her first of many thousands of public orations is lost to the ages.)

But still no sign of the Trenchers. Some of the protesters began to trickle away. At nine thirty, we ran through our three songs for practice. The effect was stirring and filled us with warmth, even as the wind began to pick up and the sleet turned to stinging frozen rain.

By ten, I'd made my way back to Dar.

"Are they scared to come out?" I asked.

"Maybe," she said. "Or scared of the weather."

We sang our three songs again. Krillgoe was enlisted to belt out a few hymns, which took hold up and down the ranks, though not with the vigor of the earlier tunes. A newspaper photographer asked Dar to climb back up on her crate and reenact her speech for some pictures. By eleven, several of the less hardy groups had come to shake Dar's hand before going home.

"A lot of old men cowering in there," gloated Gertrude, who'd also attended with the Veterans Association. "I'm pleased to have frightened them so badly, but I'm going to catch my death if I stay out any longer."

The Trenchers finally straggled out at noon. We'd lost nearly two-thirds of our number, but the remaining crowd sang lustily as a small group of old men in overcoats hobbled six blocks to the State House under cover of their umbrellas. They hadn't even worn their breastplates.

"That's it?" Dar fumed. "That was only three dozen of them!"

"Thirty-one," supplied Mayweather.

"Which one's Gannet?" I asked. I was imagining him as he'd appeared when he ran for president—a big, barrel-chested man with thick whiskers and mutton chops.

"The scrawny old one in the middle," Mayweather said.

It was a good description of pretty much all of them. Part of me wished I'd brought Mother's little pistol, though I wouldn't have known which Trencher to shoot at.

Dar shook her head in embarrassment. "I called in women from Connecticut and New Hampshire, I asked women to sacrifice a day's wages for *that?*"

"You did marvelously, Danielle," said Addams, who'd come over to join us. "You tell the newspaper men you had a thousand women, you kept the Trenchers in hiding for three hours, and the whole thing went off peacefully. Tell them you won. And you did. It'll make the next time that much easier."

Addams gave her a hug. Dar could not have looked more shocked if the Devil himself had come up from Hell to offer his congratulations.

Afterward, Dar and I filled the tub in my apartment with steaming water and climbed in together. Cramped, but sublime.

She half-lay, half-floated atop me, her head nestled against my neck.

"Corcoran and Fitzgerald from the union want to talk again next week," she said, nearly asleep as she recited the litany of women who'd sought her out. "The head girl from Wellesley. The maître d' from Tippler's."

"Who?" I asked.

"It's a restaurant. Right across the street from where we were standing, probably the nicest place in Boston. He told me to come back for dinner—someone paid for me and a couple of friends, a table for four. I said I never accept that sort of thing. But . . ."

"You want to go?"

"I've wanted to eat there for years. Was it wrong to say yes?"

"Of course not! Some rich philosopher is doing you a favor. Who was it?"

"Anonymous. In thanks for organizing."

"Then it would be an insult not to go!"

"Exactly. Would you run the hot water again?"

"And then put you to bed."

"For a week—at least. Dinner's at eight. Find a couple to go with us? Mayweather helped you with Durstman. We should ask him."

I silently cursed myself for having told Dar. "Or we could ask—"

"He'll be fun. We'll make him pick the wine."

I wrapped her in a towel and carried her to my bed.

"It's silly that I enjoy this," she said. "Dark, handsome man came out of nowhere . . ."

She sighed contentedly as she burrowed into my sheets.

"Wake me at five? Oh, and Jake, of course, if we're asking Mayweather."

In the new year, Jake and Mayweather had begun—no one quite knew what to call it: a romance, a dalliance, intensive flirting. I'd worried to Dar over Jake, whether I ought to warn her about Mayweather.

"Oh, Jake knows!" Dar had laughed. "Everybody knows. Everybody and her kid sister and her dowager aunt. He'll be a perfect lamb or Jake will string him up by his toes naked from the steeple of the Old North Church."

"He'd probably enjoy that," I'd grumbled.

And so, reluctantly, I messaged Mayweather, who cleared his social calendar to go out with us on short notice.

At seven thirty, the four of us climbed into a carriage in Harvard Square. Dar wore a low-cut green dress with a velvet bodice, a pearl necklace, and a net of fine seed pearls in her hair. Jake sported a form-fitting sheath of silver silk overlaid with a mesh of like-colored beads; it made her every movement like flowing mercury. Mayweather outfitted himself in a cream-colored three piece, with sparkling diamond cuff links. And then there was me in my sober gray suit, wearing a black Homburg that could never have been stylish in any time or place.

"Which newspapers?" Mayweather asked Dar, amid a great deal of chit-chat over the morning's protest.

"Just the *Globe*," Dar answered. "I tried everyone who ever interviewed me or came beating down my door after the disaster in Washington. I was hoping for reporters from New York and Philadelphia, maybe Detroit. But just the one."

"A pity," Mayweather said. "They'll only do an article if you're naughty."

"But no more naughtiness for Brian," Jake said as we pulled up at the restaurant. "Conduct unbecoming and all that. Did you tell them yet?"

Mayweather jumped down and gallantly extended his arm to assist Jake to the ground. I was too busy glowering at the Castle Club across the street to remember to do the same for Dar. Full of Trenchers even at that very moment.

"Not official yet," I heard Mayweather say. "Still time left for misbehavior."

Over oysters on the half shell and a bottle of Blanquette de Limoux (and I could hardly decide which I liked less), Mayweather described his most recent exploit: a commission as a second lieutenant in the artillery.

"A general for a great-uncle, I'm afraid," Mayweather said. "I report as soon as the semester's over."

"They'll let you out of your Contingency obligation to serve in the army?" I asked. I'd mused on that same question whenever the idea of taking a plush job during wartime made me feel guilty.

There followed an uncomfortable silence. Dar glared at me, but I couldn't decide what I'd said that might give offense.

"You're too generous, Robert," Mayweather said. "I haven't a prayer of passing my Contingency exam—I can't do half the sigils and that won't change in four weeks' time. So, I'll write a check to Radcliffe for my tuition and take my commission."

"Better than taking his chances in the draft and getting turned into cannon fodder," Jake added.

"Gloxinia, dear," Mayweather replied. "That's needlessly depressing. Our boys over there haven't done anything but sit on the southern end of the lines and frown at the Germans in their trenches. Not even a proper battle yet. It's the French and the British who're taking it on the chin."

"That'll change," Danielle said. "Gen. Pershing will have two million Americans in France by the end of the summer. Then he'll go on the offensive."

"That's *ages* away," Mayweather insisted. "I'll go over in June and polish my cannon and play cards. It'll probably be over before I even get there."

He topped off Jake's glass.

"Besides," Mayweather said. "We can't all be as lucky as Robert. The draft board can't touch him on his Contingency year, not with that vital work he'll be doing for the Durstmans."

I seethed at that—it was half an inch short of him calling me out as a coward in front of my girlfriend. Mayweather looked amused by my reaction. He ordered another bottle of white wine and a bottle of red. Citing Dmitri, I abstained.

"Robert's no fun anymore," complained Danielle. "He only eats rabbit food."

"Now, now," Mayweather said. "You never know—if R&E takes Robert, I want him in top form. I might have to be evacuated and I don't want some overweight—"

There was a great clanging out on the street as a fire engine sputtered past, one of the new motorized ones. I turned to catch a glimpse of it. Such things still impressed the country boy in me.

"Or perhaps Miss Stewart would fly me," Mayweather suggested. "After all, Radcliffe has to take care of her own."

Jake sighed and took a swig from her wineglass. "I tried to talk Essie out of it again yesterday—I raised my voice to her, poor girl. But tell me you wouldn't do the same."

"Of course," Danielle said. "Half of them dead or wounded every year, how could you not?"

"And yet they never have trouble finding volunteers," Mayweather mused.

I hated his snide tone.

"It's the highest good of philosophy!" I spat back. "It's saving lives. They rescued a million French and British wounded in three years. They even take German casualties when they're able—they've done it regardless of nationality in every war. It's been a vital tool of international diplomacy."

Mayweather laughed. "What book did you read *that* in?"

"*Life and Death on San Juan Hill*," said Jake. "It's every hoverer's favorite."

"Well, it's true," Danielle said soothingly. "R&E does important work. I suppose if Robert really did—"

Outside there was a dull boom. The front window of the restaurant shattered.

"What the hell?" Dar said.

Several of the other diners were pushing through the door, pointing out toward the street and shouting. I got up and followed them.

The Castle Club was in flames.

27

I've never killed a man. But I have separated many an enemy from a fresh supply of oxygen and allowed him to breathe himself to death.

Galen Wainwright, *Confessions of a Confederate Smokecarver*, 1875

I COULDN'T SPEAK. THE smell of the smoke. The flash of heat against my skin. I willed my heart to slow, but it raced away. A more primal part of me insisted, *Let them die. They tried to kill little Carla Klein like that. Plotted against Dar, against Ma. Let them burn the same way.*

Flames were shooting out of the third-floor windows of the Castle Club on all sides, thick orange fire mixed with dark black smoke, which sank instead of rising, puddling on the ground around the base of the building like a moat.

"Of course it's not natural!" Dar was saying to Jake behind me. "I put on a peaceful rally and someone buys me a front-row seat to a goddamned assassination!"

"Let them die," I whispered. My voice sounded choked and twisted.

Mayweather was the only one who heard me. He still had his wineglass in hand, the rim pressed against his lips. He raised his eyebrows at me in surprise.

The fire engine had found a hydrant and was beginning to pump water; firefighters working from horse-drawn wagons were trying to position ladders to reach the upper floors. Several firemen were kneeling around a female figure lying unmoving on the ground—they called out for a stretcher. The woman wore a heavy waterproof coat identical to theirs. A gray helmet lay beside her, as did a large utility box filled with powders. Billings' volunteer fire company had carried equipment just like that for Mother.

"Oh, Jesus, that's their smokecarver!" I said.

I hurried toward her.

"Let me through!" I shouted. "I'm a philosopher!"

I dropped to the ground beside the unconscious woman. My fingers scrabbled across her neck and found the faintest of pulses. I put my cheek above her mouth to feel for her breath. Nothing.

"Immediate evacuation," I announced, as Mother had taught me years before. The firefighters seemed to take it for granted I knew what I was doing.

I pawed through the woman's powder box—vials organized alphabetically, thank God!—until I found the silver chloride and a packet of stasis indicator papers.

"She was trying to get a cloud inside to smother it and it recoiled back on her like a hammer!" one of the firefighters told me, panic in his voice. "The way her head snapped, I thought she broke her neck."

"Fine, okay," I said.

"She's got three kids. You've got to help her!"

I squinted at the tube of silver chloride. The whitish powder was streaked with black. An old vial, partially decomposed back into elemental silver. Bad for my sigil, but I didn't have time to search for a fresher tube.

"Everybody clear!" I shouted.

I stuck an indicator to the woman's neck and drew the largest stasis I could. I pulled the strip off and checked it—eight minutes.

"Shit," I whispered.

The smoke ringing the base of the building exploded into flames and the firefighters who had been putting up ladders went running for cover. One of them—an older man—hurried toward us.

"Chief, this is a philosopher here!" the firefighter with me called out. "This man. He put Mrs. O'Sullivan under."

"You're a philosopher?" the fire chief asked. "Male philosopher?"

"Yes," I said.

"What kind of philosophy? Smokecarver? Transporter?"

"General practice. And hovering."

"A flier! That could work. Listen—there are about a dozen people trapped on the sixth floor, say the ones who got out. We're never going to get a ladder through those flames. Any chance you can fly one of my guys up there to search?"

I dusted off the knees of my suit. There was no way I was going into a building filled with Trenchers. Let them die. Let them burn.

Everyone was looking at me. I'd been at a hundred fires and cave-ins and collapsed buildings. I'd only ever been asked, *Where's your ma? Where's your sister?*

"What do you need to get in there, boss?" the fire chief asked.

"Axe," I said, before I had time to reconsider. "Helmet. Cotton webbing straps cut to twenty feet if you've got them; rope if you don't."

The firefighters rushed off to retrieve equipment. I saw Dar and Jake watching from in front of the restaurant. I waved them over.

"Jake!" I said. "Can you fly their smokecarver to the hospital? Her stasis only has seven minutes left on it."

"I'll have her there in two," Jake said. "What have we got for bags?"

There were a pair of waxed-cardboard powder tubes with disposable regulators in the smokecarver's box. The regs were nothing more than a big screw for piercing the cardboard, with a paper drinking straw attached for the powder to flow through. You pinched the straw shut or open to adjust the flow.

"These things are trash," Jake sniffed. "They either give you too much powder or none at all."

The firefighters brought me several loops of webbing. I trussed up Jake and the smokecarver with the same style harness I'd used on Gertrude.

"This is insane," Jake said.

"You always said you can fly with anything," I replied.

I lashed the tube to her side and pointed her toward the hospital.

"Brian, darling," Jake said to Mayweather. "If you try to look up my dress, I'm having Robert eunuchize you."

Mayweather blew her a kiss.

Jake launched and nearly sputtered out before her flight sigil caught and flung her toward Mass General at 190 miles an hour. She cleared a chimney by four inches. Drunk and with a cardboard regulator.

"Fucking hell!" I breathed.

"Black lace," mused Mayweather, on whom the narrowness of her miss had been lost.

I had no time to reconsider the wisdom of the homemade rigging: the fourth floor of the Castle Club was burning now, too. The firefighter who'd found us the straps helped me into a coat and helmet and handed me an axe with a spike on the back.

"What the hell are you doing?" Dar asked me.

"People trapped on the sixth floor," I said. "I'll fly up, break a window, search."

"No, you *won't*. Robert, they're—"

"I have to. It's the right thing to do. It's the highest—"

"Oh, for fuck's sake!" Danielle said.

I tied the powder tube to my hip.

"Christ, Robert," Danielle said. "If you're really going to do this, then fly in, draw a destination glyph, and let me transport a bunch of firefighters inside. They'll cover a lot more ground more quickly. Then I'll get everyone out together."

That was a much better plan. The fire chief, who'd heard about Dar's action at Gallipoli, was willing to try it. He gathered half a dozen men to transport in with her.

"What do you want for a destination glyph?" I asked Dar.

From her purse, Dar pulled a little black book—an official transporter's log of one-of-a-kind destinations, each in duplicate. She tore out a perforated sheet and took my index finger, tracing it over the figure. "That's a Lily chatterbox with double staves, slow six on the back end. Got it?" I traced it out again under her critical eye. "Close enough," she said. I stuffed the paper in my pocket.

Dar pressed a vial of aluminum into my hand. "For the destination glyph. And take this, too. I found it in her kit. In case you meet an unhappy Trencher."

It was a tube of sulfur and bone meal. I stuck the vial and tube in my waistband. Then I took two big strides, pinched the regulator tip open, and launched.

The force of my sigil caught me by surprise, kicking me back ten feet as it threw me upward. Too much flow. I drew hastily to correct, shooting up past the roof and then trying to burp my way back down. I evened out and aimed for a window.

Everyone on the ground was yelling.

"Quiet on the ground!" I screamed. Worst possible moment for a distraction.

"Sixth floor!" I heard Mayweather shout. "Down one! That's seven."

Well, I thought, with the blissful stupidity of a young man who'd never attempted something like this before, *at least I got my one mistake of the night out of the way.*

I aligned myself with the correct window, switched the reg to my left hand—thank you, Gertrude—and swung the axe with my right.

The handle twisted in my hand and the blade bounced off the glass. The recoil spun me backward and I reflexively tightened my grip on the reg, pinching off the powder flow. I dropped hard.

I heard Dar's scream above the rest.

I redrew frantically, fighting for altitude, as the reg did its best to hurl me into the side of the building. I maneuvered back up to the window and took a second swing, this time with the spiked end of the axe. The glass shattered.

I knocked the rest of the fragments out of the window frame and edged closer. The window was too small to fly through—I should have considered that while I was still on the ground. There was not going to be a graceful way to do this.

I let go of the axe. Then I grabbed the frame with my right hand, let go of the reg, and grabbed on with my left, sagging toward the ground as my thrust died. I pulled myself up and partway through, but got stuck on my powder bag. My legs flailed over the six-story drop. I wriggled my hips through and then the rest of me followed as I fell onto the glass-strewn floor.

I began choking before I could even stand up. The smoke was thicker than it had looked from outside. I used a sigil to ball up some smoke in my hands, flatten it into a sheet, and scoop out a shell around my face. Once I could breathe, I began rolling back the smoke around me and found that I was at the end of a long hall. I drew sigils wildly, squashing the smoke against the walls so that there was a tunnel of clear air.

Time for the destination glyph. I laid the page from Dar's book on the floor and used the powdered aluminum to trace out the ornate figure. Then I retreated to the window, well outside the radius of the bubble Dar would be using.

"Hey!" I screamed.

Everyone below was shouting and pointing, but not at me. Between the noise of the crowd, the pumps on the engines, and the water hissing as it turned to steam on the flames below, no one heard me. Dar had several firefighters crouched about her. Someone had found her a helmet and water-proof coat to wear. I flung the empty powder tube out the window to catch her attention and waved my arms. She didn't look up.

Mayweather noticed me, though, and called to Dar. She and the fire-fighters vanished.

"Took you long enough!" Dar said from behind me.

"What could possibly have been more interesting than watching for your boyfriend in a burning building?" I answered.

"Man on top of the turret," one of the firefighters said.

"Goddamn it, I thought they were *here*!" I said as the firefighters fanned out to search the corridors and rooms beyond.

"Maybe some here, but one on the roof for damn sure," said the fire-fighter.

I still had plenty of corn powder left. I couldn't not try.

I levered my legs out the window and worked my hips and powder bag through. My whole body revolted at the notion of throwing myself into space. But it should work. One second for the sigil to take, during which I would fall sixteen feet. Plenty of room. Easy, even.

Dead if you misdraw your glyph.

"What are you *doing?*" Danielle shouted behind me.

Too stupid. Too reckless. Climb back in and let her transport me out with the rest, man on the roof be damned.

"I'll grab the one up top," I called back. "See you on the ground."

I pushed myself out and fell.

My sigil took.

The thrust flung me up and I fought to trim, level, dip, even as I rocketed up to a hundred feet. I eased back down, buffeted by the columns of hot air rising from the flames. The whole building looked like it was burning.

I pulled hard for the roof, then pinched off my powder flow, tucking and sliding as I hit. I spotted the man on the opposite side from me, peering over the edge. There was a trapdoor with a ladder near him—he must have run up instead of down when the fire broke out. But I wasn't about to risk taking him back inside and negotiating my way down two flights of stairs to rejoin Dar.

"Hey, there!" I called to him. "I'm here to help."

A shrunken, elderly man, his head framed by wispy hair, turned toward me. His face was thin and pockmarked, his cheekbones prominent, as if his many years had stripped away all the fat and muscle. He frowned and pointed an old cap and ball revolver in my direction.

I froze. I tried to keep my breathing regular. Steady hands. I could launch, I could be gone in a second. Hard to hit a moving target at twenty feet with a pistol.

"You're with the fire department, then?" he asked, eyeing the fire coat I was wearing over my suit and tie.

"Yes," I said, desperate. My face would give me away. My naked fear, the high pitch to my voice. "Off duty."

Against all reasonable expectation, the man lowered the gun. As he moved, I spotted a black onyx ring in place of a wedding band. From bad to worse. It was a mark worn only by the most irreconcilable Trenchers—you won it by murdering a philosopher.

He said something I couldn't hear for the thudding of my heart. I pivoted so that I was facing him side-on. If he shot me, the bullet would tear into the flesh of my left side, leaving my right hand free to draw. Or was it possible he couldn't understand what I was? Was he blind to the powder bag that was even now spilling a trickle of corn dust?

"I said, how do you propose to get me down?" he asked. "I don't see a ladder."

"Pulleys," I stammered. "We have a system of ropes to lower us to the ground."

He gave a weary, sad smile.

"I offered up a prayer," he said, "and salvation came. I said, 'Heavenly Father, was it not your will that I should scour these philosophers from the earth? Did not your prophet Isaiah preach to them of their destruction?' "

He put the gun in his pocket. I resumed breathing.

He was insane, maybe. But if I needed to play the part of angel sent by God for two minutes to get him to safety, I was willing. I put an arm around his shoulders and guided him to the edge of the roof.

"It's all there," he told me. "Written twenty-six hundred years ago, all of it prophecy for today."

"Sure it is," I said. "You're gonna be just fine."

I had a reasonably good idea for getting him down.

"If you'd be so kind, could you step up onto the ledge, Mister . . ."

"Gannet," he supplied.

28

Disaster will come upon you, and you will not know how to conjure it away. A calamity will fall upon you that you cannot pay off with a ransom; a catastrophe you cannot foresee will suddenly come upon you. Keep on, then, with your magic spells and your many sigils, which you have labored at since girlhood. Perhaps you will succeed, perhaps you will cause terror.

Isaiah 47:11–12, The New Trencher Bible, 1916

THIS MAN? THIS SENILE, decrepit, used-up excuse of a man? Mastermind and assassin? The subject of a thousand childhood nightmares? The one who'd kept me up nights as a grown man, imagining how he was plotting to kill Mother, kill Dar. Imagining how I might track him down and murder him. This man?

"*Maxwell* Gannet?" I asked.

"Yes."

My hand dropped to the tube tucked in the waistband of my pants.

Sulfur and bone meal.

The sigil was just five sharp lines. Kill him myself, know it for certain, witness it. His bones would dissolve and his brain would shut down almost instantly from the sudden release of calcium. Merciful, even, compared to leaving him.

I popped the cap off the tube.

No one would ever know. Leave the body for the flames to consume.

Mother would do it. Had done it.

I grabbed hold of his shirt. As I moved, the chain with the vial of silver chloride brushed across my chest. *If you can get close enough to kill a man* . . .

But Beau and Vivian had killed. They would understand. Lew Hansen and Bertie Synge would understand. Ms. Addams would understand. Dar would—

I glanced down at the tube in my hand. Never. She was a minister's daughter, not a soldier's son.

A simple, simple glyph: *On an open count, central spine with pierced end cap, then three dropping left-to-right barbs.*

I caught Gannet's head in my left arm and pulled it roughly to the side, exposing the flesh of his neck. He looked at me dumbly, uncomprehending.

"From Beau Canderelli," I growled.

I tore the chain off my neck, twisted open the vial of silver chloride between my thumb and forefinger, and slapped a stasis sigil on Gannet's throat.

His body went stiff in my arms.

"From Emmaline Weekes," I added, and kicked him in the back so that he tumbled off the roof. His insensate body hit the ground a few seconds later.

I launched myself, too. In trying to avoid all the people in the street below, I made a hash of my landing. I hit hard and rolled, bloodying my nose. Gannet's body, by contrast, didn't have so much as a scrape on it.

Mayweather ran up beside me. "What did you do to him?" he cried.

"Nothing," I said.

"You pushed him off the roof!"

"He's in stasis. It didn't hurt him."

"Jesus," Mayweather said. "Everybody saw you. We thought . . ."

He grabbed me by the arm and dragged me away from the bystanders, who were pressing in around Gannet. Dar was nearby, talking to a detective, still wearing her fire helmet and coat over her velvet dress. Beside her, the police were interviewing several soot-covered old men—the Trenchers she'd rescued. Newspaper photographers circled, snapping pictures.

"I should add that Jake messaged," Mayweather told me. "She made it to the hospital."

"Thank God," I said. "She's okay?"

"Perfectly well, though your rope harness ruined the sequins on her—"

The Castle Club's roof collapsed, sending up an enormous, spiraling column of sparks.

"Damn!" I said. If I'd been a minute slower, I would have gone with it.

Dar saw me. She flung her arms around me and pressed her face against my shoulder.

"Don't ever!" she sobbed. "Don't ever again! I couldn't bear it."

I held her tight.

"I'm fine," I said. "Everything's fine."

Dar came away with blood from my nose running down her borrowed coat. We watched for several minutes as the building collapsed on itself.

Mayweather, who'd ducked back into the restaurant to rescue his bottle of wine and a clean glass, rejoined us. I scowled at him.

"It's an '86 Château Lafite—it would be a crime to let it go to waste!" he said by way of explanation. He took a sip and then, looking immodestly pleased with himself, extracted an envelope from his pocket. "But more important, I found *this* on our table."

Dar's name was typed on it. She opened it and nearly dropped the letter in reading it.

"What?" I said.

I looked it over with Mayweather:

You have witnessed the power of American sigilry. Those who threaten us, we will destroy. Those who aid us, we will uplift. The Gray Hats deserve a place at the negotiating table. Tell Cadwallader-Fulton. Spread the word in the halls of Washington.

Well, that certainly explained the professional-looking fire. They must have expected that we would enjoy basking in the glow of roasting Trenchers—or at least permit it to happen. Instead, we'd ruined the evening for some very deadly philosophers.

"Let's get out of here before they come back," I said to Dar.

And before Gannet woke up.

No, if it had been me, *they'd be dead*, Mother replied to the anxious message I sent that night from Dar's apartment. *This was showy and ineffective. Typical Gray Hat idiots. Jayhawks wld have don it right.*

Any rumors on whch faction? I asked.

N, Mother answered. *Hard to imagin they wld retaliate agnst Danlle or you, but possibl. I'll mak inquiries. Quietly.*

Thnks. Sorry.

Just shows I raised y right. Mayb one of thos Trnchrs will do y a good turn someday.

Dar was reading over my shoulder. "Did you tell her that you saved Gannet?"

I shook my head. "I left that out. It would have been hard to explain."

"Yeah," Dar said. Her lip curled as she said it. "It *is* hard to explain. Pulling out a half-dozen Trenchers—sure, maybe one of them will change his ways. But *him?*"

My anger boiled up.

"Don't look at me like that!" I snapped.

"Like what?"

"Like I did something wrong! Like I'm a coward."

"Jesus, Robert!" Danielle said. "I don't think you're a coward. I just said it's hard to understand."

"He was a frail, broken wreck of a man!" I shouted. "I looked him in the eye. I had him at my mercy. You don't tell someone you've come to help them and then murder them! That's . . . it's so far beyond wrong . . . it's the lowest thing . . ."

"Okay," said Dar. "It's okay."

"I don't want to be a killer!" I said, trying to get the words out before I choked up. "It's my whole family. And I love them. But I want . . . I want . . . to save lives instead of take them."

Dar stepped behind me and laid her palms on my shoulders. I lolled my head back against her. She'd had another long soak to wash off the smoke and was still in her bathrobe. I inhaled the scent of her jasmine soap.

"Oh, love," she whispered, her face buried in my hair. "I wish he were dead, but I don't wish you'd killed him."

She stroked my arm.

"I was so scared, Robert," she said. "That's the most frightened I've ever been. Gallipoli was me, alone. This was me watching you. How many times did you almost die? I can't tell you which was worse—watching you try to get in through that window or sliding back out. Or when the roof caved in and I hadn't seen you get clear."

She wrapped her arms across my chest.

"You flew into a burning building to save people who hate you," she said. "You did it because you're you. It's noble. It's merciful. I love you for it. But it scares the hell out of me."

I spent a sleepless night alone in bed.

I'd let him live. How many more people would end up dead because of it? Was it simple weakness—had I frozen up? Or was it naïveté born of too many fairy stories about Rescue and Evac? Or was it true? Did you not kill somebody you'd approached under the auspices of rendering aid, not even if he was prophet to a whole generation of Trenchers?

And then, remembering Danielle crying over me. How many times had I almost died getting in and out of that building? Six, I decided. Never again. I would be good, I would be careful, I would be wise.

Not long after dawn I heard an apologetic knock at my bedroom door.

"Robert?" came Unger's voice. "You're going to want to see this."

29

MARCH–APRIL 1918

The Wayne County Coroner's Office declared Lucretia Cadwallader's cause of death to be "accidental self-inflicted spontaneous human combustion." This only further inflamed suspicions that Cadwallader had been the victim of a Trencher assassination and intensified the First Disturbance.

> Victoria Ferris-Smythe, *Empirical Philosophy:*
> *An American History*, 1938

I STUMBLED INTO THE common room and Unger handed me a copy of the Sunday *Globe*.

A picture of Dar and me anchored the front page: Dar was wearing her borrowed helmet and firefighter's coat, which was unbuttoned to reveal her dress and pearls. We were both smudged with soot. She was clutching my arm with one hand and pointing toward the building with the other. Her face was intense and concerned, focused on whatever technicality we'd been discussing. I had my suit jacket slung over one shoulder and was laughing.

HERO OF HELLESPONT SAVES TRENCHERS: CASTLE CLUB BURNS; 24 DEAD, the headline ran.

I read a bit from the article:

Hardin fearlessly employed the same philosophical techniques she used during her famous action in the Dardanelles. After transporting firefighters to the sixth floor, she searched room to room alongside them, rolling back the smoke with her bare hands. Seven Trenchers were rescued from the labyrinthine halls, many of them overcome by the heat.

Twenty-three men on the lower floors perished. Mrs. Katie O'Sullivan, the fire department's smokecarver, was also killed while fighting the blaze.

Radcliffe freshman Robert Weekes assisted by retrieving noted orator and four-time Trencher Party presidential candidate Maxwell Gannet, who had become trapped on the roof.

"Isn't it terrific?" said Unger. He'd bought fifteen copies.

I suspected Danielle might feel otherwise. I took one of Unger's newspapers and went to visit her. She met me at the door of her apartment, wrapped in her housecoat. She wouldn't meet my gaze.

"What?" I said. "What's wrong?"

She ducked her shoulders and took a step away from me. Her eyes were full.

"Why are you crying?" I asked.

She handed me a copy of the *Boston Informer*, which had put out a special edition. They'd taken their usual editorial perspective.

RENEGADE PHILOSOPHERS MURDER 23.

And below it: EXCLUSIVE TO THE *INFORMER*: A STATEMENT BY MAXWELL GANNET.

Gannet had produced three rambling pages of madness and hellfire, but his final paragraph was coherent enough:

Robbed of control over my own body and pitched from the roof—I would have sooner died than allow that charlatan Weekes to defile me. If I'd woken an hour earlier, I would have gone over and shot the lot of them dead. So bravo, ladies and gentleman. I wish you all the joy of your murderous arson and hope that I will have the opportunity to repay you for depriving so many of my brethren of their lives.

"My God," I whispered.

"You should have left him there," Dar said. "Why didn't you leave him?"

"They'll arrest Gannet for saying that."

"No they won't. He stopped just short of making an actionable threat. But his followers know exactly what he wants them to do."

I sank down in a chair. "They can't go out and murder a couple of young, good-looking people who so recently saved their lives. It would damage the Trencher movement. That's not how you win followers."

"Gannet doesn't care about the movement," said Dar. "He thinks God put him on Earth to kill sigilrists."

She folded the paper and set it on a stack of others—*New York Times, Detroit Defender, Chicago Tribune*—all of them with the same picture of the two of us.

"I feel sick," Dar said. "I want to go home. A couple of reporters from the *Globe* came by at four in the morning to ask for my reaction. I told them to go to hell."

"Well, there you go," I said. "Go to the *Globe* and give them an exclusive right back. Tell them what you think of an organization that threatens a twenty-two-year-old girl."

Dar scowled. "I'm done with all that, with my words being twisted. Go down there yourself and do it. You'd be good at it."

"Maybe I will."

I went instead to the shooting range in the basement of the Gray Box with Mother's revolver. Every time another question bubbled up, I reloaded and popped off another four rounds at a paper target. Should I have left Gannet to burn? Should I have killed him myself? Were his acolytes plotting against Dar? Against me?

I'd been at it a good while when one of Belle Addams's men sidled up at the next spot over. He was the same one who'd spoken with me at the freshman social.

"Good morning, Mr. Weekes," he said, raising two fingers to his brow.

"Howdy," I said. I decocked my revolver. "You've come to 'prepare' me off to Ms. Addams's office?"

He waved, as if we had all the time in the world. "Many different sorts of preparedness, you know. I see you're quite well prepared with a pistol."

I smiled wanly. "It's about the smallest gun in the world."

"A Westmarch Armory four-shot revolver in .22 Short, double action," the man supplied. "They only made a hundred of them, but it's quite an admirable weapon—terrifically accurate for its size. I've always wanted to try one."

"Would you care to trade?" I asked him.

He unholstered a large semiautomatic and we switched weapons. The heavy recoil of the big gun felt immensely good to me.

"Now, that's the right-looking piece for a man," I said as I handed it back to him.

"I disagree," he replied. "Yours is more easily concealable. One could hardly blame a young gentleman for carrying it when he went out of the house."

My blood ran cold. "Is that a suggestion?"

"No—merely an observation that ours is a time that rewards preparation."

"Is there something I should be looking out for? Somebody?"

The man smoothed his hands over his vest. "It's my job to look, Mr. Weekes. It's yours to stay out of trouble."

And indeed, there was plenty of trouble.

Recriminations flew back and forth among the Trenchers over how the Castle Club had been infiltrated—perhaps the Hand of the Righteous had allied itself with a sigilrist in order to remove the older Trencher leadership.

No, it was the Trenchers from Texas and California settling an old grudge against their Eastern counterparts. No, Gannet himself had sabotaged the meeting—see how easily he'd escaped!

But the feuding Trencher groups all agreed that they had to strike back against every philosophical target they could find. Missouri and Kansas and Oklahoma were plunged into fresh rounds of murder and kidnapping; houses and effigies were set alight from Seattle to Miami.

The Jayhawks and Gray Hats retaliated in kind. A smokecarver in Kansas City swathed a Trencher meetinghouse in a cloud of vaporized kerosene, drew an ignite sigil, and ran for her life—thirty-eight souls incinerated on the spot. In Davenport, a group of young men had assembled at another meetinghouse for weapons instruction from more senior Trenchers, only to have the building transported—with them still in it—into the middle of the Mississippi River. The building sank, drowning nine boys, the youngest of whom was twelve.

That begat a retired Corps general disemboweled and hanged on her front porch, which caused a general strike of the cargo hoverers in New Orleans, which inspired someone to fire on them with a Lewis gun. And a thousand other incidents besides.

Dar gave one interview after another, pleading for an end to the violence. Despite her good intentions, both sides turned on her. The *Trencher Times* accused her of conspiring to commit murder—her protest must have provided the cover for the smokecarvers to smuggle their incendiaries into the Castle Club. Meanwhile, the *Defender* called her a turncoat for rescuing the enemy.

One of Belle Addams's men was with Dar whenever she went out. The hate mail and death threats from the public came in by the bagful.

They trickled in for me, too. By the tenth one, Addams decided I would have an escort as well.

"Until the worst of this quiets down," she pronounced during a private meeting a few days later.

"Lord," I muttered. "I wish . . ."

"No, you don't," Addams said. "You don't shoot a man in a hospital bed. You don't put a bomb in an ambulance. And you don't bonekill a man you've gone to save. I fought in a war where there were no rules and we still abided by those. You did the right thing."

"I wish anybody else agreed," I said.

"You're R&E through and through, Mr. Weekes," she said. "So, you put your head down. Train as hard as you can. Let me handle the Trenchers. I've been on Max Gannet's little lists for the last fourteen months. I'll get you through it."

Trying to spot the guards became a game for me. The man in the rain-coat, smoking on the corner, perhaps, or the gentleman in the argyle vest walking the Pomeranian, or the lad on the bicycle with two wicker baskets. Or, more likely, one of them and one I couldn't see.

I could only hope the Trenchers weren't as good at hiding in plain sight.

I tried to forget the Trenchers by sinking even more time into my prepara-tions for the Cup. My conditioning flights stretched from four hours to six as March turned into April and the weather improved. I did a hundred flare and settles a day, left-handed passes, wind sprints on the ground in full harness with sixty pounds of sandbags strapped to my back. I eked out another two miles an hour here, one mile an hour there.

I put my energy into practicing for the Contingency Exam, too, which was only days away. I spent dozens of hours on arcane sigils that I would never use again after the test: simultaneous semaphore glyphs, sigils to change red to green, the left-breaking Habbie (which seemed to have no use at all outside of cheating at billiards). Yet no matter how much I prac-ticed, little worries about the exam nagged. What if it's the one time in forty that I can't get my ignite glyph to work? The one time in two thousand that my message doesn't take? Or if I forget the sigil for manual reduplication altogether?

All the other freshman scholarship cases went around in similar blurs of anxiety—fail the exam and you had to pay back your scholarship. The single serene, unworried exception was Unger. Never a word of complaint or unease, just a little cross-eyed from all his hours of practice. For his area of specialty, he'd chosen philosophical chemistry, a subject on which he could have conducted a yearlong seminar. But that didn't matter if he failed the basic sigilry half of the test.

We did a mock exam in Essentials II, which I passed easily. I was paired with Mayweather, who blithely failed his dissipate sigil and was charmingly flummoxed by the koru for walnut trees. Mostly, he wanted to rehash the finer points of the Castle Club fire and its aftermath.

"You're holding up, I hope?" he asked.

"Sure," I said. "I told Addams don't send any of the hate mail to me unless it's a threat against my mother or something creative. Nothing so far."

"The Trenchers aren't literary types, are they?" And then, lowering his voice, "But tell me—how's Danielle? How is she *really*?"

"Aw, she's fine!" I said. The *Globe* had run an article that morning speculating that Dar was having a nervous breakdown. "It's just another smear."

"You know she did have a bit of, well, an *episode* at the end of her junior year."

"Yeah, she cussed out her French professor and walked out of the final exam to join the Corps. I know all about that."

Mayweather nodded. "She never told you the whole story, then. That was the morning that German undersea boat torpedoed the troop transport carrying two hundred newly minted corpswomen off the coast of Spain. Exploded and burned, lost with all hands."

"What does that have to do with anything?" I asked.

"Eleven of the women were Cliffes. All the girls here were in hysterics, but Danielle was inconsolable. She walked out of that exam and spent two days in her room, crying, refusing to move. The good Reverend Hardin had to carry her out of the building."

"Don't go spreading—"

"Jake had the room right down the hall. She was the one who messaged Danielle's father. I don't know why Jake's never told you."

Presumably because Dar might never forgive her.

"So be careful with her," Mayweather said. "And, goodness, if anything ever happened to you—one shudders to imagine."

On the day of the Contingency Exam, the federal examiners took over the fourth sub-basement of the Gray Box. We stood quietly in the hallways waiting to be called into one room or another so we could perform each of the basic sigils being tested.

I passed all of them without incident. Later, my hover specialty test went so well that my examiner simply shouted "Pass" halfway through and waved me down to the ground. I considered lodging a complaint—she hadn't seen a counterclockwise turn or a landing—but they had a long line of people to get through.

At the exam's conclusion, I received a strip of paper on which I was to write my preferences for positions.

I ran my finger down the list: *306: Hoverer, cargo (dock flying, logistics, freight, postal); 307: Hoverer, field (county philosopher, search and rescue, emergency stasis team); 308: Hoverer, passenger and courier (long-distance, short-distance).*

For a moment I considered doing something stupid. Surely someone needed a rough and tumble sort of philosopher out in the field—useful employment, necessary work, some adventure that even the men headed off to war would respect. Something more than being a lapdog to a future politician.

I damned myself for even thinking it. Be wise, be kind, do the obvious thing. And be a little careful.

I wrote: *308 (Durstman and Associates).*

I returned home to find Unger at the table in the common room, sitting with a bowl of ink and a stack of fresh white paper, just as he had for months. Manual reduplication—because it required the least philosophical energy of any sigil.

"I don't know what I expected," Unger said at last. "That something would be different. That I'd been using fake powder all this time, but they'd have the real stuff. You know how they kept telling us to forget what we'd done in the first room when we went into the second, not to be too excited or to let disappointment throw us off? I did that. It only began to sink in when I finished. Not that it's really sunk in, even now."

"How was the chemistry?" I asked.

He gave a heartless laugh. "Perfect score, only one of the day. They told everyone else pass or fail, but they told me the number, too."

"The Contingency Board won't give you a waiver and let you do lab work? Or theoretical research?"

He shook his head. "Practical sigilry only."

"If you need a loan—" I suggested.

"It's not the money," said Unger. "My parents won't be happy, but we'll scrape tuition together. No, it's the playacting that hurts. Me, you, everyone pretending I had a chance."

"Let me take you out for a drink," I suggested.

"I'm already going. With Mayweather and a few of the other hopeless cases."

Mayweather had passed three sigils, failed four, and then flunked the message specialty test. He, at least, had his commission to fall back on. Unger would have to take his chances with the draft.

30

The lever, the wheel, the inclined plane: break down any complex mechanism into its component parts and you'll find the same simple machines. Why not in sigilry as well? One part of the glyph to initiate, one for power, one to control the extent of its effect. Separate them out and you could modify sigils at will.

> K. F. Unger, "The Use of Laplace and Fourier Transforms in
> Analysis of Trestor Wave Patterns," Distinguished Lecturer Series
> in Theoretical Empirical Philosophy, Maria Trestor College, 1936

WITH SIX WEEKS LEFT before the Cup, the late-model regulators from Denver Custom Instruments arrived. Suddenly, the entire aerodrome was interested in training.

Essie made 400 miles an hour on her first flight with her new reg. Jake, Francine, and Tillie all easily hit 425. And my fancy five hundred dollar piece of clockwork bought me an extra—three miles an hour. I couldn't break 250.

"Again!" Brock said. "Do it again."

I ran our one-mile course, over and over, but I failed to improve: 249.

No advantage as I pushed harder on my conditioning flights, no faster even as I dropped another few pounds, no edge when we increased the corn dust ratio in my powder.

Five weeks left until the Cup, then four.

"This doesn't make sense," Brock said. "You've got to be losing energy somewhere, but I can't see it. You have no slippage. Your streamlining's fine. You have no fade or leap, so you're drawing often enough."

"Bad reg?" suggested Gertrude. "Not running rich enough?"

I traded regulators with Astrid, but nothing changed. We tried one hundred percent corn for my powder, but other than hitting me harder on my launch, it did nothing for my top speed.

"What am I missing?" Brock asked.

"He's peaked," Gertrude answered. "That's the only explanation, even if we don't want to admit it. But it's a hell of a victory! A year ago if you'd told me I could fly a man at two hundred and fifty, I would have called you insane."

"I'd hoped for a little more," Brock said. "At two hundred seventy-five you might have beaten the girls from Trestor. It's going to be an ugly loss. Do you mind, Robert? I could put you in the endurance flight, instead. We have a—how to put it?"

"We're employing novel means to win," Gertrude said. "It'll be a hoot. They'll be talking about it for years. The medals are pretty."

"Would I have any shot at a Corps invitation?" I asked.

Gertrude shook her head. "Not for the endurance flight, no."

"Then the long course," I said. "And if some theorist from Trestor kicks my ass by four minutes, I can't say you didn't warn me."

On May 1, Brock drew up our official list of hoverers. Eleven of our fliers would compete for Radcliffe's greater glory in the Cup's four events.

Most glamorous was the short course, a mile-long slalom through pylons set at irregular intervals. It required quick reflexes and raw acceleration. At Detroit and Sacramento, women spent years training for the event; they held tournaments to winnow the thousands of fliers at each school down to their two finest. Sacramento, we suspected, would send Aileen Macadoo, the young woman who'd won the event three times before and set the world speed record at 518 miles per hour. Against them, Radcliffe would fly our two most agile women: Jake and Francine.

Less prestigious, though no less entertaining, was the endurance flight. Each woman received one pound of powder and whoever traveled the greatest lateral distance won. It rewarded impeccable glyph technique and efficient body position, as well as innovations to harness and regulator design—or "cheating," if you were being strict about the rules. The list of banned technologies currently stood at forty-one. Brock was responsible for four of them and appeared to be in the midst of building a fifth. She'd moved an industrial-weight sewing machine and a small forge into her laboratory and had held several nighttime consultations with an armorer from the Museum of Fine Arts. Tillie would fly endurance for Radcliffe, as well as one of our newly minted Threes, selected (we heard it whispered) because she most closely matched Tillie's height and weight. Neither of them would say a word about what Brock was planning.

Next was the aerial pull, a sky-bound tug-of-war. Brute philosophical force was at a premium, but so was wrangling the team to pull along the same vector. That meant Astrid as captain and the four women who scored highest on a Trestor device as pullers.

Last was the long course, home to the hoverers who liked their play to look like work, the fast, ugly fliers who knew how to use a compass and tie knots. With a hundred miles and ten landings, it often got contentious; the previous year had seen an intentional collision at the eighty-mile landing field, in which a Sacramento flier had broken the arm of Detroit's best hoverer. The two teams had come to blows during the medal ceremony. Into that mess we'd be throwing Miss Etiquette herself—Essie Stewart—and the inimitable Mr. Weekes.

The University of Detroit's first reaction to our roster was that it must be a joke: a male had never flown in the Cup. Their second reaction was a strongly worded letter to Brock. Their third was an editorial in the *Defender* laying out their rationale for a boycott, unless "the man" was removed from Radcliffe's team.

"Brock has to let you fly, after all the work you've put in," Dar reassured me. "That's just ordinary fairness."

"Thank you!" I said.

"You've got to admit, though, it's a good letter."

And it was:

More and more frequently, our world requires the mixing of the sexes. We welcome men as sigilrists—indeed, the vigor of empirical philosophy demands it—but the General's Cup, with its storied traditions of sisterhood and fellowship, is not the proper proving ground for male philosophers.

Leave us our own spheres into which we may retreat. The Harvard-Yale football game is the sphere of men; Radcliffe surely would not intrude upon it by placing a woman on the field, even if she were physically able. Likewise, let us not diminish the feminine beauty and precision of the Cup by introducing the base brutishness of male flight.

Our first and foremost hoverer, Mary Fox, said it best: To the men the earth, to the women the sky, as God willed it.

"Mary Fox was wrong about plenty of things," Brock raged. "Powder ratios, sigil inversion, harness technique. Tied all her hitches backward."

"If it's going to ruin the Cup for me to fly," I suggested, "then—"

"Don't you say that!" Gertrude said. "If Detroit boycotts, you move two spots closer to an invitation to test for the Corps."

"That's the wrong way to do it," I said.

"Any way is the right way! Sarah, rig him for a hundred and eighty pounds. Start with the calisthenics your Russian invented."

Essie helped me attach five sandbags on my back and four on my chest. My legs burned as I walked back and forth across the field, touching my knee to the ground with each step. One length, two, and again. Half a mile. Then backward.

Essie, willowy as she was, did it with one hundred pounds.

"They have to let you," she gasped as we both collapsed, sweat-soaked, on the field. "No one who's actually met you—all the things they're saying about you—it's terrible. They have to let you fly."

"All the things who's saying?"

Seventy-one current Radcliffe fliers, as it turned out, in a letter to Brock published in the *New York Times*, the *Boston Globe*, the *Defender*, and anywhere else that would print it, with none of the conciliatory language of Detroit's editorial: they refused to fly until I was removed from the team.

> *Depraved experiment in social engineering . . . example of the sexual confusion that permeates American manhood in the modern age . . . a distraction—indeed, a danger—to honest women . . . blatant favoritism at the expense of philosophers faster and more talented than he is . . .*

"Stop it!" Dar said, snatching yet another newspaper clipping out of my hands. "You had your day to wallow in it. Now you have to stop. If I took it personally every time someone called me a conniving, hot-blooded African whore who was too ugly to go into politics, I would have lost my mind by now."

"They're not people you know," I answered.

Rachael Rodgers topped the list of names, as I knew she would. But forty-two of them were women I'd instructed. Most of them I had liked. Had thought they liked me.

"Lynnette Osterburg?" I said. "I promoted her from Zed. She chose my section of Ones. She told me she wanted me to teach her sister to fly when she comes next year."

"Robert—"

"Paula Andretti," I said. "She got her Two and said she wanted me to be the one who signed her card because—"

"Three hundred fliers refused to put their names down because they know you and respect you."

But I didn't have a list of their names. And Rachael—or one of her seventy lackeys—was kind enough to pin a fresh copy of the letter to the curtain of my locker room each day.

"Just have to make life harder for the rest of us, don't you?" Astrid complained, as she loaded sandbags on my back. Three members of the pull team had joined the boycott.

"I'm sorry," I said.

Astrid snorted. "Not as sorry as me. I'm going to have all freshmen. If I lose any more, I might have to start using men."

I would have given her an appropriately snotty answer, but she'd just finished rigging me with 240 pounds' worth of weight—a third more than I would be carrying in the Cup—and I had no breath left over.

With three weeks to go, Astrid's replacements quit, too.

By the hundredth death threat for Professor Brock, her mail was going through Ms. Addams as well.

Some wag with a steady hand painted an eight-foot-tall naked woman with enormous breasts on the front of the aerodrome. She was pleasuring a German soldier who sported a spiked helmet and an impressively detailed phallus. Beneath was scrawled *Deviants*.

"So, I'm a Prussian cavalry officer?" I asked Ms. Addams. "Or a well-endowed woman?"

"Unclear," Addams answered. "But I'm opening thirty letters from sigilrists furious over your participation in the Cup for every threat against you from a Trencher."

"Max Gannet is easing up, then?" I asked.

"On you, yes. I got hold of his latest list of two hundred names. He left you off it entirely."

"What!" I said, feeling almost disappointed. "After the fire he called me—"

"That was three months ago," Addams said. "Gannet's half-senile. A male sigilrist must seem as impossible to him as it does to some of the women in Detroit."

• • •

Someone messaged bomb threats in to the aerodrome every day for a whole week. We evacuated time and again so that Addams and several of Radcliffe's senior smokecarving instructors could sweep the building, using chemically treated smoke to search for explosives. They found nothing, but it was enough to persuade our second endurance flier to quit. Brock named Frieda as replacement.

"I'm going to have to modify the whole damn contraption," Brock complained to me. "But, at least I know that Frieda won't quit."

"Why's that?" I asked.

"Because she would only compete if I swore to keep you on the team."

It overwhelmed me. Frieda, who'd never had a kind word after pulling me out of the river, just cold professionalism. That anyone would care enough to say it, much less her . . .

I fought to master myself. One thing to rip your hair out in private or ball up your fists and scream in one of the soundproof practice rooms, but quite another to blubber in front of your professor.

"Christ, Weekes," Brock said, and handed me a handkerchief. "If it's too much, no one would fault you."

I left Brock's office in the basement of the Gray Box and walked home through a balmy May afternoon.

I cursed my own weakness. I cursed the whole world: the hideous flowering cherry trees perfuming the courtyards, the stupid birds singing away, sisterhood and tradition, base male brutishness, and Prussian cavalry officers.

I couldn't get the door to my apartment unlocked. Finally, I realized that Unger had dead-bolted it, a precaution we hardly ever took. I turned the bolt and threw the door open.

Freddy was sitting at the table in just his glasses and shorts, papers and bottles strewn about, a Trestor device humming on the floor. His hands were covered in something. It was streaked across his face, too. Certainly not blood?

"Don't come in!" he called out.

"Freddy, what happened?" I asked.

"I have a problem. Just back up and wait outside."

Not blood. Ink? Practicing manual reduplication, as ever.

"Freddy, wipe your hands and tell me what's wrong."

"That's just it! It won't come off!"

"Did you try turpentine? Sometimes—"

"I tried soap and water, turpentine, rubbing alcohol, soda ash solution, and mevalonate. Nothing works."

"Well, calm down. Maybe you got a bad batch of ink."

"It was coming off ten minutes ago! And then I tried a few improvements to the glyph."

I needed a moment to digest that. You didn't get a sigil to work by changing it, you got it to work by drawing it exactly like everyone else always had. If you altered the glyph there was no telling what it might do.

"You think this is . . . philosophical?" I asked, taking a step backward.

Unger raised his splotched hands in consternation.

To me, the odds of Unger making any sigil work correctly, much less inventing a new one, were roughly equal to Blind Doyle having tea with the Queen of England. But then again, if he were going to suffer a psychotic break, I would have expected it on the day when he calculated it was mathematically impossible for him to pass Essentials II.

"I'll message the philosophical containment team," I suggested. Nothing to bring a man back to reality like the emergency squad crashing into his living room.

"Please don't," he said. "I can't imagine, I mean, I shouldn't think it's *dangerous*."

I could recall several famous philosophical disasters that had involved similar phrases. I took another step backward.

"Get Murchison instead?" Freddy said. "He's a theorist. He'll know what to do."

I shut the door behind me and ran to the dean's office. Addams was sitting at her desk in the outer room, opening a pile of letters.

"What is it?" she asked, springing to her feet. "Is it her, is she—"

"It's Freddy," I said. "He said get the dean. He thinks there's been, well, maybe a slight philosophical accident."

Addams hissed through her teeth and motioned for me to follow. Murchison was sitting calm and erect at his desk, staring at his window. He had the blinds drawn.

"Lennox!" shouted Addams. The dean seemed not to notice. She rapped on Murchison's desk and he looked up. She pointed at me.

"Sir, it's about Fred Unger," I said. "He's possibly had a bit of an accident."

"What a pity," Murchison said. He resumed staring.

"A philosophical accident?" I tried. "Involving ink?"

That caught his attention. "Oh! The same ink you've got?"

"No, I didn't bring a sample."

"On your hand?"

"I didn't . . ." Then I looked at my right hand. I had ink on my index and middle fingers. Unger and I had both touched the doorknob.

"Oh, shit," I whispered.

Murchison took me by the wrist and pressed my index finger against a sheet of paper. It left a mark behind. He poured out a little of his own ink and drew glyphs, causing it to spider out across the page, forming a fine network of lines that played over my fingerprint.

After a moment, Murchison clapped his hands and laughed. At least, I assumed it was a laugh; it was more like the sound that someone who'd only ever heard a secondhand description of laughter would make.

"How droll!" said Murchison. "Did he intend for this to happen?"

"I don't think so," I said.

Murchison took a wide-brimmed hat and battered leather vest from his coat rack.

"The dean will be out the remainder of the day," he called to Addams. He grabbed a satchel from the bottom drawer of his desk and strode out the door. I hurried to keep up. It was easy to forget that the man was a physical specimen—forty years hiking through the wilderness making all those maps.

Outside my apartment, Murchison pulled on a pair of gauntlets made from fine bronze rings. "Good afternoon, Karl Friedrich!" he called as we entered. "Describe, please, the glyph that you drew."

Freddy was standing behind the table trying to hold as still as possible. "I was attempting manual reduplication, but I couldn't move enough quanta. I never can. I noticed I was hitting almost precisely one-sixty-fourth the lower limit, so I thought maybe if I doubled the initiation sequence and added a recursive suggestion, plus a couple dam lines, I could increase the gain and get it to take."

Despite having drawn the sigil in question thousands of times, I understood almost none of what Freddy had just said.

"In what *order* did you draw the parts?" asked Murchison.

"I can't remember," said Unger. "I was so excited when the Trestor device spiked that I didn't record it."

Murchison examined the sheet of paper on which Unger had drawn the reduplication glyph. In addition to the original figure, it was also covered in inky black fingerprints, as were the table, the chair, the Trestor device, and Unger's face.

Murchison lifted the sheet of paper bearing the sigil and looked at the table. The figure was replicated there, directly beneath where the paper had been.

"That's peculiar," said Unger. "I didn't put a setup trace there and it can't very well have just . . ."

Murchison dropped to his knees and crawled under the table, peering at its underside and then the floor. The sigil was repeated in black ink in both those places, too.

"I didn't draw *those*!" Unger objected.

Murchison went down one flight of stairs and pounded on Mayweather's door with his mailed fist. A minute later, Mayweather stumbled out, securing the belt on his dressing gown. When he saw the dean he went bug-eyed.

"Hello!" he said. "Is this . . . What is this about?"

Mayweather's rooms were thick with cigarette smoke, as well as something else—a thick, vegetal smell. My first thought was that he was smoke-carving, which was ridiculous. My second thought was hashish, which, as Mayweather furtively cleared away a couple of pipes and a lighter, seemed likely.

Murchison found the glyph inked on the ceiling in Mayweather's living room, right below where our table was. It was also imprinted on the expensive-looking rug on the floor. Murchison lifted the rug's edge with the toe of his boot. The figure was on the wooden floor beneath, too.

Mayweather joined us. "What *is* that?"

"Don't touch it," I said, unnecessarily. Mayweather was already backing away.

Murchison exited the room and I scrambled to rejoin him. Same story in the basement—ceiling and floor. Satisfied, Murchison led me back to my room. He used the Trestor device for a moment and asked for a logarithm table. Murchison made a few calculations and then put away his gauntlets with a look of satisfaction. He rose to leave.

"Sir?" asked Unger.

"Limiting condition on the recursive suggestion?" Murchison asked.

Unger's face fell. "Oh God!" he said. I could tell he wanted to hit himself in the head, but he had ink all over both hands and didn't want to risk further discoloration.

Murchison looked surprised at such a display of emotion. "It's safe, now," he said. He pressed his thumb down against Unger's original sigil, and lifted it away, clean and pink.

"As you drew it, the period was 0.991 seconds and it lasted 1,024 cycles."

He turned to me. "Would you be so good as to inform everyone it's harmless?"

And with that he left, humming an old sentimental tune.

I turned to Unger. "How does he know it's safe?"

In the simplest language he could manage, Unger explained that his modified reduplication sigil had continued copying itself on each available surface in line with the original glyph—the table, floor, ceiling, and presumably any pipes, earthworms, or caves that had gotten in its way. The Indian Ocean was on the opposite side of the Earth, so even if it had continued all the way through the planet's interior, we could be reasonably sure it hadn't ended up stenciled across someone's foot.

Following the initial burst, each of the glyphs had duplicated itself whenever it came in contact with another surface, which was how it had spread from the paper to Unger's hands, to the doorknob, to my fingers. After roughly twenty-one minutes, the sigil had ceased to cycle and no longer copied itself onto new surfaces.

"So it'll just wash off now?" I asked.

Unger shook his head. "There are tertiary cycles, too. You can wash it off, but it reduplicates itself back onto any original surface it imprinted on. So, I could scrub all afternoon and the water will come away gray, but the ink will still be there."

"It's *permanent?*"

"Temporarily. Until the tertiary cycle abates. But that will be at least an order of magnitude longer." By Freddy's calculation, somewhere between four days and 326 years before it would wash off.

"Temporary permanent ink," I said.

Unger cracked a smile. But a moment later Boston's Philosophical Containment Team pounded on the door and ordered us not to move. Belle Addams might be willing to allow her dean to play field scientist, but she'd also messaged the professionals. The team, protected by full bronze ring mail and carrying a bevy of Trestor devices, swept through our room.

They interrogated us for five hours, eventually reaching the same conclusion that Murchison had in five minutes: the sigil was now rendered harmless. The team confiscated the original sheet of paper and left Unger with clear instructions: under no circumstances should he attempt to re-create his experiment. It would likely lead to a repeat of the afternoon's drama. Or worse.

On the heels of their departure, Murchison's patent attorney slipped in—Ms. Addams truly did cover all the bases where novel and potentially lucrative sigils were concerned. Unger diagrammed the glyph (not difficult, given the copy on our tabletop) for the lawyer, who drew up papers. "We'll file immediately to protect your rights," she suggested. "When you remember the exact order, we'll file an addendum."

And then she, too, was gone. Unger and I sat a long, quiet moment trying to comprehend it all—the scattered papers, the stains on the floor, the legal documents.

"I always dreamed of having my own sigil," he murmured. "But I never dared imagine it might have any sort of practical import!"

"A tattoo parlor," I said. "Draw the sigil, dip your paintbrush, and turn your skin into South Seas scrimshaw without so much as a needle. Then change it for a new one in a month. Or fifty years."

"Printing presses," said Unger. "Paint it on a plate and run ten thousand newspapers without needing fresh ink."

"Shoe polish," I suggested, "house paint, hair dye . . ."

Unger sat right back down and tried the sigil again, this time adding one more line to the glyph—a limiting condition, which would prevent the image from imprinting on every surface below. On his eighth try, Unger put the pieces in the right order, mixing up a batch of temporary permanent ink that, for twenty minutes, went about merrily replicating itself.

" 'Don't try to rediscover it,' indeed!" Unger scoffed. "They probably want to patent it themselves. See if they don't try." He stared at the sheet of paper in front of him and then closed his eyes. Anyone else would have been mentally spending the millions that his sigil would rake in.

"Robert?" he said quietly. "Please don't tell anyone about this."

This with ink all over his hands, spotted on his forearms, smudged across his face.

"People may notice," I said.

"Oh, just tell them old Freddy had a bit of a mishap and it's not contagious."

I'd promised not to breathe a word about it, but Dar hardly counted. She listened with amusement, then incredulity, then amazement.

"Oh, poor Unger!" she said.

"Well, the ink will wash off eventually. In as little as a couple hundred years, he thinks." (As it turned out, thirteen years, three months, and six minutes.)

"Not that part," Dar said. "It's the sort of change that can ruin your life."

I took her in my arms. "Did Gallipoli ruin your life?" I asked.

"Only for a little while."

"May I contribute to your further ruination?" I asked.

"Please."

We thoroughly ruined each other and then lay tangled in the sheets. I stayed over, as I'd taken to doing three or four times a week.

In the middle of the night, a pounding on the door woke us. Dar grabbed me in a panic.

"Who is it?" I called out, trying to keep the terror out of my voice. Trencher or Hand of the Righteous or—

"Robert!" Freddy yelled. "Robert, get up! I've got it! It's not you, it's the glyph. You're drawing it wrong!"

31

CONWAY: *did you succeed where so many before you had perished?*

HATCHER: We flew mad. Mad as hell and scared to pieces.

JIMENEZ: Better differential equations.

HATCHER: So, we still agree on that much.

D. Priscilla Conway, "An Interview with Josofea Jimenez and
Betsy Hatcher on the Fifth Anniversary of the First Transatlantic
Flight," *Detroit Defender Sunday Magazine*, September 26, 1907

"HAS HE LOST HIS mind?" Dar whispered to me. She put the lights on and opened the door.

"Freddy," I said, "do you have any idea what time—"

"It's four fifteen! I couldn't wait any longer. You have the problem I was hoping I had: You *do* have the quanta! You're losing them to glyph failure." He thrust a piece of paper covered with handwritten tables at me.

"What are you talking about?" I asked. "Sit down."

But Unger was bouncing on his heels.

"I should have seen it the moment you said you'd lost twelve pounds and not had any change in speed—if the physics is impossible, that's a philosophical problem! I ran the numbers from Cocks and Hens. If you convert the quantal transfer rate, you should be hitting three hundred seventy-five miles an hour in the air, not two hundred fifty. So it's the hover glyph! You're drawing it wrong."

"Are you joking?" I asked.

Misdrawing the hover glyph was the kind of mistake a nine-year-old made, not a man who'd been flying for a decade. I would have bristled to hear such a thing even from a seasoned hoverer, much less the world's most inept practical philosopher. It was like a blind man mocking your handwriting.

"Robert is the most consistent flier in the aerodrome," Danielle objected. "He's not up there botching sigils."

"It's a consistent botch, then! Or consistently barely hitting! Whichever you prefer."

"I want you to leave," Dar said to Unger.

"Of course, I'm intruding, it's terribly rude! But I can prove it. We just need to run a little experiment on you. Robert, what time will you be training down at the—"

"Nine," I said. And Freddy departed, mumbling to himself about frequencies and cycles per second.

"He's cracked up," Dar said.

Unger was already down at the landing field when I got there. He was wearing one of my old skysuits, with the cuffs rolled up to fit. Essie was helping him into a harness and securing a large Trestor device to his chest.

"I can't believe you're going to permit this," Gertrude said to Brock, who was rigging to take a passenger.

"Against my better judgment," Brock said. And then to Unger: "Does Professor Yu know you borrowed that? It cost fifteen hundred dollars."

"The new model is essential!" Unger insisted. "I'll need the adjustable subtraction dampers to create a—"

"Oh, let him do it," I said. "He's at least as good with that machine as I am at flying."

We launched, with Freddy strapped to Brock's chest. She took up station a few feet from my shoulder and rolled so that Freddy and his machine were aimed at me. Brock gestured to me and I flew full out for a minute.

"Good?" Brock shouted to Unger as we slowed.

"Clear picture," he answered, still adjusting dials and making notes on an arm board. "But I need to wring out the scope in both directions. Can you give me another?"

We flew it again. Freddy began cackling madly.

"There it is!" he shouted. "A peak right at nine million cycles."

We set down.

"It's thermal bloom!" Freddy explained. "Robert can move eighteen thousand milli-Trestors per minute! He's losing a third of his energy to heat."

"Freddy, it's touching that you want to help him so badly," Brock said. "But he can't be losing that much, he'd fall right out of the air. You must be getting an echo off my glyph."

"Not at nine megahertz! Nothing else lives on that part of the spectrum. It's sigil failure!"

"You're telling me that was a failed flight?" Gertrude scoffed. "He made 249. I've only ever seen him miss a sigil with his left."

"*Partial* sigil failure. No, but see, he should be much, much faster! Robert did dozens of pushes for me before Cocks and Hens at maximum effort. So, last night I projected out how much energy he should have with the flight sigil."

"That's impossible," Brock said. "Push is a one-dimensional sigil. Hover is three-dimensional. You can't convert between them."

"Leonhard Euler devised something like it for wave equations in the 1750s! It's a second-order partial—"

"No equations," I said. "If it's failing, then tell me what part of the glyph I'm drawing wrong."

"I haven't the slightest idea!" Unger replied. "If we want a proper forensic glyph analysis we would need a highly skilled cartogramancer."

I was marched into the dean's office in full gear. Murchison covered the floor in butcher paper on which he inscribed a series of fine, gridlike lines. I would launch to a height of two feet, fly across the room, and set down. Based on how the powder fell, Murchison could tell me what was going wrong.

"Draw please," Murchison said. He was staring with immense concentration at a piece of sandstone that he was etching with a thumbtack.

I flew the length of his office.

"Failed sigil," Murchison announced.

"Lennox!" said Addams. "You didn't even look at the powder."

"Failed sigil!" the dean insisted. "Sit and draw it with a powder pencil."

A device for a child—an oversized tube filled with red sand with a pointed regulator tip on the end. Addams fetched one. I drew my flight sigil, letting the sand run onto the table.

"Incorrect," the dean pronounced without looking at it.

"What part?" asked Brock.

"Wrong hand," the dean said.

"No," Addams protested. "*Correct* hand. He's a righty."

"Wrong hand!"

We reloaded the pencil and I drew with my left.

Gertrude clicked her tongue at me. "You're flailing your elbow. You do that flying southpaw, too. Keep it in tight."

"Sorry," I said.

"Again," Murchison instructed.

I drew again, this time keeping my elbow tucked as good form demanded.

"Incorrect," the dean said.

"Oh for Christ's sake," Addams said. "It was a beautiful—"

"Oh, no, no, no!" Brock said. "Do it again."

I drew again.

Now Gertrude was aghast, too. "Up close with his off hand, it's plain as day."

"What?" I asked.

"What are the three most common reasons for hover glyph failure?" asked Brock.

That was catechism, put forth in Mary Grinning Fox's very first treatise on flying. "Mistiming, hesitation on the vertical-horizontal switch, and burying the edge on the reverse," I recited.

"You're burying the edge," Gertrude said.

"What!"

"You compensate for it by throwing your elbow, but when you don't, your tip splays. If you do it with your left hand, then you're almost certainly doing it—"

"Don't say it," interrupted Brock. "Robert, don't think. Draw with your right. Draw as fast as you can."

I drew three times with my right.

"Wrong, wrong, wrong," said Murchison, scratching away at his sandstone.

"It's subtle, but it's there!" Brock said. "Enough to weaken the sigil, but not to kill it. I never would have seen it except for the left."

Gertrude put her fingers on the flat of my hand below my pinkie and rotated it one inch. "If you supinate your wrist, you'll correct it. Practice today. We'll fly you tomorrow."

I sat that night and drew the sigil over and over with the glyph pencil. Two, three, four hundred times. Like a kid in primary school. Flat of the hand down. Hand *down*.

"I can't believe you're trying this," Dar said.

"It's just a little change in technique," I replied.

She shook her head. "You know what happens when you start thinking about your technique? It's like walking while you're thinking about it. Or breathing. Or carrying a full glass of water and looking right at it."

I refilled my glyph pencil and drew again.

"You're probably right," I said.

Hand *down*. Hand *down*.

Brock cleared the landing field the next morning except for her, me, and Gertrude.

"Do you remember when you learned to hover?" Brock asked me. "Your first time?"

"I was nine," I said. "My sister showed me. I drew the glyph a few times. She said, 'That looks good.' We went outside but it didn't work. So, she told me, 'Try harder.' I drew it a thousand times and then it worked. That's how I've done it ever since."

"I know what I'm asking is impossible," said Brock. "But something like this happens to lots of fliers who learned informally. Tillie still rotates left-side up and I'm never going to break her of it. I told Francine that she over-points her toes on her streamline, and she called me—well, if I repeat it, the devils will drag me down to Hell. Even Astrid needed three years to fix her finger slide."

"Her hands are even bigger than mine! How did she ever—"

"The important part is that she fixed it. So, here's my advice to nine-year-old Robert: try *less* hard. If you clench, you pronate your hand without realizing it. Relax your grip. Butt of the hand down. Repeat that to yourself every time you draw. Commit to it. And if you lose directional control because you're thinking too hard, I'll be flying point."

I launched and flew a lap around the landing field at low speed. I paid strict attention to my form.

"Are you doing it?" Brock called from her position above me. "It doesn't look any different."

"It doesn't feel any different," I shouted.

"Well, hit the one-mile course and see if it does anything at speed!"

I dove to accelerate, opened my reg wide, and blazed past the starting gate. Less hard. *Less hard.* Try less hard.

I knew instantly. I had a hundred tiny sensations that I'd never had while flying before: heat in the back of the calves, a tingle between the shoulder blades, the faintest taste of salt in the back of my mouth. It felt like running for the first time after spending my whole life hopping on one foot.

"Again!" shouted Gertrude, who was working the stopwatch.

I flew it again. Try less hard. Less hard. Hand *down.*

Gertrude waved me around for a third go. I flew it and landed.

Brock was crying. Big, honking sobs. "How fast?" she demanded. "Gertie!"

Gertrude didn't answer. She was humming as she showed the watch to Brock. I recognized the tune: *Highty, tighty, Christ almighty, who the hell are we? Rip ram, goddamn: flying R&E.*

"That's 341 miles per hour," Brock said.

I took a knee before I fell over from shock. Brock did the same.

"You weren't minding your posture," she said. "We didn't have you rigged low drag. And—"

I didn't hear what came after. Ten years of my life. *Ten years!* A good flier for a man. Smooth lines, pretty hands, neat form. Just never going to have the quanta—but pretty good for a man!

I was livid. I was ecstatic.

The most basic mistake an empirical philosopher could make. And no one had ever looked close enough to notice.

"All of it," I growled. "Do all of it."

Brock removed a strap here and added one there, swapped out my bag for one with an 85/15 corn powder mix, switched my helmet for one with a low-drag coating.

Three hundred forty-eight. Three hundred sixty-one.

"I'm flying to Nova Scotia and back," I snarled. I needed to do something hard before I burst.

"Save a little for tomorrow," Brock warned.

"My whole life. *My whole goddamn life!*"

Some boys can fly.

Oh lrd, son, Mother messaged. *I'm so sry.*

Working seventy hours a week to put a roof over my head. And what use did she ever have for flying above two hundred? For honest work, for carrying and hauling and lifting? None. Not her fault, not by a mile.

Really rlly? Angela asked. *Did th watch break?*

Just a child herself. I would never have been in the air without her, would never have learned any sigils at all except for my half sisters.

"That's unbelievable, Robert," Danielle said. "That's wonderful!" She was smiling like she was afraid to touch me. "Oh, you're going to have fun at the Cup!"

Fun was so far from my mind that her words barely made sense.

"Freddy, do you understand what you did for me?" I asked Unger that night. "Do you understand what this means to me?"

Unger seemed almost as pleased that his tables were correct as that I had made a breakthrough.

"The pleasure's in the thing itself, Rob."

32

We have Communists in New York City, anarchists in Chicago, and rebels in Mexico—and Miss Hardin presumes to lecture me about her *rights?* She and her mob have no more right to perform sigilry in the street than I do to commit murder. She has no more right to vote in a general election than does a child.

President Herbert Hoover, Speech Regarding
Executive Order 5901, May 18, 1932

WITH A LITTLE LESS than two weeks left before the Cup, I settled out at 375 miles per hour, just as Unger had predicted. My flare and settle was sharp, my ground technique strong, my weight at goal.

The University of Detroit decided to end their boycott and participate in the Cup after all. Their protest, it appeared, had been in part a ruse—they'd wanted to delay releasing their list of fliers until they could be sure of having Melissa Pitcairn, the former hover world-record holder, back from France, where she was flying with R&E. So, the Cup would take place with all the usual schools participating. Suddenly, the aerodrome felt friendlier.

I received my Contingency assignment: courier for the Washington branch of Durstman and Associates. Dar was overjoyed.

"You're as good as living at my apartment some weeks already," she said to me. "Maybe in a year, if you like it in Washington . . . if you decide to stay . . . we could find a place together. It would be a scandal, but—"

"Not necessarily," I said. "Not if . . ."

Neither of us needed to say it.

Danielle wrote a well-received article for the *Globe* on the rescue at the Castle Club. Senator Cadwallader-Fulton called it the finest piece by a philosopher since the war in Cuba. Danielle decided she ought to write a longer one on Gallipoli and so we went to a little shop in Inman Square to buy her a typewriter.

We squeezed down the aisles together, Dar running her fingers over one typing machine after another, delighted by the way the letters were mixed up. Moved by the spirit of extravagance, she chose an Underwood No. 5—to my eye, the largest and heaviest model in the entire shop.

"This has got to weigh thirty-five pounds," I complained as I hauled it home for her.

"That's why I'm keeping you!" she said giddily. She grabbed my arm and danced a few steps along the curb, then leaped down to the street and back onto the sidewalk.

We rounded the corner by her apartment.

I smelled the smoke before I saw it. I could barely move. My lips felt stiff as concrete.

"Run," I managed. "Run!"

In front of Dar's building, on a flimsy wooden scaffold, a woman-sized effigy had been strung up by a noose and set aflame. A hand-lettered sign reading TRAITOR was propped up against the base.

I tried to pull Dar after me, but she twisted loose.

"No," she said.

Dar strode toward the rapidly growing crowd of onlookers.

"They could still be here!" I warned.

"Oh, they've run away," Dar said. "Or if they're here, they only want to watch."

I wasn't so sure. I swept my eyes back and forth over the crowd, the rooftops, the doors and windows, searching for suspicious faces, for anyone reaching under a coat. I saw nothing. Or, rather, everyone looked like a potential threat.

In front of us, blue and yellow flames writhed over the manikin. It had been made from straw and rags doused in what smelled like kerosene. Dar surveyed the spectacle for a moment then turned to the crowd.

"You who did this!" she shouted. "You can go to hell!"

Dar kicked at the scaffold's base. The burning figure swayed. She kicked again with her heavy-soled boot and the whole thing toppled over. One of her neighbors emerged carrying a bucket of water. Dar poured it over the still-burning dummy, which now lay sprawled on the ground. The flames spat and went out.

Dar took a penknife from her workbag and hacked the rope free of the effigy's neck. She pulled it clear of the scaffolding and crossed its hands over its chest. Then she dragged the wooden beams into a pile, coiled the rope on top, and crowned it with the sign. She sorted through her handbag until she found a vial of mercury fulminate. Aiming at the pile of wood and rope, she popped the cap and drew wildly. It ignited.

Dar stood with hands on hips and reared back. "Do you hear me? Burn in hell!"

Her fists were clenched and her chin was quivering. She coughed and wiped her nose.

"Did anybody see who did this?" I called out.

"Don't bother," Dar hissed. "This is Boston. Nobody saw anything, nobody remembers anything. They never do. They hanged witches back in the day. They developed a taste for it."

Several of Belle Addams's well-prepared guards trundled us off to the dean's office while Dar's retaliatory blaze was still burning.

"This is my fault," Addams said to Dar. "I've gotten too lax about your security. I'll post someone outside your building for the next few nights, very visibly. When you go to or from the college, you'll have an escort. On campus, you should go between classes with a group of girls, never alone. If the two of you are planning to go out this weekend, I'll make arrangements for someone to follow. He'll be discreet. These are standard, sensible precautions."

"No, they're not!" objected Dar. "What would a guard have done this afternoon, search everyone for matches?"

"Miss Hardin, I wish you would take this seriously. We don't even know who's behind this—whether the Trenchers are escalating or whether you riled up the Gray Hats with your last article. God knows which would be worse."

"I *am* taking this seriously. I don't care who did it. If I don't go out in public or if I take a lot of armed men everywhere, then they've won. Because I as good as admit that a philosopher who speaks her conscience isn't safe on the street in broad daylight."

"If you end up injured, or worse, then they also win," Addams replied.

I disassembled my revolver on Dar's table to clean it. She watched with interest as I ran a wire brush down the barrel and wiped the crane and cylinder. I polished the silver plating and wiped down the pink handle.

"It's pretty," she said.

"Yup," I said. "Ma carries an old Single Action Army—the Peacemaker, they called it. Big cowboy gun. Makes this one look like a child's toy. If I were choosing . . ."

"Not the shiny little one that fits in your purse?"

"Uh-huh." I added a couple drops of lubricating oil and reassembled it.

"Robert?" Dar said. "Promise you won't kill anybody for me."

33

I've served five terms—you know how much I hate asking for help. But when you're allowed to run and forbidden to vote, that's just intolerable. They keep telling me to be good, be polite, be a lady. So, pretty please, won't you turn out on Tuesday to tell Herbert Hoover and friends that they're gutless little sons of bitches?

Rep. Danielle Noor Hardin, Speech to the Providence
Industrial Club, November 2, 1932

ONE WEEK LEFT UNTIL the Cup. I tried to set aside the effigy. Concentrate on flying. On R&E.

Monday morning, I found my makeshift changing room reeking of piss, my harness wet to the touch. I had no doubt who was behind it. Since my breakthrough, Rachael Rodgers had been even more strident in opposing my flying for Radcliffe. Plenty of my classmates still agreed with her.

I put on work gloves and picked up my rigging. To hell with them—I'd practice after I'd cleaned it. But Rachael, flanked by a dozen of her most ardent supporters, blocked the door before I could exit the building.

"What is that *appalling* smell?" Rachael asked. "Did you wet yourself?" Several of them snickered.

"It appears someone urinated on my kit," I said, trying to look perfectly unruffled.

Rachael put on a mock-sympathetic face. "Oh, you *poor* thing!"

The women stepped aside to let me through.

Once I had my back to them, Rachael called out, "You piss on tradition, then piss on you!"

They each had a cup that they flung in unison. It might have been urine, human or otherwise, or water treated with yellow food coloring, a splash of ammonia, and a drop of methyl mercaptan. But it showered down on me and stank to high hell.

"Oh God, Robert!" Jake said when I found her with the set of booms she and Francine were arranging to practice their slalom flying. "What is that—"

"What's the best way to get urine out of harness leather?" I asked her.

Jake was kind enough not to ask for more detail. "Mild soap and water."

I cleaned up my rigging and myself, then went back to the aerodrome. I mopped the floor, washed the sheet that served as my divider, hung up my tack. *Just think about doing that twice and see which one of us people call depraved.*

The following morning, I found my custom harness cut to pieces. Mother's old Springfield getup, which I kept as a backup—the one she'd brought back from Cuba—was slashed to ribbons, too. My spiral-cut regulator, smashed.

"Oh, Weekes," Brock said. She was deadly calm as she sorted through the pile of shredded straps and broken pieces of metal. "You might have told me about yesterday. We ought to have locked up— Oh my."

"Yup," I said.

It was like looking at a dismembered friend. My face went hot.

Not in front of Brock, I told myself, *not again.*

"Use one of the McCoule rigs with a chest expander?" I suggested. My voice cracked only a little.

"Oh, hell no!"

I broke down in Dar's arms. Stupid, humiliating sobs. She held me until the spell had passed.

"We could go away for the weekend," Dar suggested. "You tell me where. The mountains. New York City—we could see your sister. Go away and not hear a single word about the Cup."

"You never hid," I said.

Dar ran her fingers through my hair. "I wouldn't think less of you, Robert."

"Yeah, you would."

Dar looked sad and exhausted. "Then do it. And I'll sit in the front row."

Jake messaged every Harnemon's depot she could think of. By seven that evening, the outlet in Santa Fe had found a DCI extended-body, spiral-cut reg in their warehouse, still in its original box. They sent it express transporter line.

"Hand delivery tomorrow morning," promised Jake. "Don't let it out of your sight."

Which just left the problem of a harness. Professor Brock made special arrangements. At nine thirty that night she messaged me: *My office. Now.*

She had a short, bald man of about fifty years sitting beside her, engrossed in Unger's pages of equations for converting push energy to hovering quanta. The family resemblance was obvious.

"Your brother?" I asked.

"Steven is the lead flight dynamics engineer at Northwest Aero," Professor Brock explained.

Steven climbed to his feet and shook my hand. "The famous Mr. Weekes! We were all terribly sorry to hear about this morning. So many hours went into building that harness."

"It was beautiful," I said. "It was perfect."

"Funny you should say that, because none of us around the office in Detroit thought so," he said. "You were such an interesting problem. We kept coming back to what changes we'd make given a second opportunity, how we'd do it if price were no object. When we got Janet's message, our ad man said we ought to consider it an opportunity. Outfitting what will be the two most recognizable faces in the Cup. We sketched an idea or two—"

He riffled through his briefcase, bringing out a reduplicated drawing:

A man in a skysuit stood with his hands on his hips, four sandbags strapped across his chest. In front of him a small, thin woman was in the midst of a one-step, arm-up launch. Both wore full-body, form-fitting skysuits of a type I'd never seen before—the straps seemed to weave between layers of fabric.

The text ran: *Meet Mr. Robert Weekes of Radcliffe College. He carried 180 pounds flush using our integrated cargo strap system during the 1918 General's Cup. Flared and settled every landing. And who could mistake Miss Aileen Macadoo, world-record hoverer at 518 miles per hour? Northwest Aero's low-drag construction helped her win a fourth gold medal—in the long course, no less!*

In block letters at the bottom: NORTHWEST AERO: STRONG ENOUGH FOR A MAN. FAST ENOUGH FOR A LADY.

"That's supposed to be me?" I asked, laughing. I looked like a giant carved from granite.

"We'll take a few photographs, make it truer to life."

I studied the text again. "Does that mean Macadoo's flying the long course instead of the short?"

"That's right," Brock said. "Sacramento took a wee bit of umbrage at Detroit bringing home Melissa Pitcairn to compete. They one-upped them by switching Macadoo to the long course. I can only imagine how Detroit reacted."

"Oh, we were already out for blood and that was the final insult!" Steven said. "Sacramento making a play to steal the gold from Missy the Missile, war hero and all."

He took a set of calipers and began measuring my arms at two-inch intervals. "No allergies to spiders, I hope?" he asked. "Nickel? Latex rubber? And no objections to flying without boots?"

"None," I said, still staring at the picture. "What's it made of?"

"Cloth woven with the latest vapor deposition techniques. Smokecarved. All the best qualities of silk and steel. A hundred dollars a yard, but the publicity alone will be worth ten times that. We'll reinforce the knees and ankles with piezo-kinetic threads that go stiff when you strike—you'll be able to punch your landings and it'll absorb the shock. We offered the design to

Macadoo, but she wanted a shark-scale coating instead to improve laminar airflow. Makes her a touch faster."

"Is all that— I mean there's a rule against accepting money or gifts, right?" I asked.

Steven winked. "If you return the suit afterward, all you've done is provide a valuable service to the advancement of American sigilry by testing an experimental harness. Now, perhaps, in a couple months you'll decide you'd like to make a little money by offering your likeness to our advertising campaign . . ."

Mayweather intercepted me the moment I emerged from Brock's office.

"Could you draw a picture of it?" he pleaded. "Describe it to me at least?"

"Brian, how can you possibly know—"

"It's a custom job by Northwest Aero, so it must be Steven Brock. It's all over the betting sheets. Don't tell me you haven't looked at them."

I hadn't, though you could hardly go two minutes without hearing whispers about the odds on one flier or another—even Radcliffe's most law-abiding young ladies liked to wager a few dollars on the Cup.

"It's unethical for me to see it," I said.

"Only if you bet *against* yourself," Mayweather assured me.

He pressed a tip sheet into my hands. Four names caught my interest:

Macadoo, Aileen Marie. Sacramento. EVEN MONEY to win; 1 to 2 to medal. Fine racing form at 60 inches, 93 pounds . . . rumored to have broken her own record of 518 mph . . . plan for 3 hot landings . . . custom racing harness by Northwest Aero . . . three-time short-course gold medalist should win going away.

Pitcairn, Melissa Anne. Detroit. 3 to 1 to win; EVEN MONEY to medal. Not in peak racing condition after a year in France . . . 70 inches, 168 pounds . . . former record holder at 511 mph . . . plan for 6 hot landings . . . custom harness by Patterson & Lee . . . likely winner if ill fortune befalls Macadoo.

Stewart, Sarah Elizabeth. Radcliffe. 25 to 1 to win; 4 to 1 to medal.
Well-balanced at 65 inches, 120 pounds . . . scouted at above 410 mph . . .
plan for 10 hot landings . . . Menten-McClintock Type IX harness . . . unpre-
dictable flier with only 2 years' experience.

 Weekes, Robert Arthur. Radcliffe. 100 to 1 to win; 10 to 1 to medal.
Power flier at 72½ inches, 189 pounds . . . verified at above 374 mph . . . plan
for 10 hot landings . . . custom lifting harness by Northwest Aero . . . better
bet if high wind or rough weather.

"Ten to one to medal?" I said. That was better odds than I would have given myself.

"You'll beat both of Trestor's fliers on speed alone, so everyone is saying sixth place for you. They're wrong. I have a hundred dollars on you to finish third."

"Brian!" I said. "I don't need to know that. And that's throwing away your money."

"No, it's basic psychology: Detroit's number two knocks out Macadoo, and Sacramento's number two retaliates—that's all *three* of them injured or disqualified. Pitcairn squeaks through unscathed and Miss Stewart, provided she doesn't stop to pray over the dead, takes second. You finish third."

"That's a very dramatic idea."

"Unger agrees. 'Most probable outcome.' He's got a hundred on you, too. We're going to put someone at each of the checkpoints to tell you where things stand."

"That's absolutely forbidden."

"No, *coaching* during the event is illegal. We won't have Brock or your old lady shouting strategy, just a few like-minded young men to tell you how many seconds the next flier is ahead or behind. The crowd always yells that sort of thing, anyway. We'll do it for Essie, too. Detroit and Sacramento will be doing the same for theirs. Really, I'm doing the Cup a favor: it would be unfair for Radcliffe to be the only school *not* doing it."

"Yes, terrible that we cheat so poorly."

• • •

During the days leading up to the competition, spectators from California and Michigan poured into the city. While Boston considered the Cup an annoyance to be dealt with once every four years, the more philosophical parts of the country looked forward to it—Detroit all but shut down during the event.

Some of the philosophical tourists went looking for trouble in the Trencher enclave in downtown Boston. In the clash that followed, the Trenchers stabbed three Detroiters. The next night two Trenchers ended up bonekilled.

The *Globe* called for the Cup to be canceled. Addams put guards on the aerodrome and an extra one on me. The Corps sent three platoons of smokecarvers to see to security at the event itself. By Thursday morning they were setting up a command post in the middle of the landing field.

"Jesus," Jake said, as she watched the corpswomen unrolling razor wire and the guards patrolling with rifles on their shoulders. "It's supposed to be amateur athletics, not an invasion."

Brock pulled me out of class that afternoon, handed me a map, and said to go immediately, tell no one. I collected my gear and flew twenty minutes west, to a remote marshy patch of land with a landing zone marked with branches and an R in red and white chalk.

Gertrude and Steven were waiting.

"We were up all night at Northwest Aero finishing it, but I think you'll like it," Steven said.

He'd hung a garment bag from a tree. I opened it and found a flimsy, iridescent piece of fabric on a hanger. No wool, no leather, no buckles. It looked like a pair of silk footie pajamas. The belly was mottled sky blue and gray, the back green spotted with tan. Camouflage.

"How do I—umm—do I . . ."

"I hope you're not overly modest, we didn't design it for anything to go under."

Gertrude turned her back and I stripped. Even with Steven's help, I struggled to shove my legs into place.

"Slow and steady pressure to— no, you've got it kinked! Pull back and—"

It fit like a second skin.

"How thick?" I asked.

"Two millimeters."

The arms went easier, which just left a long open seam stretching from neck to waist.

"Snaps or pins or—"

"Self-sealing," Steven said. "Pull it snug and press the edges together."

No cap or helmet, rather an attached hood that covered my head and face, leaving only my eyes exposed.

I unlimbered my shoulders and the suit moved with me perfectly. I tried my chest thrust, hip snap, forward lean. No resistance at all.

"Straps for the sandbags?" I asked.

"The tabs on your chest and back. Also self-adhering."

They had sandbags already filled, so I lifted one into place and pulled at the tab on my suit. It stretched like putty. I wrapped it around the sandbag and stuck the end to my suit. It stayed put.

Steven helped me to kit out with my full 180-pound load and sent me up to ten feet.

"Now cut your regulator and fall!" he said.

That sounded like a horrible idea, but I allowed my sigil to fade. I assumed a crouching position and tensed my body for the terrible jolt that was sure to come.

My knees bent as I hit, but then my legs went rigid as a ripple of force ran through the fabric, absorbing the shock. I straightened against the weight and found my knees were intact, ankles intact. I'd barely felt anything.

"Damn," I said to Steven. "I love it. Have you ever flown with one?"

"Oh, I can't hover," Steven replied. "I don't have the quanta." He saw me frown at that. "At least I shouldn't think . . . well, could you imagine trying to learn at my age?"

• • •

I spent the rest of the afternoon practicing landings and attaching bags. On Friday, I cut class and flew out to the camp. Up and down. Bags on and off. There was no time to waste—the Cup was the next morning.

Brock and Gertrude joined me.

"Nobody's worked harder than you," Brock said. "No one could. Try not to get caught up in all the big talk. Sixth place would be a win."

"There are no guarantees," said Gertrude. "The Corps invitations to the long-course medalists are only customary. You might win gold and they refuse you an invite. Or maybe they give you one for finishing last."

Brock nodded. "For strategy: if you and another flier are trying to land on the same approach, cut below her. She'll have to decide whether to go around or through you. When you land, run clear of the field as fast as you can. If you dawdle, an incoming flier could drop her belly bag on you—and you do *not* want to be hit by a bunch of twenty-pound sandbags."

"Don't worry overmuch about the leaders," Gertrude counseled. "Macadoo will gain twenty-four seconds on you each leg in the air, Pitcairn nearly the same. You might win a little back with your flare and settle—Macadoo's a short-courser, so she's never had to land in competition before."

"Stay clear of the ugliness," Brock added. "They're lucky nobody died in that collision last year. Detroit will be out for revenge and they'll target Macadoo. Detroit's number two flier will be their thug; she'll attack at the second checkpoint, when she has a sandbag as a weapon. Sacramento's number two will try to protect Macadoo. Pitcairn will move to stay above the carnage and win it."

"Don't rely on following the woman in front of you," Gertrude advised. "Do your own navigation. They're a bunch of fancy city fliers who can't read a compass."

Brock, who was a fancy city flier herself, gave her a dirty look.

"Fly well," Brock said. "Fly for yourself. And know there's a nine-year-old boy watching somewhere on the course and he's going to see you and say 'I could do that.' "

34

As a girl, I was so sickly that the slightest emotional upset sent my whole body into paroxysms of shaking. It was not until I learned to master my passions that I could fly with authority. I took to waking in the morning an hour before my sisters, and a thousand times before they rose, I practiced drawing my sigils.

Lt. Col. Yvette Rodgers, *Life and Death on San Juan Hill*, 1900

I MADE MY WAY down to the aerodrome at five the next morning and found the place transformed. The landing field had been fenced off and bleachers erected with space for ten thousand people. The other spectators would find vantage points along the river from which to watch—the *Globe* was predicting a hundred thousand in all. Addams's guards were out in their red and black uniforms, patrolling the perimeter. They searched my bags and waved me through to the area reserved for the competitors. I'd expected to be the first to arrive, but Essie was already there, perched on Radcliffe's bench, studying a map of Boston and its environs.

I sat beside her. We watched the sky lighten, but there was no proper sunrise. It was an eight out of eight overcast, with a soft gray ceiling at three thousand feet, heavy gusting wind, and intermittent rain. I'd worn snow pants and my parka over my skysuit; Essie had her winter coat and a kerchief over her head. I paged through *Life and Death on San Juan Hill*, tracing out the flight sigil over and over. The print was smudged to the point of illegibility in some parts, not that I needed to see the words.

"What are you reading?" Essie asked.

I showed her the cover of my battered old paperback. She gave me the only smile she would let slip all morning. "I must have read that a hundred times as a girl."

"I read it a thousand," I said.

Frieda and Tillie made their way up to our bench, hauling thin, twenty-foot-long cases with wheels on the end. I could only think of one thing that size. It was every flier's dream.

"Are those wings?" I asked.

"Shh," said Tillie. "Don't ruin it."

"It's never worked," I said. "Mary Fox tried a dozen times."

"She used the wrong cross section," Tillie said. "She tried to make them bird-shaped. Brock did it like an aeroplane wing. If we can get up to ten thousand feet, we can glide all day. This wind is going to be murder on the ascent, though."

"After you're done, can I—"

"It won't fit you. Also, you're the eighteenth person to ask today."

The rest of our fliers trickled in and the other teams took their seats, too. You could see flashes of their skysuits—Radcliffe's red and black, Sacramento's orange, Detroit's dark purple, Maria Trestor's uniquely unfortunate shade of chartreuse. A few women stretched or did calisthenics, but mostly we waited, huddled against the cold.

At seven the grandstand opened and within minutes it had filled. Danielle sat in the front row, flanked by a pair of guards. I couldn't spot my mother and Vivian, who'd taken a red-eye transporter run in from Denver, or Angela, who'd flown up from New York, but they were somewhere in the seats.

Tens of thousands more spectators crowded onto the bridges and both shores of the Charles. We could see amateur hoverers streaking across the sky to the long-course landing fields, the list of which had just been released to the general public. (And surely they were packed a hundred deep around the twenty-mile checkpoint, where everyone was saying Detroit would make their run at Macadoo.)

At eight, Radcliffe's band struck up "Hail, Columbia." We rose and sang along. The Corps precision hovering squadron from Fort Putnam, which was supposed to do a ceremonial flyover at the end of the song, mistimed their approach and came blasting overhead in the middle of the second verse, detonating a series of blanks in a deafening salute.

"Shoddy formation flying," sniffed Astrid after we'd regained our hearing. "They were bunched up on the left. We could have put together twelve girls who fly better than that, right, Jake?"

Jake didn't answer. She and Francine were intent on preparing for the short course; they'd taken out a handheld anemometer to measure wind speed and were lost to the world as they watched it spinning wildly: thirty-one miles per hour, with gusts another twenty miles an hour above.

"You've got to wait for a lull," Jake said to Francine. "Hold in the ready position. When the wind drops, signal and start as fast as you can."

"Excuse me!" Francine snorted. "I watched my first one of these before you were born. Don't tell me—"

Uncoachable, Professor Brock had called them, *due to a surfeit of natural ability.* The announcer called for short-coursers and they were led off to a separate holding pen.

I peered out at the course along the Charles. During the night, Brock and her fellow instructors had set up ten tall, flexible bamboo towers beside the river, keeping the exact configuration of the one-mile slalom course secret from the competitors. The other fliers were buzzing over it.

"That's the most technical layout I've ever seen," Astrid whispered to me. "Poor Jake. She's gonna get creamed."

As we watched the fliers take their warm-up runs, I could see the trick. The course appeared straightforward enough to lull a careless hoverer into a false sense of security, but then placed the fifth turn so tightly that if a flier didn't start setting up two turns in advance, she was in trouble.

After a few minutes, the course was cleared and the event began in earnest. Each of the eight fliers would make three runs, with their fastest one determining their place. Francine, as the eldest hoverer competing, had the honor of opening the event. She flew all three passes cleanly, though several of her angles were less than ideal and she got blown sideways on her last run.

"Goddamn stupid tradition!" Francine hissed as she retook her seat with us. "That wind's going to drop and whoever goes last will win."

"It's not going to drop," sighed Tillie, who had taken over watching the wind gauge.

Both of Trestor's women flew competently, as did a Detroiter. Then Sacramento's number two—the long-courser who'd traded spots with Aileen Macadoo—stepped up. She wasn't accustomed to slalom flying and struggled to come out of her turns cleanly. On her final attempt, she pushed too hard and slammed into the fifth pylon. It collapsed, as it was supposed to, but the impact stunned her. She veered out of control.

When something goes wrong in front of a hundred thousand philosophers, there's a real danger that everyone will spring into action at once. But common sense won out; the crowd stayed on the ground and Brock, who was flying point, swooped in to grab the girl before her sigil died. The young woman, bruised but alive, waved to the crowd and the competition continued after only a brief delay to replace the damaged pylon.

Jake had the misfortune of going next. Her first run was unusually conservative. She looked skittish, making her turns too wide.

"Jake hit a tower really hard last year," Astrid said. "She's spooked."

On her second pass, Jake opened up, accelerating hard, only to flinch at the pylon that the woman before her had hit and make a loose, two-dimensional turn. It cost her so much time that she simply aborted the run.

"You're thinking too hard, darling," Francine muttered. "Just *fly*."

Jake waited in the starting block for the wind to drop before her final attempt. We were all sweating despite the temperature. Three minutes, then five.

The wind momentarily slowed. Jake's hand shot up to signal her start.

It was classic Jake—the stretching launch as she flung herself into the air, the lithe, sinewy turns that sliced and dropped like a circus man juggling knives.

"Yes. *Yes*," whispered Francine. "Don't think."

"Whoopsie," muttered Astrid at the same moment.

And Astrid—who inclined toward the thinky end of the spectrum herself—had called it three seconds before it happened. Jake, flying so beautifully in the moment, wasn't set up for the fifth pylon and passed it on the wrong side. We could hear her shriek of rage from eight hundred yards.

"Home field advantage my ass," Jake spat as she rejoined us. The results, announced a half hour later, did little to cheer her: of the eight fliers, Francine had taken fifth, Jake seventh.

The tug-of-war seemed our best chance to win a spot on the podium—after all, there were three medals for four teams. Radcliffe faced Trestor first. Both sides clipped the rope into their harnesses, then, on the whistle, ascended to twenty feet. On the second whistle they turned and, with their backs to each other, heaved. The theoreticians were faster on the draw, but the Cliffes had more power and applied their advantage steadily, winning a convincing victory.

"Perfect," Francine pronounced. "Astrid's got them in fine form."

Against Detroit and Sacramento, though, we were outclassed; the empirical heavyweights bulled their way through, towing our five behind them. Trestor suffered the same fate and, as expected, it was the two New England schools in the consolation round. The rematch began promisingly, with Astrid's team exerting their extra power to good effect. Trestor tried to throw them off with a series of left and right jerks, but Astrid had prepared her teammates for just such a strategy—it only lost Trestor ground. Then one of their jerks caused a Cliffe to hang up on the rope. She freed herself, but for a few seconds it was five on four, which threw our other fliers into a panic. The Cliffes lost their composure and Trestor won an upset victory.

Astrid returned with her team, scowling. "That's what I deserve for taking four freshmen," she muttered.

Detroit out-pulled Sacramento to win it.

All the while Tillie and Frieda had been watching the wind gauge.

"That's too fast," Frieda said. "We said we wouldn't use them if it was above twenty-five."

"Do what you want," Tillie said, "but I didn't come this far to fly in the old style."

Tillie uncased her wings. They were built from sheets of hammered steel, thin as a sword on the leading edge. Tillie bolted them to a metal harness that looked like a breastplate and buckled herself in.

The other endurance fliers were outfitted with similarly unusual equipage. Detroit's women had long pikes that extended from their harnesses several feet past their heads (*asymmetric bow wave disrupter, banned 1919–present*), Sacramento's had crests on the sides of their helmets that reached back to their shoulders (*cheek canards, banned 1919–present*), and Trestor's had canteens, picnic baskets, and an extra three-inch piece of tubing on their regulators (*vortex powder scavenger, banned 1919–present*—and subsequently incorporated into every standard-issue commercial regulator). Frieda wore only her regular harness.

They launched as a group and a fifty-mile-per-hour gust hit them in the opening seconds. Both of Sacramento's women had their helmets blown right off and had to be assisted to the ground. Tillie's wings flexed and bowed. Something cracked and fragments of metal came fluttering down.

"That can't be good," Astrid said.

But Tillie held her line and climbed through the clouds. The rest of the women headed southeasterly, riding the wind as best they could, each with a race official following to measure distance and carry the flier home when her powder ran out.

Frieda was the first to be brought back. She'd managed eight minutes in the air and fifteen miles covered—not terrible for a woman flying without technological assistance. "Tillie lost part of her stabilizer," Frieda reported. "She'll be able to glide, but she'll have a hard time turning if she finds a thermal."

"Does she have a chance to win?" Jake asked.

Frieda shook her head. "Detroit's are going really fast on low settings. The girls from Trestor, though—I think they're going to fly until next week." (Only until the following morning, as it turned out. Tillie, nursing her damaged wings through the gusts, managed fourth place.)

But the long-coursers didn't have time to contemplate the various new innovations. We were taken forward into the corral, issued our maps and compasses, and given five minutes to plot our route. Race officials issued us our bags and regulators, each of which had been carefully inspected. They might be willing to tolerate creativity in the endurance flight, but not the long course.

I shed my coat and snow pants. My body-hugging skysuit occasioned more than a few catcalls and otherwise enlightened commentary from the spectators.

"Jeeeesus—that one ain't no lady!"

"Show us your skirts!"

"Who's gonna carry you, sonny?"

Trestor College's fliers were laughing and pointing, too.

"Radcliffe builds them uglier and uglier, don't they?" one said to the other.

"Is it a she?" asked the second Trestorite. "It's *got* to be a she. But you can see *something* under there."

"A lifelike simulacrum," said the first, and they both snickered.

Melissa Pitcairn, who had been chatting with her number two, looked delighted by my suit. She waved at me and sauntered over, tucking her hair up under her helmet. She was unreasonably beautiful. "Too voluptuous for a sprinter" the *Detroit Defender* had called her, right up until she'd set the old world record.

"Good morning, big fella!" Pitcairn called out. "Ain't you cute as a button in that shiny little costume! Macadoo's having a fit and we haven't even launched yet. I love it!"

And, indeed, the tiny flier from Sacramento in a skin-tight orange suit quite a lot like mine was pointing me out to her enforcer—a woman even larger than Detroit's thug—and smacking one hand into the other. The Sacramento number two patted Macadoo on the shoulder, trying to calm her.

Pitcairn was eating it up. She slid an arm around my waist. "Listen, Ace," she purred. "I like you already. Maybe it's because I've got a kid brother who flies, maybe I just like seeing a big man poured into a pair of tight pants, but let me give you some friendly advice: Stay *well* fucking back. You don't want to get caught in the middle of this."

Missy the Missile looked back to make sure Macadoo was watching. She planted a big kiss on my cheek and slapped my bottom. The crowd roared.

Macadoo was bouncing on her toes. Her number two had her by the arm, but Macadoo broke away and stamped up to me.

"Making a mockery out of this!" Macadoo snarled, half drowned out by the crowd and the announcer. "Radcliffe deviants! And tell your half-Arab girlfriend the next time she saves some Trenchers to get her name in the paper, the Gray Hats will cut her head off!"

I was so far beyond angry that it was like sitting on a chair ten paces away and watching my own body, frozen in place.

"Fliers to the *ready*!" came the call.

Essie was right beside me. She whispered something to me.

"To the ready!"

"What?" I said.

"Fuck them," Essie said. She looked at me, and she didn't have the mien of a meek, anxious girl, but rather the face of a woman with deadly patience who'd waited her whole life for this.

"To the ready!" came the call a third and final time.

Then the whistle.

35

Up the Corps! Up the Corps and charge!

Mrs. Lucretia Cadwallader, Various, 1861–71

ONE-STEP LAUNCHES ALL AROUND, up and low, the entire company keeping beneath one hundred feet. No surprises as the first miles sped by. Macadoo in first, flying less than full out so that her escort could shadow her. Next, Detroit's thug with Pitcairn following—no point in them instigating just yet. Essie flew right at their heels. I was well behind despite my best effort. Both of Trestor's women puttered along in my wake.

As we approached the first checkpoint, Macadoo opened her regulator full and both of Detroit's fliers did, too. I could see it play out fifteen seconds ahead of me. Macadoo with a sharp flare, Detroit's number two diving to attack, Sacramento's number two moving to block. The Detroit thug tried to slip underneath and took a boot to the face for her trouble. Macadoo landed and sprinted for her bag, while the Detroit and Sacramento enforcers made for the ground as well. Pitcairn looped and came down practically on Macadoo's head. The two of them screamed at each other. Macadoo finished securing her sandbag and launched.

Essie flared and settled a few seconds ahead of me and was nearly away by the time I made my landing.

I grabbed my sandbag, yanked a strap out, and stuck the cargo in place. One-step launch. Level out and accelerate. Hand *down*. Hand *down*.

Macadoo in her orange suit was easily a mile ahead of me. But that was inevitable. Set it aside. Just focus on the next leg, the next minute, the next glyph. Draw for more speed. Only think about the glyph: draw, on a six count, a layered triple crescent dropping to an anticlockwise reaching spiral. Then repeat. And repeat. And repeat.

Body position. Hand *down*, elbow in, head tucked, toes pointed.

Ninety seconds.

Try less hard.

The melee at the twenty-mile mark—in the air and on the ground—has been described to me so many times that I can almost believe I was close enough to see it.

The landing field was a clearing in a pine forest, twenty feet by twenty, the bags lined up along the far edge, a rope to hold back the spectators, some fifteen thousand of them, who were crushing forward.

Macadoo streaked over, flared under full power, and hit the ground hard. She needed a moment to regain her bearings. Sacramento's number two moved to protect Macadoo from above, but mistook the charging red and black skysuit for purple. She accidentally blocked Essie, who'd slipped past the Detroit fliers. Essie tried to cut under, but flinched and was forced up and around.

That gave Detroit's number two an unobstructed path to Macadoo. The Detroit thug whipped into a dive and cut loose her sandbag, which came within a foot of crushing Macadoo. The Detroiter followed that up by slamming into Macadoo with a flying tackle. They fell to the ground together, but the Detroit woman's leg twisted and snapped. Macadoo tried to climb to her feet, but Detroit's number two—screaming in pain—clung to her.

Sacramento's enforcer got to the ground a moment later and ran to assist Macadoo. The Sacramento number two was furious: her partner had nearly been killed. She began kicking the injured Detroiter about the head and hands.

Pitcairn, who'd hung back, flared and settled. She saw her injured teammate taking a terrible beating and abandoned any thought of slipping past the chaos to take the lead.

Pitcairn spun Sacramento's number two around and slugged her in the face.

But I didn't know any of that had happened. All I could see was that Essie had been forced off her landing. As I approached and flipped into my flare dive, Essie was banking hard to come in behind me.

I somersaulted upright and drew to settle.

All four women on the ground were shouting at one another and the crowd at them. Pitcairn was standing over Sacramento's number two, who had blood streaming down her face from a broken nose. Macadoo was struggling to attach her bag; she looked dazed. The Detroit thug, with her shinbone poking through her skysuit, was lying on the ground, crying.

"Are you okay?" I called to her. She might lose the leg if it wasn't tended to promptly.

"Butt out, you stinking cunt sucker!" she screamed at me through her tears.

The other three women were shouting at me, too, in terms only slightly less vivid, as was the crowd.

"Weekes!" a man hollered. "Weekes! Get clear! Get launched!"

Mayweather, right up in the front row. For once in his life he was right—plenty of hands to provide a medical evacuation.

I dashed for my sandbag and attached it.

"Radcliffe!" Mayweather screamed. "Up Radcliffe!"

I one-stepped and was gone.

Leading the General's Cup.

Don't think it. Don't even think it. Hand down. Hand down. *Try less hard.*

Essie caught me first. She had me by fifty miles an hour; it felt like standing still while a passenger train thundered past. She gave me a hip waggle in place of a wave, which would have thrown her off course.

Then a purple suit, well off to my right, chasing Essie hard—Pitcairn at full power, better than five hundred miles an hour.

I bore down. And then there was the third checkpoint, a roped-off section of a farm pasture, crowd packed around it. Flip, flare, settle. Essie was already away. Pitcairn looked at me in disbelief as I trotted up. Then she turned and launched, too.

I attached my bag to cheers from the crowd.

"You scallywag!" shouted Osgood Fletcher. "A Cock was leading the Cup! I'll drink happy tonight!"

"Is Macadoo back up?" I shouted. "Or is she hurt?"

"Haven't the foggiest!" Osgood called back.

I checked my compass heading. I would lose sight of Essie before I reached the next checkpoint and didn't want to have to climb to spot it.

"Up Radcliffe!" Osgood shouted.

I launched.

Hand *down*. Hand *down*.

I felt the turbulence before I saw the orange skysuit, at my ten o'clock and climbing fast, searching for the next landing zone. Macadoo. She spotted it and dove. You could afford to ignore niceties like navigation when you could hit five hundred miles an hour.

She was gone before I touched down at the landing zone to tepid applause.

"Sacramento's number two is back up!" Krillgoe Hosawither screamed to me. "Thirty seconds behind you!"

Which was bad news—she'd be able to catch me, too.

I landed hard at the fourth field, but the suit did its job and dissipated the shock. I grabbed my sandbag.

"Well flown, Radcliffe!" called Steven Brock from the crowd, which was quite thin here. "You've fifteen seconds on Sacramento. Pitcairn's passed Essie."

Enough to send me crashing back to reality.

Sacramento's number two—in spite of her broken nose—passed me shortly before the fifty-mile mark. At the checkpoint, she spun out her belly bag and followed it to the ground. I flared and settled, pushing hard to the ground to shave off another second.

The Sacramento enforcer was away almost as soon as I touched, her ascent momentarily slowed as she reeled in her bag. She had me beat, though with such poor ground technique, she might not catch Essie.

Fifth place. More than respectable for a man.

I attached the next sandbag, confirmed my compass heading, and launched.

I landed alone at the sixth checkpoint and everyone was screaming.

"Macadoo's lost!" Dmitri shouted. "Way off course. Her number two's trying to help her."

If both of them—if they were lost badly enough—don't think it.

"And get your damn hips forward on your flip!" Dmitri screamed.

I flew as hard as I could for the seventy-mile checkpoint, landed—with a beautiful hip thrust, for what it was worth—and launched again.

Unger was waiting at the eighty-mile field.

"Essie's pulling even," he called calmly, in the midst of the insanity around him. "Pitcairn's belly bag is losing her too much time."

I was breathing as hard from that news as from the weight of my 140 pounds of cargo. I added an eighth bag to the load.

"Macadoo's back on course," Unger added. "Her number two's well behind, can't catch you. You've twenty seconds on Macadoo."

I didn't need Unger to do the arithmetic. Even if reeling her belly bag out and in slowed her, even if her navigation was shoddy, Macadoo had me.

I thundered down at the ninety-mile mark, striking hard enough to leave inch-deep footprints in the mud alongside the river. It smarted, but I staggered forward for my last bag.

"Low," Dean Murchison rumbled from the other side of the rope line. "Cut low."

"How far back is she?" I shouted. I didn't need a compass; I knew where the aerodrome was, ten miles downstream on the opposite bank.

I attached my bag. "How far back, damn you!"

"Radcliffe!" Murchison howled instead. "Up Radcliffe!"

I launched and screamed along the river at one hundred feet.

It was the longest minute of my life. Don't look. *Don't look.* If I turned my head, it would slow me. I couldn't afford even a second. Head tucked, elbow in, feet pointed, hand down. Hand *down.*

Macadoo whistled past me with four miles to go, ten feet above my shoulder, trying to upset me with her wake. I held my line.

Close. *So close.*

She had me by nearly three seconds per mile. Even my flare and settle wouldn't save me.

She cheated up a few feet, then a few more, trying to make sure she had a clear line of sight to the landing field. A tactical error—just the way you'd expect a short-courser to fly the long course—but it wouldn't make a difference. She was too damn fast.

Too fast! She wasn't going to be able to stop in time!

Macadoo must have recognized it, too. She whip-kicked and braked. By the time she'd stopped her forward momentum, she'd drifted two hundred feet past the landing zone. She added power to come back.

I was blistering in full bore, right at her.

Maybe she didn't see me. Maybe she thought I would pull off. Instead, I cut low: I flipped head-down into my flare, braking and putting on downward force to slide under her. My feet hit hers with me still upside down. Macadoo tumbled up and over. I fought my sigils to keep control, still diving toward the ground.

Then she was right above me. Macadoo loosed her belly bag.

It struck me on the feet. The suit warded off the blow, but it was enough to rotate me belly up. I couldn't see the ground.

Dead man. Fifty feet up, falling fast, back-first. No shock absorbers in the back.

Everything went slow. The air like water around me. Not enough thrust to stop in time. What would Dmitri say to—what would Gertrude say—what would Brock—Mother—?

But what would Robert Weekes say?

Ugly.

I directed all my power into a forward half somersault. No braking. I would hit at sixty miles an hour. More than enough to kill me.

I rotated. I'd barely gotten myself into a tuck when I struck feet-first. The impact sent me sprawling. I rolled tits over teakettle and slid to a stop on my belly. A hundred pounds of cargo on my back, eighty on my front. I couldn't breathe.

"Robert!" someone screamed over me. Tearing at the straps on my back, heaving away the sandbags.

"Robert!" Essie screamed again.

"In third place," the public address system boomed, "from Radcliffe College, in a time of nineteen minutes two seconds, Robert Arthur Weekes."

"Help," I wheezed.

"Roll him on his side," someone else said. "He can't stand up like that."

Pitcairn rolled me and helped Essie pull the tabs on my chest. The sandbags fell away.

"You alive?" Pitcairn asked me.

"Yeah." I winced.

"You just made my week," Pitcairn said.

Essie pulled me to my feet.

I stood there blinking. All of me, body and conscious mind, was trying to turn toward the next compass heading, assume launch posture, hand *down*.

Then came the irrational fear that I'd scrambled my brains and heard it wrong. Somebody else's name. Not possible that I'd—no, impossible.

"In fourth place," the PA announced, "from the Sacramento Institute of Philosophy, in a time of nineteen minutes eight seconds, Aileen Marie Macadoo."

I ripped my goggles off and flung them in the air. I pulled my hood free and let loose a yawp that had been building for nineteen years. Finally. *Finally.*

Essie was saying something to me, but I couldn't hear her over the mix of boos and cheers. I could see it in her face, too, the ferocious joy. She would have taken the whole company of fliers out to have a second run at them.

"Did you *win?*" I asked her.

She hugged me in reply and my ribs screamed.

"You made my week," Pitcairn said again.

"Obstruction!" I heard Macadoo screaming to a race official. "He cut me off at the knees! Could have killed me."

"Hey Aileen!" Pitcairn shouted. "Botched landing clears the approach for an incoming flier. It was clean. You got beat by a boy!"

And then Brock vaulted the rope, running to catch Essie and me in a sweaty embrace. "Magnificent!" She was bawling. "Both of you! Magnificent."

36

Canderelli Weekes, Robert A. (Radcliffe; 1918–21). Protégé of Janet Brock. First male to medal in any discipline. Only flier to have four medals revoked:

1918:   Long course, bronze* (stripped due to reckless flying)
1919:   Endurance flight, gold* (tie with Dmitri Ivanovich; stripped due to parasail use, collaboration, obstruction, taunting, reckless flying)
1920:   Endurance flight, gold* (tie with Michael Nakamura; stripped due to axial thrust coupler use, collaboration)
1921:   Endurance flight, gold* (stripped due to pressurized powder tank use, flying in a no-fly zone)

His career has also included numerous record-setting flights with Brock-Sudeste Aerospace and command of several former Cup fliers during his service with the Free North American Air Cavalry.

Who's Who in the General's Cup, 1939

THE CHIEF RACE OFFICIAL hung Essie's gold medal about her neck and kissed her on both cheeks. She did the same for Pitcairn and her silver. When she came to me, she handed me my bronze with a limp handshake.

She then escorted us into the aerodrome and confiscated our medals until all the complaints could be sorted out: obstruction, reckless flying, failure to yield, striking a flier. (Even Essie had cut off Pitcairn on their final landing. It would take six months for the race officials to decide that the only women not disqualified were Maria Trestor's pair—they received the gold and silver, with the bronze not awarded.)

I changed out of my skysuit in my curtained-off area. When I emerged, I found an elderly corpswoman in full dress uniform congratulating Essie.

"What a remarkable piece of flying!" she said, clasping Essie's hand. "Aggressive, neat, decisive. R&E desperately needs hoverers like you."

It was the Corps scout. And just like that, the old Essie was back, blushing and fumbling out a reply. "I . . . I have such respect for Rescue and Evacuation, but . . . I worry I would make a very bad soldier, is all."

"I think you'd make a very good one," the grizzled old lady said. "Women with calm, quiet temperaments go the furthest. Fort Putnam is testing on Tuesday morning. I would be very pleased to invite you on their behalf."

She reached into her purse and presented Essie with a card.

Then the woman turned to me. I saw the patch on the right shoulder of her jacket—an eagle clutching an olive branch in its talons—that marked her as an R&E flier. The silver oak leaves on her collar made her a lieutenant colonel. I understood almost before I saw the rest: the burn scar on her forehead with the left eyebrow gone, the scoliosis that caused her right arm to hang three inches lower than her left, the tremor in her hands when they weren't in motion.

I couldn't think of what to say.

Neither could she. But Missy Pitcairn seemed to be enjoying the scene.

"Lt. Col. Yvette Rodgers, of the United States Sigilry Corps," Pitcairn said, "may I present Robert Weekes, of Radcliffe College."

Lt. Col. Rodgers licked her lips. "I wouldn't have believed it unless I saw it," she said. "Rachael warned me. A man, self-taught, all natural ability and raw power."

"Ma'am," I said, not quite understanding. "My whole life I've wanted to fly R&E. I had all of your—"

"A rescue flier? Don't be ridiculous. A man's place is on the ground. In the army. A man in R&E would be an abomination. Not in my Corps."

I couldn't tell where my bruised ribs left off and my broken heart began. Addams had warned me from the very first. And Gertrude. And Dar. And yet, still.

"Ma'am," I said. I gave her a nod, intending to go home and find a private corner in which to curl up and die.

"Well, I'd take him for *my* Corps," Pitcairn said from behind me. "And since I'm flying in this war and you've sat out the last three, I think I get a say. Give me a card."

"Sigilwoman, you're being impertinent," Lt. Col. Rodgers replied.

"Impertinent nothing," Pitcairn said. "Somebody give me a pen! What are you carrying for paper there, Mr. Weekes?"

I tore the paperback cover off *Life and Death on San Juan Hill* and gave it to her.

"*I, Sigilwoman First Class Melissa Pitcairn,*" she pronounced as she scrawled the words on the cover's blank side, "*hereby recommend Robert Weekes as an outstanding flier and invite him to present himself for testing in the USSC at his first convenience.* Is that close enough?"

Mayweather and the Cocks had reserved us a table at Tippler's to be charged to their accounts. The sportsbooks were paying out on the time-honored principle of "as they landed," which had earned the small group of people stupid enough to bet on Weekes to finish third an enormous sum of money.

Even before we could sit, the waiters brought out snails in butter, frog legs, and three vintages of champagne. Mother and Gertrude, who'd both served in France and had fond memories of the cuisine, tried to top each other with their recollections of the little bistros in which they'd first tasted coq au vin and cassoulet and calf's liver with onions; they were delighted at Mayweather's suggestion that they order for the table. Essie devoured a leg of lamb. Dar tucked into duck à l'orange. Angela took the lead on the desserts—clafoutis and croquembouche and sweet wines.

I was ravenous but could eat nothing. I wanted to sit alone with my arms over my head and weep. *An invitation*. It had happened. Not how I would have wished, but it was real. Gertrude had assured me it carried the weight of law.

"Boo-bow?" Dar was asking Vivian.

"No, *Boo-ber*! Everybody in Billings still calls him that. They won't even recognize 'Robert' in the paper."

Brock and Essie were shaking with laughter, too, but for an entirely different reason.

"So, Sacramento hired her on the spot!" Brock roared. "Said she must be just like her auntie if she taught the two of you as well as that!"

"What will they do when they find out Rachael can barely fly?" Essie asked.

"God knows, but I'm not taking her back!"

I pulled myself to my feet, wincing. "I want to go."

"Oh, sit down and enjoy yourself!" Angela said. "That's how a celebration works."

"Don't give that appalling old woman another thought," Gertrude said. "She was a terrible commander in Cuba and everyone knew it."

"She inflated her totals," Mother said. "If Rodgers evacuated a dozen wounded in her entire career, I'll eat my hat."

"Claimed a thousand," Gertrude clucked.

"One thousand seventy-eight," I corrected, having read that part innumerable times.

"Were you there in '98?" Gertrude asked Mother.

"In '97," said Mother.

Gertrude clapped her hands. "Oh, I *do* remember you. You were the one who killed all those Spaniards outside Havana. Wasn't that you—'It's not a turkey shoot if the turkeys shoot back!' "

"Certainly one of my more memorable days in uniform," Mother demurred.

"I used you for twenty years as an example of the wrong thing to do.

Someone takes a shot while you're landing, go to full power and wave off. Or land hard. But never—"

"Return fire?" Ma finished.

"Well, you can hardly blame me, teaching a lot of green recruits. I only hope I would have had the guts to do what you did. I think your son takes after you."

"I'm sure of it," Ma said.

Mother and I spent a few minutes alone before she rode the transporter chain home Sunday morning. I admitted to her for the first time how many months I'd spent working toward R&E. I didn't know what to expect—ridicule, anger, pride.

Instead, Mother struggled to find her voice. "That Detroit girl thought she was doing you a kindness," she told me. "And I can see how much you want it. But it won't happen. They'll humiliate you, fail you, and send you home."

"Radcliffe has a connection, a brigadier general—"

"No, Robert. If she tries to take you, it'll be her last day as a corps-woman. A one-star general doesn't have the pull to do it. They'll cashier you both."

"But they're short fliers! I can do the work. I would be good at it. Tell me I would be good at it!"

Mother wiped her eyes. "You flew better yesterday than I ever have. But if you'd offered me a man of your caliber on my most shorthanded day in Manila, I would have said no. It would destroy morale. It would be impossible."

I sat there like a boxer who'd been knocked out and was too stupid to fall.

"If you love Danielle, take the job in Washington," Mother said. "Protect her and comfort her. When you're surrounded by that much danger and wickedness, sometimes the love of a good man is all that keeps you sane. Your father did as much for me. Danielle is a woman of quality—you can tell it from the first minute. She'll need you. And we're going to need her."

• • •

Sunday night, Dar held an ice pack against my bruised ribs while I lay face-down on her bed.

"I don't know how else to say it," she told me. "It's going to sound so selfish. But don't go, Rob."

"It's just to test," I mumbled into her pillow. It had her familiar smell of jasmine and lavender. "The worst they can say is no."

"No. The worst they can say is yes. Yesterday, I watched you come within a half second of dying for a bronze medal. You think you'll risk less when it's a wounded soldier?"

Dar pulled the ice pack off.

"It's R&E," I said. "It's about saving lives. Doing good."

"The Corps isn't what you want it to be," she said. "Not anymore. It's about the generals getting their names in the paper so they can move up the ranks. They take obscene risks with the girls for their own glory."

She dried my skin and rubbed liniment into the bruise. I gritted my teeth and hissed.

"Half the hoverers in France get smashed to pieces every year. *Half* of them, Robert. You want me to wait for you? Your best gal? Watching the message board every night, crying into my tea? Flip a coin—heads he comes home whole, tails in pieces. You would do that to me?"

She was yelling.

"It's not that simple," I said.

"It's exactly that simple! You came for my blessing. I'm saying no."

She sat me up and helped me into my shirt—it hurt too much to reach behind my back.

"Promise me, Robert."

37

K. F. Unger: It's never mattered that I can't do it. What the heart loves, the will chooses and the mind justifies.

D. Priscilla Conway, "Ten Male Philosophers Explain How They Settled on Sigilry," *Detroit Defender Sunday Magazine*, October 31, 1935

I DIDN'T LEAVE MY room all day Monday.

I sat with Pitcairn's introduction and my bruised chest and hopelessness. Unger brought me a sandwich for lunch. Another for dinner.

I poured the sand out of my message board. I didn't want to hear congratulations from one more person. I didn't want advice from one more well-meaning idiot. I'd dreamed of doing this my whole life! It wasn't fair of Dar to make me say I wouldn't.

Essie came by in the evening with a bag and harness—a McCoule rig with torso extender, a merely adequate substitute for the custom suit, which I'd returned to Steven Brock. She'd padded the rib straps with cotton gauze.

"Everyone says you might not go tomorrow," Essie said.

"I told Danielle I wouldn't," I said.

Even Essie, naïve as she was, understood what that meant.

"I'm leaving at six," she said. "You can meet me at the aerodrome."

Flip a coin. Heads you come back whole.

I took a quarter and flicked it to set it spinning on the common room table. I caught it between my fingers before it came to a stop. I spun it again and caught it. I spun it and caught it and couldn't sleep. I had to tell her.

I primed my message board to write Dar and then had an attack of cowardice.

I spun the quarter and caught it. Spun and caught.

Unger came out at five in the morning. He sat beside me and said nothing. Watched me spin my quarter.

"I can't do it," I said hollowly. I didn't look up from my hands. "She'll never forgive me."

"As hard as you've worked, *I'll* never forgive you if you don't."

I met his eyes.

"I love her, Fred. And it would be perfect—a little apartment in Washington and protest and pass laws. We would do good in the world. We'd be happy."

"Yet you want to travel three thousand miles to fight in someone else's war and probably get killed."

I raised my hands in supplication. "What's wrong with me?"

Freddy gave me a sad smile. "The same thing that's wrong with me. I should have been an engineer or a mathematician or a chemist. Me, with one sigil in my entire life. But I'm in thrall to it and so are you. You're called. If you don't answer, you'll lose the better part of yourself."

I spun the quarter.

Unger slapped his hand down and took the coin away.

"Do you need help dressing?" he asked.

Unger helped me shave, did up the buttons on my skysuit, buckled the straps on my harness. I could manage the pain, as long as I didn't thrust my chest out or reach backward.

He clipped my bag into place. "You have to tell her. You should do it right now."

"Not by message," I said.

"Then I'll go talk to her."

"It should be me," I said. "In person. As soon as I get back."

Unger walked me down to the street. "Do me proud. And try less hard, my friend."

I met Essie at the aerodrome. No one saw us off. We flew west to the arsenal at Fort Putnam, where the Corps held its tests.

A couple dozen sigilrists presented themselves alongside us, most of them quite young. The Corps allowed women to join at sixteen (or seventeen for overseas service). Looking at the borrowed tack and ill-fitting skysuits, I imagined most of them were desperate for a job or to flee a bad situation. No different from my mother in '71, but not the experts one hoped to see applying to the US Sigilry Corps' most elite unit. They'd all watched the Cup or heard about it. They looked at Essie with awe—she'd beat the two fastest fliers in the world—and at me with disbelief.

The flight officers took a couple hours to put us through the same maneuvers that would have earned a Two at the aerodrome. A few of the young women were borderline competent, but the rest were raggedy neighborhood fliers. The officers dismissed two-thirds of the company. Those of us remaining proceeded through the world's easiest slalom—no one allowed to fly faster than fifty miles an hour—map-reading exercises, knot tying, and an angle and tuck landing carrying a hundred-pound dummy.

The flight portion of the test ended with a one-mile speed trial. The Corps had no minimum cutoff, we were told, but we should fly as fast as we were able. Essie, though not rigged for racing, made 380 miles per hour on her pass to applause and murmurs from the handful of remaining girls.

"Weekes!" the flight officer called.

I launched, came around to pick up speed, and dropped into the course.

I was tired. My ribs were throbbing. I had the sun in my eyes. I didn't have my racing suit. It hardly mattered.

Hand *down*.

I made 348. No one clapped.

The corpswomen timing me were arguing with one another. I approached for a landing but they waved me off.

"Problem with the watch," one of them called.

I went around a second time and hit the course hard. Not quite as good as the first, but strong. Again the timekeeper waved me around.

But even my third pass didn't satisfy them.

"Left-handed, please!"

I offered up a prayer of thanks to the Great Mother Flier in the Sky— Gertrude had predicted it exactly.

I extended my right hand in a fist so that there could be no doubt and reached across my body with my left to hold the regulator. My ribs screamed.

Even after five months, I didn't have fine sigil control as a lefty. My sigil came slower, less neatly. At one point, my lines slipped and I had to redraw to avoid losing altitude. Not terrific, but still faster than everyone but Essie with her good hand. I was breathing heavily by the time I set down.

"What did they do to you?" Essie whispered as we regrouped.

"Problem with the watch," I gasped.

"No there wasn't."

I shrugged. Of course there wasn't. But what was I supposed to do?

Essie helped me out of my harness and we waited for the interviews that would conclude our day. Each woman was led into an outbuilding where she answered questions from a couple of corpswomen. Most of them lasted a quarter hour. Essie's lasted two minutes and I could see her trying not to grin as she exited.

That left just me. The flight officers huddled and then disappeared into the building. I stood in the late-morning sun for another half hour. Finally they reemerged.

"We are *not* to proceed without Gen. Blandings to grade the interview," one said, more to the others than to me.

"I thought she was in France!" said another.

"She was supposed to be at the Boston arena on the eight o'clock ser- vice. I sent a detachment. They can't find her."

They turned to me. "You can either wait or go home."

I waited another hour on my feet. Half-asleep and sweat-soaked. Dar would have figured out what I'd done. I should have sent Unger.

My eyes blinked open at a sudden motion from the east. A hoverer streaking in, making three hundred with an overseas duffel on her back, a flare and settle so crisp it made my best effort look like a wrinkled mess. She shouldered her bag and double-timed it to the outbuilding. The flight officers ran out to meet her.

"Ma'am!" one of them cried. "I had four women at the—"

"Well, they failed to find me, dear," Gen. Blandings said. She wore a workaday combat skysuit that looked as if she'd lived in it for the past week. She was short, plump, and frowny, like someone's less favorite grandmother.

"Our transporter in Greenland balked her glyph," Blandings said, explaining her tardiness. "It took them hours to clean up."

She looked at me and stopped short. "Oh, Mother Mary, *that's* him? Absolutely not. Waste of a trip."

The officers glanced at one another, before the most junior one asked, "So, shall we forgo the interview and you'll sign—"

"Oh, as a formality, then, if you prepared questions."

They led me to the outbuilding, where there was a small table and chairs. The general took out her knitting.

"Well, commence!" Blandings ordered.

Her compatriots began innocently enough by asking about the origins of my interest in the Corps. I spoke about my mother, my work at the aerodrome, my hopes of doing good in France.

"Are you a homosexual?" they asked next.

That threw me. Possibly they asked it of everyone, Sapphism allegedly being more common in the Corps than among philosophers at large. Or, they might have held to the old belief that swishy men could move more quanta (which had never been borne out scientifically, according to Unger).

"No," I said.

"Then how do you expect to control yourself in close quarters with thousands of women for months at a time?"

If it had been Mayweather being grilled instead of me, it might have been an appropriate question.

"With all due respect," I answered, "I've lived in close quarters with a thousand women for the last year without incident."

The questions continued in like fashion: What would I do if I had a field commander who wouldn't allow me to bunk with the rest of the unit? What would I say to a squadmate reluctant to fly with me because of perceived or actual deficiencies in my abilities? How would I rank myself against female fliers in general? Against the fliers that morning? If I were a wounded soldier being evacuated, would I choose a male or female corpswoman?

The general didn't ask anything. She nodded off several times. Even when she was awake she didn't seem to care what I answered. Her attention was on her knitting. And, I realized, on my hands.

Finally, she waved for a stop. "More than sufficient, thank you. For form's sake, I ought to ask one, too. Can you show me his—"

She popped on a pair of pince-nez glasses and peered at a form with my statistics from that morning's tests.

"Mr. Weekes," she said in a high burbling voice, "since you reached only a hundred sixty miles per hour in your time trial, how do you expect to compensate while flying into a hot landing field?"

Oh, how I burned at that! Left-handed, injured, on my fourth try. I wanted to damn them for a lot of hypocrites and throw the table over. Let me have a fresh run with a fair timekeeper. Then I noticed how intently the general was watching me. I recognized that the question was a wrong one— Gertrude had given me the answer the day I met her.

"Ma'am," I growled, "every hoverer is going zero miles an hour when she hits the ground. The only time the Huns can take a good shot is during the landing and that has nothing to do with raw aerial speed. I favor a flare and settle. If you like, I'll have Aileen Macadoo and one hundred thousand witnesses testify I have a pretty sharp one."

Blandings sniffed. She pointed to the door.

• • •

I struggled back into my harness and flew home.

That was it, then. In the next day or two, they would send a message beginning "Although we appreciate your interest . . ." I couldn't do anything to change it.

I tried to put the rest of my day in order. Find Dar. Confess. Beg her forgiveness, preferably with a copy of the *Washington Post* in hand and several apartments circled in the classifieds section. And flowers. Mayweather could advise on what sort you gave when apologizing for being an absolute cad.

Unger was sitting at the table with my quarter and a glazed look, as if he'd just knocked back a stiff drink.

"Robert—" he began. But I wanted none of his careful, wise sympathy.

"They didn't even give me a chance!" I raged. "Ran me through the sprint left-handed, insulted me in the interview. Then I lost my temper, gave a smart answer—"

"Robert," Freddy broke in. "I didn't mean to. You left your board set. I saw it come across. You know I would never deliberately—"

"What are you talking about?"

He turned my message board so I could read it.

Mr. Weekes,

It is with pleasure that the US Sigilry Corps offers you a commission as Sigilwoman Third Class with the Fifth Division of Rescue and Evacuation. You are to report no later than June 14 for advanced flight training at Fort McConnell, South Padre Island, Texas. Details by postal mail will follow your acceptance. Your decision is requested by message to the glyph below within 72 hours.

Sincerely,

Brig. Gen. Tomasina Blandings, USSC

38

Cadwallader delegated the matter of what equipment each corpswoman was to furnish to one of her colleagues at the University of Detroit, a certain Mrs. Peabody, who had lived her entire life within the confines of the city and had many unusual ideas as to what conditions in the field might be like. Her comprehensive list, right down to how many pairs of stockings, bloomers, and sun bonnets each woman should carry, also included a "black parasol of good-quality silk (1)" as well as a "cavalry saber, single-edged with scabbard (1; to be issued upon muster)." While it is difficult to say which item proved less useful, the Corps has since incorporated both into its standard dress uniform.

Victoria Ferris-Smythe, *Empirical Philosophy:*
An American History, 1938

UNGER WAS SAYING SOMETHING, helping me to sit.

I couldn't remember how I was supposed to feel. What I was supposed to do next.

Unger whooped and danced about the room and thumped me on the back.

They said yes, I messaged to Essie. And Angela. Vivian. Mother. Brock. Gertrude. Addams. Jake. And then, as requested, my acceptance to the glyph below. Then, I called up the message from Gen. Blandings again and stared at it for an hour.

"Robert?" Freddy said. "You have to tell her."

He went out to fetch me lunch. I continued staring.

Sometime later, I heard thick-soled boots coming up the stairs. I tried to prepare myself.

The door flew open. Danielle looked ashen, unsteady on her feet.

"So say it!" she shouted.

"I went," I said. "And they took me."

She was crying openly, which made her furious.

"You promised! You swore to me!"

"Yeah."

"Write them back. Tell them you didn't mean to accept. That it was a mistake."

I shook my head.

"Robert, if you go, I'm never speaking to you again. I'm never saying your name, I'm never thinking of you. Otherwise, every day you're over there, I'll cry my guts out. Say you're not going. *Say it!*"

I closed my eyes. "I'm going."

There followed a string of messages, the comments on my commission indistinguishable from the ones about Dar.

Have you lost your mind?

Why? Why are you doing this?

Congratulations, old boy! I knew you had it in you!

You are making a terrible mistake.

Overwhelming, terrifying silence from Mother.

Not sure if shs maddr at y or the Corps, Angela wrote. *She says Cuba & Philipns & Hawaii ruined her. Says same wll happen to y.*

Mother, who had called it impossible. Who would have turned down her own son in the field. She could go to hell.

If I set Ma aside, I fell right back into wallowing over Dar: . . . *the two of us in Washington, just write the Corps and tell them— but no, she'd been the one to manipulate me, to force me into a decision she knew was unfair, and then accuse me of— no, a clean break was simpler, don't try to apologize or say goodbye or promise to— no, come back with a whole suitcase full of medals and march into her office and then see who's too good to— no, I would die over there in some muddy ditch and they'd bury me in an unmarked grave.*

Unger found me slumped against the wall, head in hand. Maybe it was the next morning.

"Nope," Unger said. "No. You don't get to do this. Get up."

"Freddy—"

"You won. You're not allowed to quit. We'll do an hour of German. Dmitri will do an hour with you in the gym—stretching and deep breathing exercises for your ribs."

Any distraction. An hour of practice for my stasis practicum. An hour for my smokecarving class. Then I slept and divided the next day into hours too, so that I had something clear and useful to do in each and didn't think of Dar or the Corps or Washington or anything else.

I went through the next week in a stupor.

A bevy of messages came in from the Corps, plus letters, contracts, official orders. The whole thing fascinated Unger, though he was as bad as anyone for asking the "typical" questions:

Would I wear the Corps' famous full pleated skirts as my uniform? No hoverer in the field wore skirts, I explained, it was skysuits all around. For formal occasions, I would wear an army officer's uniform with Philosophical Corps insignia.

Would I be addressed as Sigilman Third Class or Sigilwoman Third Class? The latter, as a needlessly supercilious lieutenant reminded me by message board, when I used the wrong term. That was the rank, after all. No sense in proving your relative equality only to demand special treatment.

Where would I sleep? Not right alongside the ladies. While I was in training there would be a tent outside the main barracks for my use; at the front, the situation varied by locale, much to the inconvenience of my commanding officer.

When would I be going?

"I'll go down the day after exams finish," I told him. "Take the transporter chain to San Antonio, then a local jump to Corpus Christi, or if there isn't one for a couple days, fly myself the last couple hundred miles."

Unger looked forty times more excited about it than I felt.

"I'm not supposed to tell you this," he confessed, "but I'll be doing war work, too. Professor Yu found me a position with a most intriguing project—mathematical philosophical research. Highly classified. Draft waiver and everything."

"That's wonderful," I said. You couldn't wish that sort of good luck on a more deserving fellow.

"We're trying to answer a fascinating question," Freddy mused. "Given a high-energy non-vectored sigil, how would one best increase—"

"Fred, you're not supposed to talk about it, right?"

"Terribly sorry. It means we're trying to help bring you home sooner."

Even Ms. Addams dragged me into her office for one last sentimental go-around. She was wearing her dress uniform—skirts and saber and parasol and all—as was Gertrude. Murchison wore the old-fashioned cavalry blouse, tall shako hat, and jodhpurs that the Corps had issued its cartogramancers in the '70s.

They rose and saluted.

"Oh, no," I murmured. I'd walked into my frocking ceremony unshaven and wearing my gym clothes. But they wouldn't be stopped.

"It is traditional," Addams intoned, "before reporting for service, that a newly commissioned corpswoman receive the adjuncts to her uniform from a veteran not related to her by blood."

Addams put a crown woven from daisies on my head. "Daughter, we who came before call you to defend your fellow women and your country. The philosopher's war has no beginning or end."

Gertrude placed a peppermint on my tongue. "Fortune's blows are bitter but the amity of the service is sweet."

Murchison stepped forward and slapped me with his gloved left hand hard enough to leave my cheek stinging.

"Wake, daughter," he spoke. "And strike under cover of darkness."

He handed me his dress parasol. The mahogany handle was cracked, the silk panels battered, the lace trim moth-eaten.

He slapped me on the other cheek, took the saber and scabbard from his belt, and presented them to me, too.

"Wake, daughter, and stay your hand."

They saluted again.

I was trying as hard as I could not to burst into tears.

"Good grief, Lennox!" Addams said. "You're supposed to tap him, not hit him. Get that boy a chair before he collapses."

Addams was the ranking officer present, a fact not lost on Sigilwoman Third Class Murchison, who assisted me into a seat.

Brock opened the door from inside the dean's inner office to sit with us—not a servicewoman to be included in the ceremony itself, but an intimate nevertheless. She had worn her academic robes for the occasion, her velvet tam and piping in the deep purple of the University of Detroit, where she'd done her D.Em.Phil.

Brock bowed. "Congratulations, Sigilwoman. On behalf of Radcliffe College and your many admirers at Northwest Aero, may I also offer a small token? Something more practical than the baubles the Corps carries for formal occasions."

She gave me a cardboard shirt box that weighed about four pounds. I knew even before I opened it. A near twin to the first harness Northwest had made me. In beautiful thick brown leather. An unsigned note, too—*I hovered thirty feet under my own power yesterday. I can't ever thank you enough.*

"Oh my God," I whispered.

"If you think Steven's improbable, we've had a dozen men write the college to inquire about enrolling," Brock said. "One was turned down by Sacramento and Detroit. He'd never considered Radcliffe before he read about you—he's the best male flier in Japan, from what I understand. He's going to crush you in the long course when you get back."

I grinned at the thought.

"You impressed Gen. Blandings, too," Addams said. "You kept your composure through the whole morning and showed just the right amount of fight. 'Aileen Macadoo and a hundred thousand witnesses,' was that the line?"

"She did a good job of hiding it," I said.

"She hides a great deal," Addams said, turning more serious. "Blandings is an ally of this office. She shares our concerns."

"We worry about how the war will end," Brock said. "That the Germans will become desperate and attack with their Korps des Philosophs. And that we'll strike back, using our own smokecarvers."

"It'll make Manila look like a church picnic," Gertrude said.

"It will make the war after this one the last that humanity fights," Murchison added.

"So, a few of us have taken it upon ourselves to come up with more innovative solutions," said Brock.

"Blandings is one of the few in the Corps we trust," said Addams. "One of the few who cares about something larger than her career. You're one of those, too."

"We would never ask you to act against your conscience," Brock said. "But if Blandings needs your help—counting supply wagons, moving unusual persons, observing positions—we would take it as a favor."

"Like spying on the Huns?" I asked.

Addams smirked. "Your German's not good enough for that."

"On our own people?"

The four of them shared a look.

"Robert, the Corps killed half a million in the Philippines with the barest provocation," Addams said. "I did a lot of it myself, to my everlasting regret. But if we kill ten million in Europe—if we depopulate Berlin or wipe out Vienna—what future will philosophy have? It would be the best gift we could give Maxwell Gannet."

"Pray that peace breaks out," Brock said. "But if it doesn't, we'll see you in France."

"Belgium," Murchison muttered.

We all looked at him for some further explanation, but the dean only took off one of his gloves and began turning the fingers inside out.

Final exams brought me only partway back to earth. Even with the distraction of my impending departure, I could still reel off basic stases and rudimentary smokecarving techniques.

I went back to my room in the early evening after my last exam and began packing. The first southbound transporter service the following morning would leave at six. I intended to take it, much to Unger's dismay.

"You're not required to report for another week," Unger cajoled. "We never even went out to celebrate. Stay a few days."

"I want to get there ahead of time," I said. "Get the lay of the land."

"That's stupid talk," said Jake, whom Unger had invited over to help change my mind. "You're going to sit in Texas for a week with your thumb in your ear? That does nothing but mark you out as an oddity." Then, realizing the inevitability of that, "—as an *even bigger* oddity. If you're not going out, you could at least make yourself useful. Tonight's the final night-landing clinic at the aerodrome. The veterans are letting the Threes run it for once. They could use another set of hands."

"I almost got expelled the last time I helped with that."

Jake looked sideways and cleared her throat. "All right, then. Danielle messaged me this afternoon. She asked me to drop by and if I could, I should bring you."

"No."

"She asked to see you."

"I don't care," I said. "I'm going to bed."

"No," said Jake. "You're coming with me. If she's mean to you, I'll hit her. And I swear to God, if you start crying in front of her, I'm going to hit *you*. Besides, she has your necklace."

I'd taken it off while she was tending to my bruised ribs after the Cup. I'd been dreading messaging her to ask for it back.

"So, get it for me," I said.

"I'm not going unless you come."

I plunged my hands into my pockets. "Just for the necklace."

Jake knew enough not to try to make me talk as we trudged over to Dar's. My favorite of Belle Addams's men was standing guard outside the building. He put two fingers to the brim of his hat in salute. "You're a brave man to go up there, Mr. Weekes."

I fought back a wave of nausea as I climbed the half flight of stairs to the first-floor landing and the second flight up to her room. Jake put a hand on my shoulder to steady me. She knocked and the door swung open.

Danielle was less beautiful than I remembered. Her face was blunter, her lips dry and cracked, her eyes the wrong color brown. She fumbled with her hands like she wanted to fold them and had forgotten how.

She found her voice before I did.

"Would you— won't you both come and sit for a minute?" Danielle asked.

Her room was bare, with only her table, chairs, and bed remaining. We sat.

"You're already packed?" Jake asked.

"Yes," Danielle said, looking relieved to hear such a banal observation. "I sent my things on to Washington. Dad's coming out tomorrow to ride the transporter chain with me. He'll help me get settled, trap the rats out of my new apartment, all that."

Danielle shifted her attention to me and the strength ran right out of my legs. I would have fallen if I weren't sitting.

"Robert . . ." she said. "Robert, I can't leave things between us like this."

"I don't know what to say," I managed.

"Tell me you'll message every once in a while so I know you're alive."

"Okay." I wanted to offer something beyond that, to give her some better parting words, but I couldn't.

She handed me the necklace strung with the crystal vial. "I thought you'd want this back."

I nodded and slipped it over my head.

Danielle coughed, as if to cover a noise she didn't want me to hear, and turned back to Jake. They talked about some inanity—a fancy box of chocolates that a supporter had sent and could Jake take it to the aerodrome because it was unethical for Danielle to accept gifts.

"Of course," said Jake. "It'll last about ten minutes down there."

I closed my eyes. I wanted to be gone. Go to Texas and not have to nurse a broken heart or say good-bye to Unger or summon up the courage to message Mother again. Be alone.

We heard a knock—another well-wisher, probably. Jake and I rose to go while Danielle opened the door.

It was a youthful, clean-shaven man in a Harnemon's uniform. He had a box wrapped in glossy gray and silver paper, about a foot long.

Jake put a hand on my thigh and pushed me back into my chair.

"Good evening," the man said. "I'm so terribly sorry to disturb you, but I have a special delivery. You are Danielle Hardin, are you not?"

"Yes," said Dar.

"The editors at the *Globe* send their compliments. They wanted to make sure you received this before your departure. A gift in thanks for the time you've given them and in hopes for your success in Washington."

He proffered the package to Dar.

"Oh, not another one," she sighed.

Jake cut her eyes at me then smiled at the deliveryman. "Could you tell us what it is?" she asked.

The man looked to Dar, who nodded and then turned her back so she could retrieve her purse and tip him.

"It's an eau de cologne of vaporized rose petals."

"Oh, *yucky*!" Jake said. "Those always go rancid on the first warm day. But, we ought to send a note commending you on your service. A delivery at this hour. Are you out of the Cambridge depot?"

The man was watching Danielle instead of us.

"Yes," he said, "the Cambridge depot."

Jake reached across under the table and squeezed my hand. She put her left hand on top of her head as if to adjust her hair but left it there—the universal hover signal for distress.

I couldn't say how, but I knew she was right.

"If you'd be so kind as to sign the receipt," the man said, reaching under his jacket.

I stood, took two steps toward him, and drove my right foot into the side of his knee.

39

On November 21, 1897, when elements of the Spanish Army cut off two platoons of sigilwomen from the USSC encampment near Havana, Maj. Emmaline Weekes led a furious air assault to rescue them. Despite being severely outnumbered, Maj. Weekes's hoverers drove off the attacking Spaniards with small arms fire and improvised bombs, saving more than two dozen of their comrades. In recognition of her valor in actual combat against the enemy, the women of the United States Sigilry Corps, as decided by plebiscite, hereby award to Maj. Weekes the White Ribbon with Crossed Sabers.

USSC Medal Citation, June 8, 1898

THE MAN'S LEG BUCKLED. He tried to get up, but I hammered my fist into the back of his neck and he fell to the floor. I threw myself on top of him, yanked my revolver from my pocket, and stuck it into his side. Jake slammed the door and threw the deadbolt.

"What are you doing!" screamed Dar.

"He's not Harnemon's!" Jake shouted. "They haven't worn that style of hat in ten years, they don't have a Cambridge office, and it's the wrong-sized box for perfume."

Dar stared at her, incredulous.

"He doesn't have a moustache!" I added.

The man began to struggle beneath me. Jake kicked him in the groin with her pointy-toed boot. He yelped and ceased resisting.

"Stay down," I said. "I've seen her kick a lot harder than that."

"Not as hard as we'll hit the three of you," the man wheezed.

More of them?

"Dar, do you have any rope?" I asked. "Or a bedsheet to tear into strips? Something to tie him up?"

Danielle looked appalled. "I have a ball of packing twine."

"Get it," I said. "Jake, hog-tie him."

"Do what?" Jake asked.

I tried to translate that into flier-speak. "Tie him wrists to ankles behind his back with, say, a running four-corner cross cinch or—"

"Got it," said Jake.

I kept the gun pressed against his side while Jake tied him up. I found a .45 automatic in his waistband.

"Cute," I said. "What else do you have?"

A short, double-barreled shotgun tucked into a loop under his coat and a knife in his boot, as it turned out.

As soon as she saw the weapons, Dar's demeanor changed. "Who sent you?" she demanded.

The man didn't answer.

"The Gray Hats? The Hand of the Righteous?"

A thump from the window cut her short. Like a bird hitting it or a rock. The pane was cracked in a strange spiderweb pattern—not ordinary glass, but rather layers of crystal with anti-kinetic smoke webbing between. Supposedly bulletproof. We heard a second thump. The window bulged inward.

"Is somebody shooting at us?" Dar cried.

"Turn the lights off!" I shouted.

Dar ran to shut off one of the gaslights and Jake dove for the other, plunging the room into darkness. Two more bullets thudded into the windowpane, knocking it out of the frame. It fell to the floor with a tinkle.

"Everybody stay down," I hissed. Dar was pressed up against the wall a few feet from the window with Jake in the opposite corner. Both were well out of the line of fire. I kept myself flat against the floor beside the door.

"Dar, can you get us out of here?" I whispered.

"I packed my kit," she answered, "but I still have one tube in—" She scrambled for her purse, which she'd left hanging on the back of the door, and groped through the pockets. She pulled a double-sealed vial out and removed the outer tube. She had just snapped open the inner ampoule when another shot rang out. Dar dove to the floor.

"Are you okay?" I called.

"Damn it!" she hissed. "It broke."

"Message board," Jake suggested. "To Addams and copy to Brian."

Danielle sent the message and bolted back to her corner.

I could hear footsteps creeping up the stairs.

"I think there are more of them," I whispered.

I slid along the wall and handed Jake the .45. I gave Danielle the scattergun.

"They may try to rush us," I said. "If we have to shoot . . . Dar, pull both hammers back. Brace the butt against your shoulder. If they get in, fire once. If they're still standing, give them the second barrel."

I turned toward Jake, who could probably just barely fit her fingers around that enormous .45.

"Weekes, I've never—"

"It's okay. By the right side of the—of the handle. There's a lever?"

"Okay."

"That's the safety. Press it down with your thumb." I heard a click from her corner. "Grip with your right. One finger on the trigger. Left hand to steady. Elbows loose but tight."

Jake breathed the barest whisper of a laugh at the last, which was an old flier's adage.

"Get ready," I said. "I'm going to slow them down."

I pulled back the deadbolt on the door. It creaked loud enough to wake the sleeping dead. My heart's pounding shook my hands with its violence. I opened the door and slipped just far enough into the hall to get a look at the stairs.

The creak of footsteps resumed. I blew out my breath to steady my aim. As the first man rounded the corner, I pulled the trigger twice.

In the enclosed space of the hall, my underpowered little revolver thundered like an avalanche. The man fell to the ground and crawled back toward the stairs. His partner reached around the corner and fired wildly with what I suspected was a twin to the .45 I'd given Jake.

I retreated to Danielle's room, slammed the door, and threw the bolt. With a little luck, we could make their next advance even clumsier.

"Anything to burn for a smokescreen?" I asked.

"The packing twine," suggested Jake.

Dar lit the bundle of string off her stove's pilot light.

"What do you want?" she asked me.

"Anything," I said. "A semi-persistent concretion in front of the door. It'll disorient their first couple steps."

The twine put off a thin stream of smoke that Dar collected and congealed with a sigil.

"Dar," I said, "how much longer to—"

Splinters of wood exploded out from the middle of the door, leaving a gaping hole.

Dar dropped the unfinished cloud of smoke and picked up the shotgun. Jake crouched as low as she could in her corner. Another shot from the hall pierced the door, followed by the thud of a man throwing himself against the door and failing to knock it down. The man threw himself against the door a second time.

"Dar!" I called.

I waited until I thought the man was ready for his next charge then jerked the door open. The man stumbled into the room with his shoulder lowered. I ducked out of the way and Dar fired.

The man staggered but didn't go down. My ears were ringing too badly to hear the second shot, but I felt a stinging across the side of my face and neck— the shotgun must have been loaded with fine birdshot. Still, it was enough to make the man crumple to the ground and for me to drop my revolver in surprise.

A second man rushed into the room and stumbled over his fallen compatriot. Jake shot at him once and missed wide. She shot a second time and nearly put the bullet through my eye.

"Stop!" I screamed.

Jake was probably half-deaf, but realized she had as good a chance of hitting me as him. Instead, she threw herself at the man, who shoved her off. That gave Dar just enough time to scoop up the mass of semisolid smoke and apply a hasty sigil. The cloud leaped at the man, swirling about his head and sticking to his neck and chest.

It was a parlor trick, harmless, yet the man screamed and beat at the smoke with his hands. He fell to his knees in a panic, choking and blowing.

I recovered my revolver, knelt beside him, and pointed the gun at his head.

"Don't move," I said. With my left hand, I drew a glyph to disperse the smoke.

The man gasped, spittle dripping from his lips.

"Dar, the twine. Whatever's left," I said.

With the remnants, Jake tied the man up. I rolled over the one who'd taken the shotgun blasts. He moaned. His shirt was shredded. Hundreds of tiny wounds pockmarked his face and chest. Blood seeped from the holes, but he seemed in no danger of exsanguinating. He was in no danger of trying to renew his attack, either.

I put a hand to the side of my face. It was full of the same wounds, ten or twenty of them.

"Jesus," I said. My legs went out from under me.

"Robert!" cried Danielle.

"I'm okay." I tried to catch my breath. I put my head between my knees and the world spun.

"Where's he hit?" Jake demanded.

"I'm not," I managed.

"We've got to get him out of here," said Dar. "We've got to get all of us out of here."

They pulled me to my feet. Dar's eyes were furious and terrified as they searched me for some fatal injury. Jake's chin jutted haughtily forward, but her bottom lip was quivering. She kept a tight grip on the sleeve of my shirt.

"Danielle?" a woman's voice shouted from right outside the window.

"Hello?" Dar called.

"Are you okay, sister?" It was Francine—Mayweather had messaged the Threes, who'd been in the midst of their night-landing clinic and had flown over straightaway. "Put a light on and we'll get you out."

"No!" Jake cried. "There's a sniper shooting at that window."

"Astrid spotted him," Francine replied. "Dropped a spare powder bag on his head. He never even heard it coming. She's orbiting to keep watch."

Dar turned the lights on and Francine perched on the windowsill. She slid her legs through and dropped into the room.

"There were about four more people running toward the building," Francine said.

"Belle Addams's men?" I asked.

"I doubt it," Francine answered.

I relocked the damaged door and pushed the table in front. It wasn't sturdy enough to brace the door, but it might slow them down.

"We need to go," Francine said. She pointed at Jake. "Honey, let go of him and let's move."

Jake ran to Francine and flung her arms around Francine's waist. They leaned backward through the window and launched.

Tillie swung in through the window next. "Danielle!" she shouted.

Dar looked at Tillie and the window.

"I don't want to do this," said Dar. "I'll just hang over the edge and drop down to the street."

"It's seventeen feet," said Tillie. "You'll break something. Hold me around the waist. I've done this thousands of times."

Dar relented and wrapped her arms around Tillie. They were away in seconds.

Essie took their place at the window and tentatively put a foot on the sill. A gust of wind caught her and she backed off to reapproach.

"Hardin!" shouted a voice from the hall. "Give yourself up."

There was no telling how many of them there were.

"Put her out here in ten seconds or we'll shoot our way in!"

I climbed onto the windowsill and swung my legs over. Easier for me to grab Essie than for her to duck in and out.

A shotgun blast holed the door in a dozen places—definitely not bird-shot in that one. I was far enough back not to be hit.

"Hardin's gone!" I screamed.

The men outside answered with a second blast, followed by a well-placed kick to the lock, which caused the door to spring open. Three men pushed into the room, shoving the table aside. They were older than the first group and looked much more comfortable with their weapons.

Behind them hobbled a gaunt, ghostly pale figure with ecstatic eyes—Gannet. He was wearing a bronze breastplate over his shirt to protect against sigils. His hands were clasped in front of him, like he was praying.

"Disaster will come upon you . . ." he intoned in his thin, high voice.

He glanced around the room, as if puzzled to find it empty, except for a man sitting with his legs dangling out the window.

". . . and you will not know . . ."

Four men, two bullets.

". . . how to conjure it away."

I fired twice. The rounds took Gannet in the chest.

He staggered and sat down. He put a hand to his breast and pulled it away, confused. His breath came in wheezing gasps; spittle hung from his lips. He tried to say something, but couldn't get any words out. With a trembling hand, he drew his revolver.

"Robert!" Essie screamed. She was right above me.

I threw my arms around one of her legs and she clamped the other tight against me. We cleared the sill but my weight was too much for her sigil. We made a slow, graceless crash descent. I hit the ground back-first and it felt like colliding with a brick wall at a dead run. Essie landed on top of me.

Above us came the repeated crack of pistol shots through the open window.

Essie put a hand to my injured face. "Oh my God," she whispered.

"We have to run," I croaked, my lips pressing against her palm.

She clambered to her feet and pulled me up. My joints felt as if they'd all slid out of place. My ribs burned. We stumbled down the street.

A large, open-topped motorcar squealed around the corner one block from us. I raised an arm against the glare of its electric lanterns. These would be their reinforcements. We were finished.

The car ground to a halt.

"Robert!" the driver cried.

Belle Addams was at the wheel. In the back sat two of Radcliffe's senior smokecarving instructors, placid, dressed all in gray, their eyes chillingly intense. Each held a seething black cloud in her lap.

"Get in!" Addams shouted. Essie and I tumbled into the front seat beside her. She threw the car into gear and we raced toward Dar's apartment.

"Did ours make it out?" Addams asked. "Are they alive?"

"All out," I said. "We scattered."

"And the ones who did this? Where are *they*?"

"Still inside. Eight of them, I think. We took down four. I shot—I—oh God . . ."

We pulled up to the building. I could hear the whine of a police siren in the distance, minutes away.

Addams leaped out of the car with the smokecarvers on her heels.

"Lily—double breach," Addams barked to the first of her women. "Rosemary, hit the room with Billroth's mixture. I'll infiltrate around you."

The old ladies nodded. The first added a few chemicals to her roiling cloud and drew sigils to make it coil into a fist-sized sphere, which she attached to the building's door. The second poured a bottle of clear solution into her cloud and held it at the ready.

"Go!" Addams shouted.

The door exploded inward and the dense cloud charged up the stairs, unwinding itself, emitting a howling, rattling wail as it moved. The second smokecarver followed.

"The two of you, don't move," Addams said to Essie and me.

Addams took her own cloud from her handbag and sprinted up the stairs.

40

Mrs. Tyndale, advance with the left flank and end this! Give them hell and come safe home.

> Mrs. Lucretia Cadwallader, Orders at the Battle
> of Halloween, October 31, 1862

THE LATE-MORNING SUN BEAT down on the Charles River as Mother and I wound our way along the footpath. The last of the serious rowers were returning their shells to the boathouse and the first of the pleasure boaters were appearing to take advantage of an exceedingly mild June day.

"You're third on his list?" Mother asked me.

It had been a week since she'd rushed to Boston. A week I'd spent under guard—first in Moss Hall, then my apartment, and now during the daily excursions that Mother had taken to planning. I'd seen more of the city with her than during the previous year put together.

Gannet was dead, by my hand.

No, I chided myself, *call it by its right name.*

I'd killed him, though not cleanly.

Addams had incapacitated the Trenchers with smoke; the police had arrived moments later. They'd hauled Gannet to Massachusetts General, where the doctors had found he had a fractured sternum, collapsed lung, and internal bleeding from a nicked artery—probably survivable if he would have consented to surgery with a smokecarver to see to anesthesia and a stasis to help fix the blood vessel. Gannet had refused.

He'd lasted three hours, using his last breaths to draw up his final list of the two hundred philosophers whose deaths would destroy sigilry for all time.

"Yeah," I said. "The detective only let me look at the first page. It's not spelled right, but it's me."

My name had followed only Danielle Hardin and Senator Josephine Cadwallader-Fulton. Rarified company.

"I can't believe the police are going to allow it to be published," Ma said.

"It's the ramblings of a dying man," I answered. "He didn't know what he was saying—half the people on it are already dead. The Trenchers will see it for what it is. They're not going to dig up Comfort Tyndale just to kill her a second time."

But despite my bluster, I knew the Trenchers were salivating over the list. "Holy writ," the *Boston Informer* had called it, part of the rumors and innuendo surrounding Gannet's death. Why, it was common knowledge that a Bible in his pocket had stopped two bullets! Barely had the wind knocked out of him, but the hospital smokecarvers engineered his demise. Only the power of the good Lord kept him alive long enough to record his final prophecy.

It would make me a marked man. Dar, too. She and her father had holed up in a hotel—even I didn't know where—with the Corps sending a detail to protect her. We'd exchanged messages, but I hadn't been allowed to see her.

According to the Trenchers who'd been captured, they'd been watching Danielle's apartment and had planned to attack the next morning along with another half-dozen men in hopes of taking her alive. But then I'd visited and the opportunity to eliminate both the Hero of the Hellespont and "the deviant male" who had defiled the blessed Gannet with a sigil had been too good to pass up.

My favorite of Addams's men, who'd been guarding the front door, had been shot and killed when the first wave of Trenchers rushed him. Gannet's acolytes, however, had all survived. The sniper on whom Astrid had dropped the powder bag was paralyzed below the neck; the man Dar had hit had been blinded, both his eyes shredded by the birdshot.

As I'd had time to reflect, though, my own actions frightened me more than any of the rest. How indifferently, how automatically I'd gunned Gannet down. In all my hours of imagining horrible ends for him, I'd expected to feel celebratory, self-righteous, smug. Instead, I was left with a gnawing ache right in my middle.

The police had called it the most justifiable case they'd ever seen. But I could have dropped out of the window, even if it meant a broken leg. Gannet would be rotting in jail on three charges of attempted murder, instead of being held up as a martyr.

"You wouldn't have wanted him in court," Mother said. "A chance to rant in front of an audience? It would have done more harm than good."

"Sure," I said. "Might have been safer for me, though."

"The Trenchers won't be able to touch you once you're with the Corps," Mother replied. "They'd have the fury of a thousand smokecarvers on them."

"The training officer on the message board last night agreed," I said. "But she thought a change of name might be prudent all the same. I hope you don't mind."

And then I felt very shy.

"Did you take Beau's name?" Ma asked.

I nodded.

"I went by Mrs. Canderelli for a time. It's damn hard to spell."

Mother sighed and kicked a stone clear of the path.

"Robert Canderelli was the name on your birth certificate," she said. "I changed it to Weekes when we moved back to Guille's Run after the Second Disturbance. It was simpler that way. Too many wanted posters with the name Canderelli."

"Was that his real name?" I asked.

"God, no. His family caused all sorts of trouble—he had a few different names growing up in Santiago. Canderelli is the one he liked best."

"So, what does that make me?" I asked. "Half-Chilean?"

"It makes you his son," Mother said. "And mine. He would have been proud as hell. I am, too. But I'm terrified of what's going to happen to you. It's an evil thing—over there and back here. It works evil on every soul that touches it."

"Well, *you* came through it okay."

"I came through it mean. I wasn't hardly a mother to you."

"Ma . . ."

I put my arm around her shoulders and we stared out at the water together.

"A man ain't supposed to say his mother's his hero," I managed before my voice cracked. "But I never wanted no hero but you."

I saw Ma off to the transporter arena that evening and returned to my apartment to find Unger in an agony of indecision, all 159 bow ties spread across his bedroom. He looked me over with distress. "Jake is coming for us in twenty minutes! You can't possibly mean to go dressed like that."

Radcliffe's end of the year party was being held at the Smoke and Mirror, the most chic venue in town. It served as a wild celebration of the end of classes, a "bon voyage" for the Contingencies heading to their jobs, and a more sober farewell to the outgoing corpswomen.

I hadn't, until a few hours earlier, planned to go. I had no desire to face my classmates. The attack had violently upset Radcliffe's student body; the volunteer campus patrols and nightly reports of suspicious men had only just begun to die down. Everywhere I went, they pressed me for details. Was it true I'd murdered a man in cold blood? Had Dar mistaken me for one of them or did I think she'd shot me on purpose? Had I seen Gannet in his death throes, all bloody and gasping and crazed?

Then in our last exchange of messages, Danielle had declared she would attend. *A few pictures of me, alive and healthy, for the* Globe, she'd explained. *Put a little spirit in my fellow Cliffes. Talk to you for a minute, face-to-face, if you'll let me.*

The thought of her made me queasy. I hadn't seen Danielle since Tillie had flown her out the window—Addams had kept us in different buildings to ensure that a single Trencher attack couldn't kill us both. Our conversations by message had been terse. We'd avoided talking about Gannet. Or the Corps. I was frightened of what Danielle might say to me but I couldn't bear not to see her.

I did my best to tamp down my feelings. I straightened my shoulders and put on my gray suit and a red cravat in lieu of a bow tie—not that anyone was at risk of confusing Unger and me.

We heard the growl of an engine followed by honking: Jake, feverish with delight, piloting Radcliffe's custom Packard automobile, Addams sitting stiffly beside her. They'd been doing lessons, ostensibly in recognition of Jake's valorous action during Gannet's attack, but also, one suspected, because Addams wanted to bask in a little secondhand joy.

Mayweather was in the backseat smoking a cigarillo. Unger and I piled in with him. Jake pulled away from the curb and floored the accelerator, grinding the gears.

"Easy!" Addams barked. "Let the clutch out. No!"

"She never handles quite the way you think she will the first time," Mayweather jibed.

"And the last time if you're not more careful than that," Addams said. "Turn it, no, toward—*toward*—"

She lunged for the steering wheel.

"We're worried *these* are going to replace hovering?" I wondered aloud, my knuckles white with holding on to the seat.

Jake drove us, without actual damage to the car or our persons, to an anonymous building in the North End. There was no sign to denote the place, only a glass door and two large windows blacked out with crepe paper.

Addams positively refused to allow Jake to park. Mayweather offered Jake his arm and the two of them entered the building.

"I'll be arranging your ride home, Sigilwoman Wee—er, Canderelli,"

Addams said to me. "Check in before you leave. Miss Hardin will be along in a few minutes. She's finishing up photos for the newspapers."

Freddy and I went inside.

My first impression of the interior was of overwhelming darkness. The walls, the floor, the tables and chairs, the bar—all of it was painted a black of such richness and totality that light simply died when it struck. Only the barest hints of edges. Yet I could see Unger clearly and the liquor bottles sitting on their nearly invisible shelves.

The ceiling provided the illumination. It was a vast, glowing, philosophically built mirror that stretched the length of the dining room. But the closer I looked, the less sense it made: I couldn't see my own reflection in its surface. Unger and the hostess weren't in it, either. Faint lines of color rippled across the image—a tapestry woven of light-emitting smoke, perhaps? The difficulty of synthesizing threads in a thousand different colors, much less annealing them, would be extraordinary.

Unger coughed. The hostess was holding his coat and hat. I handed over mine as well. "The ceiling," I said. "Is it a fluorescent particulate thread in a Robechon matrix?"

"Goodness, no," the hostess said, looking pleased with the question. "Though that's not the worst guess I ever heard. Come back in fifty-nine minutes and then you'll see. If you look quickly—" She pointed.

In the artificial image I saw the barmaid enter through the back hallway with a rag and wipe down a section of the bar where the black was a little lighter. Then she exited. But when I looked back at the real bar, the barmaid was standing right there, mixing a drink.

"So not a tableau," I murmured. A recorded image? I hadn't known such a thing was possible.

Unger and I walked down a hallway lit only by thin, luminescent strips of wainscoting. The corridor ended in a V. To the left, glowing cursive letters in red spelled out HELL; glowing blue ones on the right read HEAVEN.

"Shall we start at the bottom and work our way up?" suggested Unger.

Hell had been cleared for dancing. A piano player banged out a spirited tune and everyone was doing a fast, high-stepping waltz I'd never seen before. The room's only obstruction was a huge crystal punch bowl mounted atop a pedestal. It contained a liquid that changed colors right on down the rainbow, from red to ultraviolet and back again. Intrigued, I ladled out a glassful and sipped at it. When it was red, it tasted of tropical fruit and grain alcohol. When it was orange . . . exactly the same. I'd been hoping for a full complement of flavors to accompany the colors, but it seemed there were limitations to what even smokecarvers could do with mixed drinks.

I put the glass to my lips again and found it empty.

"Son of a gun!" I muttered.

"You'll want to drink it quickly!" called Krillgoe Hosawither, who cut quite a figure in a Navy dress uniform rather than his absurd Cocks regalia. He and his dance partner spun toward me. "Once it hits your glass, it evaporates at the end of the cycle."

Anyone who wasn't dancing was looking at the ceiling, waving and gesturing or acting out elaborate pantomimes. Rather than our own reflections, the ceiling displayed an entirely different group of people who waved back from a brightly lit white room decorated with puffy clouds.

Simultaneous two-way visual transmission, Unger explained. A network of smoke fibers absorbed the light on one side, shuttled it over to the other, and re-emitted it.

I picked out Jake in the reflection. She motioned to come over.

I exited Hell, turned the corner, and entered Heaven, where a string quartet played a musty old piece. There were tables set with lace doilies and flutes of champagne in neat rows. Jake sat slouched in a chair, her feet up on the table, smoking one of Mayweather's cigarillos. She reached into his breast pocket and proffered one to me. I held it, unlit, between my teeth.

"You're shipping out tomorrow?" she asked.

"First thing," I replied. "Essie and I will take the same transport down."

"You'll need this, then," Jake said. "From me and the Threes. Come safe home."

Jake handed me an old bronze coin the size of a nickel that had been mounted so it could be worn on a necklace. It showed the profile of a hand-some young man with curly hair who wore a bowl-shaped helmet with wings—the god Hermes, the original flier. I strung it beside the vial of silver chloride on my chain and tucked it beneath my shirt. One couldn't possibly have too many good luck charms.

"Most of the sigilwomen carry one of Athena—I already gave Essie hers—but that didn't seem right for you," Jake said.

In the ceiling we spotted Essie back in Hell, dancing closely with Krill-goe, who'd changed partners. Any girl's dream, but who could have imag-ined Essie being audacious enough to ask him a month ago? Or even one minute ago?

"Though one suspects Ensign Hosawither is only Sigilwoman Stewart's *second* choice for a dance partner," Mayweather whispered.

"Brian!" Jake said.

Mayweather stubbed out the end of his cigar. "They had a fling, you know, in the old books. Clever Hermes and solid, sensible Athena, shield and spear and all."

"Athena was a maiden, unless I misremember," I said.

"I've heard *that* one before," chuckled Mayweather.

"No," Jake said. "Your job is to be her big brother. You bring her back alive. I can't go through all that again, especially not for Essie. Or for you."

Mayweather squeezed her shoulder.

We watched in the ceiling as the song ended and Krillgoe gave Essie a peck on the cheek. They separated and young Miss Stewart retreated to a corner of the room to whisper with several other girls. Standing nearby was Danielle.

The Hero of the Hellespont stood rigidly, arms crossed, scanning the dance floor. As if she could sense my presence, Dar glanced up at the ceiling and caught me watching her. I looked away.

"A goddamned tragedy," Mayweather lamented. "His stock is never going to be higher and instead of playing the field, here he sits, pining for—"

"You should ask her to dance," Jake said.

Dar looked healthy and well rested. She was dressed luxuriantly in a yellow silk dress and white gloves, hair done up, rouge on her cheeks. She wore an almost maternal expression of concern—these were her girls, her charges to protect, even if they didn't know it. Whoever was protecting *her*, I couldn't spot.

"Ask her to dance," agreed Mayweather.

So I did. Dar saw me reenter Hell with more than enough time to turn and run or transport herself home. But she held her ground.

"Would you like to dance?" I asked grimly.

She opened her mouth then shut it again with a look of incredulity not so very far removed from a smile. "You want to *dance*?"

"Yes."

"Do you know how?"

I looked around at the couples holding each other close, rocking and turning to a slow, warm song. "I can manage."

I took her familiar hand in mine and put an arm about her waist. Her hair brushed against my cheek and caught on the bandage.

"God, I'm sorry about your face," she said.

"My fault," I said. "I should have ducked better."

"I just can't believe it. You or me or any of it. Robert, when they came through the door . . ."

"I know," I said.

We turned a couple of circles together. "Are you doing okay?" I asked.

"I'm better than I was. My dad's been an absolute rock. He says he doesn't know if everything happens for a reason, but that he wouldn't have us change a single thing we did."

I nodded. "How's Mrs. Hardin taking it?"

"Badly. It's the sort of thing Mom always said would happen. When I left home, she was worried sick about Boston and then petrified about Gallipoli. She's sure Washington will be even worse, a den of iniquity and peril. When I told her we weren't together anymore, it was the maddest I've ever seen her—she wanted to meet you."

"Probably safer for me that I didn't."

"Yes! Nobody's ever been good enough for her little girl. Then when I'm not with someone, she worries philosophy has turned me on to women."

Dar shifted her hand to a more secure grip on my shoulder. "So," she said. She had a nervous little smile. "I've decided that for a liar and a coward, you're awfully brave. Even with the bandage, you're middling handsome. So, I'm going to reserve the right to visit you."

That was so unexpected as to be incomprehensible.

"Where?" I asked. "In France?"

"Of course in France! I can hop the transatlantic chain to Le Havre. From there, a good transporter can always find a way into your tent in the middle of the night. Your wingmates wouldn't even know."

I grinned at the thought. "That doesn't sound like a good idea."

"It's a *terrible* idea. You're also not going to say no after you've been over a few weeks."

"Paris?" I countered. "I'll get a couple days of leave every three months."

"Name the date."

The weight of what Dar was saying came roaring over me. The smell of her jasmine perfume filled my nostrils and the semi-vaporized smokecarver alcohol burned through my veins. I gave a guttural yowl, caught her under the arms, and spun her round and round. We were both laughing like maniacs and fighting back tears.

"I'll write you every day," I said.

"No, you won't. But frequently? Please?"

I stepped on someone's foot and nearly dropped Dar. People were staring. I didn't care. I set her down and kissed her until I had to come up for air.

"When I get back—" I said.

"Don't," she said. "We'll talk about it when you get back."

"But what does that make us?" I asked.

"I don't know. I don't have a word for it. I mean, if you meet a pretty little Sigilwoman First Class over there, I expect an invitation to the wedding. But if you don't—"

I leaned back in and kissed her again.

In the months that followed, when the thunder of distant artillery kept me up at night, when I sat in the mess tent scrubbing bloodstains out of my backup skysuit, when I went into no-man's-land to retrieve my lieutenant's body on a day my division suffered a third of our number killed or wounded—always, that was the kiss I remembered.

Then Unger was pulling at my elbow, worked into a lather about something, something I absolutely had to see.

"Good-bye, Robert," said Dar. "Come safe home."

"Give them hell, Danielle," I said.

She smiled tightly and turned to watch over the party. I tried my damnedest not to look back at her so that she couldn't see me crying.

"There are only seven possible topologies," Unger explained as he dragged me out to the club's front room, where the regular dinner crowd was sipping drinks from double glasses that coiled around each other. "And this should be the fifth confirmation, I believe. I do hope we haven't missed it." He consulted his pocket watch.

"What aren't we missing?" I asked.

Unger pointed at the ceiling, which depicted the same front room, albeit nearly empty, with only the hostess making a note at her station and the barmaid folding napkins. The bottles shone like gemstones in a hundred different colors, but the rest of the image was murky and lightless. We watched as the reflected door opened. In walked Unger, cool and collected, and me, gawking about. My image turned its face up to the ceiling, staring almost directly at where I was standing in the present moment.

My reflection, younger than me by one hour, looked drained and tense, but its anxieties melted away as it gazed upon this fresh wonder, at a new corner of the world that seconds before had been beyond any imagining.

APPENDIX

Adapted from Robert Canderelli Weekes, Pilar Desoto, Michael Naka-mura, Edith Rubinski. *A Primer for Practical Sigilry.* Matamoros University Press. 1937.

EMPIRICAL PHILOSOPHY IS BEST learned from another practitioner. However, in the current political environment, finding a mentor is increasingly difficult, obtaining high-quality powder has become prohibitively expensive or outright illegal, and actually *practicing* sigilry may involve substantial risk to life and liberty. As a result, we've written this book in hopes of introducing the adult learner to the fundamentals of several basic sigils so that she can learn basic practical philosophy in the privacy of her own home. (Children may prefer a less complicated text such as *Sigilry 1-2-3* or *Miss Goodbody's Book for Girls.*)

We've begun with a brief overview of eleven useful sigils, each of which has its own chapter devoted to more advanced topics.

While the written word can never hope to fully capture the subtleties of counting and hand position which are vital to drawing sigils, understanding the broad movements and shape of each glyph is an essential first step. Practice with pen and paper or with a powder pencil (see Chapter 4—Improvised and Homemade Equipment) has helped many students to progress rapidly when they begin formal instruction. And in many cases, it really is possible to learn a sigil with only a printed description and a good deal of practice.

KORU

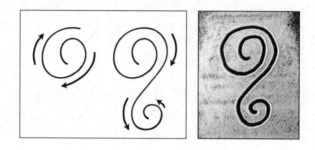

THE DISCOVERY OF THE koru glyph in 1873 ranks among the most serendipitous moments in empirical philosophy. The eight-year-old daughter of wealthy amateur sigilrist Bertha Moss often drew ornate figures in the steam that condensed on the frosted glass door of her bathtub. One day, Mrs. Moss noticed that a potted philodendron in the opposite corner of the bathroom had grown to enormous size. Correctly deducing that a novel sigil must be the cause, Moss and her daughter spent several weeks attempting to re-create the glyph, eventually calling in the entire four-woman faculty in empirical philosophy at nearby Radcliffe College to assist. The famous photograph in the *Boston Globe* of the six women standing in the bathtub peering through the glass has come to embody the unexpected nature of many philosophical breakthroughs.

METHODS AND MATERIALS

Coat a square piece of glass (typically three-by-three inches) with a fine mist of water, then draw the figure with bare finger on glass, aiming at the nearby plant or seedling. Avoid using glass with a wooden frame or other ergonomic "improvements" as these often trap water droplets, making the sigil unreliable. Any mister is suitable for home garden use, though philosophers working on a commercial scale or with particularly delicate plants (e.g. citrus trees, figs, vanilla orchids) may wish to invest in a high-quality adjustable atomizer.

Distilled water is strongly preferred, as minerals in groundwater can cause sigil failure. As appealing as many of the heavily-advertised "elixirs," "tonics," and "patented anti-smear solutions" that claim miraculous effects on the sigil can be, they all perform worse than plain water, often at a cost of several dollars per quart.

Koru is among the most widely researched sigils, with thousands of customizations for latitude, soil quality, plant age, agricultural goal (larger fruit or faster maturation), and expected rainfall. These modifications generally involve adding loops, drawing certain lines more heavily or decorating the tail end of the glyph. Though the possibilities can seem overwhelming, *Canul's Annual Koru Advisor* is an invaluable guide that will allow you to quickly arrive at the right figure for your individual circumstances. The glyph shown above is the standard starting point; for most crops, it will decrease time to harvest by roughly 65 percent and increase yield by 150 percent. However, results may vary dramatically.

COUNTING

Koru is drawn on the four-count, with two beats for the upper spiral, one count for the transitional line, and one count for the lower spiral. This requires smooth deceleration into the transition and decisive acceleration into the final spiral.

SMOKECARVING
(COHERENCE)

WITH LUCRETIA CADWALLADER'S INVENTION of smokecarving in 1843, empirical philosophy advanced from a tradition-based, frequently superstitious discipline to one fully invested in the scientific method. Today, smokecarving remains a vital technique for medicine, high-rise construction, fashion design, and hundreds of other industries.

METHODS AND MATERIALS

All smokecarving begins by cohering a cloud of smoke into a persistent mass. The left hand is held cupped over the smoke source—tallow candle, smudge pot, or lampblack vaporizer—and the coherence sigil drawn with the right hand. In the Originalist American style, the glyph is drawn on the gaseous smoke with a jackknife or scalpel; in the German style, with knitting needles; and in the New American style, with a fingertip. Cohering is a messy but necessary first step; the inevitable smoke stains have led most smokecarvers to dress in gray, as Cadwallader did. Bottled smoke varies tremendously in quality, but if you find a reliable supplier, having ready-made condensed high-soot material can dramatically speed larger constructions.

COUNTING

The usual teaching is "agitate for three, tease for one, draw in zero," with the repetitive, diminishing strokes of the agitate drawn parallel to each other, the linear zig-zagging motion of the tease drawn perpendicularly to the agitate, and the three strokes of the main glyph drawn as rapidly as possible with sharp, slashing strokes. Most experienced smokecarvers perform the first two steps so quickly that they slur into the first slash; beginners should not imitate this style.

MESSAGE

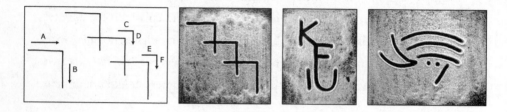

PRIOR TO THE ESTABLISHMENT of the Federal Glyph Registry, American sigilrists had chosen their own message glyphs for nearly 200 years, often using several different glyphs for communication with different people—for example, two lovers might develop their own set of figures for private communication. Nearly all personal glyphs were abstract, nonrepresentational symbols, though they possessed a handmade artfulness that has been lost in the era of mass-produced glyphs created by lock and tumbler machines.

METHODS AND MATERIALS

On a plate of glass backed with silver leaf, pour out a thin layer of sand and level it with a board scraper. To send, the originator draws her own personal glyph in the left upper corner using a finger or blunt stylus, draws the recipient's glyph in the right lower corner, writes the message, and finally draws the transmit glyph center-right. To receive, the steps are reversed; the transmit glyph is drawn first in the right lower corner, followed by the recipient's personal glyph in the left upper.

COUNTING

While a personal glyph is usually counted in four, what matters most is that the timing be consistent. The transmission glyph is also drawn in four, with each segment drawn faster than the last.

STASIS

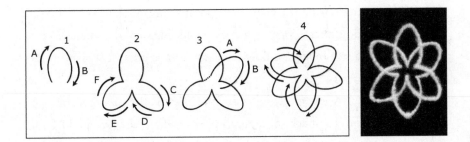

STASISRY IS A RELATIVELY new discipline, first described in 1891 by anthropological philosopher G.H. Wilson and traditional healer Namagiri, in Madras, India, after the two women traced simplified Hindu mandalas on research subjects with over 2,100 different compounds. These early experiments are now widely viewed as unethical for using inmates in a local insane asylum as "volunteers," as well as for failing to report dozens of adverse events including strokes, permanent paralysis and death. (Wilsons' refusal to include her co-investigator on her enormously valuable American patents is also the subject of multiple ongoing lawsuits more than four decades later.)

Nevertheless, the sigil has done enormous good in the world. More elaborate forms of the stasis glyph can numb individual nerves to provide anesthesia, terminate seizures, slow the growth of tumors, and stop the flow of blood in targeted parts of the body, allowing for bloodless surgery. These advanced figures are notoriously difficult and require years of dedicated study. Most sigilrists who earn a doctor of medical philosophy (DMP) train in both smokecarving and stasisry. The proper title for a woman holding a DMP is "doctor," not "miss."

METHODS AND MATERIALS

Fresh, high-purity silver chloride is essential, as is use of smoked glass tubes for storage, since sunlight causes the powder to decompose into elemental silver and chlorine. Powder can be synthesized in a home laboratory from silver nitrate (which is more stable) and sodium chloride; this is a classic test for an aspiring amateur chemist. Gloves should be worn when handling silver chloride (except when drawing the glyph itself), as it stains the skin. For advanced figures, a dissecting microscope or loupes are mandatory to accurately place the glyph, as is a sub-milligram flow regulator—these are not sigils to be attempted lightly.

For a standard wide-spectrum stasis, the chest is the most reliable spot to place the glyph; the neck, head and upper back are also acceptable. The three-and-three-petal figure above is the most widely used form, as it balances ease of drawing with effective full-body stasis. Longer effect for similar powder mass can be achieved with an eight-petal figure (the so-called "Corps four-by-four"), though it is more difficult to draw. The simplest form, the two-petal "propeller" or "two-by-none," can be drawn in under a second and is a useful defensive technique for incapacitating an attacker, though it lasts only a few minutes.

While drawing, it is essential to smoothly interrupt the powder flow when switching from the first circuit of petals to the second. If the sigil fails, this is almost invariably where a philosopher has gone wrong.

COUNTING

Each stroke of each petal should be drawn in an equal length of time. The glyph is traditionally counted in four (three four-counts for the glyph above), though advanced forms vary.

HOVER

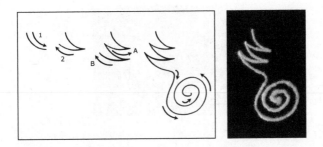

THE AUTHORS WOULD DISCOURAGE readers in the strongest possible terms from attempting to fly for the first time without the supervision of an experienced hoverer. As the adage among hoverers goes, Mary Fox was the only woman who ever taught herself to fly and even she crashed into Lake Erie thirty-three times. (It is illustrative that while Fox did not require her first class of hoverers to have any prior philosophical experience, they did have to pass a one-mile open water swim test while wearing full hover kit.)

METHODS AND MATERIALS

Harnesses, bags, and regulators are covered in detail in Chapter 9, as are grinding your own corn powder with a hand mill and selecting sand/desiccant mixes for stabilization. The hover sigil is drawn with the regulator held between the thumb and forefinger in a pencil-grip. The terminal spiral should trail in the opposite direction of the thrust vector, as if the sigilrist is pushing herself in the desired direction of travel.

COUNTING

The hover glyph is the only sigil drawn on a six-count, which may explain why experienced philosophers who have practiced mainly four-count sigilry often struggle to learn it. One beat is devoted to each of the three sawtooth crescents, one to the transitional line, and two counts for the terminal spiral.

Transport

Destination sigil placed in downtown
Boston, February 1918.

DUE TO THE EXTRAORDINARY physical risks to passengers, nearby buildings (as exemplified by the Battle of Berlin during the closing minutes of the Great War), and the sigilrist herself, transporting remains one of the most highly self-regulated forms of philosophy. The sigil should be learned after the onset of puberty from an expert practitioner.

METHODS AND MATERIALS

Because finely milled aluminum powder oxidizes quickly, it is generally sealed in an ampoule, which is itself sealed inside a second tube filled with nitrogen. Increasing powder mass increases the radius of the bubble; longer point-to-point jump distance results in greater weight loss for the philosopher.

By convention, destination glyphs are drawn with all lines starting at the left side of the figure (nine o'clock position), proceeding anticlockwise. To transport to that position, the transporter draws the same lines in clockwise order. Thus, it is vital that the original destination glyph be drawn with correct line progression and accurately logged.

COUNTING

As all destination sigils are unique, they are drawn on an open count with precision and line progression as paramount goals; counting is of minor concern.

Eupheus

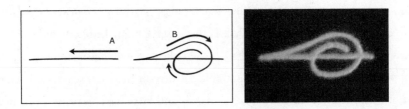

SIGILS TO SUMMON THE east wind first came into prominence in 1843, when a caravan of sail-powered wagons made the trip from Independence, Missouri to the Willamette Valley in Oregon in only 10 days, thanks to hurricane-strength philosophical winds. One badly jostled settler remarked upon disembarking, "Had I been stuffed in a sack and beaten by devils for a week, I should be less thoroughly bruised. Surely no one shall ever attempt this again."

That proved not to be the case. Over the next four decades, as aerodynamic wagons with advanced leaf-spring suspensions were developed and steerable traction kites replaced sails, wind-powered vehicles easily reached sixty miles per hour over flat terrain, with a much smoother ride. Kite coaches were used by prospectors during the California gold rush, Mormon pioneers during the settlement of Utah, and for regular passenger service throughout the American Southwest. Kite-bandit attacks on wagons carrying US Army payroll inspired the creation of the US Kite Marshallry, which paired sigilrists and lawmen to make long-distance patrols across the West. Chief Marshall Edwin Fitzenhalter's aphoristic eighty-four-page memoir *Fresh Gale on the High Sonora* is an excellent account of this era. Despite widespread rumors of immorality and sexual depravity on these extended missions, the marshals were fiercely protective of their female counterparts; Fitzenhalter famously shot a cowboy who fondled his longtime philosopher, Mrs. Gower.

Unfortunately, the eupheus sigil suffered from several serious flaws: it could only create winds that blew from east to west (meaning that kite wagons were packed up in California and shipped back east by sea); the glyph required pure crushed silver, making it relatively expensive; and it failed in humid climates or near water. Kite coaches disappeared almost overnight after the establishment of the National Transporter Chain. Eupheus did enjoy a resurgence after 1905, when the crushed silver powder was amended with 90 percent graphite, making it suitable for use on the high seas. Since then, large windjammers hoisting dozens of sails and kites have become a practical means of hauling bulk cargo on easterly routes from America to Asia.

The name "eupheus" is believed to be a corruption of the classical Greek name for the east wind, eurus, considered an unlucky wind since Biblical times.

METHODS AND MATERIALS

The glyph is drawn with a tube of crushed, untarnished silver, which may be cut with graphite up to a 9:1 ratio. It is a difficult sigil despite its structural simplicity, as small distortions can cause brief-lived, weak or choppy winds that make propulsion impossible. Contrariwise, wind fronts that fail to break up and die on schedule mean that hurricane-force winds may continue unchecked for hundreds of miles, causing considerable destruction. The Great Texas Dust Bowl of 1880 was one such disaster.

COUNTING

The sigil is counted in four, with two beats for the central line and then a sharp reverse, with one beat for overhead curve, and one to finish the spiral. Fitzenhalter, who himself could do no philosophy, rightly called the reverse "the toughest backhand in sigilry."

DISSIPATE

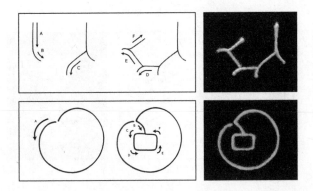

EMPIRICAL PHILOSOPHERS HAVE KNOWN since the mid-eighteenth century that all forms of bronze interfere with sigils; drawing the dissipate sigil strengthens that native quality a thousandfold or more. There are currently thirty-eight distinctive forms of dissipate (each with dozens of subtypes), now all believed to be cross sections or "shadows" of a single, unified eight-dimensional figure. Numerous defensive strategies employing the interfaces between stacked dissipate glyphs were developed by the Radcliffe Working Group in the final months of the Great War, but outside of specialized military philosophy and theoretical research, the sigil is rarely used.

METHODS AND MATERIALS

Individual dissipate glyphs vary widely in shape, strength, and persistence. Ideal powder for each varies, but contemporary bronze, with 88 percent copper, 11 to 12 percent tin and trace amounts of zinc and antimony will produce consistent effects with all known glyphs.

COUNTING

For the Reverse Pearl Standard shown above, the glyph is drawn in four beats. The initial anticlockwise circle receives one beat, then one for the bridge and two for the inner square. Counting for the Philippine Figure 3 is idiosyncratic and beyond the scope of this introduction.

Bonekill

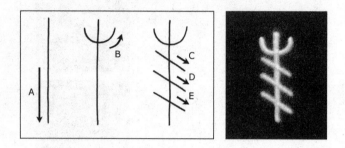

SO MUCH MISINFORMATION SURROUNDS bonekilling that the authors decided an accurate description would do more good than harm. After all, if a philosopher is hellbent on murder and able to get close enough to draw a bonekill, there are numerous simpler methods for taking a life.

Bonekill came into use around 1895 and was employed by all sides during the guerilla actions in the Philippine-American War. While gruesome, it kills quickly and death is painless (so far as we can tell). Powder must be applied directly to the skin of the target; it cannot kill from a distance. A failed sigil does not cause brittle bone disease, as is popularly believed.

METHODS AND MATERIALS

Powder is a 7:1 mix of bone meal and elemental yellow sulfur. The bone meal should be ground from human bones—a femur if possible. The powder tends to stick and come out of the tube in a single clump; this is especially problematic in vials carried in a purse for years or worn in jewelry intended for self-defense. The central stem is drawn first, with the arced end-cap next, followed by the three barbs. Strokes should be fast, precise, and decisive.

COUNTING

Drawn on an open count, though each barb should receive equal time.

PROPHYLAXIS

ENTIRE BOOKS COULD BE written on what the prophylactic glyph does *not* do: it does not terminate pregnancies, rather it prevents them from occurring in the first place; it does not increase the incidence of ovarian or breast cancer; it does not cause pathological increase of the sex drive; it does not cause subsequent infertility.

Much of the challenge lies not in the glyph itself, which is relatively simple, but in not knowing immediately whether the sigil has taken and in the fact that it cannot be redrawn with hope of efficacy until at least twenty-eight days have passed. For that reason, even though prophylaxis is among the most widely practiced sigils in the world, many women prefer to visit a specialist or medical philosopher for one minute each month to have it drawn for them. A prophylaxis sigil should not be neglected until the heat of the moment, when inevitably a bottle of saline can't be found or one's hands are shaky.*

---

*Failure rates of the prophylaxis sigil are often used as an example of independent probability in introductory theoretical empirical philosophy textbooks. To wit: the probability of at least one unintentional pregnancy over a lifetime is the probability of a successfully drawn glyph raised to the power of the number of months on which it is drawn (often estimated at 360 months, or thirty years). With a 99.5 percent success rate (one miss in two hundred—an enviable percentage), probability of at least one lifetime miss is 83.5 percent, which most women find unacceptably high. By contrast, a client of a specialist able to achieve 1 in 10,000 miss rate has a lifetime risk of unintentional pregnancy under 5 percent.

METHODS AND MATERIALS

Early practitioners believed that water from the Dead Sea was preferable for drawing glyphs, but it is far too salty, aside from being expensive to import. A simple 3 percent saline solution is preferred; this can easily be made by putting three grams of table salt in a graduated cylinder and adding water until one hundred milliliters of solution is reached. The old shortcut of half a teaspoon of salt in one-third cup of water will also work in a pinch.

The glyph is generally drawn one day following the end of menses and then each twenty-eight days thereafter. Specialists can make small adjustments to the glyph if it is being drawn at a different point in the menstrual cycle, as well as for age and number of previous pregnancies.

COUNTING

The glyph is drawn on the four-count, with two counts on the opening loop, one on the middle curve, and one on the final three-quarters loop, making it a classical accelerating glyph.

MANUAL
REDUPLICATION

THE MERIWETHER LEWIS EXPEDITION famously lost its cartogramancer, William Clark, when he wandered away from the rest of his party only three miles outside St. Louis. Though his compatriots believed him dead, Clark nevertheless emerged in San Francisco ten years later, having made fabulously detailed maps of much of the American West. (His survey of the Yellowstone River Valley in Montana and Wyoming proved so accurate that it is still used as the basis for topographical maps of that region more than a century later.) Clark also devised a sigil and philosophical ink system by which he could make perfect copies of his maps.

Clark's reduplication glyph was used without modification by nearly every clerk and bookkeeper the world over, until investigations by KF Unger in 1918 revealed it had many other useful properties, making it a cornerstone of the modular glyph movement. Temporary-permanent ink and a variety of related selective-binding emulsions have proven vital to fields of basic research ranging from cellular biology (where they are used to tag microscopic structures) to astronomy (for tinting telescope lenses so that stars are visible in daylight). However, none of these specialized versions has surpassed Clark's original glyph for usefulness.

METHODS AND MATERIALS

Clark's preferred ink, made from walnuts and naturally occurring magnetite, provides unparalleled image quality for copying maps and pictures. Most modern inks use iron filings instead, which have proven easier to work with, much less expensive, and perfectly adequate for duplicating documents.

For maximum fidelity, the glyph is drawn on the original sheet of blank paper by a fingertip dipped in ink and then on the sheet on which the copy is to be produced. The picture, map or document is drawn with the same ink on the first sheet; following this, a small amount of ink is spilled out onto the second page. The ink droplets will skitter across the page and into position before binding to the paper, making a perfect one-for-one copy. Copies can also be made of an existing printed or written page, though these duplicates are inevitably of poorer quality than the original. A tertiary copy (a copy of a copy of a copy) tends to be the last level at which handwriting is still legible.

COUNTING

Reduplication is among the simplest four-beat glyphs, with equal time given to the two curved strokes and two crossing lines. It makes for an ideal first sigil.

AUTHOR'S NOTE

WHERE POSSIBLE, I HAVE preserved the names and dates of historical events, including key moments in the Civil War, the Spanish-American War, the Philippine-American War, and World War I. The most notable exceptions are the Battle of Petersburg (which was horrendous in other ways) and the Dardanelles Campaign, which I have prolonged by roughly one year.

Maxwell Gannet's sermon is inspired by a 1978 speech by radio personality Paul Harvey. *Hovering Emergencies and Recovery* is a nod to Judith Tintinalli's *Emergency Medicine*, a book that changed the way I look at the world. Brock's "malevolent presence" is an homage to Tom Wolfe's demon that lives at Mach 1. Fox's Prayer is an adaptation of the Astronaut's Prayer, sometimes attributed to Alan Shepard. The song that Gertrude hums after Robert's breakthrough is based on a paratrooper marching cadence. Northwest Aero's advertisement is a parody of a Secret deodorant slogan. In his meditation on not being able to perform practical sigilry, Unger quotes Thomas Cranmer without attribution.

ACKNOWLEDGMENTS

THIS STORY HAS BEEN many years in the writing.

My thanks to: Let's Go, Inc. for sending me to New Zealand, where Lennox Murchison and smokecarving came to me while I was lost on a five-day hike; my fellow writers at Notre Dame's MFA program, especially William O'Rourke, Valerie Sayers, and Steve Tomasula, who met Lucretia Cadwallader in 2005 and didn't send me straight back to the farm; and my colleagues at the University of Wisconsin Department of Emergency Medicine, who encouraged me to continue writing, particularly Dr. Mary Westergaard for engineering a soft landing.

Thank you to my early readers for their enthusiasm and advice: Kay Miller, Jarrett Haley, Jim McCarthy, Thomas and Patricia Miller, Brian Suffoletto, Sumner and Lucy Brown, and Dan and Nate Carlin.

Thank you, Alexandra Machinist, my agent, to whom I owe a blood debt. Thank you to my three extraordinary editors, Sarah Knight, Ben Loehnen, and Zack Knoll.

Thank you most of all to Abby, who was Robert's first fan and staunchest supporter. And thank you, Owen, for riding in the backpack and listening while I mow the lawn and talk about imaginary people.